The Lighthouse on Plum Island

Cobble Beach Romance — Book 1

AMY RAFFERTY

Copyright © 2024 by Amy Rafferty

All rights reserved.

No part of this publication may be reproduced, stored, distributed, or transmitted in any form or by any means, including photocopying, recording, or other electronic or mechanical methods, without the prior written permission of the publisher or author. For permission requests, contact the author.

The story, all names, characters, and incidents portrayed in this production are fictitious. No identification with actual persons (living or deceased), places, buildings, and products is intended or should be inferred.

Images inside were designed using resources from canva.com and bookbrush.com

First Edition 2024

VIP READERS

Don't want to miss out on my giveaways, competitions, and

'hot off the press' news?

Subscribe to my email list.

It is FREE!

Click Here!

FOLLOW ME ON MY SOCIALS HERE

Not only can you check out the latest news and deals there, you can

also get an email

alert each time I release my next book.

Follow me on BookBub

I always love to hear from you and get your feedback.

Email me at ~ books@amyraffertyauthor.com

Follow on Amazon ~ Amy Rafferty

Sign up for my newsletter and free gift, Here

Join my 'Amy's Friends' group on Facebook

TABLE OF CONTENTS

1. CHAPTER 1 — 1
2. CHAPTER 2 — 17
3. CHAPTER 3 — 33
4. CHAPTER 4 — 50
5. CHAPTER 5 — 65
6. CHAPTER 6 — 86
7. CHAPTER 7 — 103
8. CHAPTER 8 — 124
9. CHAPTER 9 — 145
10. CHAPTER 10 — 166
11. CHAPTER 11 — 187
12. CHAPTER 12 — 203
13. CHAPTER 13 — 223
14. CHAPTER 14 — 239

15.	CHAPTER 15	255
16.	CHAPTER 16	272
17.	CHAPTER 17	293
18.	CHAPTER 18	314
19.	CHAPTER 19	335
20.	CHAPTER 20	356
21.	CHAPTER 21	375
22.	EPILOGUE	394
	CONTINUE THE SERIES	400
	COBBLE BEACH ROMANCE SERIES	414
	ALSO FROM AMY RAFFERTY	415
	MORE BOOKS BY AMY RAFFERTY	418
	BOOKS BY AMY RAFFERTY & ROSE RYAN	422
	ABOUT THE AUTHOR	425

CHAPTER 1

Caroline Shaw's heart raced with exhilaration after her meeting with Travis Danes. As she strolled through the bustling streets of New York alongside her lifelong friend, Jennifer Gains, palpable excitement filled the air. Travis had wholeheartedly agreed to her terms, and within three to six months, a film crew would descend on Plum Island to bring her beloved "Cobble Cove Mysteries" to life on screen. It was a dream unfolding before her eyes.

"Can you believe it, Jen?" Caroline gushed, her hazel eyes sparkling with joy. "He actually agreed to everything! The film crew will be on Plum Island soon, and we'll be making magic together!"

Jennifer, who had been Caroline's unwavering source of support since childhood, beamed in response. "I always knew you could do it,

Caroline. Your writing is brilliant, and now the world will not only read your work but see it come to life."

Their destination was Jennifer's favorite coffee shop in Soho, a haven of creativity and conversation. Just as they arrived at the charming spot, Jennifer's phone rang, and she sighed regretfully.

"It's work," Jennifer said apologetically. "I'm so sorry, Caroline. I have to take this."

"No worries," Caroline replied with a reassuring smile. They were close to the cafe entrance, and she gestured for Jennifer to go ahead. "I'll have a coffee and write while you handle business. We can catch up later at your place for our celebration dinner."

Jennifer made sure the owner of the coffee shop noticed them and guided Caroline to her usual table by the window before rushing off to attend to her call. Caroline settled into her seat, and Simon Newbury, the cafe's owner, greeted them warmly.

"Good afternoon, ladies," Simon said with a charming smile. "You both look lovely today."

"Thank you, Simon," they chimed in unison, and Caroline took a menu.

"Why are you still standing?" Simon inquired with a quizzical look at Jennifer.

"Because I have to get back to work," Jennifer groaned, and then she added, "Please put Caroline's order on my tab."

"You don't have to do that," Caroline protested.

She felt her cheeks flush as she accepted Jennifer's offer. The cafe's prices were exorbitant, and even though Simon's coffee and treats were top-notch, they didn't warrant such costs.

"Nonsense," Jennifer insisted. "Consider it my treat. Besides, consider it a business expense, with you being my top client."

Simon turned to Caroline. "Can I get you your usual coffee while you peruse the menu?"

"Yes, please, Simon," Caroline replied with gratitude. Simon nodded and excused himself to fulfill their orders.

"I'd better get going," Jennifer said, her tone apologetic. "I'll see you back at my place this evening."

Caroline bid her friend farewell and Jennifer left the cafe, disappearing into the bustling city. As Caroline settled in, her coffee arrived, and she decided to forgo any food and instead set up her laptop. The cafe's creative ambiance was infectious, and she was eager to dive back into her writing.

With her laptop screen glowing before her, Caroline's thoughts drifted back over the past three years. Her father had passed away from a heart attack just two months before she'd discovered her husband,

Robert Parker, was cheating on her. Two weeks after that revelation, she lost her job as the head of NYU Libraries.

Robert had insisted on keeping their house, a brownstone on the Upper West Side of New York, leaving Caroline and their twelve-year-old daughter, Jules, with nowhere to go. Jennifer had graciously taken them in, and they had lived in her three-bedroom Soho apartment for nearly six months, depleting Caroline's meager savings as she desperately searched for new employment.

However, there weren't many opportunities for a forty-four-year-old librarian in New York City. During Jules's school hours and between interviews, Caroline had begun writing "Cobble Cove Mysteries." Writing had become her refuge, a way to escape her shattered marriage, fading career, and the resentment of her now fourteen-year-old daughter.

Jules had been furious when Caroline uprooted their lives and moved them back to Plum Island, her small hometown in New England. She held Caroline responsible for the divorce and blamed her for everything that had gone wrong. However, their bond had recently started to mend as they collaborated on Caroline's new book, and the prospect of the TV series had brought them closer.

Caroline sighed contentedly and turned her attention back to her writing, eager to immerse herself in the world of her characters once more. However, her solitude was short-lived as a tall, impeccably dressed man approached her table. He appeared slightly flustered but politely asked if he could share her table.

Caroline surveyed the crowded cafe and realized that every seat was taken. She offered a friendly smile and gestured to the empty chair. "Of course, please have a seat."

The man smiled gratefully and settled into the chair across from her. He seemed like a creature from a different world, with his expensive attire and an air of sophistication that contrasted sharply with the cafe's casual atmosphere.

A server promptly arrived at their table, and the man ordered a sugary designer coffee concoction, which didn't take long to arrive. Caroline couldn't help but suppress a shudder at the sweetness overload. The man seemed to notice her reaction and chuckled as he took a sip.

"I have a sweet tooth," he confessed, striking up a conversation. "My parents are always on my case about it. Even my sixteen-year-old son shakes his head at me when I have to satisfy my sugar cravings."

"My teenage daughter has a sweet tooth, too," Caroline mused.

"Really?" He chuckled. "Teenagers and their sweet tooth! It's a universal struggle, it seems." He held out his hand. "I'm Brad."

"Caroline." She shook his hand and noticed his handshake was firm but not rough.

As Caroline sipped her coffee, she soon found herself engaged in a pleasant conversation with Brad. While they chatted, Caroline couldn't help but observe him discreetly. Brad was a striking figure. She estimated his height to be roughly six foot three inches, just like her brother. His stylish, short, straight, jet-black hair was graced with subtle streaks of gray at the temples, framing a strong and handsome face that looked like a great artist chiseled it. Brad's piercing blue eyes sparkled with a warmth that drew you in, and when he smiled, it was nothing short of heart-stopping.

Their discussion meandered from favorite books to travel destinations, and Caroline found herself genuinely enjoying Brad's company. It was a rarity for her to strike up conversations with strangers, especially a strange man. Caroline learned that he was from New York, but his job in the entertainment industry took him all over the world. He had a sixteen-year-old son, Connor, who was his pride and joy. The two of them had been close since his wife left them when Connor was eight months old. Except for a few visits, Connor didn't know his mother well, and he shied away from what he did know.

"I'm thankful that my son and I have such a close bond," Brad told her. "I always worried when I was younger that my kids wouldn't be as close to me as I was with my parents."

"Are your parents still around?" Caroline asked.

"Yes, my mother and father are still both fit and don't look a day older than fifty-five." Brad laughed. "Or so my mother likes to tell everyone."

"I was close to my parents, too," Caroline admitted.

"By was, you mean—" Brad's brows crinkled as he looked at her questioningly.

"My mother passed away ten years ago from cancer." Caroline swallowed the burning lump, thinking about her mother still brought to her throat. She cleared her throat. "My father passed away three years ago from a heart attack."

"I'm sorry." Brad's eyes filled with compassion. "Do you have siblings?"

"Yes, I have an older brother. He also lives in New England," Caroline told him. "Well, he's actually my half-brother. His mother passed away during childbirth."

"Oh, no, that's horrible," Brad said.

"My mother was a doctor at the hospital in Boston where my brother was born," Caroline explained. "His mother had a complicated pregnancy and had been hospitalized for her last two months."

"How did your parents end up getting together?" Brad's brows tightened in a curious frown.

"A year later, my father took my brother to the hospital because he was having breathing problems and was sent to a specialist at Boston General, where my mother worked." Caroline had no idea why she was blurting out her family history to a complete stranger, but Brad seemed genuinely interested. "They ran into each other again, and as my brother had to stay in hospital for tests for nearly two months, they saw each other daily." She smiled, thinking about the story her father told her. "One thing led to another, and they fell in love. My mother fell in love with the small town where my father lived and started a small practice on the island."

"You never wanted to become a doctor?" Brad frowned.

"Oh, no." Caroline's eyes widened. "I can't stand the sight of blood." She shuddered. "I was always more of a bookworm who loved to read. All I ever wanted to do was lose myself in stories."

"That's why you became a librarian." Brad smiled and sat back in the chair. "I'm glad libraries still exist with the internet being around."

"They do, but sadly, most of the books are being overlooked for the computers libraries have now." Caroline sighed. "I've just realized my life may seem such a bore compared to your jet-setting one."

"My life is tiring, and between you and me," Brad leaned forward and lowered his voice, "I'm actually afraid of flying."

"Oh, me too." Caroline nodded, wide-eyed. "I'm nervous while in the air, but I think the worst parts are the—"

"Take-off and landing," they said in unison and laughed.

"You know, I've always wanted to visit New England," Brad admitted. "The historic towns and the coastal beauty all sound incredibly charming."

"I can't believe you've been nearly everywhere there is to go in the United States, the world, and you've never been to New England." Caroline's eyes lit up as she spoke about her hometown. "It's a wonderful place. Although I spent most of my adult and married life in New York, my heart was still firmly planted in New England."

"Well, it's true," Brad assured her. "I've skirted around the area." He leaned back in his chair, a thoughtful expression on his face. "But hearing you talk about it and seeing how your eyes light up when you explain it, I'm definitely going to make an effort to get there."

Their conversation continued to flow effortlessly, touching on a myriad of topics. As the minutes turned into hours, Caroline found herself captivated by the man and surprised by the connection they were forming. It was a rare and unexpected pleasure, and she couldn't deny the sense of warmth that had enveloped her during their conversation.

The bustling coffee shop around them seemed to fade into the background as they shared stories and laughter. Time flew by, and Caroline couldn't help but feel a pang of disappointment when she realized how late it had gotten. She glanced at her wristwatch and then back at Brad.

"I should probably be heading back soon," Caroline said reluctantly. "The friend I'm staying with while I'm in New York will be waiting for me, and I have to check in with my daughter, who's staying with her father while we're in New York."

Brad nodded, a hint of regret in his eyes. "Of course. It's been a pleasure getting to know you."

Caroline gathered her things and stood up, and Brad stood with her. Her heart was heavy with the knowledge that she would have to say goodbye. But as she prepared to leave, Brad surprised her by extending an invitation.

"I know this is sudden, but would you like to join me for dinner tomorrow night?" Brad asked, his eyes filled with sincerity. "I'd love to continue our conversation."

Caroline hesitated for a moment, her mind racing. She barely knew Brad, and yet there was an undeniable connection between them. With a smile, she decided to take a leap of faith.

"I'd like that," she replied, her heart pounding with anticipation.

"Why don't we meet back here tomorrow evening around six?" Brad suggested.

"That sounds like a plan," Caroline said, hoping he couldn't hear how heavily her heart thudded against her rib cage. "Until tomorrow, then."

Brad raised her hand to his lips, gently kissing her knuckles. "Until tomorrow, Caroline."

Brad's smile was heart-stopping, and Caroline had to force her knees not to buckle under its impact. She gave herself a mental shake and gathered all her strength to walk out of the coffee shop without him seeing her jelly legs or collapsing in a puddle of mushy goo.

As she made her way to Jennifer's apartment, her mind was filled with images of Brad and how she'd had her first serendipitous moment. Caroline's footsteps echoed down the quiet corridor as she approached Jennifer's apartment. She couldn't shake the excitement from her chance encounter with him, the intriguing stranger who had entered her life so unexpectedly. Thoughts of their upcoming dinner date warmed her heart, and she couldn't wait to share the details with Jennifer.

As she reached Jennifer's door, Caroline fumbled for her keys, eager to get inside, but the door flew open before she could open it. Her anticipation turned to concern when she noticed Jennifer staring at her with an expression of a mixture of relief and worry.

"Caroline!" Jennifer exclaimed, her voice edged with worry as she grabbed Caroline and hugged her before pushing her away to look at her. "Where have you been? I've been trying to call you for ages. I was about to phone the police!"

Caroline checked her phone and was shocked to find a barrage of missed calls and messages from both Jennifer and Jules. She had been so engrossed in her conversation with Brad that she hadn't noticed her phone buzzing in her bag.

"I'm so sorry, Jen," Caroline apologized, feeling guilty for causing her friend so much distress. "I lost track of time. Let me check in with Jules. She's also been messaging."

Jennifer nodded, her concern easing. She stepped aside for Caroline to enter. Caroline dialed her daughter's number as she walked inside. Jules answered after the third ring. Before Caroline had finished greeting her daughter, she learned that Jules was upset because her father and his new wife were planning to convert her childhood bedroom into a nursery for their expected baby. Caroline did her best to placate her daughter, promising to talk to her father about finding a solution.

Once she hung up, Caroline hurriedly got ready, feeling a sense of urgency to make amends for her absence. Jennifer, who had been patient throughout, smiled as she saw Caroline's anxiousness.

"Don't worry," Jennifer reassured her. "We still have time to make our reservation at 'Le Petit Lueur.' It's one of the finest restaurants in Soho, and I'm sure you'll love it."

"I'm sure I will," Caroline said. "You know how much I love French cuisine."

Forty minutes later, they made their way to the restaurant. It was a hidden gem nestled in the heart of Soho. Its exterior was unassuming, but they were greeted by a warm, intimate atmosphere as they stepped inside. Soft candlelight flickered on white linen-covered tables, casting a romantic glow. The aroma of exquisite dishes filled the air, and the gentle hum of conversation added to the restaurant's charm.

Over a sumptuous meal, Caroline explained why she'd been so late returning to Jennifer's apartment. She shared the story of her chance meeting with Brad and how she'd agreed to go on a dinner date with him.

"Caroline, I can't believe you, of all people, agreed to go on a dinner date with a complete stranger!" Jennifer stared at her in disbelief.

"We spoke for hours," Caroline reminded her. "So, we're technically not strangers anymore."

"It is good to see you so perky and dreamy again." Jennifer smiled. "Maybe a New York fling will be good for you."

Caroline couldn't help but smile at her friend's openness to new possibilities. She agreed to download a tracking app on her phone, allowing Jennifer to keep an eye on her during the date, which put Jennifer's mind at ease.

As they finished their meal and took a leisurely stroll back to Jennifer's apartment, Jennifer finally revealed the reason behind her rushed meeting earlier in the day. Her voice carried a hint of sadness as she spoke.

"The truth is, the publishing house isn't doing well," Jennifer confessed. "They've decided to downsize, and I'm one of the people being laid off. In six months, I'll be unemployed."

Caroline's heart ached for her friend, knowing how much Jennifer had dedicated herself to her career in publishing. But she also saw an opportunity, a chance to inspire Jennifer to follow her own dreams as she'd done for Caroline.

Taking a deep breath, Caroline stopped walking and faced Jennifer. "Jen, I know this is a difficult time, but it might also be a chance for you to pursue what you've always wanted."

Jennifer looked puzzled, and Caroline continued, her voice filled with conviction.

"Remember how you've always wanted to open your own Entertainment Management firm? Publishing was supposed to be a stopgap until you could afford to do it. Maybe now is the time."

Jennifer's eyes widened as Caroline's words sank in. She had indeed dreamed of running her own company, guiding talent in the entertainment industry, and shaping careers. But life, with its demands and responsibilities, had pushed that dream aside.

Caroline placed a reassuring hand on Jennifer's shoulder. "Jennifer, this setback could be the universe's way of telling you it's time to follow your passion. It's never too late to chase your dreams, my friend." She smiled. "Isn't that what you told me not too long ago? And look, I've got a book deal for my series and a television series."

Jennifer's face slowly lit up with hope and determination. "You know what? Maybe you're right. Perhaps it's time I took that leap of faith."

They continued their stroll. Caroline could see the weight of uncertainty lift from Jennifer's shoulders. As they walked together under the city's glittering skyline, Caroline couldn't help but feel that life had a way of weaving unexpected threads into their stories, leading them toward brighter tomorrows.

AMY RAFFERTY

CHAPTER 2

Brad left the quaint coffee shop with a sense of lightness he hadn't felt in years. The chance encounter with Caroline had injected a burst of unexpected excitement into his otherwise predictable life. As he strolled down the bustling New York City streets, his thoughts were consumed by the intriguing woman he had met.

Caroline...

He couldn't help but smile as her image danced through his mind. She stood at about five foot six inches, her figure slim and graceful. Styled in a loose bun, her sandy blond hair, the color of sun-kissed wheat, framed her face. Her captivating hazel eyes were set beneath long, thick lashes and hidden behind a pair of glasses. Caroline's face bore no heavy makeup. Just a touch of mascara accentuated her natural beauty. It was evident that she possessed flawless skin, a fact that only enhanced her charm. But what truly drew him in was her dimpled smile, which radiated warmth and kindness.

While some might label her appearance as "mousy" and stereotypically librarian-like, Brad found her endearing and refreshingly genuine. What was even more appealing was that she seemed oblivious to his identity. Or, if she did recognize him, she was a masterful actress, adept at concealing her knowledge. It was a rarity he hadn't experienced in a long time.

Lost in his reverie, Brad meandered along the sidewalk, oblivious to his surroundings. He was so absorbed in thoughts of Caroline that he didn't hear his son's voice calling out to him. It was only when Connor shouted from the town car that had pulled up next to the curb that Brad snapped back to reality.

"Dad!" Connor's voice held a hint of exasperation as he leaned out of the car window. "Are you coming?"

Brad shook his head to clear his thoughts and grinned at his son. "Sorry, buddy. Got a lot on my mind."

Connor rolled his eyes playfully. "You wouldn't happen to be thinking about a summer vacation to California, would you?"

Brad settled into the plush leather seat next to his son. The town car pulled away from the curb, navigating the busy Manhattan streets.

Brad found he had to force his mind from drifting back to Caroline, leaving a bemused smile on his face.

"No, son, we're not going to California so you can spend your days surfing while I watch from the shore, holding my breath and willing all the sharks away." Brad looked at him.

Brad's thoughts of Caroline remained his own as he refrained from sharing them with Connor. After all, parents generally didn't discuss their dates with their sixteen-year-old children. Although, for some reason, Brad found himself wanting to tell whoever would listen about his meeting with Caroline.

The town car finally arrived at their stately townhouse, situated in one of the upper-class neighborhoods of New York. The building was an architectural masterpiece, boasting elegant brownstone façades and a charming front garden with meticulously manicured hedges and flowers in full bloom. Its elegant exterior showcased timeless wrought iron railings and a carefully landscaped garden that burst with vibrant colors each spring. Inside, high ceilings with intricate moldings, large windows, and rich dark wood floors created a luxurious and inviting atmosphere. The décor was a harmonious blend of classic and contemporary, reflecting Brad's family's refined taste.

Dinner that evening was relaxed in the spacious and tastefully decorated dining room. Connor, who had been eagerly awaiting this conversation, wasted no time diving into his favorite topic.

"Dad," Connor began, his eyes shining with excitement, "please, can you at least think about going to California this summer?"

Brad raised an eyebrow. "Why are you so adamant about California?" He watched his son closely. "There are loads of other surfing spots around the country and overseas, for that matter."

Connor leaned forward, his enthusiasm shining in his blue eyes that mirrored Brad's. "There's this big surfing competition I want to enter." His eyes widened in excitement. "It's the same competition that started Finnster's surfing career."

Brad smiled, fully aware of Connor's passion for surfing. His son had idolized legendary surfer Finnster since he was a child. Finnster's remarkable career and his status as a surfing icon had inspired Connor to pursue his own dreams on the waves since Brad had bought him his first bodyboard at the age of six.

That was the year they'd watched Connor's first surfing competition, and he'd been hooked. Every chance Connor got, he'd hightail it to Rockaway Beach in Queens when they were in New York or one of the many popular surfing spots when they were at Brad's family home in the Hamptons.

"I take it you're talking about the West Coast Classic Surfing Competition?" Brad leaned back in his chair.

"Yes, you know it's been my dream." Connor's expression was full of hope as he stared at his father.

Brad sighed with mock exasperation. "How can I say no to making whatever dreams of yours I can make come true?"

Connor beamed. "Does this mean we're going?"

"It means I'll think about it!" Brad grinned. "And what is your report card going to tell me?"

Connor's face lit up with excitement. "Thanks, Dad! You're the best!"

"Don't thank me just yet, young man," Brad warned him. "You've still got one week of school left, and we're not making any plans until we know you don't have to attend summer school."

"Dad!" Connor harrumphed. "When have I *ever* had to attend summer school?" He gave his father a comical look. "You know I'm a genius and I've never gotten lower than A's."

"There was that one time you got an A minus." Brad stood once they'd finished their meal and thanked Rosa as she came to clear away their plates.

"Would you like beverages in the living room?" Rosa asked them.

"Can I have cold chocolate milk, please?" Connor asked, standing up.

"Of course." Rosa smiled at him fondly. "I was going to bring you one anyway."

"Thanks, Rosa." Connor kissed her on the cheek, making her blush as always.

Rosa had been with Brad's family since his father was a young man. She'd helped Brad raise Connor when his wife had left him with an eight-month-old baby. Rosa adored Connor as if he was her own son.

After dinner, father and son retreated to the living room, where a massive flat-screen TV dominated one wall. It was Connor's favorite spot in the house, where he could indulge in his virtual surfing game, a gift from his grandparents. Brad wasn't too keen on his son having a game console at first. But then it became a way to bond with his son, and now their nightly challenges had become a cherished tradition.

As they settled in for their gaming session, Brad couldn't help but reflect on the day's events. A chance encounter with Caroline had filled him with newfound hope and anticipation. At the same time, Connor's dreams of surfing in California had reignited his own sense of adventure. Little did they know that the summer ahead would be a season of transformation and discovery, where dreams would take flight, and destinies would be woven together in unexpected ways—which Brad was to find out early the following day when his father called to schedule a meeting as soon as Brad got to the office!

Having dropped Connor off at his exclusive private school in New York City, Brad navigated through the morning traffic to reach the imposing glass-and-steel skyscraper that housed Danes Productions. He'd been driving the same route for years, but today felt different. The chance encounter with Caroline still lingered in his thoughts, infusing his day with a sense of anticipation he hadn't felt in years for their dinner that night.

As he pulled into the parking garage beneath the office building, he couldn't help but think about how life had taken an unexpected turn. Brad had grown up in privilege, inheriting wealth and, hopefully soon, the family business. His father, Travis Danes, had taken his family's already impressive production company and turned it into a powerhouse. Danes Productions was a formidable force in the entertainment industry.

Brad had always felt like he was living in his father's shadow, trying to prove himself worthy of taking over the family empire. Granted, he had made some bad choices in the past that had hurt his family and broken his father's trust, all in the name of love. Brad shook his head, thinking of what a fool he was nineteen years ago when he'd fallen head over heels for Debbie Attwood. Little did he know her father,

Shaun Atwood, who owned Atwood Finance Brokers, was about to get indicted for fraud and insider trading.

Brad's parents had warned him that Debbie was nothing more than a scheming socialite trying to save face by hitching her name to theirs. Brad didn't want to know as his parents had never liked the Attwoods, whom his father had never trusted. But Brad was so besotted with Debbie that he didn't see the signs his family and friends did. Until it was too late, and he'd been cut out of the Danes empire. He had to earn a salary at a television news network, where he was hired as a production manager.

Debbie had stuck out their marriage for exactly three years and five months. She'd even allowed herself to fall pregnant. While Brad had convinced himself Debbie wanted to start a family with him, it was just a ploy to get them back into the Danes empire. While his parents welcomed Connor, they still didn't welcome Brad back into the family while he was married to Debbie.

When Connor was eight months old, Brad came home from work one day to find Rosa at their house with Connor and all traces of Debbie gone. She'd left. The only thing she left behind were divorce papers. Six months after their divorce, Brad discovered his mother and father had paid her off to stop her from demanding full custody of Connor. Brad was furious, but his father told him not to underestimate the Attwoods, and he'd ensured she could never try to get custody of Connor or squeeze them for money again.

Brad became a single father, and to this day, although he dated, it was never anything serious, and he was very wary of their motives. His heart and family legacy were well guarded, especially now that he had Connor to care for. Brad's son came first in his life, and he made sure anyone who wanted to be a part of his life knew that. After years of not feeling anything but respect and enjoyable companionship for the woman he dated, he felt light and excited about going on a date since meeting Caroline.

The lift from the parking garage dinged, snapping Brad out of his thoughts. He exited the top-floor elevator and greeted Grace at the front desk before heading down the hallway. His father had called him early that morning to meet him as soon as Brad got into the office. That's why he bypassed his own corner office and headed straight for his father's, hoping that one day soon, it would be his office to occupy.

Travis Danes was deep in conversation on the phone when Brad entered. He gestured for Brad to sit and continued his call. Brad leaned back in the plush leather chair, his eyes scanning the impressive office that had always seemed so out of reach. The walls were adorned with framed posters of iconic movies and television shows that Dane Productions had brought to life over the years.

Finally, Travis hung up the phone and fixed his gaze on his son. "Brad, thank you for coming in right away." He sorted a few papers on his desk. "We have something important to discuss."

Brad leaned forward. His curiosity piqued. "What is it, Dad?"

Travis leaned back in his chair, his expression serious. "We're making a television series."

Brad raised an eyebrow. Danes Productions hadn't taken on a television series in years. "A series? What's it about?"

Travis's eyes sparkled with excitement. "It's called 'Cobble Cove Mysteries,' and I believe it will be a hit. Picture this, Brad: Jessica Fletcher meets the twenty-first century with a younger lead, and it's all set on Plum Island in New England."

A shiver swept up Brad's spine at the mention of New England, which immediately brought images of Caroline to mind, and he couldn't believe the path fate was leading him down. Now, his interest really was piqued. It had been a while since their company had ventured into the world of television series, and this concept seemed intriguing.

"Plum Island? That's an unusual choice for a filming location." Brad sat back and rubbed his chin thoughtfully.

Travis smiled and nodded, his voice earnest. "Exactly, and that's where you come in, Brad. I want you to oversee the entire production, from casting to locations, wardrobe, scriptwriting—everything."

Brad hesitated. That was a big undertaking and different from his usual job description. "Who's the creator of this series?"

Travis smiled. "A newcomer to the industry, Carrie Lines. She initially wrote it as a book series, but after reading it, I knew it had the potential to become a successful television series."

"A newcomer, Dad? Really?" Brad couldn't help but feel skeptical. "This is risky, and why Plum Island? Why not choose a location that viewers have actually heard of?"

Travis's expression turned serious. "Because, my boy, Plum Island has a unique charm and mystery that will set our series apart. I've already secured the rights to film there, and the locals are excited about it. It's an opportunity we can't afford to miss." He steepled his fingers in front of him. "It is also part of the contract I signed for the television series deal with Carrie Lines."

"Dad!" Brad sighed. His father was always doing things like that.

While Travis Danes was no fool, he still had a soft spot for newcomers and loved giving them their first big break. But in so doing, he did things like agree to film in locations like Plum Island.

"Listen, son, some of the most successful television mystery series have been filmed on small obscure islands," Travis reminded him. "Viewers love the small island atmosphere." He grinned. "And you can take Connor. There are some good summer surfing spots there. I did some research. Guess who's originally from Plum Island?"

"No way!" Brad said in disbelief.

"Uh-huh." Travis nodded. "Finnster was born and raised on Plum Island."

"I knew he was from New England, but I didn't know it was Plum Island," Brad gave a low whistle. "Connor will be ecstatic."

"I know," Travis said. "Be sure to tell him Gramps sent you there."

"Dad!" Brad rolled his eyes. His parents doted on Connor and would move the moon for him if he asked them to. "Sure, I'll tell him." He laughed. "When do you want us to go?"

Travis leaned back in his chair, a sly smile playing on his lips. "In two weeks. You'll need to head to Plum Island and set everything up. Find suitable locations for filming, arrange accommodation for the crew, and ensure everything runs smoothly. Think of this as your final step to taking over from me."

Brad's heart sank as he considered the timing. "Two weeks? That's not possible, Dad. Connor wants to participate in a surfing competition in California."

"What competition?" Travis raised an eyebrow. "And when is this competition?"

"West Coast Classic Surfing Competition," Brad told him. "It's during the first week of the summer vacation, and he's been looking forward to it for months."

Travis sighed, torn between business and family. "Alright. After the competition, you can head to Plum Island. But we can't afford any other delays."

Brad nodded, grateful that his father had relented, if only slightly. "I'll make it work, Dad."

Travis leaned forward, his tone encouraging as he said, "You know, I've been to Plum Island. They used to make the most delicious beach plum desserts and jellies." He sighed. "And Connor might enjoy it there. It has some good surfing spots. His surfing hero is from there." His grin grew. "Who knows? Maybe Connor will even get to meet the man."

"I doubt it!" Brad ran a hand through his hair. "After that mess with his ex-wife, Finnster seemingly disappeared off the face of the earth years ago." He sighed. "But even with the man now a ghost, Connor idolizes him."

"Well, then, you have two things in common with Finnster. Your son idolizes you." Travis pointed out before giving a lopsided smile.

"And you both have bad taste in women who've led you down a bad path."

"Okay, Dad!" Brad's heart slammed against his ribs. "It's been almost nineteen years. When are you going to let it go and forgive me?"

"When you find actual happiness with someone who deserves you and will love your son as much as they love you!" Travis gave him a smug smile. "Believe it or not, your mother and I only want you to be happy and find the kind of love we have."

"What you and mom have is one in a billion," Brad told him. "I don't think another relationship can top yours."

"You're wrong, son." Travis corrected him. "Your mother and I are not perfect. We have our flaws. But what we have is real. When love is real, it can conquer and survive anything."

"You make it sound so easy!" Brad mocked and looked at his wristwatch. His mind once again conjured images of Caroline, and his heart skipped a beat as he thought of their dinner date later. "Send me everything I need to know about this television series."

"Harriet already has it," Travis assured her. "It's a pity you and she—"

"Dad!" Brad hissed in exasperation. "We've been over this a million times. Harriet is my executive assistant and a good friend—*nothing more!*" He shook his head. "We just don't feel that way about each other."

"Such a pity." Travis sighed. "She might be tough, but she has a good heart. She's loyal and protective."

"You make her sound like a German Shepherd." Brad shook his head. "I must go. I have a meeting in twenty minutes, and I still need to review a few things."

After the meeting with his father, Brad returned to his own office, his mind abuzz with plans and preparations. He understood that the forthcoming weeks would whirl by in a frenzy of activity, and he realized the importance of assembling a capable team to assist with scouting and logistical arrangements on Plum Island.

While he diligently made calls and sent out emails, thoughts of his serendipitous encounter with Caroline continued to weave through his mind. It had ignited a chain of events that promised to reshape the trajectory of his life, both on a personal and professional level. Unbeknownst to him, the enigmatic island of mysteries held a trove of surprises and secrets poised for discovery.

Fate, it seemed, had cast its gaze upon him, and the journey ahead was poised to be a transformative odyssey, steering him through a turbulent but exhilarating course that would leave an indelible mark on his life.

AMY RAFFERTY

CHAPTER 3

Caroline's day had been nothing short of tumultuous, a rollercoaster of emotions that had left her drained yet strangely exhilarated. She had found herself thrust into the middle of a feud between Robert, Jules, and Tanya—one that had escalated far beyond the issue of Jules's childhood bedroom.

What had started as a seemingly simple attempt to find an amicable solution quickly transformed into a therapy session. Caroline had found herself consoling Tanya, who was overwhelmed with insecurity and doubt. Pregnancy hormones had a way of amplifying every emotion, and it was clear that Tanya was struggling.

Caroline had done her best to reassure Tanya, even though a nagging feeling tugged at her conscience. She couldn't help but wonder if

Robert was already subjecting Tanya to the same emotional turmoil he had once inflicted upon her during their marriage. The guilt weighed heavily on her, knowing she was lying to a pregnant woman to protect her from the painful truth.

After hours of mediating and offering support, Caroline had finally managed to bring some semblance of peace between the feuding parties. Jules would have the loft room at their Plum Island home, and she was free to bring whatever belongings she wished from her father's house. It was a small victory, but it was one that had left Caroline emotionally drained.

With the family drama temporarily resolved, Caroline shifted her focus to the upcoming meeting with one of Danes Productions' scriptwriters for the Cobble Cove Mysteries series. The discussions had been creative and engaging, filled with excitement and potential. It was a welcome change of pace from the earlier turmoil, and it reminded Caroline of why she had chosen the world of literature and storytelling in the first place.

As the meeting concluded, Caroline's thoughts inevitably turned to her impending date with Brad. A smile tugged at her lips, and her heart danced with a newfound sense of hope and anticipation. It had been so long since she had experienced such elation, and the feeling was both foreign and enchanting.

Caroline's preparations for the date had been meticulous. She had selected an outfit that struck the perfect balance between casual and chic, wanting to make a good impression without appearing overly eager. Her fingers traced the delicate fabric of her dress as she admired her reflection in the mirror. She had forgotten how exhilarating the prospect of romance could be.

Just as Caroline was about to head out the door, Jennifer intercepted her, a determined glint in her eyes.

"Can I borrow your phone quickly?" Jennifer asked her, and Caroline handed it to her.

With a swift motion, she took Caroline's phone and proceeded to download a "Find My Friends" app, linking it to her device.

"What on earth, Jen?" Caroline frowned while her initial unease was replaced by gratitude for her friend's concern and the feeling that at least Jennifer would know where she was.

"Well you did agree to this and you're going out with a man we don't know, and I haven't even met." Jennifer raised her eyebrows. "You don't even know his last name."

"I'm sure we'll get to exchanging those tonight," Caroline promised.

"You'd better!" Jennifer demanded. "At least then I can Google him or ask my friend at the FBI to run a background check."

"You're joking, right?" Caroline was a little alarmed.

"No!" Jennifer shook her head and presented Caroline with a small gift, elegantly wrapped. "I'm not. Times have changed since you were last on the dating scene."

"I'm not on the dating scene, and I most certainly didn't expect to have a chance meeting with a handsome stranger that I hit it off with, and he asked me to dinner." Caroline couldn't help the goofy smile that spread across her lips, spurred on by her fluttering heart.

"Oh, well, that makes it so much better!" Jennifer mocked. "Now open your gift, or I won't allow you out the door."

Caroline's curiosity piqued. She eagerly unwrapped the gift. Inside, she found an exquisite smartwatch, its design both modern and sophisticated.

"Jenny, this is gorgeous and must've cost you a fortune." Caroline looked at her friend in awe. "I can't accept this. It's just too much."

"You can never be too careful in the city," Jennifer warned, then beamed. "And you can consider it a gift from your future literary manager."

Caroline was touched by the gesture, her heart warmed by Jennifer's unwavering support right before her friends' words sunk in, and her eyes widened in surprise.

"Does this mean you're considering my idea?" Caroline's heart lifted even higher.

"I'm more than considering it," Jennifer told her. "I've already started the ball rolling." She gave Caroline a sheepish grin. "Honestly, I was going to follow you tonight and ensure you were okay." She laughed when Caroline rolled her eyes. "But I'm going to be networking at a media function tonight. I got the watch as my spy instead so I can find out where you are at all times."

She took Caroline's watch off her and made her put the new smartwatch on, deftly helping her fasten it. Caroline couldn't help but feel a sense of security knowing that her friend was looking out for her. She was even happier about Jennifer's new venture.

"Oh, Jen, I'm thrilled for you," Caroline said gleefully. "This is so exciting. Both of us are taking strides towards our dreams."

"Okay, slow down there, Speedy." Jennifer laughed at her enthusiasm. "While you're flying to the top, I'm starting out with one client—you!"

"I know you, Jen," Caroline encouraged. "When you put your mind to something, it's not without the force of your heart and soul behind it." She gave her a big smile. "That's why I know you will be a *huge* success."

"Thank you for your vote of confidence," Jennifer told her. "I need as much of that as I can get." She checked Caroline's new wristwatch. "I've already linked it to mine. There's a panic button if you need me."

Jennifer gave Caroline a crash course on how to use the watch. With a final embrace and a few words of encouragement, Jennifer finally allowed Caroline to leave. Nervously, she made her way to A Cup of Soho, the coffee shop where her chance encounter with Brad had unfolded. Her steps were light, but her heart raced with anticipation.

As she pushed open the café's door, a wave of relief washed over her. Brad was already waiting for her. A smile lit his face that mirrored the fluttering excitement in her own heart when he saw her. The evening ahead held the promise of new beginnings, a chance to leave behind the trials of the day and embrace the hope of a romantic adventure.

The quaint ambiance of A Cup of Soho enveloped them as they settled into a cozy corner, the world outside fading away. Brad and Caroline's evening had begun, and it was filled with the promise of a delightful dinner with engaging conversation. They shared a bottle of red wine as they read over the menus.

"Do you come here often?" Caroline asked after noting how well Brad seemed to know all the staff.

"I know the owner very well," Brad informed her. "We were at school together. I like to support his business, and Simon makes the best fancy coffees, food, and desserts in New York."

"Ah, the decadent coffees and desserts are how he keeps you coming back here, I bet." Caroline laughed.

"Oh, definitely," Brad agreed. "I noticed you were also on good terms with Simon yesterday." He noted. "Did you come here often when you lived in New York?"

"No, only in the last six months when my daughter and I moved in with my best friend," Caroline explained. "I like the ambiance here, and Simon makes the best coffee." She glanced at the dinner menu. "I've never come here for dinner, though."

"What do you feel like eating?" Brad asked.

"I was thinking of seafood," Caroline said, eyeing the menu again.

"Then I can recommend the grilled salmon," Brad told her. "It's exceptional and a personal favorite of mine."

"Then I'll try that." Caroline closed her menu and sipped her wine.

"Excellent choice. I'm having the same." Brad hailed the server, who took their order and disappeared as quietly as he'd appeared. "Tell me a bit about yourself." He smiled, picking up his wine.

"What do you want to know?" Caroline's heart raced.

"Everything!" Brad's voice was low, deep, and hoarse. His eyes darkened with emotion. "And anything you want to tell me."

"I hope you'll return the favor and tell me about yourself," Caroline prompted.

"Of course." Brad grinned, sipping his wine and staring into her eyes. Making her breath catch in her throat for the umpteenth time since she arrived at the restaurant. "I'm an open book. You can ask me anything."

"Okay, how about your last name?" Caroline asked him. *There, Jennifer will feel better.* She ignored the little voice at the back of her mind that whispered. *And so, will you.*

"Beckett," Brad answered her question.

"Hello Brad Beckett, it's nice to meet you." Caroline playfully held out her hand and then nearly melted when he took it and kissed it. "I'm Caroline Parker."

She had no idea why she gave him her married name, which she'd stopped using over a year ago. But it was too late to change it now, and it could be seen as an honest mistake, especially after fifteen years of marriage.

"It's nice to meet you, Caroline Parker." Brad linked his hand with hers and kept them on the table in front of them. "Do you like the theater?"

Starting a possible romance was like getting a new puzzle. There was the extreme patience you had to have while you sorted through all the pieces and painstakingly sorted them into piles. The excitement of finding each piece and then finding where they fit. Sometimes, you got all the pieces, which clicked into place, creating a beautiful picture. Other times, the puzzle pieces might fit, but at the end of putting the puzzle together, you find the picture it made wasn't for you. Then, there were times when the puzzle was a complete dud, and none of the pieces fit correctly, or they had to be forced into place.

So far, the pieces to the puzzle Caroline and Brad were sorting through seamlessly fitted into place. While they waited for their food to arrive, the conversation flowed naturally, like two old friends catching up after years apart. They laughed and regaled their way through a myriad of topics. They found out that they had a lot of shared likes and dislikes.

"I love the theater, and it's one of the things I miss most about New York," Caroline admitted. "And you?"

"I love it too." Brad raised an eyebrow. "Would you like to go to a show tomorrow night?"

"I'd love to, but I promised Jennifer I'd go to a work function with her." Caroline's heart sank.

"Another time then." Brad's easy smile sent more electric shock waves through her system and gave her goosebumps.

Their conversation shifted to their movie preferences. They found even more common ground. Other than their shared and deep appreciation for the theater, where they relished the magic of live performances, they both agreed that their favorite nights out often revolved around the anticipation of a gripping mystery or thriller at the movies.

Dinner arrived—an array of tantalizing dishes that delighted their senses. Amidst bites of exquisite cuisine, they continued to share stories and laughter. Time seemed to slip away, and neither of them was in any hurry for the evening to end. The conversation eventually fell on the subject of music.

Brad, an avid music enthusiast, shared his eclectic taste, which ranged from classical compositions to the electrifying beats of rock. Caroline found herself captivated by his enthusiasm and shared her own love for music, mentioning how her daughter, Jules, was a talented pianist who often filled their home with melodies.

Mentioning Jules turned their conversation to a deeper personal level when Caroline shared the challenges she had faced with her daughter since her divorce. She explained how her ex-husband had remarried and was now expecting another child, which had created an even rockier relationship between Jules and her father.

"Of course, I'm the one to blame for all of it." Caroline laughed. "Although I think I'm slowly winning her back after this visit. She's gone from blaming me for everything to asking me to help her sort out difficult situations between her father and his new wife." She shook her head. "We're slowly getting back to the mother-daughter relationship we had before the divorce. We were close. Now and then, I see a glimpse of my pre-divorce Jules right before she remembers she vowed to hate me for all eternity."

Brad listened attentively, his empathy evident in his eyes. "That sounds tough," he said softly. "I can imagine how challenging that must be for both you and Jules."

Caroline nodded, appreciating his understanding. "It's been a journey, that's for sure. But we're working on it."

Brad then opened up about his family, particularly his son, Connor, who was passionate about surfing. He spoke fondly of Connor's dedication to the sport and how it had become a significant part of their lives. Brad proudly told her that he never had a problem with Connor. He was such a well-adjusted kid and a straight-A student.

"Well, there was that one time he got an A-minus for pottery." Brad grinned.

"Pottery?" Caroline said in disbelief. "It's not as easy as it looks, you know."

"Oh, I know." Brad nodded teasingly. "But it's nice to have something to tease my bright, polite, happy, well-adjusted kid about."

"My daughter was all that." Caroline sighed and reluctantly pulled her hand away from Brad's when their desserts and coffee arrived.

As they savored their confectionery and sipped their coffee, the conversation meandered to other subjects, such as places they had always dreamed of visiting.

"I've had this lifelong dream of exploring Paris and Italy," Caroline confessed, her eyes gleaming with wanderlust.

Brad leaned in, a smile tugging at the corners of his lips. "I've been fortunate enough to visit both places," he said. "Paris is a city of timeless beauty, and Italy's art and history are breathtaking. If you ever decide to go, I could recommend some must-visit spots." He idly stirred his coffee. "And if you go to Italy, make sure to visit the smaller towns. You won't regret it. The people are friendly, warm, and inviting. And the food is out of this world."

As the evening drew to a close, Caroline felt a sense of reluctance. Time had flown by, and she had enjoyed every moment spent with Brad.

As they walked out of the eatery, Brad turned to her and smiled. "Thank you for tonight. I had a great time." His eyes reflected his reluctance for the evening to end. "I don't know when I last had such a good time."

Caroline's eyes twinkled with agreement. "I also enjoyed our time together. It's been a while since I've had such a wonderful time too."

Under the enchanting city lights, they stood, caught in a moment where words seemed unnecessary, their connection palpable.

"Can I get a cab to take you home?" Brad's courteous offer to arrange a cab hovered in the air.

With a gentle smile, Caroline declined his offer. "I only live a block away."

Brad's eyes brightened with pleasure, and he extended his arm toward her. "Then may I walk you home?"

Caroline's heart skipped a beat at his gallant gesture. "I'd like that," she replied, her smile mirroring her genuine delight.

A delightful shiver of anticipation coursed through her as she linked her arm with his. It was as if a dormant part of her had suddenly awakened, a symphony of emotions, and her heart felt like it was bursting into a spectacular fireworks display. Together, they began their short walk down the city streets, the world around them fading into insignificance as they reveled in the simple joy of each other's company.

But too soon, they came upon Jennifer's apartment building, and Caroline knew it was truly the end of the evening.

"This is me!" Caroline pointed to the building.

Their eyes met and held once again, each mirroring their reluctance to say goodnight.

Under the dimly lit street lamp, they shared their first kiss, a sweet and lingering connection that left them both breathless. When they finally pulled away, Brad looked into Caroline's eyes.

"Would you have lunch with me tomorrow?" Brad's words were a hoarse whisper as their foreheads touched.

Caroline's heart danced with delight, and she smiled warmly. "I'd love to."

Brad's face lit up, and he leaned in for one more kiss, a promise of more to come. "I'll pick you up at noon," he whispered.

Caroline nodded, her anticipation growing. "I'll be ready."

With one last sweet kiss, Brad stepped back, leaving Caroline standing outside Jennifer's building. They exchanged warm goodnights. Her heart filled with excitement for the day that awaited them.

As Brad walked away, he turned and smiled, waving back at Caroline before hailing a cab. Caroline watched him disappear into the night, and she smiled as her emotions shivered in anticipation of their lunch date the next day.

THE LIGHTHOUSE ON PLUM ISLAND

She walked into the apartment building feeling like a giddy school girl who'd just had her first kiss, and it was from the high school heartthrob. Caroline sighed as she walked into the empty apartment and went to prepare for bed, not that she thought she'd get much sleep. She was getting a bottle of water from the refrigerator when Jennifer arrived home.

"Hello!" Jennifer seemed surprised to see her. "You're home early."

"Jen, it's past one in the morning," Caroline pointed out.

Her eyebrows shot up in surprise, and she looked at her wristwatch. "Oh, it is!" She pulled a face, kicking off her ridiculously high Jimmy Choo's as she walked to the kitchen. "How was the date?"

"All kinds of wonderful!" Caroline sighed, getting another bottle of water for Jennifer and handing it to her.

"Uh-oh!" Jennifer looked at her with concern. "I've seen that starry-eyed look before, and you ended up marrying Robert the rogue."

"Oh, no!" Caroline fobbed her off. "This is just a look of me enjoying a moment I haven't had in a long, long time."

"If that's all it is." Jennifer popped the bottle of water open and took a sip. "Then I'm glad, and it's nice to see that sparkle in your eyes. You deserve some fun and a whirlwind romance."

"Thank you!" Caroline grinned before stifling a yawn. "How was your networking night?"

"A lot more lucrative than I thought it would be." Jennifer's eyes lit with excitement. "I've got another three potential clients. I'm meeting with them tomorrow."

"And your work won't mind you taking time off to conduct personal business?" Caroline teased.

"Nope." Jennifer shook her head. "Even if they did, I'd just take a few personal days, and I have way too much leave saved up."

"I thought as much." Caroline nodded and sipped her water. "You've hardly ever taken a vacation since you started working."

"Did you get Brad's last name?" Jennifer changed the subject.

"I did." Caroline beamed. "It's Beckett."

"Brad Beckett!" Jennifer rolled the name off her tongue. "Sounds like the opening of a tongue twister."

"Be nice," Caroline warned her teasingly. "He's a great guy."

"You know that after a chance meeting and one date?" Jennifer looked at her skeptically. "You and I both know that people rarely present who they are even after you've known them for a hundred years."

"Is this your way of telling me you've been lying to me about who you really are, and you're really a cyborg alien here to destroy Earth?" Caroline grinned.

"Wow! You've truly become an author, my friend." Jennifer laughed. "There were a million different ways you could've addressed that, but your imagination went straight to fiction."

"I'm embracing my new craft." Caroline gave a slight bow.

"Or you're floating on cloud nine from a chance meeting with the gorgeous Brad Beckett!" Jennifer teased.

"You're not going to stop saying his full name, now are you?" Caroline rolled her eyes.

"Nope!" Jennifer shook her head, taking a big sip of water before following Caroline from the kitchen. "And now I'm going to have to say goodnight because I have to be up early for a meeting and need some sleep."

"I'm also tired and have a date with Brad at noon." Caroline hugged Jennifer. "We're going for lunch."

"As long as you remember, we have the gallery function in the evening," Jennifer reminded her.

"I know," Caroline assured her as she headed for her bedroom. "I won't forget."

Caroline drifted off to the feel of Brad's lips still imprinted on hers and his face floating through her dreams.

CHAPTER 4

The following day, Brad sat in his spacious corner office, engrossed in a conversation with Lucy Woods' manager. The actress was a potential candidate for the lead role in the upcoming television series. Brad's executive assistant, Harriet Joyce, had suggested her for the part.

As he hung up the phone, Harriet entered his office, holding two advance copies of "Cobble Cove Mysteries," the books that were the foundation for their television series. Brad couldn't help but admire the sleek cover designs, a tangible representation of the project they were about to embark upon.

"How did it go with Lucy Woods' agent?" Harriet inquired, her sharp eyes assessing Brad's expression.

Brad sighed and shook his head. "Not well, I'm afraid. Her agent was on board until I mentioned that the Blackwell brothers would be producing the show."

Harriet rolled her eyes, a gesture she often employed when discussing Brad's father, Travis Danes. "Why is your father so insistent on hiring the Blackwell brothers for this series?"

Brad leaned back in his chair, pondering the question. "Because they're the best at what they do. Their track record speaks for itself. When you want a successful movie or television series, you get the Blackwell's."

"Talking about the Blackwell brothers, have you spoken to them yet about directing and producing the show?" Harriet enquired with raised brows. "They may not be available, and you've started throwing their names around in association with this production."

"I'll talk to them tomorrow before their birthday party on their yacht. I know they'll accept the gig," Brad told her, sitting back and raising a knowing eyebrow. "Have you decided if you're going to attend the party tomorrow?"

Harriet had found a perfect excuse to avoid the party and raised the advance copies of the books. "I'm afraid I'll be too busy." She gave him a smug smile. "Someone has to read these books to get acquainted with the material."

Brad chuckled, appreciating her dedication. "Have you started reading them yet?"

Harriet nodded, holding up the first book. "Just started book number one." She looked at the cover. "I have to admit, it's darn good."

Brad nodded. "Let's hope it translates into a decent series." He tilted his head. "Have you managed to secure one of the scriptwriters on my father's list?"

"I did!" Harriet told him, and he had a feeling he wasn't going to like who she managed to secure. "Despite your rather public humiliation of her and the fact she swore she'd never work for Danes Productions again if it meant you were involved, I managed to secure Dawn Vanderbilt."

Brad closed his eyes briefly, a shadow of the past crossing his thoughts. He remembered his relationship with Dawn, which had been one of his longest since his divorce. They had been together for three years, even engaged for two, until Brad realized that she wasn't the right fit for him. Unfortunately, their breakup hadn't gone as planned, and he shuddered at the memory, pushing it aside. He hadn't seen Dawn in two years.

"You couldn't get one of the other two writers on my father's list?" Brad looked at her hopefully.

"No, your father told me that Dawn was the first one to try and the scriptwriter *he* wanted working on this project," Harriet told him. "I felt awful having to use my friendship with her to twist her arm and assure her she wouldn't have to deal with *you!*"

"Great." Brad gave a resigned nod.

"It goes without saying that I'll be the one working with her throughout the production," Harriet warned him.

"Agreed!" Brad glanced at his wristwatch. "Besides, the past was in the past. I'm willing to move forward in the best interest of the project and the upcoming series."

"How gallant of you!" Harriet mocked. "Especially when you were the one that humiliated Dawn."

"Thanks, Harriet. I still have vivid memories of the episode and don't need a reminder," Brad assured her.

"Oh!" Harriet said, snapping her fingers as a thought struck her. "There's a quaint hotel on Plum Island called the Summer Inn that I believe can accommodate us and most of the team. There are a few bed and breakfasts on the island that will take the overflow."

"Good news," Brad said.

As Harriet prepared to leave his office, she paused, studying him intently. "There's something different about you today," she remarked.

Brad raised an eyebrow, feigning innocence. "Oh? What do you mean?"

"Something is going on with your face!" Harriet circled with her hand, her eyes narrowing suspiciously. "You've been smiling, looking far too happy. What's up?"

Brad couldn't help but laugh. "Things are looking up, Harriet," he replied, intentionally omitting the cause of his happiness. "The clouds are lifting, and the sun's starting to shine through again."

"Does that mean your father's finally retiring?" Harriet's eyes widened with excitement. "Remember you promised I would get your job and this office."

"I haven't forgotten!" Brad laughed and shook his head. "Especially as you remind me every opportunity you get."

With that, Harriet left his office, and Brad watched her go, a sense of optimism lingering in the air. He noticed it was time to call the town car, and his heart did a weird tap dance in his chest because it was finally time to meet Caroline.

Brad sat in the back of his sleek town car, the leather seats cradling him in comfort as he glanced out of the tinted windows at the bustling streets of New York City. The soft hum of the engine and the gentle sway of the car provided a sense of calm amidst the urban chaos. He was accompanied by his professional chauffeur, a seasoned driver with years of experience navigating the city's labyrinthine streets.

As the car glided through the city, Brad's mind wandered to the afternoon he had planned with Caroline. He couldn't shake the feeling of excitement and nervousness that had taken root in his chest. The prospect of spending more time with her, getting to know her better, and deepening the connection they had established sent a thrill through him.

Brad's thoughts drifted to the romantic picnic he had arranged in Central Park, complete with all the elements of a perfect date. He hoped the day would be memorable for both of them, a shared experience that would continue to draw them closer. Brad gave himself a mental shake. He felt like a schoolboy on his first date with the head cheerleader.

The car maneuvered through traffic with precision. Brad's heart skipped a beat as they approached Caroline's apartment building. Brad's driver pulled up in front of the building, and Brad took a deep breath, his anticipation building. He knew this was the beginning of something beautiful, a new chapter in his life that fate had unexpectedly written.

Wow, I have got it bad! Brad shook his head. He couldn't remember when last he'd felt like this and after only two dates.

Although the first day he'd met her was more a twist of fate than a date. It was worth getting stuck in Soho when his town car had been stuck in a major traffic jam after having collected Connor from his field trip.

Brad couldn't help but feel a surge of nervous energy coursing through. He couldn't believe how anxious he felt, like a teenager about to ask someone out on a first date. Even his palms were slightly sweaty. Taking a deep breath, he gathered his composure and stepped out of the car.

The doorman, a friendly older man in a crisp uniform, greeted him with a nod. "Good afternoon, sir. Who are you here to visit?"

Brad smiled warmly. "I'm here to see Caroline Parker." He frowned. "She's a guest of Jennifer..." He didn't know her friend's last name.

"Of course, sir." The doorman nodded and smiled. "I know Mrs. Parker." He pressed the intercom button, and Brad heard Caroline answer. "Mrs. Parker, I have a guest in the lobby for you."

"Thank you, Harry. I'll be there in a few minutes," Caroline told him.

"If you wouldn't mind waiting a few minutes, sir, Mrs. Parker will be here in a few minutes." Harry indicated towards the plush chairs in the waiting area of the lobby.

"Thank you." Brad nodded but didn't feel like sitting.

Luckily, he didn't have long to wait. Within a few minutes, the lift door dinged open, and Brad's breath caught in his throat as Caroline stepped out. She looked radiant in a soft rose cotton shirt that gently hugged her slim figure, flowing cotton pants in light gray, and strappy sandals. Her sandy blond hair was swept up in its usual messy bun, and her glasses perched on her nose added to her charm. Her glossy lips curved into a smile as soon as she saw him.

"Hello, Brad," she greeted him warmly.

"Hi," he replied, equally pleased to see her.

They exchanged pleasantries, and Brad couldn't help but admire how effortlessly beautiful she looked. He offered her his arm, which she graciously accepted, and they headed back to his town car.

Their destination was Central Park, where Brad had arranged a romantic picnic complete with a wicker basket filled with delicacies like fresh strawberries, artisanal cheeses, and crusty baguettes. Champagne chilled in an ice bucket, and there were even chocolate-covered strawberries for dessert. Brad had made sure to include an array of different choices, not knowing what her tastes were. He wanted to make this day special for her.

They spread out a soft blanket under the shade of a towering oak tree, the dappled sunlight filtering through the leaves, creating a tranquil atmosphere. Brad poured champagne into crystal flutes, and they toasted to the beauty of the day and the promise of the afternoon.

As they enjoyed their meal, their conversation flowed naturally like it had the night before. It was filled with laughter, and they shared stories about their lives in New York. The conversation moved on to their favorite books.

"I have many of those," Caroline admitted. "Sadly, I haven't had much time to read in the past two years." She sighed. "I've secretly moved from reading to writing in the spare moments I used to ferret away for reading."

"Ah, the reader is becoming an author." Brad raised his glass to her. "I know authors don't like to talk about their work in progress. But may I ask what it's about?" He grinned. "You can give me a vague description."

"Oh, it's just a mystery novel," Caroline said, waving it off.

"I hope you'll let me read it when you're done." Brad refilled their glasses.

"Maybe," Caroline said with a soft laugh.

"I'll take that!" Brad smiled. "Are you and Jules doing anything special for the summer vacation?"

"Not, really," Caroline told him. "How about you and Connor?"

"We usually spend most of the summer vacation at my family home in the Hamptons," Brad told her. "Connor loves it there as we live close to some of what he calls the hottest surfing spots, and he has all his surfer buddies."

"I'm familiar with surfer lingo." Caroline laughed. "As I mentioned last night, I grew up with an older brother who was an avid surfer. He was always chasing the best waves. My father spent a fortune on him as he traveled all over America looking for the perfect waves." She shook her head. "He was delighted when we had big storms in New England because it meant great waves."

"I remember Connor and his friends wanting to surf the storm breaks." Brad's eyes widened. "But I wouldn't let him. I draw the line at things like that."

"I don't blame you." Caroline sipped her champagne. "My brother and his best friend, who happens to be Jennifer's older brother, did that, and I swear he's the reason my father went gray so young."

"I'm sure my son and your brother would get on well then." Brad laughed, his heart jolting and a warm feeling washing over him at the thought of introducing Caroline to Connor.

"And my nephew, who shares his father's love of surfing, but thankfully not to the same extent as my brother." Caroline leaned against the tree trunk and spread her long legs in front of her. "Are you and Connor going to the Hamptons this summer?"

"Sadly, no," Brad said, shaking his head. "He's managed to twist my arm into allowing him to enter a surfing competition in California."

"Do you mean the West Coast Classic Surfing Competition?" Caroline impressed him by asking.

"Yes, that competition." Brad nodded.

"Yeah, my brother used to go to that competition every year," Caroline told him. "Be sure to get there early because that place fills up quickly, and take a beach umbrella."

"Thank you for the advice," Brad said. "I'll be sure to heed it." He smiled and shook his head. "That stretch of the shore gets jammed packed as it's during summer vacation. I can only imagine what it's like when it draws in the kind of surfing talent that competition does."

"It's unbearably busy." Caroline finished her drink and refused another refill. "No thanks, I've reached my limit." She smiled and returned to the conversation about California. "Even with all the hustle and bustle, I envy you and Connor getting away for a summer vacation." Her eyes reflected a deep longing. "Jules and I haven't had a proper vacation in over four years." she sighed.

Brad empathized with her situation. "Well, I know we've just met, but you are both welcome to join us," he suggested with a playful grin.

Caroline smiled warmly and appreciative, but she shook her head gently. "Thank you. That's so kind of you, but I have a lot going on this summer, and Jules has already gotten a summer job."

Brad nodded understandingly. "Of course. Maybe some other time, then."

Caroline's hazel eyes sparkled with sincerity. "I'd like that."

"Where does the time go?" Brad looked at his wristwatch.

"I know." Caroline agreed.

She helped Brad pack away their picnic items before he helped Caroline to her feet. His heart went wild as her soft hand touched his. They took a leisurely stroll through the park on the way back to the town car. As they walked, they savored the beauty of their surroundings and the pleasure of each other's company. Eventually, they found themselves near the park entrance, where a line of horse-drawn carriages awaited.

"I haven't been on one of those in about ten years," Caroline's eyes lit with excitement.

"I might not be able to take you on vacation," Brad said. "But I can certainly take you for a carriage ride if you have time?"

"Do you have the time?" Caroline asked, her eyes filled with hope.

"I can make the time." Brad hailed one of the carriages.

They climbed aboard, settling onto the plush seats. The carriage driver gave them a warm smile and set the horse in motion. The rhythmic clip-clop of the horse's hooves added a romantic soundtrack to their ride.

As they meandered through the park, Brad couldn't help but steal glances at Caroline, her profile soft and serene in the gentle afternoon light. He had to stop himself from pulling her to him and crushing his lips to hers. She was one of the most amazing people Brad had met. Her sincerity was refreshing, and he knew she wasn't a gold digger. Caroline had no idea who Brad was. She seemed to like him for who he was. Guilt at having lied to her about his last name sliced through him, but he pushed it aside.

"What a wonderful ending to an enchanting picnic," Caroline turned and smiled at him, making his heart stop for a few seconds.

"Yes, it is," Brad agreed.

The carriage ride was a fitting end to their day together. It was a slow and graceful transition from the enchanting picnic to the real world beyond. Brad didn't want the day to end, but sadly, he had a meeting he was already running late for.

All too soon, the carriage ride ended, and they went back in Brad's town car, heading towards Caroline's apartment building. Once they arrived, he helped her out of the car and kept her hand in his as he walked her to the door. The doorman opened it, and they walked to the elevator.

"I had a wonderful time today," he said sincerely.

Caroline smiled, her cheeks dimpling delightfully. "Me too."

Brad pulled her to him, their lips met, and the world around them no longer existed. His phone buzzing made it abruptly come crashing back, and he pulled away.

"If you're not busy tomorrow, would you like to join me at my friend's birthday party?" Brad asked her. "It's on his yacht docked at the New York Yacht Club." He smiled. "You can bring Jennifer."

"That sounds nice, but are you sure your friend won't mind you adding two guests to his birthday list?" Caroline's brows shot up.

"Trust me, they won't even notice," Brad assured her. "If you give me your phone number, I'll send you the name of the yacht and where it's docked." He took his phone out and bit back a wince when he saw all the missed calls and angry messages from Harriet. "The only catch would be that I'd have to meet you there as I have business to attend to before the party."

"Okay," Caroline said, an uncertain frown creasing her brow as she took her phone from her purse and they exchanged numbers.

"I'll send my town car to pick you up," Brad offered, shoving his phone into his pocket.

"That's okay. I'm sure we can find our way there," Caroline told him.

"I'll send you the details," Brad promised.

Once again, his fingers curled around hers and drew her toward him for another kiss. The annoying buzzing from his pocket wouldn't stop, and he pulled away from Caroline. Their fingers reluctantly parted as Brad stepped away.

"Until tomorrow, then," Brad said.

"Until tomorrow." Caroline smiled warmly.

Brad turned and walked back to his town car. He felt like he was floating on air and couldn't wait to see her again the following day.

CHAPTER 5

Caroline stood amidst the glamorous crowd at the art show function, her feet aching in the ridiculously high heels that Jennifer had insisted she wear. The heels perfectly matched the expensive A-line dress that clung to her figure, stopping just above her knees to showcase her shapely, tanned legs.

Jennifer had whisked her to the hairdresser's immediately after her enchanting lunch date with Brad. Caroline was still trying to get used to her sleek new hairstyle. The soft bob now framed her face, the highlighted honey-gold tresses falling gracefully to her shoulders. Her eyes had only just stopped burning from the contact lenses she was wearing. Every time she caught her reflection, she couldn't help but marvel at the stunning transformation of it, thanks to Jennifer's expert makeup application.

Caroline felt like she'd been transformed from her usual understated, almost mousy appearance into someone entirely different. The attention her new look attracted made her self-conscious, even though Jennifer insisted she looked stunning. Caroline struggled to remember their names after being introduced to a never-ending stream of people. The wine she had been sipping was starting to make her feel a bit lightheaded as she and Jennifer strolled through Rad Ripley's art exhibition.

Rad Ripley's modern art was a sight to behold. His pieces were a mix of vibrant colors, intricate designs, and abstract forms that seemed to challenge the boundaries of imagination. Caroline marveled at how each piece conveyed a different emotion or story, and she couldn't help but get lost in the world of art, if only for a moment. She leaned closer to one of the paintings, examining the brush strokes and how the colors blended and danced on the canvas.

Jennifer, who had been chatting animatedly with a group of art enthusiasts, noticed Caroline's fascination with the artwork. She excused herself from the conversation and joined Caroline by the painting.

"Quite something, isn't it?" Jennifer remarked, her eyes fixed on the canvas.

Caroline nodded. Her gaze was still captivated. "It's incredible how art can evoke such powerful emotions and thoughts. Each piece tells a unique story."

"Art or your new romantic interest?" Jennifer teased her friend. "You're positively glowing and not just from your make-over."

Caroline blushed slightly. "I can't help it. It's like I've stepped into a different world."

Jennifer chuckled. "Well, I'm glad you're enjoying yourself for once. And I must say, you look like you belong here among all these art aficionados."

Caroline's cheeks flushed with a mixture of embarrassment and gratitude. "Thanks, Jennifer. I owe it all to you and your magic makeover."

Jennifer waved off the compliment. "Oh, please, it's not just about the makeup and the dress. You've always had this beauty inside you, Caroline. It's just that sometimes a little external transformation can help us see what's been there all along."

Caroline smiled, touched by Jennifer's words. "You're too kind."

As they continued exploring the exhibition, Jennifer introduced Caroline to more people, including some artists and collectors eager to discuss Rad Ripley's work. Caroline was drawn into conversations about art, culture, and creativity, topics she had rarely explored before.

A sense of wonder and excitement gradually replaced the wine-induced light-headedness.

As the evening wore on, Caroline's feet began to protest the relentless high heels. She discreetly slipped them off under a table and sat to catch her breath and relax. Caroline couldn't help breathing a sigh of relief when Jennifer joined her at the table, glancing at her watch. "It's getting late, and I can see you're ready to head home."

Caroline nodded. "Yes, my feet have had enough excitement for one evening."

Jennifer chuckled as Caroline groaned and slipped the shoes back on. They made their way towards the exit, bidding farewell to the vibrant world of art and culture that had enveloped them for the night.

Outside, a cool breeze greeted them, carrying with it the scent of the city. Caroline took in the familiar sights and sounds of New York, feeling a sense of contentment wash over her. Despite her initial reservations, the art show had been an eye-opening experience, and she couldn't help but be grateful to Jennifer for pushing her out of her comfort zone.

As they walked towards a waiting cab, Caroline reflected on the evening. It had been a whirlwind of colors, conversations, and creativity. She realized that sometimes stepping into the unknown, even if it meant wearing uncomfortable shoes, could lead to unexpected discoveries and a deeper appreciation for life's beauty. Her heart fluttered as Brad's face flashed before her, and she couldn't stop a smile from spreading across her lips.

As the cab made its way back to Jennifer's apartment, she took out her phone and found a message from Brad reminding her about the yacht party. At the end of the message, he gave details of the yacht and a time.

"Jen, do you have plans for tomorrow?" Caroline hadn't told Jennifer about the party. She was waiting for Brad to message her with the details.

"It's your last day in New York, so I thought we'd spend it together." Jennifer's brows knitted together as she watched Caroline suspiciously. "Unless you're going to ditch me for Brad."

"No," Caroline said, smiling at Jennifer. "How would you like to go to a yacht party in the afternoon?"

"A yacht party?" Jennifer looked at her, intrigued. "Tell me more."

"Brad has invited *us* to—" Caroline looked at his message and read, "The Blackwell's birthday party upon the Black Tulip docked at the New York Yacht Club."

"Did you just say Blackwell's?" Jennifer gasped. "

"I believe so!" Caroline frowned as she looked at her friend.

"The Blackwells?" Jennifer asked her to clarify.

"That's what Brad's message says." Caroline nodded.

"Yes!" Jennifer nodded. "Wow! Caz!" She breathed excitedly. "That's fantastic."

"Who are the Blackwells?" Caroline asked her.

"How can you not know who the Blackwells are?" Jennifer gaped at her.

"I don't!" Caroline shook her head as the cab pulled up in front of Jennifer's apartment building.

They climbed out after Jennifer paid the cab driver and they hurried inside.

"Don't you ever read a magazine?" Jennifer said in exasperation as she let them into her apartment. "They're only *the* most sought-after production talents in the country, if not the world."

"Oh!" Caroline said, with a shrug as she pulled the torture devices, she thought Jennifer had paid way too much for, off her feet. "Anything you have to pay as much as you did for these shoes should at least be comfortable."

"Beauty is pain, my friend." Jennifer laughed. "Are we still going to that *man's* house tomorrow?"

"If by that *man*, you mean Robert, then yes." Caroline nodded. "We have to mark the items Jules wants to have shipped to Plum Island from her childhood bedroom."

"Fine, anything for Jules." Jennifer got them each a bottle of water from the refrigerator. "Let's go early." She suggested, taking a sip of water. "Because afterward, you and I are going shopping."

"For what?" Caroline asked.

"Outfits befitting a Blackwell yacht party!" Jennifer stated excitedly. "Do you know the kind of networking I can do for our new business ventures there?" Her eyes lit up. "That party will be filled to the brim with entertainment royalty."

Caroline sighed resignedly and knew she wouldn't talk Jennifer out of the shopping spree, but secretly, she was pleased her friend had suggested it. She knew Brad was rich because of his expensive clothing and his family home in Rhode Island.

"Fine, but you have to promise you won't do your usual interrogation procedure when I introduce you to Brad," Caroline told her.

"Nope, sorry, I can't promise that," Jennifer said honestly. "I know you're having a fabulous time, and Brad has put a sparkle in your eyes I've not seen in years." She took another sip of water. "But while you're all starry-eyed, I have to be the one to make sure what's starting as a sweet romance doesn't turn into a country and western song."

"Not all country songs are about heartache, you know." Caroline rolled her eyes.

Jennifer hated country music. She said it was always full of granny falling out of wheelchairs, freight trains running over Peggy Sue, hearts being ripped out, and so on. Caroline still wasn't quite sure what country music her friend had listened to, but she got the gist of Jennifer's warning. Caroline knew Jennifer was only looking out for her, and she loved her all the more for it. Jennifer was her best friend, and she knew Caroline better than anyone else in this world did. They had each other's backs.

"Of course it is!" Jennifer shuddered. "Give me good old rock and roll any day."

"Can we talk about the party?" Caroline changed the subject.

She knew their current conversation would probably lead to Jennifer wanting to play some of her favorite rock ballads. While Caroline loved all kinds of music, her feet ached, and she was tired. She didn't want to go to the yacht party with dark circles under her eyes.

"We're going!" Jennifer stated and stifled a yawn. "And on that note, I suggest we get to bed." She grinned. "We have a big day tomorrow."

The following day, Caroline and Jennifer were up early. Caroline was amazed to find that she was still strangely energized even after a few late nights in a row.

"I still believe you should've got the house in the divorce," Jennifer said, pulling her shades from her face as they pulled up in front of Robert's brownstone.

"I couldn't afford to keep it back then," Caroline reminded her as they climbed out of the car.

They had just started climbing the few steps to the front door when it flew open, and Jules flew out, wrapping her arms around Caroline.

"Mom!" Jules said, hugging her tightly. "I'm so glad to see you."

Caroline and Jennifer exchanged shocked glances. It had been a while since Jules had greeted Caroline like this.

"Hi, sweetheart," Caroline greeted her, kissing her daughter's blonde head. "Is everything okay?"

"Yes." Jules stepped back and looked at her mother quizzically before hugging Jennifer. "Hi, Aunt Jen."

"Hey, kiddo." Jennifer returned the hug. "How's things at your father's house?"

"Oh, you know." Jules shrugged. "It's been good to see my friends."

"That's great." Jennifer smiled and wrapped her arm around Jules's shoulder as she led them inside.

"Dad isn't here," Jules said, turning to close the door, then stopped and looked at Caroline in surprise. "Mom!" She gasped. "You look beautiful."

"Oh!" Caroline felt her cheeks heat.

"I gave her a makeover," Jennifer said proudly. "Your mother's heading for fame and fortune. I thought she should look the part."

"I always knew you were gorgeous!" Jules smiled.

"Thank you!" Caroline wasn't quite sure how to take that.

"Caroline!" Tanya's voice drifted to them from the sweeping staircase.

"Hello, Tanya," Caroline greeted the woman, forcing a smile and doing their usual air kiss greeting. "You're looking radiant."

"Fat, you mean!" Tanya pouted. "And don't even look at my swollen ankles." She moaned, forcing them to look at her ankles. "See. They are now *cankles*."

"They're not that fat!" Jennifer said, and Caroline bumped her warningly. "I've seen worse."

Caroline shot Jennifer another warning glance and rolled her eyes at her.

"Thank you." Tanya sniffed and hugged Jennifer, taking her sarcasm as a compliment. "Can I get you something to drink?"

"No, thank you, Tanya," Caroline declined her offer. "We don't have a lot of time."

"I'm sure," Tanya said, dabbing her eyes with a crumpled tissue. "You're a celebrity now."

"Well, I wouldn't go that far," Caroline said, quickly changing the subject. "Should we go to Jules's room?"

"Yes, of course." Tanya nodded and led them up the stairs. "I'm sorry we have to move Jules to another room. But with the baby coming, we need her room."

"And one of your other six bedrooms wouldn't suffice as the nursery?" Jennifer raised her eyebrows in disbelief.

"Jules's room is next to the main bedroom," Tanya pointed out. "We're going to join the two rooms."

"Oh, nice," Caroline said, feeling hurt. She'd begged Robert to do that when Jules was born, but he'd refused.

Tanya's gaze fell on Caroline, and she frowned. "Have you cut and colored your hair?" she asked, making Caroline feel her space was being violated as Tanya touched one of her golden locks. "And you're wearing contact lenses."

She stepped back and ran her eyes over Caroline's attire. She wore designer jeans that fit her without being too tight and a cream cotton shirt with soft pink roses. Instead of her usual comfortable sneakers, her perfectly pedicured pink toes popped out of a pair of sandals.

"You're even dressed differently," Tanya noted. "You look gorgeous." She surprised Caroline by complimenting her. "Success suits you."

"You really do look gorgeous, Mom," Jules whispered, her eyes shining with pride as she smiled at her mother. "Can I have my hair cut too?"

"We'll make a day of it when we go shopping in Boston to pick out items for your new loft room," Caroline promised, her heart lifting at Jules's new attitude toward her.

An hour later, Caroline, Jennifer, and Jules had marked all the items Robert would have to send to Plum Island. Tanya had gone to nap, and Jules was leading them out of the house, reluctant to let them go.

"What time will you be picking me up tomorrow?" Jules asked Caroline.

"Are you actually eager to go back to Plum Island?" Jennifer looked at Jules in mock disbelief and then playfully mussed Jules's hair, making her laugh. "Who are you, and what have you done with Brattigan Jules?"

"Hey, I'm not a brat!" Jules laughed at Jennifer, fending her off from tickling her. "Not that much anyway."

"We love you, brat and all!" Caroline grinned and kissed her daughter goodbye.

Jennifer and Caroline had just walked through the front gate when they ran into Robert, who stopped dead and did a double-take seeing Caroline.

"Caroline!" Robert sputtered, his eyes widening in disbelief. "Wow!" He gave his head a vigorous shake. "You, uh—" He cleared his throat, attempting to regain his composure. "You look amazing."

"She does, doesn't she!" Jennifer chimed in with a smug expression. There was no love lost between Jennifer and Robert.

"Yes," Robert replied absentmindedly, not even sparing a glance at Jennifer. His gaze remained transfixed on Caroline. "You're gorgeous," he added, his voice barely above a whisper.

"Thank you," Caroline replied, feeling a sense of satisfaction despite the pettiness of it all. She knew she shouldn't let his compliment affect her, but it did.

An awkward silence hung in the air as Robert continued to gape at her, seemingly at a loss for words.

"Well, this hasn't been fun at all," Jennifer drawled, tugging Caroline's arm. "We have a yacht party to get to at the New York Yacht Club." She casually dropped the name. "We wouldn't want to be late." Jennifer shot Robert another smug smile. "Goodbye, Robert." She playfully pointed at his mouth. "You might want to close your mouth and wipe away the drool."

With that, Jennifer led Caroline away, leaving Robert dumbfounded and gaping as Jennifer drove off. Caroline couldn't help but smile. She no longer had any romantic feelings for Robert. Still, having him look at her like she was the most desirable woman on the planet was undeniably satisfying. It gave her a significant confidence boost.

"That must've felt good," Jennifer remarked as they headed toward Fifth Avenue.

"I know it's petty," Caroline replied, her voice filled with elation, "but it really did. It felt really, really good."

A few hours later, dressed in a chic, soft pastel A-line vintage pleated flare-style dress made of soft linen that breezed around her figure, Caroline looked radiant. The hemline stopped just above her knee, showcasing her toned legs, accentuated by matching wedge heels that weren't too high. Her newly styled hair bobbed mischievously on her shoulders, framing her lightly made-up face that highlighted her most outstanding features. Without her glasses, her hazel eyes stood out, showing off her naturally long, thick lashes. Her soft pink lips shone with a touch of gloss, and two deep dimples punctuated her smile.

"You look breathtaking," Jennifer complimented as they exited the cab upon reaching the yacht club.

"You always look like you're ready for the runway," Caroline laughed nervously.

Jennifer linked her arm with Caroline's. She stood three inches taller than Caroline, with dark auburn hair, big blue eyes, and a stunning natural beauty. Jennifer's long, elegant figure was highly toned from regular exercise, and she had an effortless glide to her walk. The two of them turned heads as they made their way to the yacht, where they could hear the party had begun.

"Wow!" Caroline murmured as they stopped near the yacht. "That's not a yacht," she spluttered. "That's a mini cruise liner."

"Come on," Jennifer said, barely containing her excitement. "Let's go find this man of yours."

An usher greeted them as they reached the boarding stairs for the yacht. "Good afternoon," the man in a tuxedo greeted them. "May I have your names?"

"Caroline and Jennifer Parker," Caroline repeated the names Brad had added to the guest list.

"Ah, of course." The usher nodded. "Please, mind the step at the top and enjoy the party."

"Thank you," Caroline and Jennifer said in unison, feeling like movie stars as they walked up the boarding stairs to the yacht. Caroline couldn't help but whisper to Jennifer, "Wow! This is amazing."

"I know," Jennifer whispered, encouragingly squeezing Caroline's arm. "I've been to A-lister yacht parties before, but this is like a New York royalty party."

Caroline and Jennifer stepped onto the massive super yacht, the gentle sway beneath their feet a testament to its size and grandeur. The yacht gleamed under the soft glow of strategically placed lights inside. The air was filled with laughter, clinking glasses, and the soothing melodies of a live jazz band. Waitstaff moved gracefully through the crowd, offering trays of champagne and hors d'oeuvres. It was a scene of opulence and sophistication.

The sea sparkled beyond the yacht, a breathtaking view that stretched to the horizon. The boat was docked in a prime spot, offering a stunning panorama of the New York City skyline, with its iconic buildings illuminated against the afternoon sky.

As they navigated through the well-dressed guests, Caroline and Jennifer couldn't help but marvel at the extravagance of the event. The guests were dressed in casually elegant attire, and the women wore a mix of stunning dresses, shorts, and pantsuits, with jewelry that sparkled in the sunlight. The men wore a mixture of slacks or chinos, polo shirts, or linen shirts. It was like walking into the pages of an elite yachting magazine.

Jennifer took two sparkling glasses of champagne from a waiter who stopped in front of them. She handed one to Caroline, who sipped the bubbly liquid, which was crisp and refreshing.

Caroline leaned into Jennifer and spoke over the soft jazz music. "This is beyond anything I could have imagined."

Jennifer chuckled. "I told you the Blackwells know how to throw a party."

Caroline nodded in agreement. "It's incredible. I can't believe I'm here."

"It's a pity you're meeting Brad." Jennifer flashed a mischievous smile. "You've caught the eye of quite a few very well-known gentlemen already. I told you that makeover was a game-changer."

Caroline blushed but appreciated the compliment. "Well, I must admit, I'm not used to all this attention. It's a bit overwhelming."

Jennifer laughed softly. "Welcome to the world of New York's elite." She glanced around the yacht. "And by the looks of it. If things work out between you and Brad, you'll have to get used to it."

As they strolled through the opulent yacht, Caroline couldn't help but feel like an outsider in this world of extravagance and glamor. Her heart raced with nervous excitement, and she kept her eyes peeled for any sign of Brad. The yacht was a floating palace adorned with lavish decorations, crystal chandeliers, and fine art. The guests sipped on glasses of expensive champagne, their laughter mingling with the soft melodies of a live jazz band.

Jennifer nudged her gently. "Don't be too overwhelmed, my friend. You belong here just as much as anyone else."

They continued their search for Brad, ascending to different decks of the yacht. Each level outdid the last in terms of luxury and entertainment. There was a cozy lounge area with plush sofas, a fully stocked bar, and a dance floor where couples twirled to the music. On another deck, a gourmet buffet showcased a mouth-watering spread of dishes from around the world.

"I see someone I know," Jennifer told her. "I'll come find you."

"Okay," Caroline said, though deep down, she felt a twinge of anxiety.

Caroline moved through the crowd, her heart pounding in her chest. She couldn't help but feel out of place among the glittering elite of New York. Every familiar face Caroline recognized sent a wave of shock and awe through her. It was surreal to think she was at a party mixing with celebrities and influential figures.

As she ventured further into the yacht, she heard a warm, rich laugh that made her heart skip a beat. She turned and saw Brad engaged in conversation with another man, equally as tall and striking. Her eyes widened as she realized who the man was—a Blackwell brother, a name synonymous with Hollywood royalty. Jennifer had given her a quick lesson on the Blackwells and had shown Caroline their pictures in a magazine over breakfast.

Suddenly, her shyness overwhelmed her, and she retreated behind a pillar, her heart racing like a trapped bird. She observed them from a distance, her gaze fixed on Brad, who looked dashing in dark linen trousers and a polo shirt. His casual elegance made her breath catch in her throat.

"I saw you having a picnic in the park yesterday, old man," the Blackwell brother told Brad.

The Blackwell brother's words reached her ears, and her heart sank. They were talking about her. Anxiety coursed through her veins as she listened to their conversation.

"Oh, right!" Brad said, with a nod, taking a sip of his drink. He scanned the room before turning his attention back to the man in front of him.

"Was it a blind date? Maybe lose a bet? Or were you interviewing a nanny or tutor for Connor?" The Blackwell brother persisted.

"Not that it's any of your business. She's just a friend who's in New York for a few days," Brad replied in what Caroline interpreted as a bored, disinterested tone, sending a mix of emotions through Caroline.

She strained to hear the rest of the conversation while not being seen.

The Blackwell wiped his brow teasingly. "Phew, that's a relief. For a moment, I thought you might be going through a mid-life crisis. The mousy librarian type is certainly not the kind of woman you usually have gracing your arm." He laughed. "That would be like trading in an elegant racehorse for a nag."

Caroline's heart ached at the words, and her cheeks flushed with humiliation. Before she could process further, a stunning woman approached Brad, and they walked away for an intimate conversation. The sight shattered Caroline's confidence, and she turned to flee.

Humiliation, anger, hurt, and betrayal overwhelmed her as she pushed her way through the crowd, desperate to escape the painful scene. She finally found Jennifer, her emotions a tumultuous storm.

"Caroline!" Jennifer gasped, concerned by the devastation on her friend's face. "What's the matter?"

"Please, can we leave?" Caroline's voice quivered as she clung to her last shreds of dignity and forced herself not to burst into tears. "Please, please don't ask questions. Let's just go."

"Of course," Jennifer said, her eyes filled with empathy as they rushed off the yacht.

They remained silent for the cab ride back to Jennifer's apartment. As soon as they were in the familiar surroundings of Jennifer's apartment, Caroline's pain, humiliation, and heartbreak finally burst forth.

She crumpled on the sofa, wrapped in her friend's arms, recounting the painful incident. One thing was clear to her—she and Brad were from two very different worlds, and she didn't fit into his.

CHAPTER 6

"Okay, Brad," Harriet hissed. "I've been here for three hours, and that's three hours too long."

"I'm glad you came," Brad told her.

"It's not like you gave me much choice," Harriet reminded him. "I did what you asked, and we have the Blackwell brothers committed to the Cobble Cove Mystery series." She repositioned her clutch beneath her arm. "Now, I'm going home." She turned and grabbed an unopened Krug Clos d'Ambonnay champagne bottle from the ice bucket. "Nice," she said, eyeing the label. "I'll see you on Monday."

Harriet kissed his cheek and walked off, skillfully dodging Alex Blackwell as she made her way to the exit. Brad sighed and ran his hand through his hair, glancing at his wristwatch and frowning as he wondered where Caroline was.

Brad pulled his phone from his pocket. His heart dropped when there were no calls or messages from her. He was about to send her a message when he stopped himself. He didn't want to seem too eager or come off as stalkerish. Brad decided to give Caroline another twenty minutes before trying to call or message her.

After thirty minutes with no Caroline, Brad tried to call her, but the phone went straight to voicemail. He stood on the deck of Alex's yacht, the Dark Ocean, and stared at his phone, a frown marring his brow.

"You look like you've been stood up!" A familiar female voice from behind him made his jaw clench.

His grip on his phone tightened before he turned to see the tall strawberry-blonde woman staring at him with a raised eyebrow that arched over jewel-green eyes. She was breathtakingly beautiful and dressed in a stylish sun dress that dropped to her knees. The dress topped long, tanned legs accentuated by heels that added at least two inches to her height.

"Hello, Dawn," Brad greeted her. He hadn't seen her since their breakup two years ago. "You're looking as gorgeous as ever."

"You don't have to flatter me, Brad." Dawn's expression didn't change. "I've already signed the contract to write your father's new project."

She stood with her purse clutched beneath one arm, and a glass of what he knew would be sparkling apple juice in the other. Having grown up with an alcoholic mother, Dawn didn't touch alcohol.

"It's not flattery when it's the truth, Dawn," Brad assured her. He gave her a tight smile and sighed. "I know this is long overdue and probably won't mean a thing." He pocketed his phone. "I'm sorry about what happened."

"Is the apology for publicly humiliating me at the launch of a novel?" Dawn tilted her head slightly. "Or for you having cheated on me twice?"

"Both!" Brad said and sipped his drink. "I never meant to hurt you, and for the record, I never cheated on you. I was having a business dinner with Daphne Rose, and she *kissed* me as we exited the restaurant." His jaw clenched. His life always had a spotlight on it. "I think she'd set the whole thing up as the press were waiting for us as we walked out." He pinched the bridge of his nose. "And you know that thing with Vanessa Turner was completely staged by her." He blew out a breath. "But the worst was using the Vanessa thing to call off our engagement in front of the press. I should never have said the things I did to you so publicly."

"I never needed the explanations," Dawn told him. "I understand how things work in our business. But I'll take the apology." She raised her glass to him. "I didn't walk over to you to dredge up our past." She sipped her apple juice. "I came to call a truce. I know I'll mainly be working with Harriet. Still, we'll cross paths during the project, and it wouldn't be professional to let our personal life interfere with our working relationship."

"Thank you." Brad's smile broadened, and he leaned against the railing. "At least something good has come of today."

"So, someone really stood you up?" Dawn's brows rose, and she pulled a face. "That must be a first for you."

"I've been stood up more than once," Brad assured her with a soft laugh.

"Don't worry," Dawn said, a smile spreading across her beautiful mouth. "We've all been there." She stood next to him, leaning against the railing with him. "Would you mind some company?" She looked around the room. "I only came here because Harriet dragged me here, and then she took off."

"That's Harriet for you." Brad shook his head. "When you're going out with her—"

"Always come in your own car or have your own transport," Dawn finished for him, and they laughed.

It felt good to be on speaking terms with Dawn again. They may not have worked as a couple, but they had been friends, having grown up in the same circles before that. Brad had four best friends, and Dawn used to be one until they started dating, and he'd missed her. Brad knew this truce didn't mean their friendship would pick up from where they'd left it and become romantically involved, but it was a start.

"Her ex did a number on her," Brad said before thinking, and he gave himself a mental shake.

"Yes, Joel was a bigger jerk than you were," Dawn said, giving him a lopsided smile. "Sorry, I couldn't help myself."

"No need to apologize," Brad told her. "I was a jerk." He glanced down. "I hurt my best friend."

Brad turned, and their eyes met.

"As much as I want to blame you for *everything* that happened," Dawn admitted, "I played my part in the demise of our relationship."

"Is that an apology for breaking my nose?" Brad asked with a grin.

"Yes." Dawn grimaced. "If it's any consolation, I broke two fingers punching you." She looked at the hand she was holding her glass in. "It was not my finest moment."

"It wasn't either of our finest moments." Brad sighed. "I know better than to go a few rounds with duking Dawn."

"How come the press called you blindsided Brad, and I was called duking Dawn?" Dawn shook her head.

"Because you did blindside me," Brad reminded her. "With a right hook to my nose."

"I warned you to let go of me," Dawn defended her actions.

"You were about to rush off in a fury, and we both know that you tend to rush off blindly when you're *that* angry," Brad told her. "I was just trying to calm you down and put you in a cab."

"Here's a tip for you for the future." Dawn's eyebrows rose. "Trying to show off how much stronger you are than an angry woman by restraining her when she's told you to let go of her is *not* the way to calm her down."

"Yes, I learned that the hard way." Brad gave his nose a wiggle.

"The plastic surgeon did a great job on your nose, by the way." Dawn grinned. "For the record, I wasn't aiming for your nose or even your face. You ducked your head as I swung."

"I've still got the picture of you punching me in the nose," Brad told her. "Connor wanted to frame it. He didn't speak to me for weeks after we broke up."

"Connor told me he wasn't speaking to you." Dawn's words didn't shock him.

Brad knew how close she and Connor were even before they started dating. His friends had also helped him raise Connor.

"Then you know he took a *break* from me and went to live with my parents." Brad shook his head, remembering the trouble his and Dawn's public break-up at her book launch had caused.

"Yes." Dawn nodded. "I told him not to. I'm sorry about that."

"Connor loves you," Brad told her. "To be honest, I was so proud of how he defended your honor and stood up for what he thought was right."

"He stuck up for you too, you know." Dawn smiled at his surprised look. "He said that his father wasn't usually such a jerk. Connor said that you were usually a man of honor. Still, you were just a man caught in the gravitational pull of a cunning woman."

"He said that?" Brad looked at her in surprise.

"He did." Dawn sipped her drink. "Although I can't lie and say that I didn't feel a little smug when I saw Daphne had moved onto the arm of Alex and then her new co-star, Davin Giles."

"I promise you, there was nothing between Daphne and I." Brad stopped. He closed his eyes and shook his head before looking at her.

"Sorry, that was a lie. We had a few dates, but only *after* you and I broke up."

"And Daphne got exactly what she wanted." Dawn did a mock toast. "Publicity."

"And what she deserved after the trouble she caused," Brad reminded Dawn. "She may have managed to trap the dashing Davin into marriage, but now they're both struggling to get roles."

"The industry we work in is a fickle one." Dawn sighed. "That's why I'm so glad I'm not directly in the limelight."

"Unfortunately, we were born into the limelight." Brad ran his hand through his hair. "Your parents are two of the most famous people in our industry. You are like the entertainment industry royalty."

"And you're not!" Dawn raised her eyebrows and glanced around the yacht. "One of the reasons I took the script writing job for Cobble Cove Mysteries is the location." Her eyes darkened. "I hate being unable to do anything without my every move being documented by some reporter or person with a mobile phone. I might get a moment of freedom on Plum Island."

Brad pulled his phone out of his pocket and saw Caroline still hadn't answered his message.

"Yes, phone cameras make it difficult for well-known faces to hide in plain sight these days." Brad put his phone away, his heart feeling heavy.

"Not even a call?" Dawn's voice was soft.

"Sorry?" Brad's head shot up, and he looked at her questioningly.

"Your date." Dawn pointed to where he'd pocketed his phone. "She hasn't called?"

"No!" Brad sighed, deciding to be honest no matter how disappointed he felt.

"I'm sorry," Dawn said, and he could see she meant it. "As one of your oldest friends, I'll say whoever the woman was, it's her loss."

"I just thought—" Brad stopped. His jaw clenched and he shook his head.

"Thought?" Dawn encouraged him to speak to her.

"That she was different," Brad admitted.

He turned to look out over the darkening ocean as the sun slipped beyond the horizon, and the night started to sprinkle out its inky carpet of stars. Brad finished his drink as Dawn turned to look at what he was, and they stood in companionable silence. His heart felt like someone was squeezing it as he thought about Caroline. She'd told him she and Jennifer were attending the party. Worry zipped through him as he wondered if something had happened.

Brad was about to send Caroline another message when the photographer he had been dodging since he'd gotten to the party interrupted Brad and Dawn.

"Hi, would you mind if I took a picture of the two of you for Alex and Ethan's birthday memories?" The photographer asked them.

Dawn and Brad turned toward the man.

"They're fifty, not twelve," Brad told the man.

"It's a milestone birthday." Dawn laughed at him. "If you remember, their mother insists on their birthday memory photo shoots every five years."

"I know." Brad grimaced and gave in. "Sure."

"Thank you," the photographer sighed in relief. "The two of you have been the most elusive of this crowd to get photographs of. Would you mind standing a little closer?"

Brad and Dawn moved closer, putting their arms around each other. Dawn rested her head against his chest, and he placed his head on hers, putting on their best smiles before the flash nearly blinded them. The photographer checked the photo, said his thanks, and took another sneaky picture of them before disappearing.

"What's the bet that picture lands on some tabloid cover in the morning." Dawn's eyes flashed angrily before she placed her glass on the tray of a passing server. "And with that, I'm going to call it a day."

"Can I give you a lift home?" Brad asked.

"Thank you, I'd appreciate that," Dawn accepted his offer. "Harriet took my car."

"So, you didn't follow the *going out with Harriet rule*." Brad air quoted, laughing as he escorted Dawn out of the party, skillfully avoiding anyone who might detain them.

Brad and Dawn spoke about Cobble Cove Mysteries as they drove into Soho. They passed the Cup of Soho, and Brad swallowed as his heart lurched. He looked at his wristwatch and had to curb the urge to ask his driver to take them to Jennifer's apartment so he could find Caroline.

"Brad?" Dawn's voice broke through his thoughts. "This is me."

Brad's head shot up. He'd been so lost in his thoughts of Caroline he hadn't realized the car had stopped. Brad climbed out of the vehicle, helped Dawn out, and walked her to the door of her apartment.

"When did you move to Soho?" Brad asked her as the doorman opened the door for her.

"About two years ago." Dawn grinned. "You know I always wanted to move here." She looked up at him. "Thank you for the ride home."

Dawn leaned forward and kissed his cheek before giving him a hug.

"Of course," Brad said, sighing as he hugged her back. "I know it's only an olive branch," he kissed her head before stepping back, "but I'm glad we've started to sort things out."

"Me too," Dawn said. "Goodnight, Brad."

Brad watched Dawn walk into her building before walking back to his car. He stopped before climbing into the back seat. His eyes widened as he realized where he was. Dawn's apartment was across the road from Caroline's friend Jennifer's apartment. Brad was about to throw all reasoning from his thoughts and rush over there, but his phone rang. It was Harriet.

"Hello," Brad answered. "Is everything alright?"

"No!" Harriet hissed. "What is wrong with you?"

"What do you mean?" Brad asked, a frown creasing his brow.

"Where are you?" Harriet asked him.

"I just gave a friend a lift home," Brad hedged. "Why?"

"I think you'd better get over to my place *now*!" Harriet ordered.

"Okay!" Brad's heart jolted as he slid into the car's back seat and told his driver where to go. "I'm on my way."

As they drove off, Brad didn't see the person standing across the road staring at him. They pulled up outside Harriet's house in the Upper East Side. The car had barely stopped when the front door flew open, and Harriet stood silhouetted beneath the door frame.

"She looks angry," Brad's driver commented as he opened the back door for Brad.

"She does." Brad agreed, his frown deepening as he walked up the stairs to face Harried. "What's going on?"

"Are you crazy?" Harriet's eyes blazed angrily at him, and that's when he saw the rolled-up document in her hands.

"What's going on?" Brad asked her, confused.

"Here, I printed the latest headlines from a few tabloid blogs." Harriet shoved the document at him before spinning and marching into the house.

Brad followed her, unrolling the documents. His eyes widened as he saw the latest story.

Duking Dawn and Blindsided Brad have hung up their differences—BrayDawn back together.

The picture of Brad and Dawn posing for the photographer on the Blackwell's yacht was splashed all over the pages. He shook his head and drew in a breath.

"This is not what it seems," Brad told Harriet, following her into one of the many living rooms. He slammed the pages onto the coffee table. "We were posing for the compulsory birthday memory album."

"Really?" Harriet drawled in disbelief. "Then explain this."

She shuffled through the papers and pointed to a picture of Brad and Dawn hugging on the steps of her Soho apartment.

So, this is why Brad has been sighted in Soho for the past week.

"What the..." Brad hissed, his blood running cold as he shoved the page away and looked at Harriet.

"You have had that—" Harriet splayed her hand out and circled it at his face, "thing going on with your face lately." Her eyes narrowed. "You know that look you get when you're all starry-eyed over a woman."

"I'm not starry-eyed over anyone!" Brad plonked down on the sofa opposite Harriet and ran his hand through his hair.

"Your father is going to freak!" Harriet warned him. "You'd better have a good explanation ready for tomorrow."

"Maybe he won't see this!" Brad knew he was grasping at straws.

"Who do you think called me to tell me about it?" Harriet sat back, shaking her head. "Brad, we need Dawn to write the script for this series."

"I know!" Brad assured her. "And for the record, Dawn and I started to patch things up tonight."

"What?" Harriet looked at him in disbelief. "I thought you said this was *not* what it seems."

"It's not." Brad realized he'd worded his last sentence wrong. "I apologized. Dawn and I have called a truce, and we spoke about what happened."

Harriet sat staring at him through narrowed eyes for a few seconds.

"Seriously?" Harriet's gaze didn't waver.

"Yes." Brad nodded. "Dawn and I have started to move past our last encounter." He glanced at the articles on the table. "Although I'm not sure what she'll think about those."

"I'll handle it." Harriet sighed. "This is why I'm so glad I don't have photographers hounding me."

"Only because they're scared of you." Brad laughed at the look she shot at him. He looked at the documents on the table. "Dawn said the picture would be out in the world by tomorrow." He sighed and flopped back against the sofa. "Thanks to the internet, it would be out within a few seconds."

"Yup!" Harriet drew in a breath. "Welcome to the age of big brother."

Brad glanced at his wristwatch. "I'd better get home and talk to Connor before he sees this."

"Too late!" Harriet told him. "Who do you think told your father?"

Brad's body went slack as he looked at the ceiling in exasperation. "Good grief."

"I've already spoken to Connor," Harriet informed Brad. "I told him it was publicity because Dawn's working on the Cobble Cove Mysteries project."

"Thank you." Brad breathed a sigh of relief. "What would I do without you?"

"End up in a big mess," Harriet grinned smugly. "Now go home so I can finish reading."

"That's why we all love you so much, Harry," Brad teased, standing and turning to leave. "You don't mince your words. When you want someone to leave, you kick them out."

"Don't call me Harry," Harriet threw a cushion at him before standing and following him to the front door. "I don't kick everyone out." She grinned. "Just you and the Blackwells because you guys don't always take a hint."

"Noted." Brad opened the front door and stepped outside. "Thanks for the heads up."

"Someone has to look out for you." Harriet took the cushion he'd caught from him.

"Goodnight, *Harry,*" Brad teased and stepped out of the way before she could hit him with the cushion.

"Try to stay out of trouble from here to your house," Harriet told him. "I really want to finish the book I'm reading."

Brad saluted her and climbed into the car. As they pulled off, he took out his phone to see there were still no messages from Caroline. He couldn't believe how much he'd wanted to find a message from or missed a call from her.

I hope everything's okay.

He stared at the screen, hesitating to send the message, then deleted it and pocketed his phone before giving in to temptation. Brad laughed at himself, taking in the city's lights on the way to his house. He was acting like a high school boy with a crush and promised himself he'd try Caroline again in the morning just to find out if everything was okay.

CHAPTER 7

Caroline tried to clear her mind as she got ready for work, but it wouldn't switch off images of her last night in New York. It had been almost six weeks, but that night still tormented her. Caroline couldn't believe she'd let herself get caught up in a fairytale whirlwind romance with a mysterious, handsome, wealthy man. She snorted.

I should write a tragic romance novel about my love life next. Caroline sighed as she looked at her image in the bathroom mirror.

She still couldn't get used to her chic hairstyle as she ran a brush through it before pulling it into a loose bun, not bothering to stop a few rebellious strands from falling loose. Caroline put some mascara on her lashes and a pearl pink gloss on her lips before rushing out of her room.

"Honey, are you ready?" Caroline called to her daughter as she checked her purse to make sure she had her phone and wallet.

"'Yes!" Jules grumbled, shuffling down the stairs from her new loft bedroom, yawning. "I'm going to Uncle Finn's house after my shift at the restaurant." She stretched. "It's Tucker's birthday party."

"Oh no, I forgot about Tucker's birthday present." Caroline slapped her forehead as she remembered she'd left her nephew's gift at the library. "It's at the library."

"Can you bring it to me before the party?" Jules asked. "Like at the restaurant?"

"Don't worry." Caroline pulled a face. "I won't make you seem uncool by showing up at the party and asking for you."

"Please don't ever say *uncool* again." Jules held up her hand, looking horrified. "There are just some words that aren't parenty."

"Sorry!" Caroline jiggled her head. Her eyes caught the time. "Shoot. We have to go."

They rushed out the door and nearly ran over a woman about to knock on it.

"Oh, geez!" Jules skidded to a halt. "I'm sorry."

"It's okay." The woman smiled.

Caroline's eyes narrowed as she looked at the woman who looked familiar to her.

"Hi, can I help you?" Caroline stepped beside her daughter.

"Yes, I'm looking for Carrie Lines," the woman said.

"That's my mom!" Jules said proudly, her eyes sparkling with excitement as they caught Caroline's.

"Me, I'm mom." Caroline laughed.

"Hi, I'm Harriet Joyce from Danes Productions," Harriet introduced herself. "I'm Mr. Danes' Executive Assistant."

"Oh!" Caroline blinked as it suddenly hit her that Harriet was from the production company. *That's where I must've seen her before.*

"Do you have a moment?" Harriet asked.

"We're actually just heading out," Caroline told her. "I have to drop my daughter at her job and then get to work."

"No problem," Harriet smiled. "You work at the library, right?"

"Correct." Caroline nodded.

"I was asked to set up a meeting with you and Mr. Danes," Harriet told her. "Can you join him for lunch at the Summer Inn today?"

"That's a bit sudden," Caroline said, frowning and slightly annoyed that they would assume she didn't have lunch plans. "I can't make lunch today."

"Mom!" Jules looked at her in disbelief. "What plans?"

"I have plans!" Caroline felt a little offended by her daughter's skepticism. "You know." She gestured with her hands. "Meetings and things."

Jules looked at her questioningly.

"Let me see," Harriet said, swooping her finger over her phone. "Can you meet this evening?" She smiled. "At, say, six-thirty for an early dinner, perhaps?"

"Yes, she can," Jules answered for her mother.

"Jules!" Caroline looked at her, annoyed, before giving Harriet a tight smile. "Sure. But I can't have dinner. I have a birthday party to get to."

Jules's eyebrows rose as she looked at her mother, knowing she was lying.

"I'll explain that to Mr. Danes," Harriet assured her. "It was nice to finally meet you. I love your books and am honored to be working on this project."

She said goodbye and walked back to the limousine awaiting her.

"How much do you think executive assistants earn?" Jules gave a low whistle as they watched the limo drive away.

"I think the word executive in the title means it must be a pretty penny with perks like limos," Caroline told her, hurrying to the car. "We have to hurry."

As they drove toward the Cobble Cove Restaurant, Jules looked at her mother suspiciously. "You lied."

"Excuse me?" Caroline glanced at her daughter, hoping she didn't look guilty.

"You told Harriet that you had plans for lunch," Jules pointed out.

"That wasn't a lie," Caroline defended her actions. "I'm bringing Tucker's birthday present to you."

"That takes like fifteen minutes." Jules pursed her lips. "I thought you were excited about the television series and couldn't wait for it to start filming."

"I was—" Caroline paused. "I am." She smiled at Jules as she pulled into the restaurant's parking lot. "But they're here a week early, and I'm still handing all my duties over to Daniella." She stopped the car. "We were going to have lunch at the restaurant."

"It's okay to be nervous, Mom," Jules surprised her by saying. "This is huge and overwhelming. I still can't believe my mom is a famous writer now."

"Well, not famous, honey," Caroline smiled lovingly at her daughter. "Ah, there's Carly. You'd better go."

"What time are you picking me up from the party?" Jules asked, sliding out of the car.

"Eleven," Caroline told her before warning her, "And Jules, be good."

"Always!" Jules said, closing the door and rushing off.

Caroline watched her daughter. She couldn't believe how much their last visit to New York had changed their relationship for the better. At least two good things had come from the trip to New York. Caroline had signed a television series deal, and her daughter had finally realized that Caroline was not her enemy. She grinned as she drove away from the restaurant, thinking about her and Jules's shopping trip to Boston.

They had decorated the loft and set it up as a bedroom for Jules, which looked great. Caroline was going to use it for her home office, but it was worth setting up Jules' old bedroom as her office instead for the sake of her daughter's happiness. Caroline was snapped out of her thoughts as she turned into town, headed towards the library, and saw the movie crew heading down the road.

Her heart jolted, and her fingers tingled from the waves of excitement that zapped through her. They were in town to shoot Caroline's television series. A surreal feeling engulfed her, and she felt like she was floating in a bubble as she turned into her parking space behind the library.

Caroline was barely out of her car when her young library assistant, Tanith Willis, came flying toward her. Excitement shone in her eyes.

"Caroline!" Tanith called. "Did you see the movie crew is here?"

"I know." Caroline smiled. "I saw them when I drove into town." They walked into the library. "They're a week early."

"It's the movies!" Tanith stated. "They roll in when they roll in."

"Uh-huh!" Caroline nodded as she headed toward her office. "Is Daniella in yet?"

"No." Tanith shook her head and went to the service desk. "She called and said she couldn't make it today."

"Oh!" Caroline frowned. "That's a shame." She bit her lip. "Is she sick?"

"She didn't say." Tanith shrugged. "Do you want me to call her and ask?"

"No!" Caroline shook her head. "That won't be necessary, thanks." She sighed. "Daniella doesn't officially start at the library until next week. She's not obliged to be here."

"Are the movie crew going to come to the library?" Tanith asked.

"I'm not sure," Caroline said, glancing at her wristwatch. "Don't you have cataloging to do?"

"Yes." Tanith nodded and got to work.

Caroline breathed a sigh of relief that Tanith's questions had finally stopped as she moved into her office. Caroline always left her office door slightly ajar to see part of the service desk, and Tanith could hail her if it got busy. She put her purse in a desk drawer and slid into her office chair. There was a lot to get done before Plum Island Junior High came to the library in an hour. Caroline had a meeting, and then a large conference was booked in their conference room that afternoon.

The library kept its doors open by using some of its many rooms for different activities. Like the conference room, a functions room, a recreation room, a music room, a gymnasium, a hall with a raised stage, and a few quiet reading rooms.

The recreation room was one of Caroline's favorite projects, and she was sad that she couldn't dedicate as much time to it as she used to, now that her writing had taken off. The recreation room provided an excellent place for the younger generation on the island to meet and mingle. It had game consoles, game tables, and a juice bar. The library would host a movie night in the room twice a month.

Their gymnasium was rented out for modern dance lessons, gym lessons, ballet, basketball, and volleyball. The schools used the hall for various assemblies, graduations, and staged drama productions. It was also used for weddings, other celebrations, funerals, and dance and music recitals. Caroline's second favorite room was the music room. It was where she'd found out what a talented musician Jules was. Her daughter loved trying her hand at different musical instruments, like the guitar, piano, cello, drums, and violin. But Jules's favorite musical instrument was the piano.

Caroline sighed. She was going to miss the library. She glanced at the crack in her office door at the few neat rows of shelves stacked with books. The library had been her savior after Caroline's divorce had left her homeless and penniless. This building had also once been hers and Jennifer's haven when they were kids. They'd come to mingle in the rec room or study in the library. The Saturday Morning Reading Corner was Caroline and Jennifer's regular weekend activity. They loved sitting around Mrs. Trumble, the head librarian, as she took them into another world, reading stories to the kids gathered around her.

Caroline's smile grew as her memories played through her mind, and her heart filled with nostalgia. Plum Island had always been her shelter from the big wide world. The tether to her sanity and the calm for any storm raging inside her. Her phone rang, snapping her back to reality.

"Hello?" Caroline answered it.

"Hey, you," Finn, her older brother's voice, filtered through the receiver. "I see the film crew has arrived."

"Yes, I think the whole island has seen them," Caroline moaned.

"Feeling a little overwhelmed?" Finn's voice was soft and gentle. His *Caroline soothing voice* was what she called it.

"Have you been speaking to Jules?" Caroline smiled.

"No." Finn denied. "But I do know you. While you've been excited about your series being published and then picked up for television, I know that inside your soul is shaking with fear."

"That's quite an image." Caroline frowned. "But really descriptive, and yes, I feel like my body is shaking from the core." She pinched the bridge of her nose. "I'm sorry they arrived today on Tucker's sixteenth birthday."

"Are you kidding me!" Finn laughed. "He wants to invite the film crew to his party tonight."

"I can imagine." Caroline shook her head. "Speaking of Tucker. I did try to call him to wish him, but he didn't answer his phone this morning."

"He's been at the Surf Shack since dawn getting it ready for the party tonight," Finn told her.

"He's excited." Caroline picked up her pen and started drawing shapes on her writing pad. "You are going to be there to chaperone, right?"

"Of course," Finn assured her. "As you know, your good friend Jennifer's brother, Liam, my best friend, is back in town."

"Why do you always do that?" Caroline clicked her pen thoughtfully. "You don't have to remind me who Liam is. I grew up with him hounding Jennifer and me."

"You and Jennifer hounded us," Finn corrected her. "As for reminding you who Liam is, I'm just making sure you don't forget him—*again!*" Finn teased. "You know, like when you didn't send him an invitation to your wedding."

"Good grief!" Caroline rolled her eyes. "That was fifteen years ago, and I didn't forget him. *Liam* lost the invitation. He never liked Robert and made no attempt to hide it."

"No, Caro, Liam didn't lose the invitation." Finn's voice became grave. "Now that you're no longer married to Heart Robber..." He paused, and Caroline could picture the mischievous glint in his eyes. "Sorry, *Robert* didn't send it."

Caroline Frowned. "Jennifer told me Liam didn't get an invitation after the divorce when we had our *no more Robert* party."

"You two are still so freakin' weird," Finn said. "So, are you going to answer my initial question and reason for this call?"

"I did answer it," Caroline reminded him.

"No, you didn't," Finn pointed out. "You gave me a brief answer and then moved the conversation full steam ahead to something else."

"Yes, I'm feeling overwhelmed, scared, and like I'm in some weird altered reality," Caroline admitted. "I have to meet Mr. Danes tonight for dinner, but I found myself making excuses not to go."

"Ah!" Finn said. "Do you want me to go with you?"

"Thanks, big brother," Caroline said. She and Jennifer had gotten the best of the bunch when it came to big brothers. "But you have your son's sixteenth birthday party, and I'm a big girl now. I have to do this on my own."

"No, you don't, Caro," Finn told her. "I've always got your back whenever you need me. But I understand, and I'm a phone call away."

"I know, and I love you for that." Caroline's eyes moved to her office door, where Tanith was trying to get her attention. "I have to go. Tanith is about to break her arm, waving it so vigorously to get my attention."

"Okay, little sister," Finn said. "Let me know how your meeting with Mr. Danes goes."

"Will do," Caroline promised before saying goodbye and hanging up.

She stood as Tanith got to her door, popping her head through the crack and hanging on the handle, keeping it partly closed.

"Caroline, there's someone to see you," Tanith's voice was hushed.

"I don't have time," Caroline told her. "The middle school's principal will be here in fifteen minutes to discuss the science fair, and then the junior high school is arriving in an hour." She gestured frustratedly with her hand. "Can't you ask them to come back?"

"He said it was urgent and couldn't wait." Tanith pulled a sorry face. "And he's not easy to say no to."

"Tanith, you must learn to be sterner with people no matter who they are." Caroline shook her head impatiently before giving a resigned sigh. "Fine, send him in, but make sure he knows I've only got a—"

Her words were cut off as a deep, familiar voice floated around her door.

"Sorry for the intrusion and stopping in without an appointment—" The subtle scent of sandalwood, patchouli, musk, and vanilla wafted along with the voice.

"Sir, I asked you to wait at the—" Tanith moaned at the man who rudely pushed the door wider.

Tanith stood in front of the tall man who loomed behind her and turned to Caroline, shrugging and mouthing, *I'm sorry.*

Caroline's heart froze in her chest, and her breath caught in her throat as her eyes collided with the startled ones of Brad.

"Caroline?" Brad's voice echoed the shock in his eyes.

"Brad?" Caroline spluttered back.

She gripped the edge of her desk as the sight of him made her legs turn to jelly, while a handful of butterflies went wild in her stomach, jolting her heart to start racing. A frown creased Caroline's brow as she tried to remember if she'd told him where she lived or worked.

"What are you doing here?" Caroline and Brad chorused together, gaping at each other in shock.

"I'm here to meet Carrie Lines," Brad said distractedly before his brows shot up thoughtfully. "You live here?"

"Well, no, not here." Caroline swallowed as her throat was feeling dry.

"You don't live on Plum Island?" Brad's frown deepened, looking at her in confusion.

"I do." Caroline nodded. *Shoot. Get it together, Caroline.* "I meant I don't live in the library." *What the heck, Caroline!* She gave her head a slight shake, holding up her hands. "I work here in the library. What are you doing here?"

"You two know each other?" Tanith looked from Brad to Caroline, and they both nodded.

"We met on my trip to New York," Caroline's eyes finally broke away from Brad's to look at Tanith.

"Wait!" Tanith's voice dipped. She raised her hands before her, and a mischievous glint sparked in her eyes as she looked from Caroline to Brad again. She pursed her lips and pointed at each of them. "So, you two know each other but obviously don't *know* each other." She snorted. "Oh, this is so good."

"Tanith, what is wrong with you?" Caroline asked her angrily. Her shock over seeing Brad looming in her doorway faded into anger as the last time she saw him flashed through her mind.

Brad's eyes narrowed as he looked at Tanith.

"I really don't have time for this," Brad said impatiently. "I have a busy day, and I thought you were taking me to meet *Carrie,* not Caroline."

The name Carrie shot through Caroline like a volt of electricity, sending pinpricks of shock through her nerve endings as her jaw slackened and she gaped at Brad in disbelief.

Did he just say, Carrie? Caroline gave herself a mental shake. *Did I hear him right?*

"Did you say Carrie?" The words popped through her lips before she could stop them.

"Yes, I'm here to meet Carrie Lines." Brad glanced at her coldly and gave a curt nod before turning away from Caroline as if dismissing her and addressing Tanith. "If you could please take me to her. I have a busy day and am in no mood to be fawned over by adoring fans."

Anger at his words and the blatant brush-off coursed through Caroline. *The nerve of the man!* Her eyes narrowed, her jaw clenched as she straightened her shoulders and lifted her chin. *Adoring fans?* She was about to give him a piece of her mind before swatting him off his high horse when Tanith beat her to it.

Tanith raised an eyebrow at Brad, not flinching under his angry, impatient gaze or letting his words rile her. She tilted her head to one side before saying sweetly. "While I'm certainly *not* a fan of yours, whoever you are," Tanith's gaze never wavered as Brad's eyes narrowed warningly. "I am a *huge* Carrie Lines fan." She bowed slightly at the waist and used her hands in a dramatic sweeping gesture toward Caroline, like a talk show host introducing a famous guest. "I give you Carrie Lines."

Tanith turned and gave Brad a smug smile as his face fell and his eyes registered his shock. "Call me if you need me," Tanith said to Caroline before giving Brad a mock salute and marching off.

Brad and Caroline stood staring at each other again for a few minutes before Brad spluttered in disbelief, "*You're Carrie Lines?*"

"Yes." Caroline raised her chin a little higher, staring at him down her perfectly straight nose defiantly. "And *I* currently don't have time to deal with *fawning fans!*"

She took immense pleasure in throwing his rude words back at him.

How dare he think they were fawning fans just because he was a wealthy playboy who mingled in high society? Just because he was a hot-shot producer? Her eyes widened as a thought struck her, and her breath again caught in her throat. *Oh no! Please no!*

"Why are you looking for Carrie Lines?" Caroline asked, afraid that she already knew the answer. *Does he work with the Blackwells?* Jenny had mentioned earlier that week that the Blackwells were directing the series.

"We're supposed to meet later, but I was hoping to change Carrie's mind about lunch," Brad told her. His eyes held hers and still shone with disbelief.

"Why would I be meeting you this evening?" Confusion washed over before a thought struck her. *Brad must work for Danes Productions.*

His brows shot up as he stared at her. "You made an appointment with Harriet this morning."

"Is Mr. Danes unable to make the meeting tonight?" Caroline was starting to get a sinking feeling as a thought she refused to acknowledge nagged at the back of her mind, trying to make itself clear.

"No!" Brad's brows crumpled into a tight frown as he stared at her, mystified for a few minutes before something sparked in his eyes. "Oh!" He nodded as understanding dawned on him. "I'm Brad Danes—you made an appointment with my executive assistant, Harriet, to meet with me."

A whooshing noise resounded in Caroline's ears, and she gasped at the information, feeling as if she'd been punched in the stomach, winding her. She forced air into her lungs when she started to feel lightheaded and made herself focus as she made sense of it all.

Brad was Brandon Danes—Travis Danes' son! Caroline's mind whirled. *How didn't I piece that together?*

Brandon Danes' name had come up a lot when she was speaking to Travis in New York. Caroline was supposed to have met Travis's son, but he'd been unavailable at the time.

"You're Brandon Danes?" The word shot out her mouth before she could stop them. *Fate really has an evil sense of humor!*

"You're Carrie Lines!" Brad's eyes narrowed suspiciously, and he gave his head a shake. "How did I miss that?"

"I'm asking myself the same thing!" Caroline's brain fog started to lift, spurred on by another painful surprise. She knew where she'd seen Harriet before. She shared an intimate moment with Brad at the yacht party in New York!

Anger, humiliation, and hurt spurted through her as the image of Brad and Harriet together flashed through her mind. But before they had a chance to say another word, Tanith reappeared.

"Caroline, Principal Becks is here for your meeting." Tanith's breathless voice cut through the tension building between Caroline and Brad.

Caroline dragged her eyes away from Brad and glanced at Tanith. Her cheeks were flushed, and her eyes had that dreamy look she had always gotten when the handsome young Principal Tanner Becks was around.

"Take him to meeting room one, offer refreshments, and let him know I'm on my way," Caroline instructed Tanith, grateful for the distraction.

She scooped her notepad and pen off her desk then walked to the door. But Brad stepped in front of her, completely blocking the exit as his tall, broad-shouldered frame dominated the doorway.

"Please let me pass." Caroline's eyes narrowed. "I have a *scheduled* meeting."

"Caroline, wait!" Brad stepped closer to her, and she automatically stepped back, making him stop and run a hand through his hair as their eyes met and held. "Can we please talk?"

"I'm sorry, but I have to go," Caroline said. She felt like she was sleepwalking through a bad dream.

She tried to sidestep him, but Brad reached out and grabbed her arm to stop her, making her skin tingle where he touched her and her treacherous heart leap, stirring up the butterflies in her stomach.

"Please, have dinner with me at Summer Inn tonight," Brad's voice was soft. "We have a *lot* to talk about."

Caroline swallowed and took a breath to control her wayward emotions before glancing pointedly at his arm, which he immediately dropped.

"As I told your *executive assistant* this morning, I'll be there to discuss the television series, but I cannot stay for dinner as I have a previous engagement," Caroline told him in a cool, professional manner. "I'll meet you at six thirty at the Summer Inn. Now, if you'd please excuse me, I have someone waiting for me."

Brad sighed, nodded, and stepped aside. "Fine, I'll see you at six-thirty."

Caroline walked away on shaky legs, trying to control her erratic heartbeat. She didn't allow herself to look back as she walked into the meeting, filing away the questions reeling in her mind.

CHAPTER 8

Brad slid into the limo's backseat, his mind reeling with the events that had just unfolded in the library.

Caroline? Brad swallowed as he leaned back against the plush leather seats. *Caroline lived on Plum Island!* He ran a hand through his hair. *And she's Carrie Lines!*

Brad had felt like he'd been hit in the face when he'd pushed the door open and saw her standing behind her desk. She looked different with her new chic haircut, contact lenses, and neat suit that emphasized her slender figure while showing off her shapely calves. Caroline seemed like a completely different woman to the one he'd met in New York. The only thing that hadn't changed about her was her soft, tantalizing scent.

Brad rubbed his eyes and let out a breath as he played their time together in New York over in his head. His heart did the little skip it always did when he thought of her—which had been more than he'd have liked over the past six weeks. California had been loaded with women wanting his attention, but Brad's mind had been too full of Caroline. He'd even taken up surfing to try and get her out of his mind, but it hadn't worked. Instead, he was plagued with wondering what had happened that she'd never shown to the party and then just left without a word.

Brad had tried to call Caroline's friend, Jennifer Gains, but the woman hadn't been helpful or friendly. In fact, Ms. Gains had been cold and rude to Brad over the phone and warned him not to call her again. Thoughts of Jennifer made his brows shoot up, remembering she was also Carrie Lines' publisher and liaison with Danes Productions for the television series.

"I should've put it together!" Brad slapped his forehead.

"Are you going back to the hotel, Sir," the chauffeur, Sam Donovan, slid the partition window down and turned toward Brad.

"Actually, could we go to Cobble Cove?" Brad asked him. "I'd like to see the lighthouse."

"That's private property," Sam, a local to Cobble Cove, informed him. "I do know the owner. I can call her and ask if I can take you to look around."

"Who's the owner?" As the words left his mouth, Brad already knew the answer.

"Caroline Shaw," the chauffeur confirmed Brad's suspicions. "The Shaw's once owned that entire side of Plum Island."

"Oh?" Brad's interest was piqued. "What happened that they no longer own it?"

"Stuart Shaw had medical bills piling up," Sam told him. "He sold Mid-Point of Cobble Cove to the long-term tenants, the Swan family. A few years later, he sold Lookout-Point to the Donovan's. A year before Stuart passed away, he sold the Summer Inn on Lower-Point to Liam Gains." He gave Brad a tight smile. "But the Shaw's still own a large part of it, including the Cobble Cove reserve."

"Cobble Cove plays a major role in Carrie Lines' books," Brad told him. "I'd like to see the area and get a clear picture."

"Let me call Caroline," Sam said, pulling out his phone and calling the woman who had been haunting his days.

Brad's heart made a few loops around his chest as he waited for Caroline to answer Sam's call, but it went to voicemail.

"I'll try her brother." Sam turned toward the front of the car to make the call. This time, someone answered. "Hello, young man, it's Sam here." Brad overheard the conversation. "I'm driving Mr. Danes around the island, and he'd like to see the lighthouse."

Brad watched Sam nod a few times. "We can be there in …" He turned to get a time from Brad.

"Twenty minutes, I'd like to fetch my son," Brad said.

"Twenty minutes?" Sam asked Caroline's brother, then turned to smile and give Brad a thumbs up before ending the conversation. "All set." He adjusted the mirror, and Brad nodded. "I'll take you to the hotel."

Sam was about to slide the partition up, but Brad stopped him.

"Would you mind being my guide while I'm here?" Brad asked him.

"Of course," Sam nodded enthusiastically. "I'd be glad too."

Sam skillfully steered away from the library, directing the car towards the Summer Inn. The short journey unfolded smoothly, ending in a seamless parking maneuver right in front of the establishment—a place Brad insisted transcended the conventional notion of an inn; it was more like a small modern-style hotel. The building gracefully formed a square U-shape, with broad windows and balconies that wrapped around the front, ensuring every room in the hotel embraced a breathtaking panoramic view of the sea.

Sam climbed out and opened the door for Brad.

"I'll meet you in the foyer in ten to fifteen minutes," Brad told Sam, who nodded and left.

Brad stepped up to the front sliding doors that opened automatically, inviting him to step inside the sleek building that had been cleverly designed with a mix of modern architecture that blended with the coastal charm of the area.

The foyer was bright from the natural light of the floor-to-ceiling glass windows that ran the length of the front of the inn. The check-in and concierge desks occupied the right corner closest to the doors, making guests feel like they'd stepped into a seascape painting. Seating areas lined the front section of the entrance area with glass doors on either side of the lounge area. One led to the long sparkling pool that ended a few feet from the beach's white sand, outlined by an outdoor cocktail bar.

Brad's eyes scanned the scene in front of him. The inn could rival any five-star hotel Brad had ever stayed in. It boasted twenty luxury rooms, a fully equipped gym with an indoor pool, a mixed cuisine restaurant, and a full-service spa. Brad, Connor, and Harriet were stunned when they first arrived at the hotel. They expected a quaint small-town inn, not a five-star hotel with modern amenities set against the breathtaking backdrop of the Atlantic Ocean.

His eyes moved to the left, where the first few slips had been built for the small marina that the owner of the Summer Inn had installed to accommodate the Blackwell's yachts. Thinking of Ethan Blackwell broke Brad's reverie, and he shook his head, thinking of what they'd put the Summer Inn owner through to accommodate the Dane Productions crew. Brad had to remember to get Harriet to ensure Mr. Gains was adequately compensated for his efforts. He glanced around the foyer once more.

Brad knew many A-listers who would love to know about this place. He went to the elevator, where he went to the top floor. Brad, Harriet, Alex Blackwell, and Dawn were occupying the four suites of the inn. As the elevator stopped and opened, Brad was greeted by Harriet and Connor.

"Hey, Dad," Connor greeted him. "We were on our way to the beach."

"I see that," Brad said, eyeing their swimming outfits. "But I'm afraid you're going to have to put something else on as we're going for a quick tour of Cobble Cove, including the lighthouse."

"Seriously?" Connor's eyes grew wide with interest. "Cool!" He spun on his heels and raced back to the suite.

"Wow!" Harriet breathed. "Teens are so fickle!" She watched Connor disappear through the door. "We were going to check out the *scenery* on the beach."

"I'm sure you were!" Brad laughed, getting her meaning loud and clear. "But I'm afraid the *scenery* is going to have to wait. We've got a tour of the lighthouse in fifteen minutes."

"I hope you're going to change out of that stuffy suit?" Harriet circled her hand with her fingers splayed out around his suit.

"I'm going to wear shorts and a linen shirt," Brad assured her. "Besides, it's too hot to be in this stuffy suit."

They walked down the hall together, stopping at Harriet's door. "Good, and please don't wear that ugly red shirt with the yellow swirls on it."

"They're flowers!" Brad defended his island shirt. "I'll have you know I got that in Hawaii."

"This isn't Hawaii!" Harriet pointed out and gave a snort. "And I'm sure Hawaii was glad to see that shirt leave the state."

"Rosa's Hawaiian, and she likes my shirt!" Brad raised his chin.

"No, Rosa doesn't!" Harriet shook her head and pursed her lips. "But she loves you. You're like a son to her, and that's what mothers do. They lie so they don't hurt their kid's feelings." She stopped and frowned. "Or at least that's what good mothers do. Not my mother, though." She widened her eyes and shuddered. "Queen Julie was born emotionally impaired."

"Harry, you've got to stop beating your mother down." Brad sighed. "She's trying."

"Yeah, like forty years too late!" Harriet opened her room door. "I won't be long. I'll meet you at the elevator."

"Okay!" Brad walked off and heard her door click closed as he neared his suite.

He was about to reach for the door handle when the door flew open.

"I'm ready!" Connor stood facing him.

"I'm not!" Brad indicated his suit by sweeping his hand over it.

"Ah!" Connor nodded and stepped back to allow Brad into the suite.

"I'm going to find Sam," Connor told him eagerly, his eyes shining with excitement. "Do you know that he knows the Finnster?" He followed Brad to his room and stood at the door. "He was friends with the Finnster's father. Sam said he'd introduce me to him."

"That's nice of him." Brad pulled off his tie and started to undo the buttons of his shirt. "I won't be long."

"Okay, I'll meet you at the limo." Connor turned and disappeared.

Ten minutes later, dressed in tailored cotton shorts, a linen short-sleeved shirt, and sneakers, Brad met Harriet. She'd changed her beach outfit for a soft blue summer dress, low-heeled matching sandals with her hair swept back into a loose knot and her designer shades hanging from her hand.

"Oh, thank goodness you didn't wear the red eye-sore." Harriet grinned at the black look Brad shot her. "I had visions of spilling red wine on it, so you'd have to take it off."

"We're not having red wine. We're going sightseeing." Brad hit the elevator button.

"Oh, I organized a glass to be ready at the concierge desk," Harriet told him as they stepped into the elevator.

A few minutes later, Brad, Connor, and Harriet were heading down the coastal road toward Cobble Cove lighthouse. When they turned out of the inn's parking lot, Sam took a right toward the lighthouse instead of a left to the small town of Plum Island. The road was a long downhill curve that eventually evened out as it rounded Cobble Cove Beach.

"From the ocean, looking onto Cobble Cove, you'll notice that it's shaped like the number three," Sam explained. "There are three cliff points that jut into the sea."

When they were level with the beach, it wasn't visible through the thicket of trees that hid it from the road. Two car parks fed the beach. A smaller one on the side of the beach and a larger one across the road. Brad noted that restrooms and signs pointed to Cobble Cove Nature Walk and camping grounds.

"What are the camping grounds like?" Brad asked Sam.

"Oh, I'd love to go camping, Dad." Connor's head swiveled toward the camping ground side of the road.

"I wouldn't mind a camping trip." Harriet surprised them all by saying. "My father once had a tent pitched for us in the back garden of our home because my brother and I wanted to camp." She sighed. "It wasn't the camping trip we envisioned."

"Maybe we can go camping for a few nights while we're here?" Connor turned to look at his father, hopefully.

"I'll keep the idea in mind," Brad promised.

"It is a lovely camping ground. Especially at this time of year," Sam informed them.

The car rounded into a steep incline with Brad, Harriet, and Connor captivated by the breathtaking scenery of the white beach flanked by cliffs jutting out into the sea zoomed out into the distance behind them. As the road climbed, a granite wall rose up beside them, blocking the view of the ocean while the reserve, a mesh of trees and local fauna, ran along the other side.

"If you look back, you'll see Lower Point, where the Summer Inn is," Sam instructed. "We're nearing Lookout Point, the highest part of Midpoint. You can't see it from here, but there is a wonderful restaurant and lookout stop on the cliff. My niece owns it." He boasted and ducked his head to look at the cliff. "From up there, you can see the whole of Cobble Cove and the rest of Plum Island."

"Do you have to walk to get to the restaurant?" Connor asked Sam because they were still climbing, and there was no turn-off to the top.

"No, there's a turn-off up ahead." Sam pointed to it. "Although there are some lovely walking trails you can hike up to the top."

They drove a little further, and the road started flattening out as they neared a turn-off with a sign pointing to Lookout Point and Beach Plum Cottage.

"Was that where Beach Plum Cottage Furniture, Crafts, and Homemade Goodies is?" Harriet's eyes widened, her head turning as she kept her eyes on the sign when they drove past it.

"Yes, that's it." Sam smiled at Harriet in the mirror.

"Why did it close down?" Harriet asked Sam.

"It's a long story. One of legend, heartache, and a family feud!" Sam glanced at his passengers in the mirror, grinning. "But, that's a story for another day."

"I'm going to hold you to that," Harriet warned Sam.

"She will, too!" Brad told him. "Harriet loves stories like that."

"I promise to tell it to you before you leave," Sam promised as he skillfully maneuvered the long vehicle through the next long sweeping curve.

"If you look ahead, you'll see the red and white dome of the lighthouse peeking out of the thicket of beach plum trees surrounding it." Sam pointed ahead. "We're almost at Top Point." The car started to curve with the road.

"What's in the reserve?" Connor looked out the window at the reserve as the tall trees fell away, leaving an expanse of sea plants for a few miles toward the other end of the cliff they were driving on.

"Oh, various species of ocean-side flora, different bird and small animal species," Sam answered as he slowed down and turned into a driveway.

Brad's heart jolted, knowing they were driving onto Caroline's property. His eyes caught the tall tower of the lighthouse that rose above the hedges and trees, staring out across the ocean. The building was white, with the octagon-shaped dome perched on top of it painted red. The windows that were the dome's eyes glinted in the sun sunlight

"Wow!" Connor breathed as the tower seemed to get taller the closer, they got to it.

The long hedge-line driveway opened into a parking lot with picnic tables and chairs off to the one side. Sam drove past the area through another path of tall hedges until they popped into an opening in front of a whitewashed double-story house with a slanting red roof and attic windows. The driveway curled around a large boulder with a bronzed commemorative plate. Sam pulled into a parking off to one side and switched off the engine.

Harriet, Brad, and Connor stepped out of the car, taking in the quaint double-story house linked to the towering lighthouse by a single-story cottage. The warm breeze rattling the leaves of the tall beach plum trees engulfed them in the fresh tang of the sea air. As Sam led them toward the house, they were serenaded by the call of the gulls that soared above their heads and the sounds of the ocean as it crashed against the rocks below.

"It's lovely out here," Harriet commented. "The white picket fences holding back the hedges around the property make a perfect sea cottage picture."

"This is kinda what I thought the Summer Inn was going to look like," Connor admitted.

The barn-styled door of the main house swung open, and for a moment, Brad held his breath, hoping Caroline would appear in the doorway. Instead, they were surprised to be greeted by Liam Gains, the owner of the Summer Inn.

"Hi." Liam sported a warm smile, offering his hand first to Brad, whom he'd met earlier that day. "It's good to see you again, Mr. Danes."

"Please, call me Brad." Brad shook his hand. "I don't believe you've met my colleague, Harriet Joyce, and my son Connor."

"Hi," Liam greeted them warmly, shaking their hands before looking past them to wave at Sam, who'd stepped back when Liam had appeared. "Hey, Sam."

"Hi, Liam." Sam raised his hand.

"Hey, I know you!" Connor's eyes widened in recognition. "You're Riptide Gains."

"Wow!" Liam laughed. "I haven't heard that name in a very long time."

"So, it is you!" Connor stared at Liam in fascination. "You grew up with the Finnster until you retired when you finished college."

"Ah!" Liam raised an eyebrow. "You're a surfer."

"And a *huge* fan of you and the Finnster," Connor admitted.

"Then you're in luck, kid." Liam grinned. "Because the Finnster happens to be living in Plum Island again. But don't tell him I told you when we *bump* into him."

"You'd introduce me?" Connor's eyes widened a little more with excitement.

"Of course." Liam nodded and looked at Brad. "How long are you all in town for?"

"Four weeks initially," Brad told him. "Why do you ask?"

"Because I'm sure Connor would love to meet some of the local kids his age," Liam said, his grin widening at Connor's enthusiastic nod. "Most of them surf."

"Why not bring him to Tucker's sixteenth party tonight?" Sam suggested.

"I was just about to invite him," Liam told Sam and looked at Brad for approval. "If your father doesn't mind you going?"

"If you're sure it's okay to crash the party?" Brad said.

"It's fine." Liam waved off Brad's concerns. "All the teens in Plum Island are invited."

"All of them?" A thought struck Brad. *I wonder if that's the party Caroline's going to. Her daughter must be invited to it!*

"Yeah!" Liam nodded and looked at Connor. "You can go with my daughter and her best friend."

"Cool!" Connor said, turning to Brad. "Is that okay, Dad?"

"I guess!" Brad nodded. "What time is the party and where is it?"

"It's right next to the Summer Inn at the Beach Hut on Cobble Beach," Sam answered for Liam.

"Oh!" Brad's eyebrows raised up. "That's convenient."

"Yeah, the kids love the Beach Hut," Liam told them. "It's a shop, restaurant, and hang-out for anyone who goes to the beach."

"Thank you!" Connor smiled in appreciation.

"No problem." Liam turned toward the house. "I was told you wanted a tour of the lighthouse."

"We would love that!" Harriet answered before Brad could. "When I was here this morning to meet Carrie Lines, I must admit how intrigued I was by the lighthouse."

"You've met Caroline?" Liam turned his attention to Harriet, and she nodded.

"Yes, and she seems lovely," Harriet said.

"Yeah, Caro's the best." Liam nodded in agreement. "She and my sister grew up together."

That information stopped Brad in his tracks as the puzzle pieces fell into place. *Gains isn't Caroline's last name. It was her friend Jennifer's.* "You're Jennifer Gains's brother?"

"Yes," Liam confirmed, stepping aside for the three of them to enter before him. "Caroline's older brother and I are best friends. He was supposed to meet you, but it's his son's sixteenth birthday, so he's a bit rushed to get everything done for this evening."

Liam followed Brad, Harriet, and Connor into the large kitchen.

Brad looked around the room. It was a haven of simplicity, adorned with blue-and-white checkered curtains and mismatched ceramic dishes. An old farmhouse table, polished by countless meals and conversations, stood beneath a vintage pendant lamp that Brad could picture casting a gentle light over gatherings of family and friends.

"This way," Liam was about to lead them through the house when Sam appeared at the door.

"Sorry, but I have to go. My niece called for help," Sam apologized. "She needs me to get some food and supplies to the Beach Hut for Tucker's sixteenth. She's catering the party."

"I can give you a lift back to the Summer Inn." Liam looked at Brad for permission.

"Yes, of course, that's fine, Sam," Brad told him. "Please, take the rest of the day. We're not going anywhere tonight."

"Thank you," Sam said gratefully before saying goodbye and leaving.

Liam turned and exited the kitchen, stepping into a cozy living room. A wood-burning stove stood proudly at the heart of the room. Brad could picture it radiating comforting warmth on cooler evenings. Nearby, a worn leather armchair sat beside a table piled with books and a notepad. A smile touched his lips as he pictured Caroline curled up on the chair reading.

Brad's eyes traveled around the room. The house seemed like it was frozen in time. The interior was a warm blend of nautical accents and New England nostalgia. Whitewashed breadboard walls framed the living area, adorned with sea-inspired artwork and shelves of well-loved books. Soft sunlight filtered through the lace curtains, casting a warm and welcoming glow on the worn hardwood floors.

Through the windows was the blue expanse of the ocean pushing waves against the rocks below while seabirds rode the winds in the distance and the sun reflected off the water in a kaleidoscope of color. He turned, hearing the chinking of a key chain, and saw Liam fiddling with keys looped on a large metal ring.

"I keep telling Caroline she doesn't need to lock this place up like a fortress," Liam grumbled, finally finding the key he was looking for and inserting it into the lock of the wooden door. "But, like my sister, she's lived in New York for too long and hasn't been able to shake the habit."

"It is a different world out here," Harriet told him and frowned when she noticed Liam hesitate before pulling open the door. "Is there a problem?"

"Have you seen any animals around?" Liam's brow creased as he cocked his head, listening for something.

"No," Harriet and Connor, standing near the door with Liam, chorused.

"Shoot!" Liam hissed. "That's not good."

"Why?" Brad asked.

He started to make his way to the front door as Liam cautiously pulled it open, then jumped back, pulling Harriet and Connor with him. Before Brad could react, a large, long-haired, ginger-striped cat shot through the door like a furry bullet. It bounced off the wall straight into Brad's chest, nearly knocking him off balance. As he steadied himself, he felt the sting of sharp claws dig into his skin. Brad grabbed the squiggling, hissing fur ball, ripping it off his shirt and holding it away. The cat clawed out of his hands and vaulted toward the living room.

"Watch out!" Harriet yelled as Brad recovered from his tangle with the angry cat.

Harriet's warning was followed by someone shouting, "Onward!"

Brad's eyes widened, and his feet froze to the floor as he gaped at the black and gold German Shepherd sprinting toward him with a big blue and red parrot on its back, egging the dog on.

The strange duo was a few feet away from him when a female voice barked from behind him in the living room. "Stop it! Slow down, you two!"

The dog plopped its butt on the floor and slid into Brad's legs. He managed to steady himself against the wall as the parrot flew off the dog's back and into his face. Brad got a mouth full of feathers, and sharp talons gripped the side of his face as the large wings flapped about.

"Blue Beard!" The female echoed around him. "Bad bird."

The bird let go and flew off over Brad's shoulder. His vision cleared, and he plucked feathers from his shirt and a few out of his mouth before his eyes landed on the young girl standing in front of him.

"Oh no! Your face and hands are bleeding." The teenage girl pointed out before looking past him and calling, "Mom! Blue Beard hurt someone. Bring the first aid kit."

Brad touched his cheeks and flinched as he felt the burning sting of the scratches and claw marks on his skin.

Harriet walked toward him, a mix of concern and amusement she was trying to stifle in her eyes. "Are you okay?" She pulled his hand away from his cheek. "Don't touch it." She told him.

"It's just a scratch," Brad assured her. "Nothing that some disinfectant and a band-aid can't fix."

"I have the first aid kit. Who got hurt—" The feminine voice made him freeze.

His breath caught in his throat as he slowly turned and faced a startled Caroline.

CHAPTER 9

Caroline's hands tightened around the first aid kit as she took in the unexpected scene. Brad stood in her hallway with blood on his face. The room seemed to shrink around her as his eyes locked with hers, pulling memories of their time in New York to the surface.

"Caroline!" Brad's voice echoed with surprise. "What are you doing here?"

His question snapped her from her shock, and her eyes widened. "I should be asking you that!"

"I thought your brother called you?" Liam appeared beside Brad.

"Liam?" Caroline's brows rose a little more as she shook her head. "What's going on?"

"I'm giving Brad, Harriett, and Connor a lighthouse tour," Liam explained. "They wanted to get a feel for it as it is a major part of the first episode."

"Sorry." Harriet popped up from behind Brad. "We should've called you."

Caroline noticed the woman slip her hand through Brad's arm, and her heart jolted as images of Harriet and Brad on the yacht flashed through her mind. She bit back her emotions and forced herself to concentrate on the present.

"Hi!" As Jules squeezed past them, a tall, good-looking young man stepped beside Liam. The young man leaned forward politely, holding out his hand. "I'm Connor, Brad's son."

Jules took the initiative and shook Connor's hand. "Hi, I'm Jules, Caroline's daughter."

"Hi." Connor gave Jules a small wave.

"Hello, Connor," Caroline greeted the young man, plastering a smile on her face. "It's nice to meet you." Her attention turned to Jules. "Please go find Blue Beard and his chaotic posse."

"Sure." Jules nodded. "Would you like to come with me?"

"Not if you're going near that vicious bird and cat!" Brad's hand shot out, placing his hand on Connor's chest as he was about to follow Jules.

"I promise you, Blue Beard is not vicious," Jules assured Brad. "You probably startled him."

"I'll be fine, Dad." Connor pushed past his father and took off after Jules.

"They'll be fine," Liam confirmed Jules's words. "Blue Beard loves Jules, so he'll behave."

"He hates Liam!" Caroline told them.

"Yeah, that bird and I have never gotten along!" Liam shook his head.

Caroline pointed toward an armchair. "If you sit, I'll disinfect those scratches."

"I'm sure they'll be fine." Brad waved her off. "I'll get some disinfectant from the hotel."

"I think you should let Caroline help you now." Harriet gave him a bump toward the living room. "It's an animal. You don't know what germs are coating its talons."

Brad reluctantly sat on the chair.

"How about I take you to look around outside while we wait for Brad?" Liam looked at Harriet and offered.

"I'd like that," Harriet said, and Liam led her out the front door.

Caroline's hand shook slightly as she opened the first aid kit and put it on the table beside Brad, focusing on the task and pushing the questions in her mind aside. As Caroline treated his wounds, the room filled with a heavy silence, broken only by the distant squawks of Blue Beard and the muffled sounds of Jules and Connor's voices.

"I'm sorry we came here unannounced," Brad apologized as she gently dabbed the scratches on his face. "Sam assured me that your brother gave us permission to look around the lighthouse."

"I'm sure he did." Caroline felt him flinch as the disinfectant touched his torn skin. "Sorry." She pulled a face. "I'm almost done with your face." She glanced at his hands clenched around the chair's arms. "Did Blue Beard scratch your hands as well?"

"Oh, no, that was a mini tiger," Brad told her, and despite herself, she felt a smile tug her lips.

"You met Melton," Caroline told him. "Jules's cat. He can be a little jumpy around strangers."

"Well, he used me as a springboard," Brad lifted his hand slightly. "They're not that bad."

"I'm sorry about the animals," Caroline apologized. "They can be lunatics at times."

"The parrot was riding the dog and squawking onward!" Brad gave a soft laugh. "Is that a common sight?"

"I'm afraid so." Caroline sighed. "Sandy's a stray that was dumped in the cove when she was a puppy. Blue Beard found her and stayed with her until my father and Jules went looking for him, and they've been inseparable ever since."

"And the mini tiger?" Brad's eyes watched her every movement, making her feel self-conscious.

"Jules rescued Melton from the pound," Caroline answered. "He was a ball of ginger and white stripes. Jules thinks he's a cross between a Persian and Garfield."

"He looks like a long-haired Garfield," Brad agreed. "I know he has a bad attitude. Does he eat pizza and lord all over the place?"

"That's Melton." Caroline laughed as she finished patching Brad up. "There, all done."

"Thank you," Brad said.

As Caroline leaned toward the table to grab the first aid kit, Brad stood, and they collided, sending Caroline flying backward. Brad's hand shot out and caught her, pulling her toward him, and she landed against his solid chest. Caroline heard him suck in a breath. As she stepped back, she noticed tears in his shirt with blood spots on it.

"On, no, your chest!" Without thinking, Caroline reached out and touched his chest.

Heat shot through her arm and pierced her heart. She snatched her hand away as if Brad had burned her.

"That must be where Melton sprung onto my chest." Brad cautiously touched his shirt.

Caroline bit her tongue, stopping herself from offering to pay for the shirt. She didn't have to be a fashion expert to know it came with a huge price tag, and besides, *Brad* was in her house, uninvited!

"This is why you don't wander around people's houses without them there!" Caroline said before she could stop herself. She skirted around him and picked up the first aid kit.

"Again," Brad's eyes shone with regret, "I'm sorry we intruded like this."

"It's fine." Caroline held up a hand, her eyes catching the time on the clock perched on the mantel. "Shoot, is that the time?"

Brad glanced at his wristwatch and was amazed to see it was after lunchtime.

"I have to get back to the library." Caroline looked at Brad. "Please, continue your tour of the lighthouse." She pointed toward the front door. "Liam knows this place as well as we do. He knows more about its history than I do, so he's the best person to show you around."

"You're not going to join us?" Brad's eyes flashed with disappointment, making Caroline's heart bounce. She ignored the fluttering starting in her stomach.

"Sorry, I brought Jules back because she's forgotten her outfit for her cousin's party," Caroline explained, and a thought hit her. "Connor should join her and Liam's daughter. They are best friends and are going to the party together."

"Actually, Liam already invited Connor and suggested the same thing," Brad informed her.

"Great!" Caroline nodded. "Connor seems like a polite young man." Brad nodded. "He looks a lot like you."

"Don't tell him that." Brad gave a soft laugh. "He hates being compared to me."

"I think all teens are like that." Caroline gave him a tight smile, torn between wanting to turn and flee his company and staying where she was.

Luckily, her phone rang, making the decision for her. She pulled it out of her pocket and saw it was her brother.

"Excuse me, I have to take this." Caroline pointed at her phone, answering. "Hi, can you give me a minute?"

"Sure," her brother said from the other side of the line.

"I'll go find Harriet and Liam." Brad pointed toward the door.

They gave each other a nod before Brad turned and walked out the front door.

"Ah, is our company still there?" Finn asked.

"You could've called and given me a heads-up!" Caroline hissed. "I came home to chaos."

"Chaos?" Finn's voice filled with worry. "What happened?" There was a pause. "They didn't try to walk over the old boardwalk, did they?"

"No." Caroline's eyes widened, and concern filled her. She glanced out the living room window. "They're with Liam, so he won't take them to the boardwalk."

"What happened?" Finn asked.

"Melton, Sandy, and Blue Beard happened." Caroline sighed and rolled her eyes. "Melton used Brad as a springboard and scratched his hands and chest while Blue Beard scratched his face."

"How the heck did that happen?" Finn wanted to know.

"I'm not too sure," Caroline told him, making her way through the kitchen. She started packing away the few groceries she'd bought. "But at a guess, I'd say they were stalking Liam as usual but got Brad instead."

"Ah!" Finn said in understanding. "Blue Beard still has a problem with Liam."

"Well, Liam shouldn't steal his crackers!" Caroline pointed out. "You know how that Macaw is with his treats."

"Yes, I have the scars," Finn reminded her.

"Did you want something or is this the call you should've given me an hour ago when you agreed to let strangers wander around my house?" Caroline finished packing the groceries.

"I really meant to, Caro." Finn's voice was filled with apology. "But today has gotten away from me." He paused. "You don't usually mind allowing the odd person to look at the lighthouse."

"Yes, but not Brad Danes!" Caroline bit out, lowering her voice. "I just found out who he is and that he's in charge of the production of my series."

"Do you know him?" Confusion was evident in his voice. "When I spoke to Liam, he told me Brad was here with the television crew as he was with Danes Productions."

He is Danes Productions. Caroline corrected her brother in her mind.

"We met in New York!" Caroline told him and realized she'd said too much, so she changed the subject. "Did you need something?"

"Yes!" Finn said. "Liam messaged me to let me know that the director's son is coming to Tucker's party."

"Connor." Caroline frowned. "Why is it a problem?"

"Not at all," Finn said. "Tucker is cool with it. I just needed to know if there's anything the kid can and cannot eat. You know we have to check for allergies. Especially the rich and famous. I don't want to get sued."

"Can you ask Liam to ask Brad?" Two encounters with Brad in one day was Caroline's limit. "I—Uh—I have to get back to the library, and they're with him right now. I must take Jules back to the restaurant to finish her shift."

"I've been trying to call Liam," Finn told her. "I called the library and found out that you had to take Jules home, so I thought I'd give you a try."

"I'll tell him," Caroline promised. "I have to go."

They hung up as Jules and Connor walked into the kitchen.

"Do you want some juice?" Jules asked Connor.

"Yes, please," Connor accepted the offer.

"Connor, my brother wants to know if you have any allergies or have a special diet," Caroline asked him.

"Nah!" Connor shook his head, taking a glass of juice from Jules. "Thank you."

He smiled at Jules, making her blush, and Caroline's eyes narrowed suspiciously. The last thing she needed was another Shaw's heart being broken by a Dane.

"I eat everything," Connor assured her.

"Great, I'll let my brother know." Caroline looked at her daughter. "Jules, get your things. We have to leave."

"I'm ready," Jules told her. "Can Connor come to the restaurant?" She looked pleading at Caroline. "I've already texted Carly, and she's cool with it. Reef's there as well."

Something flashed in Jules's eyes, and her cheeks pinkened once again at the mention of Reef Donovan. Caroline sighed. She wasn't ready for teenage crushes and the drama that went with them.

When did my baby grow up? Caroline wondered as she watched her daughter and Connor interact.

"Please, Mom?" Jules turned to Caroline once again.

"You'd better ask Connor's father," Caroline told her and looked pointedly at her wristwatch. "Please hurry. I have to get back to the library."

The teens nodded, downed their juice, put the glasses in the sink, and dashed from the kitchen while Caroline messaged her brother to tell him Connor had no allergies. Twenty minutes later, Caroline drove Jules and Connor to the Cobble Cove Restaurant.

"I'll see you after the party tonight," Jules leaned over and pecked Caroline on the cheek.

She smiled. She was still getting used to this new loving Jules. "Okay, honey. Please be careful and safe."

"Don't worry, I'll look out for her," Connor said gallantly.

"Thank you, Connor." Caroline watched them pile out of her car.

"Love you, Mom," Jules called, blowing a kiss before slamming the car door.

Caroline saw Reef walk out of the restaurant, and her eyes narrowed when she noticed how Reef and Jules looked at each other.

"Nope!" Caroline muttered, shaking her head as she started reversing out of the parking space. "I'm not ready for teenage crushes!"

At least Jules's crush was Reef Donovan, Carly's teenage son and Tucker's best friend, and not a Danes. Although Connor had surprised her at how he'd immediately stood up and took responsibility for Jules's safety. It was gallant and sweet.

Caroline drove the winding road into Plum Island. She went down Main Street, turning off when she came to the library and pulling into the back-parking lot. Caroline parked in her parking space with her name on a small board. When she exited the car, she stopped and looked at the trim board with her name on it. Her heart felt heavy in her chest. This wouldn't be her allocated spot in a few weeks. It would be Daniella's.

Caroline entered the library, the familiar creak of the old door accompanying her entrance. The air inside was a comforting blend of aged paper and polished wood—a scent that held the essence of countless stories and memories. As she strolled through the central area, the shelves stood like silent sentinels, each book a portal to a different world. The soft murmur of pages turning and distant whispers of conversations added to the symphony of the library.

Her gaze wandered over the well-loved reading nooks, where patrons had spent hours lost in the magic of words. The cozy chairs, bathed in the warm glow of reading lamps, beckoned with the promise of literary adventures. A nostalgic smile played on Caroline's lips as she remembered the countless hours she had spent here, escaping into different realms crafted by wordsmiths.

The library had been a second home to her, a sanctuary where creativity flourished and imaginations soared. She glanced at the recreation room, remembering the vibrant energy that filled the space during community gatherings and events. The upcoming changes weighed on her, and a subtle melancholy settled in her heart.

Caroline meandered past the shelves, her fingertips lightly tracing the spines of familiar titles. The music room whispered memories of Jules's laughter as she explored her musical talents. The gymnasium echoed with the sounds of lively activities and celebrations that had brought the community together.

Stopping in the middle of the library, Caroline allowed herself a moment to absorb the atmosphere. With its multifaceted rooms, the library held the essence of a shared history—a chronicle of joy, sorrow, growth, and connection. It was a place where stories unfolded within the pages of books and in the lives of those who frequented its halls.

As Caroline walked further, she reached the recreation room, a space that had been a labor of love for her. The memories of shared smiles, laughter, and the vibrant energy of the younger islanders flooded her mind. The room had become a haven for community bonding, and the bittersweet realization that she would soon part ways with this cherished space tugged at her heart.

Caroline continued her journey through the library, reliving moments etched into its walls. Each room held a piece of her past, and as she approached her office, a mix of nostalgia and gratitude enveloped her. The door to her office stood ajar, and as she entered, the familiar sight of her desk, adorned with notes and manuscripts, brought a sense of closure.

With a deep breath, Caroline embraced the transient nature of life. The library, with its timeless stories and the imprints of countless lives, stood as a testament to the enduring spirit of Plum Island. As she lingered in her office, a silent acknowledgment passed between her and the space that had been an integral part of her journey.

"Caroline, the high school bus has pulled up," Tanith's voice echoed from behind her, breaking the nostalgic spell.

Caroline turned toward Tanith, nodding. She picked up the clipboard on her desk. "Everything's ready for them." She straightened her shirt and smoothed her skirt. "Let's go welcome our guests."

"I know most kids hated summer school," Tanith said, following Caroline out the library's front door. "But I loved it. Especially all the trips to the library."

"I loved summer school too," Caroline confessed.

"You went to summer school?" Tanith gaped at Caroline in disbelief. "I always pictured you as a straight-A student who wouldn't have to attend summer school."

"You're right." Caroline nodded. "I got excellent grades. But I helped by tutoring the other kids who needed summer school."

"You really are a saint!" Tanith breathed in awe. "I'm going to miss you when you leave."

"I'm not leaving Plum Island," Caroline reminded her. "Now that my writing career has taken off, I can't balance the library and my writing."

"Daniella is going to run a small surgery while doing the job!" Tanith's brows raised.

"Daniella is going to be relying on the best assistant librarian in the county to help her keep it running smoothly when the clinic opens,"

Caroline explained. "Besides, the clinic will only be open three days a week and mornings only."

Tanith's eyes narrowed suspiciously. "What does that mean? The part about Daniella relying heavily on me to keep the library running smoothly."

"We weren't going to announce it until after Daniella officially started as head librarian," Caroline told her, watching as the doors to the school bus opened. "But you're going to be training as head librarian, and we're hiring another assistant librarian."

"What?" Tanith's jaw dropped. "Are you kidding me?" Excitement made her eyes sparkle.

"Nope!" Caroline shook her head. "I signed the paperwork two days ago."

"Thank you, thank you, thank you," Tanith squealed, wrapping her arms around Caroline's neck as a busload of summer schoolers descended on them.

"You're welcome, and you deserve it," Caroline grinned. "Now, as your first assignment. Why don't you assist Miss Kruger?"

"On my own?" Tanith's brows shot up in disbelief.

"Yes, unless you don't think you can handle it?" Caroline tilted her as they turned to greet Miss Kruger, the teacher accompanying the high schoolers.

"Oh, no," Tanith assured Caroline. "I've got this." Tanith took the clipboard Caroline handed her and greeted the teacher. "Hello, Miss Kruger."

Caroline watched Tanith skillfully guide their guests into the library and felt a swell of pride. Tanith had come a long way since those early days when she first entered the library as a troubled youth on probation. As Tanith ushered the visitors, Caroline stepped back, her gaze lifting to the venerable structure that held decades of history within its walls.

The library, originally an eighteen-hundreds double-story mansion, stood as a living testament to Plum Island's past. The exterior exuded a timeless charm, with its weathered brick facade and imposing architecture that spoke of a bygone era. Ivy tendrils crept up the sides, adding a touch of nature's embrace to the stately structure.

Over the years, the mansion had undergone thoughtful renovations and expansions, morphing into a multifaceted haven for literature and community. The amalgamation of styles hinted at the evolving purposes the building had served, from a residence to its current role as a beloved library. The additional wings, seamlessly integrated, bore witness to the library's commitment to adapt and grow.

Caroline's eyes traced the lines of the building, noting the Victorian-inspired windows that punctuated the facade, each pane reflecting the changing light. The double-story mansion retained its character by carefully preserving original features like the ornate wooden trim and the imposing entrance door that had welcomed generations of islanders.

As she gazed up, Caroline couldn't help but feel a connection to the past, to the visionaries who had seen potential in this old mansion and transformed it into a cultural cornerstone. The library's charm extended beyond its architectural grandeur; it resonated with the stories of countless lives that had intersected within its walls.

The entrance beckoned with a sense of anticipation, and the expansive windows hinted at the treasures held within. The library had become a living organism, with each room and corridor telling a unique tale. Caroline felt a swell of gratitude for the dedicated individuals who had contributed to its legacy, ensuring that it remained not just a repository of books but a vibrant hub for the community.

The library's interior unfolded like a literary labyrinth, with winding corridors leading to different sections. A grand staircase, resonating with the echoes of countless footsteps, connected the two stories.

With its rich history, architectural grace, and the heartbeat of the community pulsing within, the library stood as a sanctuary for the islanders, a haven where stories intertwined and the magic of literature came alive. Caroline couldn't help but smile, knowing that although her time here was limited, the library would continue to be a beacon for Plum Island, guiding the way for generations to come.

It had been her haven and the inspiration that drove her to where she was today. Caroline saw the library as an old friend, a keeper of secrets and dreams. As she walked through the familiar corridors, memories flooded her mind like well-worn pages of a cherished book. She could almost hear the echo of her younger self, the aspiring writer who had found solace and inspiration within these walls.

As if thinking of old friends conjured her up, Caroline's phone rang with a call from Jennifer. She walked into her office, sitting as she hit the accept button on her phone.

"Hello," Caroline answered the phone enthusiastically. "I was going to call you later today."

She'd wanted to call Jenny since Caroline had found out who Brad was when he pushed his way into her office earlier that day.

"I would've hoped you'd call me when *Brad* showed up on Plum Island!" Jennifer hissed through the receiver.

"How did you know about Brad?" Caroline's brow furrowed.

"It's a teeny tiny island, *Caroline*!" Jennifer reminded her, and Caroline knew how upset Jennifer was with her when she used Caroline's full name. "What is he doing there? Stalking you?"

"What?" Caroline's confusion grew. "Wait!" Her chin drew back, and her brows creased tighter together. "What were you told about Brad, and who told you about Brad?"

"Does it matter?" Jennifer asked impatiently. "I'm your best friend. I'd have expected you to have called me the minute you bumped into him."

"I didn't *bump* into him," Caroline told her. "Brad found me at the library."

"Oh!" Jennifer said. "How did he find you?"

"You really don't know?" Caroline asked, amazed. "Please tell me who told you about Brad."

"Alright, I promised not to," Jennifer said. "Finn called me to ask if I knew who Brad was and why the man seemed to upset you."

"Finn called you?" Caroline shook her head.

"Yes, he was worried that Brad was the man who'd broken your heart when you were in New York six weeks ago," Jennifer told her.

"Wait!" Suspicions pricked down Caroline's spine. "How would Finn know about my New York romance?"

"Uh—" Jennifer hesitated. "I may have told him." She could picture the sheepish look on her friend's face. "In my defense, I was worried about you and didn't want you pining away or closing up your heart again, so I told Finn."

"Great!" Caroline sighed, knowing she couldn't be mad at her friend when she was just looking out for her. "That's all Finn told you about Brad?"

"Yes," Jennifer nodded.

"Then he left off the best part," Caroline informed her. "Brad didn't come to Plum Island looking for me. He came to Plum Island for the Cobble Cove television series because he's Brad Danes."

Just mentioning the man's name did weird things to her heart, even though she knew he was in town with his girlfriend, who was also his executive assistant. While her heart felt bruised, she couldn't help smiling as she heard Jennifer start to choke with disbelief on the other end of the line.

"I'll be there in a few days," Jennifer spluttered.

CHAPTER 10

Brad stood in front of the bathroom mirror after his shower, looking at the slashes across his chest, face, and hands from his introduction to Caroline's pets. The thought of her made his blood zing in his veins, and he had to admit to looking forward to meeting her in twenty minutes.

As he dressed, his mind played over the events of the day. It had been a shock to find Caroline in the library, and he'd thought he was hallucinating for a few minutes, only to be bowled over when he found out she was Carrie Lines. Could fate get any more twisted than that? He gave himself a mental shake as he pulled on his gray chinos and soft blue cotton shirt. Brad's eyes moved to the shirt he'd worn earlier.

"That's ruined," Brad muttered, shaking his head before spraying deodorant, brushing his teeth and hair, then exiting the bathroom feeling refreshed.

"Hey, Dad," Connor flew out of his room and into the kitchenette area, grabbing a bottle of water and a snack. "Jules and Lila are in the foyer waiting for me. We're going to walk to the Beach Hut. It's not far, and the hotel has beach access."

"Okay, son, please be careful," Brad told him. "And don't get back too late."

"I won't," Connor promised, waving as he slammed his way out of the suite.

"Why can't kids ever just close a door without having to slam it off its hinges?" Brad rolled his eyes and glanced at the clock on the wall in front of him.

Brad decided to go to the restaurant bar and wait for Caroline. It had a lovely ocean view, and he was told that spotlights lit the beach at night. Brad made his way down to the foyer.

"Good evening, Mr. Danes," the concierge greeted him. "Are you going through to the restaurant?"

"I am," Brad confirmed.

The concierge picked up his desk phone, and within a few seconds, the restaurant hostess came to meet him.

"Good evening, Mr. Danes," the woman greeted him. "Your table is booked and ready for you, but you can wait at the bar until your guest arrives."

"I'll go to my table and order a drink there," Brad told her.

He followed the woman into the restaurant. Brad's eyes took in the large room with low lighting. Two of the glass roll-back doors were open to a spacious terrace adorned with fairy lights, allowing a gentle breeze to drift in. The scent of blooming flowers and the savory aroma of culinary delights created an inviting atmosphere.

The interior boasted an elegant blend of modern design and rustic charm. Marble floor tiles gleamed beneath the soft glow of hanging pendant lights. A series of intimate tables, topped with crisp white linens and sparkling glassware, were strategically arranged to offer a mix of privacy and a view of the vibrant terrace beyond.

The walls were decorated with tasteful artwork, capturing the essence of Plum Island's coastal beauty. Large windows framed the breathtaking vista of the white beach stretching to the sea. No curtains obstructed the panoramic view, allowing guests to enjoy the beauty of nature as they dined. The low hum of chatter and laughter intertwined with the soothing notes of background music, creating a harmonious ambiance.

In one corner, a well-stocked bar showcased an array of spirits, and a skilled mixologist crafted signature cocktails with precision. The clinking of ice and the gentle pour of liquids added to the symphony of the restaurant, creating an inviting backdrop for guests seeking relaxation and indulgence.

As Brad followed the woman to his table, he couldn't help but appreciate the attention to detail that defined the Summer Inn's beautiful restaurant and warm ambiance.

"Your waiter will be with you shortly," the woman told him.

"Thank you," Brad took the menu she handed him.

The woman left him alone at a table near the window. Brad turned to see the setting sun slowly dipping below the horizon in a dramatic splash of gold as it bid farewell to another day. In the distance, the moon, a silvery crescent poised on the canvas of the twilight sky, awaited its turn to cast its luminous glow. Back home in New York, Brad couldn't remember the last time he'd watched a sunset. As a boy, it had been his favorite time of day when he'd sit outside and watch the sun make way for the moon like one gracious actor exiting the stage to let the following one enter and captivate the audience.

"Right this way, Miss Shaw," Brad heard the hostess say.

Brad turned, and his breath caught in his throat when he saw Caroling walk toward him. Her honey blonde hair teased her shoulders in a chic bob and a rose cotton dress with shoestring straps. The dress gently outlined her upper body, falling into a soft cinch in the waist before flowing elegantly around her thighs and ending just below her knees, showing off her tanned, toned calves and pink-tipped toes encased in elegant rose sandals.

Brad swallowed as his throat went dry, and his heart lurched. She was gorgeous and walked with a newfound confidence he'd also noticed earlier. Caroline's transformation from shy, unassuming librarian to the woman before him both saddened and intrigued Brad.

"Hello, Brad," Caroline greeted him as he politely stood to seat her.

"Hi," Brad walked to his chair and sat. "I'm glad you could join me tonight." He glanced out the window. "It's a beautiful evening."

Caroline's eyes followed his, "When you live in the city, you forget what an amazing artist Mother Nature is."

Brad turned to look at her. Her voice softened, and her features became wistful as she watched the sunset.

"I love watching as daylight gracefully surrenders to the night, and the moon's glow intensifies, heralding the arrival of a celestial masterpiece as the night sky unfurls above." She sighed. "Adorned with millions of sparkling stars, to create a dazzling spectacle that turns the vast inky expanse into a cosmic work of art."

Brad sat staring at Caroline in awe. Her words captivated him, enabling him to picture the scene she described clearly in his mind.

"It's like having a front-row seat to a celestial ballet," Brad murmured, and she turned toward him.

Their eyes locked while the air carried a gentle breeze, whispering secrets they couldn't understand but were somehow soothed by. The rhythmic lull of the waves in the distance added a soothing undertone to the atmosphere.

"May I take your drink order?" The waiter's voice shattered the moment.

Brad felt like he'd been rising into the clouds, elated only to be dropped and come crashing back down to earth when Caroline turned to give her attention to the waiter.

"I'd like a pot of tea, please," Caroline ordered, and the waiter nodded, turning to Brad.

"I'll have a coffee," Brad told him.

The man turned and walked away to get their beverages, leaving Brad and Caroline in an awkward silence, which Caroline was the first to break.

"Did Jules and Lila meet Connor to take him to Tucker's party?" Caroline asked.

"Yes, they did," Brad said. "Thank you for making them include him. I was worried Connor wouldn't have a good time while we were here."

"I can assure you I didn't make my daughter or Lila do anything," Caroline clarified. "They were only too happy to take Connor with them. He'll have fun as the kids here love meeting new people and are very hospitable."

"That's good to know," Brad said, fiddling with the menu. "Liam told me that most of the kids on the island surf, which Connor is really pleased about." He grinned. "That and the fact that he got to meet one of his surfing idols, Riptide."

Caroline rolled her eyes at the mention of Liam's surfing nickname. "Yes, Liam and my brother were Plum Island surfing royalty."

For the first time since meeting her again, Caroline smiled. It lit up her eyes and transformed her features, making her breathtaking, and Brad's heart did crazy things in his chest. He swallowed and rubbed his neck, suddenly feeling nervous. Something he hadn't felt on a date since he was sixteen.

This isn't a date! Brad reminded himself. *We're here to talk about the television series.*

Their beverages arrived, and Brad was grateful for the distraction. The waiter put a menu in front of Caroline.

"If you'd like to order food, just call me," the waiter told them before leaving.

Brad opened the menu and scanned it. It was a mix of cuisines inspired by local flavors and global influences, offering dishes from fresh seafood caught off the island's shores to handcrafted desserts. The Surf and Turf, a mix of perfectly seared beef filet, prawns, and crayfish, caught his eye, making his stomach gently rumble as it reminded him he hadn't eaten since breakfast.

"Are you sure I can't talk you into having dinner with me?" Brad tempted her by looking at a dish on the menu that he remembered Caroline telling him she liked. "They have crayfish with different sauces and side dishes." He turned a few pages. "Oh, and a selection of mousse desserts."

Caroline took a sip of tea before sitting back in her chair and looking at him. "I am quite hungry," she admitted. "I've been so busy today that I didn't get time to eat." She looked at her wristwatch. "I guess I could be tempted to have a light dinner."

"Great!" Brad breathed a sigh of relief. "Because I haven't eaten since breakfast, and I'm starving."

"You won't be disappointed with the food here," Caroline assured him, and he watched her stiff posture relax as she picked up the menu and read through it. "What were you thinking of having?"

"The Surf and Turf?" Brad looked at her questioningly.

"That's my brother's, his son's, and my daughter's favorite," Caroline told him. "They swear it's the best dish they've ever eaten."

"That's settled then." Brad snapped the menu closed. "Surf and Turf, it is."

Brad caught the waiter's attention when Caroline was ready to order along with a bottle of wine. Soon, they fell into comfortable conversation. They talked about their kids, Plum Island, and the television series as they skirted around the topic of their New York romance.

"The lighthouse is amazing," Brad said as the conversation turned to the first episode of the Cobble Cove Mystery series based around the lighthouse. "The Blackwells will arrive within the next few days along with the screenwriter, Dawn Vanderbilt. I'm sorry, but we'll have to intrude into your home once again as they'll want to see it."

"That's okay," Caroline told him, "If you give me advanced warning, I'll make sure Jules puts her animals away so there are no more incidents." She glanced at his hand. "How are you feeling?"

"The scratches are fine," Brad lied. They stung like heck! "I promise to call you before exploring your property again." He grinned.

"That's wise." Caroline nodded. "Especially as I have a house filled with crazy critters and can be treacherous to navigate."

"Liam told me about the crumbling boardwalk," Brad told her, leaning back in the seat. "I've already organized a team of engineers to look at it so we can fix it."

"Oh, no!" Caroline looked embarrassed. "There's no need to do that."

"Caroline, your property is the main focus of the series," Brad explained, watching her eyes widen in surprise. "It needs to be up to a certain safety code. You do realize we'll be filming there a *lot*?"

"Honestly, I didn't really think about it," Caroline admitted.

"It's something we'll have to discuss when we meet with the Blackwells and Dawn," Brad warned her. "I know they're quite a trio, but I'd like to get our animal expert in to find out if we can work with your parrot, dog, and cat."

"Blue Beard's a Macaw," Caroline corrected him.

"There's a difference?" Brad's brows drew together.

"Technically, Macaws are parrots, but they are bigger with longer wingspans, more colorful, and have bare patches of skin on their face," Caroline told him distractedly. "Wait! You want to write my animals into the series?"

"Yes." Brad nodded. "I think they'll add a bit of fun, and they are such unique characters they will appeal to the audience." He fiddled with the stem of the wine glass. "I'm sure Dawn will agree as she loves writing unique animal characters into her screenplays."

"I still can't believe I will be working with Dawn Vanderbilt!" Caroline's eyes sparkled with excitement. "She's an amazing writer."

"Dawn is the best," Brad agreed. Even though he and Dawn were back on speaking terms, he still felt uncomfortable talking about her. "So are the Blackwell brothers." He took a sip of the wine. "You really impressed my father as he insisted that only the best of the best for you."

"Really?" Caroline's eyes widened in surprise, and her cheeks pinkened.

Brad smiled to himself as his spirits lifted. *My Caroline is still in there!* He'd been worried that her walk into fame and fortune was changing her into the many other rising stars Brad knew. Many started off sweet and unassuming, as Caroline when he'd first met her, only to change as success took them, changing them into entirely different people. One of the reasons Brad had been enamored with Dawn was because even though she'd grown up in the industry with her famous family, she'd remained down to earth.

Brad shook thoughts of Dawn away as he and Caroline finished their meal and ordered dessert. While he was dying to ask Caroline what had happened that night when she never showed up at the party and then ghosted him, Brad was enjoying her company too much to ruin it. So, he let it go for the moment and decided he would find out when the time was right, which wasn't that evening.

"Yes, really!" Brad finished his wine and dessert. "Would you like a coffee?"

"No, thank you," Caroline declined. "I'm so full."

She glanced out the window, and Brad caught their waiter's attention before following her gaze. A wistful smile played on Caroline's lips.

"It's a lovely night," she remarked, her eyes reflecting the moonlit serenity that stretched across the beach.

Brad, captivated by the magic of the moment, leaned in. "How about a stroll on the beach?" he suggested, his eyes catching a subtle hesitation in Caroline's expression.

A mischievous glint sparked in Brad's eyes.

"Or," he proposed, "How about we go on a spy mission and check on the kids at the party?" His gaze met hers, and he couldn't help but add, "I was going to go anyway, but I'm not sure how to get there, and I tend to lose my way in the dark. As a local, I'm sure you know the way no matter the time of day."

Caroline eyed him suspiciously for a brief moment before a playful smile broke through. "To be honest, I was planning on stopping by. I haven't had a chance to wish my nephew a happy birthday in person today, and it would be a good excuse to do some spying."

"And I'd like to meet your brother and nephew to thank them for including Connor even though they didn't know him," Brad reasoned, signing the bill to his suite when the waiter quietly handed it to him.

With a shared understanding, they left the restaurant. They stepped through the glass doors into the breathtaking panorama of the night. The moon hung heavy in the sky and looked so much bigger than he'd ever seen it, casting a silver glow on the ocean, and the stars glittered like diamonds overhead.

As they stepped onto the sandy shore, shoes in hand, the cool grains embraced their toes. A contented sigh escaped Brad, and Caroline noticed the pleasure he took in the action.

"Feels good, doesn't it?" she commented, her voice soft in the night air. "No matter how often I walk on the sand, it never gets old."

Brad nodded, his eyes tracing the path ahead. "It's like letting billions of grains of sand massage your feet."

Following the paved walkway surrounded by swaying palms and lush greenery, they approached a well-lit path adorned with flickering torches. A small bridge led them across to Cobble Cove Beach, where spotlights danced on the sand, and the lights from surrounding houses twinkled on the cliffy hills ahead.

The Beach Hut came into view, a lively hub of music, laughter, and conversation. The sounds of a celebration spilled into the night, creating an inviting atmosphere.

"Looks like the party's in full swing," Brad observed.

Caroline nodded, leading the way with a graceful stride. "I'm so glad there is such a good turnout for it."

They ventured toward the heart of the festivities, the lively ambiance of the Beach Hut enveloping them. The music swirled around them, the beat echoing the rhythm of the ocean waves. Caroline's eyes scanned the crowd as did Brad's, each looking for their children.

"There's Jules," Caroline pointed out, spotting Jules amid friends, her laughter carrying on the breeze.

It didn't take Brad long to spot Connor standing next to Jules and another teenage girl he assumed was Lila, Liam's daughter. From the look on Connor's face, he seemed quite taken by the girl with her long golden red hair and big brown eyes.

"Is that Lila?" Brad asked Caroline. "My son can't seem to take his eyes off her."

"Oh, yes, that's Lila," Caroline confirmed with a soft laugh. "Most of the young men on the island stare at her like that."

"Yes, she is lovely," Brad commented, and his eyes moved to Jules, who was just as beautiful as Lila, only Jules had a more refined air about her. Which Brad knew would scare most teenage boys except for the tall, good-looking, blue-eyed hulk towering over her. "Who is the boy behind Jules?"

"*Reef Donovan!*" Caroline shook her head. "He's my nephew's best friend. Reef's mother, Carly, owns the Cobble Cove Restaurant on Lookout Point."

"He seems smitten with Jules," Brad knew it was the wrong thing to say the instant the words left his lips.

If he had a daughter, it's not words he'd want to hear either at their age.

"Oh, no!" Caroline's chin pulled in, and her eyebrows raised as she eyed the situation between Jules and Reef. "She's only fourteen, and I'm not ready for teenage girl crushes."

"I have to say I don't blame you," Brad told her. "I've only just met Jules, but I, too, don't like the way Reef is looking at her, and she's not even my daughter."

"Reef's not a bad kid." Caroline craned her neck to watch the four teens walk to where others were dancing. "I just don't think Jules is ready for the dating scene."

"Rather, she's open about it than going behind your back!" A female said from behind them, making them both swirl to see Tanith holding a bottle of water. "Hi!" She gave them a wave before looking accusingly. "Are you two spying on your teens?"

"Guilty!" Caroline sighed.

"I take it the handsome new teen is your son?" Tanith asked Brad.

"Yes, that's Connor," Brad answered. "I was worried he wouldn't fit in, but I guess it was for nothing. He seems to be having fun."

"He is!" Harriet stepped into the light. "I thought you weren't going to spy on Connor?"

"Why are you here?" Brad avoided the question and looked at her suspiciously.

"The owner of the Summer Inn asked her if she'd like to chaperone with him," another female that made Brad's hackles rise instantly stepped next to Harriet. "Hi, Brad."

"Hello, Clover, what are you doing in Plum Island?" Brad's eyes narrowed. "I thought you were arriving with your brother in a few weeks."

Brad couldn't help the annoyance that crept into his voice. His father had wanted Rowen Ashton to play one of the male characters in the series. Rowen agreed to take the role with the condition that his sister get a job on the crew so she could learn about the world of movie production. Brad had never liked Clover. Something about her made him uneasy, and it wasn't just how she stared at him all the time.

"As Harriet's assistant, I thought she'd need me to help her as I know she has a lot to do before filming can begin," Clover explained. "So, I came early."

"That's nice of you." Brad gave her a tight smile before turning his attention back to Caroline. "Should we make our presence known to our kids?"

"No!" Harriet stepped in between Caroline and Brad, linking her arms through theirs. "I'm here keeping an eye on them. Moms and dads are not allowed here tonight."

"Caroline is worried about Jules and that teenage boy she's dancing with," Brad told them, looking for an excuse to stay so he could keep Caroline with him for a while longer.

"Reef is harmless, and I know he really likes Jules," Tanith told them.

"You know about this?" Caroline looks at Tanith in surprise. "Why didn't you tell me?"

"Because Jules told me in confidence, and I thought it was better to trust me and talk to me than to have no one to talk to," Tanith reasoned. "Don't worry. If I thought there was anything you needed to know, Caroline, I promise I'll tell you."

"I think knowing my daughter has a crush on a boy is something I need to know," Caroline pointed out.

"I'm sure Jules will tell you when she's ready," Tanith assured her. "And before you get cross with me, it's like I said, it's better if she's talking about it than hiding it."

"True," Harriet agreed and smiled warmly at Caroline. "As we've been teenage girls, we can understand that."

Caroline sighed and agreed, "I guess you're right." She glanced at her wristwatch. "I'd better get going." She looked at Tanith. "You'll keep an eye on Jules for me?"

"Of course," Tanith promised.

Caroline looked at Brad, and his heart sank. He had to refrain from reaching out and begging her not to go; he wasn't ready for their night to end.

"Thank you for tonight," Caroline said to Brad before looking at Harriet. "It was good to see you again." She turned to Clover, holding out her hand. "Hi, I'm Caroline."

"Clover," Clover introduced herself, shaking Caroline's hand. Her eyes scanned Caroline's face before realization dawned on her. "You're Carrie Lines?"

"She is," Tanith said proudly.

"If you're returning to the inn, I'll walk you," Brad offered.

"No, it's okay," Caroline held up her hand to stop him. "I'll be fine."

"We'll walk back with her," A male voice followed a man from the direction of the Beach Hut. "Hi, I'm Trent Becks." He introduced himself.

"Trent?" Caroline looked at him in surprise. "What are you doing here?"

"I invited him," Tanith held up her hand as she answered, then quickly changed the subject. "We were going to the Summer Inn to get more ice."

"I'll go back with you," Brad insisted.

"Stay," Harriet pleaded with him. "We haven't had a fun night in ages."

Brad didn't want to stay, and he was about to say so when Caroline said, "Please, stay and get a taste of Plum Island hospitality."

"Yes, and come meet Caroline's brother." Harriet grinned. "You'll never guess who he is."

Brad looked at Caroline questioningly, "Is your brother a celebrity?"

"Sort of!" Caroline waved her hand in the air.

"Oh, don't be so modest!" Harriet gushed and turned to Brad. "Caroline's brother is none other than The Finnster!"

Brad looked at Caroline in disbelief. "Your brother's The Finnster, a surfing legend and Connor's hero?"

"Afraid so!" Caroline rolled her eyes. "On that note, I'm going to say goodnight."

Brad stopped himself from trying to tempt her to stay as Caroline said goodnight and walked off the way they'd come with Tanith and Tanner.

"Clover, can you get us each a refreshment, please," Brad heard Harriet ask Clover as he watched Caroline disappear through the curtain of the night.

He stood staring in the direction she'd gone and barely heard Clover leave.

"Oh no, you don't!" Harriet hissed, startling Brad as she appeared in front of him.

"What?" Brad looked at her, confused.

"No!" Harriet shook her head and wiggled her index finger in front of his nose. "Don't you dare." Her eyes narrowed warningly.

"Dare what?" Brad's brows knit tighter together.

"Fall for Caroline!" Harriet said through gritted teeth. "This assignment is too important to us for you to mess it up by falling for the author of the series."

"Then we have a problem," Brad told Harriet honestly, his eyes meeting hers. "Because I fell for her six weeks ago."

A lone figure stood listening to the interaction between Brad and Harriet. Hearing Brad's confession drew a soft gasp from them before they turned and silently walked away.

CHAPTER 11

The night was wrapped in a tapestry of darkness, with the headlights of Caroline's car illuminating the way as she navigated the winding road that hugged the cliffside. The tires of her vehicle hummed against the smooth tar of the road. The moon hung high in the sky, casting an eerie glow over the landscape, revealing glimpses of the sea below. The gentle waves sparkled in response to the moon's tender caress with splashes of white as they crested and hit the shoreline.

But Caroline hardly noticed the fine display Mother Nature put on as frustration lingered in Caroline's chest like an unwelcome guest. Each twist and turn of the road seemed to echo the turmoil within her. She replayed the dinner with Brad, the beach walk, and the party in her mind, a reel of regret that played against the backdrop of the night.

The cool, salty coastal breeze swept through the open car window, tousling her hair as if nature sought to untangle the knots of her conflicting emotions. She couldn't shake the annoyance at herself for allowing Brad to weave his way back into her life, disrupting the carefully constructed boundaries she had set.

The familiar scent of sea salt and pine greeted her as she turned onto the long driveway leading to Cobble Cove Lighthouse and Cottage—her home. Shadows danced beneath the trees, playing a nocturnal symphony as the long line of bushes and trees guarding the driveway parted to reveal her house.

As she stepped out of the car, the distant crash of waves against the cliffs provided a soothing background melody. Caroline noticed a solitary light flickering in an upstairs window.

"Liam must've left that on," Caroline muttered to herself, closing the car door and heading for the back door of her house. She turned her head to the right, tilting it back to look up at the ghostly shadow of the dark lighthouse. Caroline's gaze lingered on the once vibrant sentinel that stood in the process of repair and modernization, a necessary evolution that left it silent and lonely.

THE LIGHTHOUSE ON PLUM ISLAND

A nostalgic smile played across her lips as memories of the lighthouse's former glory tugged at her heart. Once, its light had cut through the night, a steadfast guardian guiding ships safely home. Now, a more efficient technology had taken over, casting the lighthouse into obsolescence—a poignant relic of a bygone era.

Caroline sighed as the ghosts of past moments with Jules, like the first stirrings of a childhood crush, flashed through her mind. It was a stark reminder that nothing ever stayed the same; time, relentless and unforgiving, pressed forward, reshaping the landscape of memories into a mournfully beautiful tapestry of change.

Entering the kitchen, Caroline braced herself for the usual cacophony of greetings from her furry companions. Sandy, Blue Beard, and Melton – a trio of companions who usually filled the house with chaos and warmth – were conspicuously absent. A frown etched across her face.

"Oh, no, I hope Liam didn't lock them out the front!" Concern nagged at her as she closed and locked the back door.

Her first thought was of the potential hazard the currently off-limits boardwalk was for her adventurous pets. Wanting to find her pets, Caroline quickly closed and locked the back door as Jules was staying at Lila's. She hung up her keys and was about to rush to the front door when she froze at the sound of footsteps creaking along the floorboards upstairs.

Panic knotted Caroline's stomach as she stood for a few seconds. Her senses heightened as she listened, and the steps moved towards the stairs. There was definitely someone in her house!

Her eyes widened with fear as her heart started to hammer in her chest. Caroline's eyes darted around the kitchen, settling on a skillet she lunged for. Gripping the handle of the makeshift weapon with both hands, Caroline moved slowly and cautiously into the dark living room.

She was about to round the corner that split into the hallway when the figure materialized before her, and two screams reverberated through the house. Caroline's instincts kicked in. She swung the skillet, which vibrated through her hands as it hit its target, accompanied by a thump and a yelp of pain.

"Did you just hit me with a skillet?" the familiar voice hissed indignantly.

Caroline reached out and flipped the light switch, which flooded the room in light to reveal Jennifer nursing her bruised hip.

"Jenny?" Caroline spluttered, relief flooding her before wrapping her arms around her best friend. "Thank goodness it's you. I thought there was an intruder in the house."

"Clearly!" Jennifer pointed at her hip where the skillet had whacked her. "Do you have ice?"

"Yes, of course." Caroline's eyes landed on Jennifer's hip, and she pulled a sorry face. "I'm so sorry about that." She walked into the kitchen and plopped the skillet on the counter before going to the freezer and getting her friend a frozen bag of peas. "What are you doing here?" She handed the peas to Jennifer. "I thought you weren't here for another few days."

"I decided to come as soon as I learned who Brad was," Jennifer told her, taking the frozen peas and putting them on her aching hip. "I took the first flight to Boston, rented a car, and drove here." She glanced at the kitchen clock. "I got in an hour ago. I did try to call you numerous times during my journey, but it went straight to voicemail."

"Sorry, my phone died, and I left it in my bedroom charging," Caroline explained before her brows knitted with worry. "Did you see the animals when you came in?"

Jennifer shook her head. "No, I didn't." She glanced toward the back door. "I did think it strange that they weren't at the door trying to knock me over as I came in." She frowned. "But I know they like walking down by the cove."

"That's what's worrying me." Caroline walked to the living room window and looked out into the night. "I hope if they are at the cove, they used the stairs to get there, not the boardwalk."

"Is that thing still not fixed?" Jennifer stared at her in disbelief.

"Do you know how much it costs to repair it?" Caroline asked wide-eyed. "I don't have that kind of money lying around right now."

"Well, you will soon have money from the television series!" Jennifer pointed out.

"I think Danes Productions is going to take care of it," Caroline told her.

Jennifer's knowing look didn't go unnoticed. "I take it you had your meeting with Brad this evening?"

"Yes." Caroline nodded, moving toward the front door and avoiding the topic of Brad.

She kicked off her sandals and reached for a pair of rain boots perched on the shoe stand beside it. "I have to go look for my animals."

"I'll come with you." Jennifer put the peas down and reached for another pair of rain boots. "Where are the flashlights?"

She looked at the stand next to the shoes, and it was empty.

"Shoot!" Caroline sighed. "They must be in Jules's room. She and Lila camped in the front garden the other night."

"Ah, the front garden camp nights!" Jennifer signed nostalgically. "I used to love sleeping beneath the stars with the waves crashing against the cliffs below us."

Jennifer followed Caroline up the stairs to the attic on the second floor

"No, you didn't!" Caroline laughed. "You were always worried about tidal waves sweeping us away while we slept."

"Not always," Jennifer reminded her as she eyed Jules's new attic room. "Oh, this is lovely."

"Jules loves it." Caroline's eyes swept the room until they found all four flashlights on one of the dressers. "There they are."

She moved into the room and grabbed the flashlights from the dresser, knocking Jules diary off it.

"Shoot," Caroline said.

Reaching down to pick up the book that had fallen open where Jules had propped her pen between the pages, her eyes landed on the words written in her daughter's neat handwriting.

"Don't!" Jennifer shouted and lunged for the book, snatching it off the floor before Caroline could. "This is Jules's personal diary. You know how sacred these are to a teenage girl."

Caroline felt her cheeks heat with guilt. She'd only caught a few words, but they'd made her go cold as they were about Reef Donovan.

"I didn't see..." Caroline's eyes fell on the book clutched in Jennifer's hands. "Much. Just a few words about *Reef Donovan!*"

"Oh, my!" Jennifer's eyes widened in realization. "Does our baby girl have her first crush?"

"Don't look so excited about it!" Caroline growled. "Jules isn't old enough to have her first crush yet, and I'm not ready to deal with all that entails."

"When does life ever happen to a schedule?" Jennifer pursed her lips and raised her eyebrows. "And Jules is fourteen. We had our first dates at that age."

"To a school dance!" Caroline reasoned. "It was hardly a date."

"You went with the guy you'd had a huge crush on since the previous year!" Jennifer reminded her smugly before putting the diary back where it had been. "Now, let's go find that crazy trio of unlikely friends." She took two flashlights from Caroline.

They grabbed yellow rain jackets as they slipped through the front door, heading for the steep stone stairs carved into the cliff wall that separated Cobble Cove from an expanse of sea.

Caroline and Jennifer stepped onto the stone stairs that carved a winding path down the sheer cliff face. A cool breeze cut through the balmy night air as they gripped the hand railing to steady themselves on the slippery rock stairs beneath their feet. Above them, the stars blinked against the brightness of the full moon reflected in the dark ocean running beside them.

The beams of their flashlights illuminated the stone, revealing its weathered yet resilient surface. Although undergoing upgrades through the years, the stairs had been etched into the cliff centuries ago. They served as the passage to perfectly arched Cobble Cove below.

As they descended, the rhythmic crashing of the waves below became more pronounced. The sea roared, a symphony of nature echoing in the hidden cove. Cobble Cove lay shrouded in darkness, its secrets concealed beneath the cloak of night as Caroline and Jennifer stepped onto the pebbled shore.

"Are you okay, Jenny?" Caroline eyed her friend, who sounded slightly winded. "Are you out of breath?"

"I've just had my hip injured." Jennifer pointed out. "Navigating those treacherous stairs in the dark was a little hard for me."

"You're going to hold the hip injury over me for some time, right?" Caroline helped Jennifer down the last trick stair and onto the cobbles that tiled the floor of the cove.

"I'm not letting it go anytime soon, no!" Jennifer warned her. "You hit me with a skillet!" She looked at Caroline accusingly. "A cast iron skillet."

"I said I was sorry," Caroline reminded her. "And you were the one who broke into my house."

"I didn't break into your house. I have a key." Jennifer pointed out.

Caroline turned and started to make her way across the arched cove, calling for Sandy a few times before glancing in the direction of Beach Plum Cottage, an outline in the distance.

"Why didn't you stay at your Aunt's house?" Caroline aimed her flashlight at Beach Plum Cottage perched high above the facing cliff.

It was where Jennifer and Liam had been raised by their Aunt Betty.

"Aunt Betty's in Boston visiting friends," Jennifer explained. "You know I don't like staying there on my own. Besides, I thought staying with you would be more convenient for us working on the television series."

"Are you still afraid of the ghost of Beach Plum Cottage?" Caroline couldn't hide her amusement at the thought. "You know that's just one of Aunt Betty's wild stories."

"You didn't live there!" Jennifer scanned the cove with her flashlight. "Where are these animals?"

Caroline shone her flashlight over the boardwalk, and there was no sign of them. They walked over the rocky shelves scattered around the coves until they neared the Midpoint and stood staring at the rock face.

"You don't think they've gone in there?" Caroline shuddered as she aimed her flashlight at the three openings in the rock that formed into a cave.

"I hope not." Jennifer also gave a little shudder. "After the last time we went in there, I swore I'd never do it again."

"Agreed!" Caroline nodded and drew a breath to calm her hammering heart at the thought of entering the caves. "Let's get closer to the entrance, and I'll yell for them."

As they neared the cave entrance, their attention was caught by excited barking and squawking coming from the stairs that led to Beach Plum Cottage.

"Oh, thank goodness." Jennifer's hand splayed out on her collarbones as she breathed a sigh of relief. "Now we don't have to yell into a cave filled with bats."

Caroline shared Jennifer's sentiment as a flood for relief washed away her worry over her pets. She turned and hurried toward the stairs, where three excited animals greeted them.

"Hello." Caroline's voice became animated as she patted Sandy's head before catching Melton, who leaped at her. At the same time, Blue Beard perched on her shoulder.

"You look like a character from a Disney movie laden with all your critters." Jennifer laughed as they made their way back toward the lighthouse.

"I'm just glad they're alright," Caroline said, glancing back toward Beach Plum Cottage. "I wonder why they were at your Aunt's cottage?"

"Aunt Betty has told me they visit her often," Jennifer informed her. "But usually when you're at work, and Jules is at school."

"Maybe they went there because Jules and I were out for the evening." Caroline shrugged. "I hope they don't make a nuisance of themselves when they visit Aunt Betty?"

"No, she loves it and keeps treats especially for them." Jennifer ran her hand over the soft fur on Sandy's back. "I was thinking of asking Jules to find Aunt Betty a dog as a companion."

"That's a good idea," Caroline agreed as they started to climb the stairs to her house.

"The sooner you have the boardwalk fixed, the better," Jennifer puffed as she climbed the stairs behind Caroline. "I know it will make Aunt Betty's life easier. I don't like her walking up and down those steps every day."

"Your Aunt has walked along the cove every day since she was a child," Caroline reminded Jennifer. "I think out of all of us, she's the fittest navigating those stairs each day." She glanced over her shoulder at Jennifer. "Even when the boardwalk was functional, Aunt Betty used the stairs. She said the boardwalk was touristy and for people who couldn't use the stairs."

"Yes, that sounds like something my aunt would say." Jennifer sighed.

Caroline and Jennifer were nearly at the top of the stairs when Sandy's ears perked, and a low growl echoed in her throat before she skillfully dashed up the last of the stairs.

"What on Earth?" Caroline turned and looked at Jennifer.

Blue Beard shrieked in her ear and flapped his powerful wings while Melton leapt from Caroline's arms, and they took off after Sandy. As Sandy's barks echoed through the night, Caroline and Jennifer quickened their pace up the stairs, their curiosity piqued. The floodlights illuminated the front garden, casting long shadows that danced like ethereal spirits along the cliffs.

Blue Beard's vibrant feathers ruffled in agitation, and Melton scampered along, tail puffed. The unusual commotion suggested something was amiss at the lighthouse.

"What's got them so worked up?" Jennifer wondered aloud, her eyes scanning the well-lit front garden.

Caroline shrugged, concern furrowing her brow. "I don't know. Sandy rarely acts like this unless…"

Her voice trailed off as they approached the front door, where Sandy barked fervently, scratching at the wood as if signaling urgency. The unusual behavior heightened the tension in the air, and Caroline's hand trembled slightly as she reached for the doorknob.

As the door swung open, Sandy darted inside, followed by Blue Beard and Melton. The chaotic trio raced through the hallway, their footsteps echoing in the silence of the night, and they pounded up the stairs.

"Did you leave a window open?" Jennifer asked, scanning the living room for any signs of intrusion. "Maybe a raccoon got in."

"No, everything was locked up tight." Caroline's gaze darted toward the staircase, her instincts tingling with unease.

Sandy's bark reverberated from upstairs, and the two women exchanged a worried glance before hurrying after their furry companions. The wooden steps creaked beneath their weight, adding tension to the situation like a scene from a horror movie when you knew the characters were walking into danger.

At the top of the stairs, Caroline and Jennifer reached the hallway, where Sandy's bark seemed to lead toward Caroline's bedroom. The door stood slightly ajar, an unexpected invitation into the heart of her personal space.

The feeling of intrusion clawed at Caroline's nerves. "I didn't leave the door open," she whispered to Jennifer. "I close it because Blue Beard steals my pillows."

Before Sandy and her friends could enter the room, the door was slammed shut with a force that sent shivers down their spines. Panic gripped Caroline as the realization hit her—someone else was in the house.

Without hesitation, Jennifer surged forward, her expression fierce and protective. With a swift push, she flung the bedroom door open. Sandy rushed in, creating a commotion that echoed through the room.

Caroline's eyes widened in shock as a figure, donned from head to toe in black, raced toward her. The intruder clutched Caroline's laptop under their arm, moving with a speed that caught her off guard.

"That's my laptop!" Caroline yelled.

Instinct kicked in, and Caroline attempted to intercept the thief, but a mighty shove sent her sprawling. The impact with the floor was abrupt, and a sharp pain radiated from her head. Before she could comprehend what had happened, the world around her blurred. The last thing she heard was Jennifer's enraged voice, the subtle scent of clean sheets dried by the sun. As she faded into unconsciousness Sandy's fierce barking resounded around her like a cacophony of chaos.

CHAPTER 12

The Beach Hut pulsed with the rhythm of laughter and music, the sounds of the sixteen-year-olds reveling in the freedom of a summer night. Brad stood watching the flashing lights move to the beat of the music and the mix of teens and adults crammed onto the dance floor.

The adults, a diverse group bonded by their love for the island and the sea, swayed to the music, momentarily lost in the carefree spirit of youth. Brad had been introduced and welcomed by them as if he was a long-lost relative they were happy to see. He and Harriet had been amazed at how warm and inviting the locals were and soon found themselves enjoying the evening.

Brad took a moment to observe each face, remembering the connections he'd made earlier that night: Daniella was poised to become the head librarian and the town's doctor, Liam, the Summer Inn owner and once a surfing hero known as Riptide, Tanith, the library assistant and the youngest of the group, and Tanner, the headmaster of the middle school and a volunteer medic.

His eyes shifted to the tall man who stood at least a head above the rest of the group —Finn, the proud owner of the Beach Hut, Caroline's older brother, and the legendary surfer known as The Finnster. The man who was also Connor's all-time surfing hero. Brad was still amazed at what a small world was. Six weeks ago, he'd met Caroline in New York—a chance meeting at a coffee shop. Today, his son met his surfing hero, who happened to be Caroline's brother, and only because Caroline's books she'd written had brought them here. Fate worked in mysterious ways.

Brad's eyes moved a little to the left to find Harriet teaching Caroline's daughter, Jules, and Reef a dance that looked vaguely similar to a group dance they used to do as teens. He laughed softly as the rest of the dance floor joined them, and the DJ changed the song to a more appropriate one to suit the dance. Brad sipped his beer, watching the laughter and camaraderie between the different age groups as they joined the fun together.

He sighed, thinking about how different parties were back in New York. The younger generation would never think to join in like that—at least in their social circles. Something inside Brad twinged as he saw how happy and relaxed his usually socially reserved son was, unless he was with this surfing crowd, that is. Connor was happier with people he called *real people*. He thought everyone in their social circle was stiff, pretentious, and *totally* boring. Now, he was showing his moves on the dance floor, flirting with a teenage girl, and laughing like he'd never seen Connor laugh.

My father's right. Cobble Cove is going to be good for Connor! Brad thought, catching Harriet's eyes. *Uh-oh!*

Brad quickly lost eye contact and stepped onto the deck before he was roped into another dance as he'd hit his dance quota for the night. A fresh breeze swept in from the sea, carrying the scent of salt and wet sand. The moon glowed silver over the beach, and the rhythmic waves provided a soothing backdrop to the vibrant scene.

Finn joined him first, a knowing look passing between them. "Quite a night, isn't it?"

Brad nodded, his eyes fixed on the illuminated beach stretching out to meet the dark expanse of the ocean. "I could get used to this."

Soon the others joined them on the deck, and Brad, seizing the moment, turned to Finn. "Ever surfed around New York?"

Finn's eyes lit up, memories of the waves intertwining with the sparkle of curiosity. "Sure have. There's Long Beach and Rockaway. You get some great breaks, especially during storms."

The conversation flowed, with each group member sharing stories of their favorite surfing spots around New York. With his gentle demeanor, Tanner reminisced about hidden gems known only to the locals around New England. Tanith contributed tales of Plum Cove, capturing the group's imagination with the simplicity and serenity of the spot.

As the group delved into wave-riding nuances, Brad interjected with a touch of pride. "Connor and I just returned from a surfing competition in California."

Danniella's emergency phone disrupted Brad's sentence, and she excused herself, leaving the group to continue their discussion.

"Was that the West Coast Classic Surfing Competition?" Finn asked.

"Yes. Connor surfed in it and did pretty well." Brad's sense of pride grew. It was the first time he'd told people who he felt were genuinely interested and impressed.

"Wow, I haven't been to that competition in a good few years," Liam told him.

"Liam and I used to go nearly every year in our teens," Finn explained. "It was the highlight of our year."

"And where these two rose to fame!" Tanith added, rolling her eyes. "My granddad was always regaling us with stories of how Finn and Liam were doing in whatever competition they were surfing."

"I recall surfing changed your life!" Liam reminded her.

"Oh?" Harriet looked at Tanith inquiringly. "How so?"

"I was a bit of a juvenile delinquent!" Tanith admitted. "After my parents split and left me with my grandparents, I got a little rebellious."

"She smashed the windshield of the cop's car that arrested her for shoplifting," Finn told her, laughing when Tanith punched him on the arm.

"I've always wanted to do that." Harriet stared at Tanith in admiration. "Take a baseball bat to a cop's windshield."

"I've told you a million times that parking meters need to be fed every hour!" Brad rolled his eyes and shook his head. "Harriet has this little green Mini Cooper S that she thinks the cops won't notice if she doesn't feed the meter."

"I have a bunch of parking tickets," Harriet confessed. "But recently, after a fight with a policeman, I've started parking in my allocated bay in the office building."

"Harriet was taken to court for ripping up the parking tickets a cop wrote her." Brad grinned at the black look Harriet shot him.

"You don't usually go to court for that!" Liam noted.

"You do if you rip up their ticket pad." Brad oomphed when Harriet elbowed him in the solar plexus.

"The woman was being abusive and very offensive," Harriet defended her actions.

Before anyone could comment on Harriet's parking indiscretion, Danniella rushed back, her urgency visibly noticeable on her face.

"Tanner, we need to go. We've been called out on an emergency," Danniell's voice was soft but commanding as she took control of the situation.

"What's going on?" Finn asked Daniella. "Where's the emergency? Do you need help?"

She hesitated momentarily, and Brad noticed her eyes darken with emotion as she reluctantly answered, "The call came from the lighthouse."

"Cobble Cove Lighthouse?" Finn's face fell, his eyes shadowed with disbelief, and his voice dropped.

The news sent shockwaves through Brad, and he held his breath, waiting for Daniella's answer.

"I'm afraid so," Daniella confirmed with a nod. "We have to go."

When Finn echoed his thoughts, Brad had to stop himself from demanding he go with them, too.

"I'm coming with you," Finn stated, only to have Liam grab his shoulder to stop him as Daniella held up her hand.

"No!" Daniella's voice brooked no argument. "You'll only get in the way. We'll call you as soon as we know anything."

"But—" Finn started to argue, only to have Daniella shake her head, cutting him off.

"Finn, we'll wait here. Let Daniella and Tanner do their job!" Liam held Finn back.

Finn relented, and Brad was about to excuse himself to find Sam or a cab to take him to the lighthouse as worry combined itself with fear in his gut for Caroline. He was pulled from his thoughts as the sirens for the emergency vehicle split through the night.

"To heck with that!" Finn's voice was filled with determination. "I'm going after them."

"I'll join you," Brad said.

"Me too!" Harriet held up her hand.

"Then I'm coming as well," Liam told them. "One of us has to have their head on straight." His shrewd eyes took in the looks of panic, fear, and worry on their faces.

"I'll stay here and adult," Tanith offered. "But please let me know what's going on as soon as you get there!"

"I will do that," Harriet promised, then glanced around the room. "Where's Clover? I should let her know we're leaving."

"I think she left hours ago," Tanith told her.

"It is three in the morning," Brad pointed out, pulling Harriet along.

Brad, Harriet, and Liam followed Finn to his SUV. As they piled into Finn's SUV, the night air held a sense of foreboding, the laughter of the party fading behind them as they headed toward the darkened silhouette of the lighthouse, standing sentinel against the vast expanse of the night.

The night was tense as Finn's SUV approached the Cobble Cove Lighthouse. Emergency vehicles with their lights flashing, painted the scene with vibrant colors. Two police cars added to the heightened sense of urgency.

Finn leaped out of the SUV without bothering to close his door, driven by an urgent need to reach the entrance. Brad, Harriet, and Liam followed suit, their expressions reflecting the gravity of the situation. The pulsating lights of the emergency vehicles cast an eerie glow on the surroundings.

Liam's voice cut through the silence. "That's Officer Crowley and Jones' car. They must be here with the dogs."

The mention of the K-9 unit added another element of concern to the silent urgency enveloping them as they approached the cottage entrance. The door was ajar, beckoning them into an unknown realm of anxiousness. Finn, who was at the forefront, opened the kitchen door. The well-lit room greeted them, casting away the shadows of the outside.

Without exchanging words, they hurried into the lighthouse cottage. Their footsteps echoed through the house, the suspense growing as they drew nearer the living room. Finn led the group into the living room, which was usually cozy and inviting but now appeared disturbed. Books were scattered in disarray, ornaments had been toppled to the ground, and the coffee table had been pushed aside.

They stopped looking on in disbelief as the scene unfolded before them. Caroline, looking grumpy, was being examined by Daniella, with Tanner hovering over them.

"I'm telling you I'm fine, Daniella," Caroline's voice was impatient. "I need to console my animals. They must be distraught."

"Don't worry, Jenny has them locked in a bedroom upstairs," Tanner tried to console her. "We can't have those characters interfering with the police dogs or officers."

"And you need to come with us to my emergency room so I can keep an eye on you and give you a proper examination," Daniella insisted. "That's quite a bump you have on your head, and Jenny told us you were out for a good two minutes."

"Seriously, I'm fine. I don't even have a headache," Caroline told her.

"That's a lie," Daniella stated and sighed. "If you don't come to the emergency center, I'll have to stay here."

"Fine, you can have Finn's old room." Caroline shrugged.

Brad's attention was caught by Jennifer as she told a police officer what had happened.

"As we returned from the cove, Sandy rushed to the front door and anxiously tried to get into the house," Jennifer explained. "When we opened the door, Sandy, Blue Beard, and Melton rushed up the stairs, and we followed. Caroline's door was ajar." She glanced at Caroline, shaking her head. "Caroline never leaves her bedroom door open because Blue Beard steals all her pillows. And I knew it had been closed when Caroline had come home. We walked to the door, and suddenly, this person dressed in black flew out of the bedroom. Caroline tried to stop them, but they pushed her flying into the wall."

"Did you notice anything that might lead us to identify them?" The officer asked Jennifer.

"I heard a scream from downstairs, but I was caring for Caroline. As soon as Caroline could walk, I helped her downstairs, and the living room was in this state." Jennifer swept her arms around the room, twirling to see four sets of eyes staring at her in shock. "Liam!"

Jennifer flew over to her brother to embrace him, then looked at Finn and hugged him. "Thank goodness you're both here."

She barely noticed Harriet and Brad standing rooted to the spot. His eyes never left Caroline as he watched Daniella attend to her.

"Caro!" Finn left their side and rushed to his sister when Daniella stood to address Tanner.

"Finn." Caroline was about to stand, but Tanner touched her shoulder to stop her.

"No, stay seated," Tanner warned her, stepping out of the way as Finn reached down to engulf her in a hug.

"I've been so worried," Finn told her, pulling back to examine the lump on her temple. "Good grief, Caro. I agree with Daniella. You need to go to the emergency room for the night."

"I'm not going anywhere," Caroline said stubbornly. "I'm fine."

Daniella glared at Finn, her eyes widening in surprise as she noticed his three companions who walked over to where Caroline was sitting. "I thought I told you to stay away?"

"You also knew I wouldn't listen," Finn pointed out, perching on the arm of Caroline's chair.

"Liam, Harriet," Caroline exclaimed in surprise, her eyes meeting Brad's. "Brad?"

"We were at the party when Daniella got the call," Harriet explained when Brad seemed to have lost his tongue. "We came with Finn because we were concerned about you."

"Sorry to interrupt," the officer interviewing Jennifer pushed through the group, "but if you're up to it, Caroline, I must ask you a few questions."

"Of course." Caroline nodded.

Brad felt cold when her eyes left him to give her attention to the officer.

"So you're *Brad*!" Jennifer's voice made him turn to look at her.

"You must be Jennifer Gains," Harriet interrupted the exchange as the air started to tense when Brad and Jennifer looked at each other with mistrust. "I'm—"

"Harriet Joyce," Jennifer finished for her, shaking the hand Harriet had extended.

"And I see you know Brad Danes." Harriet smiled at Jennifer, who didn't return the warmth but nodded. "What happened must've been so harrowing."

"Did Caroline get a look at the person who attacked her?" Brad asked.

"I don't know," Jennifer told him. "We didn't get much of a chance to talk about it. I was too busy worrying about her and trying to fight the terrible trio into a room."

"The terrible trio?" Brad frowned.

"I believe you already met them this afternoon." Jennifer pointed to Brad's face.

"Oh, right!" Brad's eyes widened in realization, and he nodded.

He had heard Jennifer telling the cop she'd locked the animals up, but he'd been too concerned for Caroline to register.

"Caroline, you shouldn't be standing up!" Daniella's voice drew their attention away from Jennifer to see Caroline pushing through them.

"I told you I'm fine," Caroline grumbled. She looked at the cop as her brow furrowed. "The intruder had blood on their arm where I think Sandy must've bitten them." She looped her fingers around her wrist. "It was on the wrist area."

"Brad and Harriett," Caroline walked toward them. "Thank you for coming. It was sweet of you. I'm sorry to have interrupted your evening."

"Are you kidding?" Harriet looked at her in disbelief. "We were worried about you." She shuddered. "I was mugged once and know how awful it is to be attacked."

"Oh, how awful," Caroline's voice was laced with compassion. "It's terrible to think someone has so little disregard for another's personal property or space that they'd do these things."

"How are you feeling?" Brad asked her, his eyes scanning her face worriedly.

"I'm fine," Caroline assured him with a small smile. "Getting annoyed with everyone—" Her eyes traveled toward Daniella, Tanner, and Finn, who were hovering near her. "Fussing around me like I'm going to break."

"That's a bad bump you have on your temple," Brad pointed out. "They're going to fuss in case you have a concussion or something more serious."

"Thanks for making me feel better." Caroline laughed, her head swiveling when there was a bang followed by exuberant barking from upstairs. Her eyes flew to Jennifer. "What on earth?"

"I'll go!" Finn said, turning and rushing toward the sound.

"I'm going to talk to the officers with the dogs," the officer told them, excusing himself and walking toward the kitchen, where they heard a yell and the officer shout. "My word. Are you alright?"

Brad, Caroline, Daniella, Harriet, Jennifer, Tanner, and Liam rushed to the kitchen to see the officer disappear through the backdoor. Curious, they went to see what was happening when there was a commotion, and the police dogs started barking.

"Stop it, get away!" A female voice echoed from outside.

As the group stepped through the back door, they found Clover clutching something muddy in her hand and looking like she'd just been dragged through the mud.

"Clover?" Harriet said in amazement. "What are you doing here?"

"I was on my way back to the party after going to the hotel to get changed into something more appropriate for a beach party when I saw you all leaving," Clover explained, wiping mud from her face with the back of her hand. "I followed you here. As I got to this area, something ran in front of my car. So I stopped right there, and when I got out of the car." She pointed to the one dog that was barking at her. "That dog came dashing through the hedges and scared me. I tried to run for the door but skidded on this." She handed the item to the policeman, who picked her up from the mud. "It was lying in that patch of mud."

"That's my laptop," Caroline blurted, pushing past the group to get to where Clover and the officer stood. Her eyes fell on Clover's arm.

"You've hurt yourself." She turned and gestured to Daniella. "Can you come and have a look at Clover's arm?"

Daniella nodded and headed over to help Clover. "Come into the kitchen, and we can get you cleaned up, and I can get a better look."

Clover nodded and followed Daniella into the house. The policeman handed the laptop to Caroline, who wiped the mud from it and confirmed it was her laptop.

"We're going to have to take it with us, I'm afraid," the officer told Caroline, pulling an evidence bag from his pocket and dropping the laptop into it.

"For how long?" Caroline asked him. "That has all my writing on it."

Brad stepped up next to Caroline. "Do you have a backup of your work? I can get you another laptop by tomorrow."

"Yes, my daughter set it up to back up to the cloud every hour," Caroline told him, smiling gratefully. "I can go to Newburyport tomorrow and get one."

Brad nodded, not wanting to intrude or push his help on her.

"We're going to wrap up here for now," the police officer told them as the other three officers appeared, greeted them, and made their way to the police cars. "I'll be by in the morning."

"It is morning," Jennifer pointed at the horizon to where the sun was starting to push through the night. "The sun is already lifting the blinds of the night."

The officer smiled. "We'll be back later today," he corrected before taking his leave.

"Can I make everyone some coffee?" Jennifer offered. "I know I need some."

"I'd love a cup," Harriet said, following Jennifer.

"I'll have a coffee," Tanner said, walking after the women.

"I—" Caroline stopped and pinched the bridge of her nose.

Brad's eyes widened in alarm as he watched her face go gray.

"Caroline?" Brad's hand reached out and circled the top of her arm as he looked at her.

"I—" Caroline flinched. Squeezing her eyes tightly together. "Ow, my head."

Brad turned to call Daniella as he felt her sway. "Daniella!"

He called as Caroline rocked forward, landing against him. Brad's arms encircled her. As her body went limp, he managed to grab onto her and swing her into his arms.

"Brad?" Daniella rushed toward him with the rest of the group standing by the kitchen, staring at them.

"It's Caroline," Brad turned with an unconscious Caroline in his arms.

"What did you do?" Jennifer hissed as she ran to them.

"We were talking," Brad mumbled, his eyes scanning Caroline. "She grabbed the bridge of her nose, winced, and collapsed."

"I told her to stay in the chair!" Tanner said, shaking his head and stepping up to them.

"Quick, get her into the van," Daniella rushed to the passenger van that had been kitted out as a small ambulance. "Tanner, get the gurney ready."

Tanner nodded and jumped into the back of the vehicle.

"Caroline!" Finn's voice broke through to them. "What's going on?"

Finn skidded to a stop near the van, his eyes glued to where Brad wouldn't let Caroline go, and carefully stepped into the van to lay her on the gurney.

"I'm going with her!" Finn insisted and was about to climb into the back of the van, but Liam stopped him.

"We should go back to the party and wind it down. Then you need to let Jules know what's happening," Liam suggested, looking at Brad. "Jen, go with Brad and Caroline to the emergency room." He looked at Harriet. "We'll need you to stay here with the animals."

"Me?" Harriet choked. "The last time I was near them, they tried to kill me."

"They'll be fine," Liam assured her. "Just lock the house up, and we'll be back in no more than an hour."

"I'll stay with you, Harriet," Clover offered.

"Okay," Harriet nodded at Clover.

"I'm sure Caroline won't mind if you take a shower and wear some of her clothes," Finn offered Clover.

"I have a bag in my car," Clover told him. "But a shower would be good." She looked at her mud-stained clothes and patted her hair.

Before Tanner closed the back door, Harriet popped her head in. "Please let me know how she is."

Brad couldn't find his voice and nodded, not wanting to take his eyes off Caroline for too long in case she woke up.

"You don't need to be here," Jennifer said through gritted teeth as she put on her seatbelt. "I can stay with Caroline so you can get back to Harriet."

Before Brad could answer, Daniella looked at them. "Brad, maybe you should stay with Harriet." She picked up her phone and messaging.

"I'd rather stay with Caroline," Brad told them.

"But Harriet may need you when the police return," Daniella told him. "I'm just messaging Office Crowley to let him know that wasn't a scrape on Clover's arm. It was a dog bite."

CHAPTER 13

Caroline slowly opened her eyes, squinting against the unwelcome intrusion of light. Her surroundings appeared blurry and unfamiliar, and her head throbbed painfully, sending waves of discomfort through her entire being. As her vision adjusted, she realized she was lying in a small emergency room bed. The sterile scent of disinfectant lingered in the air.

Confused and disoriented, she groaned softly, bringing a hand to her forehead. A sharp, pulsating pain shot through her temples, causing her to wince. The events leading to her current situation were a foggy puzzle in her mind.

"Caroline?" Brad's voice called out, full of concern.

Her eyes strained to focus on the figure hastily rising from a nearby chair and hurried to the door.

He popped his head through and shouted, "Daniella, Caroline's awake."

"Why are you yelling?" Caroline groaned and tried to sit up.

Brad dashed to her side.

"Easy there," Brad said, his eyes filled with worry and an underlying emotion that Caroline couldn't quite decipher. He gently pushed her back into a lying position. "Don't move until Daniella gets back."

Caroline squinted at him, trying to make sense of the situation. "What happened?" she asked, her voice a hoarse whisper. "Why am I in the clinic?"

"You passed out," Brad replied, taking her hand.

At that moment, Daniella entered the room in her crisp white doctor's coat. Brad stepped back, allowing her to take charge.

"Hello, sleepyhead." Daniella's expression remained professional but concerned as she examined Caroline. One of the first tests was to shine a small flashlight into Caroline's eyes. The light felt like a red hot laser beam piercing her eyeballs, making her wince as the pain in her head intensified.

"Do you have to do that?" Caroline placed a hand over her lids, seeing dots swimming before her eyes.

"I have to check you over, Caroline," Daniella told her. "You've got a bad concussion. In order to make sure that's all it is, I'd like to take you to Newbury Port for a CT scan."

Caroline hesitated, feeling a sense of unease at the thought of undergoing more tests. "I'm fine, really. No need for a CT scan."

Brad interjected, his tone gentle yet firm, "Caroline, it's important. As you're now an important client of Danes Studio, I must insist you go, and I'll be right there with you."

Her apprehension eased at his offer. The genuine concern in his eyes comforted her. Daniella continued, explaining the potential risks of a severe head injury, using medical terms that danced over Caroline's comprehension. The mention of being in and out of consciousness for the past twenty minutes sent a chill down her spine.

Her eyes moved from Daniella to Brad. While she appreciated his concern and the concern of Danes Production, she didn't like feeling as if they somehow owned her. If she didn't want to go for a check-up, no one was going to make her.

"I really don't need a CT scan," Caroline said stubbornly. "All I want to do is go home, climb into my comfortable bed, and sleep for a couple of hours."

"You need more than a couple hours of rest," Daniella told her. "But I'm sorry, I can't discharge you. I have to insist you go for a CT scan."

"You can't keep me here either," Caroline reminded her.

"Caroline, please do as Daniella advises," Brad tried to reason with her. "You have a lot going on, and the pressure will increase now as we scan locations. Per your contract and my father's insistence, you have a say in where you want various scenes shot." He took her hand once again. His eyes gentled as he smiled at her. "We need you fit and healthy."

She was about to firmly put her foot down and insist she be released when Jules and Finn rushed into the room, their faces a mix of relief and worry.

"Mom!" Jules flew to her mother's side like a bowling ball, heading for the pins as Daniella and Brad scattered to the side to let her through. "I was so worried."

Jules wrapped Caroline in her slim arms, and Caroline pulled her daughter close.

"I'm okay, honey," Caroline reassured her daughter.

"Please don't stress Caroline," Daniella warned them. "We want to take her to Newbury Port for a CT scan to rule out anything more serious than a concussion."

"A CT scan?" Finn and Jules echoed. Their worried eyes landed on Daniella.

"It's just a precaution," Daniella reiterated. Her eyes narrowed on Caroline. "But Caroline is being stubborn and refusing to go."

"Mom, you have to go." Jules looked at her with wide, pleading eyes. "Please, Mom."

"Yeah, Caro, you can't mess with your health," Finn said, his voice brooking no argument.

Caroline looked at the four pairs of eyes staring at her, waiting for her response, and she knew she was outnumbered. Reluctantly, Caroline agreed to go, "Fine, let's get this over with."

Daniella nodded and glanced at her wristwatch. "I have to get the van ready." She walked to the door, stopping to look back at them. "I'm sorry, but you can't ride in the van this time. You're welcome to follow us, though."

Finn nodded at Daniella and looked at Jules, then Brad. "We can go in my car."

"Great! Tanner will be here in a few minutes to take Caroline to the van," Daniella concluded before leaving the room.

It wasn't long before Tanner walked into the room, pushing a wheelchair. "Hey, everyone." His eyes crinkled as he smiled warmly at Caroline. "I've come to collect the patient." He bowed over the wheelchair. "Your chariot awaits, my lady."

Jules laughed at his silliness, but Caroline eyed the chair in disgust.

"I'm not riding in the chair." She ignored the pain and woozy feeling as she pushed herself into a sitting position. "I'll walk."

"No, you won't!" Three voices chorused as their eyes pinned her warningly.

"I swear, Caro, if you don't get in that chair, I will hoist you over my shoulder and carry you," Finn threatened.

"You know Uncle Finn will do it, Mom," Jules warned her mother.

"I'm sorry, but I must side with your brother and daughter on this one." Brad held his hands up in surrender when Caroline looked to him as an ally.

Traitor! Caroline thought as she sighed and let Tanner help her in the chair.

The journey to the Newbury Port Hospital took a few minutes, but it had felt like hours to Caroline as every bump in the road felt like a hammer to her brain. She also hated being wheeled into the hospital on a gurney. But there was nothing she could do but lie on the uncomfortable bed with wheels as she was swished into a room to get ready for the scan.

A few minutes later, Caroline felt a sense of vulnerability as she lay on the hospital gurney, clad in a thin hospital gown, being wheeled toward the ominous-looking CT scan room. The rhythmic clattering of the gurney wheels echoed through the sterile corridors, adding to the surreal atmosphere. She wondered if Jules, Brad, and Finn were at the hospital and pictured them pacing the waiting room for news.

Entering the CT scan room felt like stepping into a futuristic chamber of medical wonders. The large machine dominated the space, its circular opening intimidating yet strangely intriguing. A technician welcomed her before helping Caroline off the gurney and onto the cold, hard table. The coolness seeped through the thin gown, making her shiver involuntarily.

As the technician positioned her, Caroline glanced at the door as Daniella, donned in scrubs and wearing an air of calm professionalism, joined them in the room. She explained the procedure to Caroline, her voice a steady reassurance in the face of the unknown.

"Caroline, the CT scan is a painless and quick procedure. You'll feel the table move as it slides you into the machine, and there might be some whirring and clicking sounds. Just relax and keep still. It'll be over before you know it," Daniella explained, her tone soothing. "I'll be back there talking to you through the scan. If you start to feel discomfort at any time, let me know."

Caroline nodded, trying to suppress the rising tide of anxiety within her. The sterile room, the clinical scent of disinfectants, and the looming machine all contributed to the uneasy feeling gnawing at her core.

The technician secured a brace around her head as she lay on the table to keep it still. The alien sensation heightened her sense of vulnerability. Daniella stood by her side, a steady presence amid the mechanical hum of the CT scan machine.

The table slowly glided into the circular opening of the machine, and Caroline's pulse quickened. Daniella and the technician left her alone in the tunnel. She lay there feeling her heart beat like a trapped bird. She nearly jumped out of her skin when Daniella's voice came through the comms.

"Caroline, the scan is about to start," Daniella warned her. "Lie still and remember I'm right here."

"Okay," Caroline stammered. "I think I'm ready."

The whirring and clicking sounds enveloped her, creating an otherworldly symphony that seemed to echo her own internal apprehension. Caroline's eyes moved, wondering if they should also be still. She then gave herself a mental shake for being silly. Of course, her eyeballs could move, but her head and body had to remain still.

She was so caught up in trying to distract herself from the weird sensations of the machine that she nearly screamed this time when Daniella spoke to her.

"Caroline, you're doing great. Just a few more moments," Daniella's voice floated through the machine's noises, offering a lifeline of support.

Caroline closed her eyes and focused on the rhythmic sounds, trying to find a calming rhythm within the cacophony. She tried to imagine her family and Brad in the waiting room, and knowing they were there calmed her. Suddenly, Brad's face popped into her mind with his piercing blue eyes and sexy smile. Caroline could still feel his lips against hers as he pulled her into his strong embrace and then skidded her thoughts to a halt.

No, Caroline. Remember, he's with Harriet! Caroline pictured herself drawing over Brad's face with a black marker pen, but his face just reappeared clean to haunt and torment her. There was no mistaking the look of worry and a much deeper emotion when she woke up to see him next to her at the clinic. Then there was their dinner at the hotel and...

No, no, no!

"Almost done, Caroline," Daniella's voice snapped her out of her reverie and brought her back into the reality of her being in a weird tube that could see through her skin and bone.

Suddenly, the scan seemed to stretch into eternity, each passing second intensifying the feeling of confinement. The mechanical whirring and clicking became a relentless soundtrack, a stark contrast to the serenity Caroline sought and the pain in her brain. Caroline wondered if they would ever make a machine that could see a broken soul and find a way to mend it. That's what she needed right now because as much as she hated to admit it, Caroline still had feelings for Brad. Feeling that deepened every minute she was in his presence, and she knew that she had to somehow get over him fast, especially if she was going to be working with him for most of the production.

Finally, the table moved back, retracting her from the machine. The sudden release from the confines of the CT scan offered a rush of relief. The technician approached, helping Caroline sit up as Daniella offered a supportive hand.

"You did great, Caroline. We'll get the results soon, and then we'll have a clearer picture of what's going on," Daniella reassured her, a genuine smile softening the clinical environment.

A mixture of gratitude and vulnerability lingered as Caroline stepped down from the table. The ordeal had been a stark reminder of life's unpredictability, and the supportive presence of those around her provided a semblance of comfort.

She was helped back onto the gurney and wheeled into a room where she had to wait for the results that would unveil the mysteries within her head. If only it would be that easy to show the secrets of the heart and how to fix them. The room door opened before Caroline could get lost in her thoughts once more. Jules came in, cuddling a teddy, followed by Brad. Her heart skipped a beat, and her stomach knotted when she noticed the flowers in his hand.

"How was it?" Jules asked her, hugging her.

"Weird!" Caroline told them.

"Here, this is for you." Jules held up the teddy with a heart on his belly, and *I Wuv you Beary Much* on it. "We had to buy them at the little gift shop in the hospital."

"They only had these daisies," Brad said, handing them to her. "We were going to sneak you a coffee but thought better of it."

"We didn't know if you were going to need further treatment," Jules explained. "If you don't, I'll get us a coffee."

"Nice try," Caroline told her daughter with a grin. "You can have a tea or cocoa."

"It was worth a shot." Jules shrugged and sat in a chair beside the bed. Brad sat next to her.

"How long did Daniella say the results will take?" Brad asked.

"I'm not sure," Caroline answered. "But if you need to go, I'm sure Finn can take us home." She frowned and craned her neck, looking through the door. "Where is Finn?"

Brad and Jules looked at each other before he answered, "Finn had to get back to the lighthouse to help—"

"He went to help Jennifer and Harriet," Jules finished Brad's sentence, making Caroline suspicious.

"What did they need help with?" Caroline's eyes narrowed.

"Something to do with the lighthouse," Jules told her, moving the subject away from Finn's absence. "Do you think they'll serve you breakfast?" She glanced toward the door. "I'm starving."

"You also need to get some sleep." Caroline realized what the time was as she looked at the clock hanging over the door, and her eyes collided with Brad's. "You both do."

"We'll be able to sleep once we know you're alright," Brad said. His eyes were still shadowed with concern for her, making her heart do more crazy flips.

As if on cue, Daniella walked into the room. "Good news." She put the tablet she was carrying under her arm. "Your scan came up clean. But you still have a concussion, and we need to keep you here for twenty-four-hour observation."

"I don't have twenty-four hours to lie around in bed," Caroline moaned. "I want to go home. I have a lot to do today."

"Which is why you're not going anywhere, Mom," Jules told her, suppressing a yawn and glancing at the soft family recliner in the corner.

"I'm going to get you a new laptop." Brad smiled at the look she shot him. "I insist. It's the least I can do. Jules said she'll set it up for you and download all your information from the cloud."

"Thanks, honey." Caroline took her daughter's hand and squeezed it. "And thank you for getting me another laptop." A thought popped into her head. "I have some locations listed for various places I thought would be great for filming some scenes."

"I'd love to go through them with you," Brad said. "Why don't I go organize your laptop." He smiled warmly at Jules. "You can take a nap in the comfy chair." He looked at his wristwatch. "I'll be back in two hours with it, and I'll check with Daniella if I can bring some decent coffee and cocoa for you."

"Ooh, can you get some breakfast?" Jules asked him.

"Jules!" Caroline admonished her.

"It's okay." Brad laughed. "I was going to offer."

Jules gave him her breakfast order, which had Brad looking at her in awe, wondering if such a tiny teenage girl could eat all that.

"Trust me, she'll put all that away and then some," Caroline read Brad's thoughts.

"Wow!" Brad grinned. "You and Connor under one roof would eat us out of house and home."

The thought of her and Brad living under one roof with their teenagers made her heart jolt and her mind want to meander into a dream world about it. But she once again gave herself a mental shake. That was *never* going to happen. Brad was with Harriet, and she had to remember he'd taken her on more than a few dates in New York while with Harriet. He'd even had the audacity to invite her to a party. Brad had probably thought Harriet wasn't going to be there.

Anger shot through her like a lightning bolt, and she had to stop herself from snorting at her thoughts. Caroline took a deep breath to steady her emotions as she reminded herself that Brad was being nice and they had to work together for half a year. She bit down her anger and plastered a smile on her face.

"How did you get here if Finn didn't bring you?" Caroline asked, hoping her voice didn't sound like she was gritting her teeth.

"We drove in a limo!" Jules's eyes widened with excitement. "It was awesome."

"Finn offered me his car, but I contacted Sam as I didn't want to put him out," Brad explained. "Besides, Sam was already waiting for us when Jules and I got to the hotel to organize a car to get here."

"Sam said he'd drive me to my senior prom," Jules told Caroline.

"Honey, you have another few years before you get there." Caroline didn't want to think about her baby girl graduating high school.

"I know, but it's good to book in advance," Jules said, stifling another yawn. "I think I'm going to have a lie down for a while."

"Take the blanket from the end of my bed," Caroline offered and pulled a pillow from behind her. "And here's a pillow."

"Thanks, Mom," Jules organized the chair and curled up in it, instantly falling asleep.

"Is she asleep already?" Brad stared in astonishment at Jules.

"Yup!" Caroline nodded, smiling at her beautiful daughter, who was sleeping soundly in the corner. "She's a deep sleeper. Although she can hear a candy bar being unwrapped through four walls and a thunderstorm—that's the one thing that would wake her."

"Connor's the same." Brad laughed and looked at his wristwatch. "I must go. I have a few things to attend to. I want to go back to the hotel, shower, and get changed before returning to Newbury Port, pick up your new laptop, and then I'll be back."

"You really don't have to go to all that trouble if you have a busy day." Caroline hoped she sounded sincere when her heart was screaming *please come back*.

"I have nowhere to be today other than here with you." Brad's voice dipped and hoarsened while his eyes darkened with emotion. "So, if it's okay with you, I'd like to come back and help you get through your twenty-four-hour hospital observation."

"I'd like that," Caroline replied. Her voice sounded as hoarse as his, her eyes locked with his, and she felt herself being pulled under his spell.

They stared at each other, and the hospital room started to fade into the distance until the clatter of a bedpan in the hall burst their bubble. Brad straightened and stood, bending over to kiss her aching forehead.

"Get some rest." Brad's voice was soft. "I'll be back soon."

Caroline watched him walk through the door, taking her heart with him.

CHAPTER 14

Brad stepped out of the hospital, the crisp air hitting him with a rush of reality. His mind buzzed with thoughts of Caroline, the worry, and the relief that she was going to be okay. The night had taken an unexpected turn, but the promise of her recovery was a big relief.

"How's Caroline?" Sam asked as he pulled the waiting limo door open for Brad.

"Her CT scan was clear, but the doctor is keeping her in hospital for a day for observation," Brad informed Sam as he slid into the car.

"I'm glad to hear Caroline is going to be okay," Sam told him. "The whole town is abuzz with news of a break-in." He closed the back door, walked around the car, and climbed into the driver's seat.

"Nothing like this happens in our little corner of the world, so it shocks the town folks."

The news shocked Brad as he stared at Sam. "How does the town already know?" His brow furrowed.

"It's a small community." Sam shrugged. "Word spreads quickly." He glanced at Brad in the mirror. "I must warn you, though, that they're already blaming what happened to Caroline on the film crew coming to town."

"They're already jumping to that conclusion?" Brad's eyes widened.

"I wouldn't worry about it," Sam reassured him. "The head of the town council says it's good for the town and will help keep it going. The residents have been advised to be more vigilant for a while."

"I must remember to thank the head of the town council." Brad breathed a sigh of relief.

"You're welcome." Sam grinned at the look on Brad's face.

"You're a man of many talents." Brad shook his head.

"I wear many hats around this town," Sam said proudly. "I've lived here my whole life, as did my parents and their parents before them going back another two generations."

"That's amazing." Brad looked out the window unseeingly, his mind filled with the events of the evening.

"Are you going back to the Summer Inn?" Sam enquired.

"Yes, please, Sam." Brad nodded. "If you'll excuse me. I need to make a phone call."

Sam rolled up the partition and Brad pulled out his phone. His mind replayed the moment when Daniella informed him and Jennifer about the nature of the wound on Clover's arm—a dog bite. It added another layer of complexity to the already perplexing situation.

Brad was going to stay behind, but Jennifer had stayed. Her logic was that she was less likely to spook Clover into realizing they knew her wound was a dog bite and suspected her as the burglar. Brad had reluctantly let her stay, torn between his worry for Harriet and Caroline.

Jennifer hadn't given him much choice when she jumped out of the ambulance, and Daniella pulled off. Brad still felt guilty about leaving them alone to deal with Clover, even more so since they'd been locked in the lighthouse.

The limo glided through the streets of Newbury Port. With Caroline stable, his immediate concern shifted to Harriet, Jennifer, and Liam. Pulling out his phone, he dialed Harriet's number, the anticipation building with each ring as he wondered if they'd been freed.

"Brad?" Harriet's voice was sleepy as she greeted him.

"Are you okay?" Brad's voice was laced with urgent concern.

"We're all fine," Harriet told him, and he heard her yawn. "Oh, excuse me."

"Were you sleeping?" Brad asked, frowning. "Since when do you sleep when the sun is up?"

"When I've had no sleep for two nights in a row and got locked in a dark, creepy old lighthouse," Harriet informed him sarcastically.

"Of course!" Brad sighed and rubbed his eyes. He was also starting to feel tired as the strain from everything that happened began to wear on him. "I'm sorry I woke you. I was worried when I didn't hear from you or anyone else that you'd been freed from the lighthouse."

"I should've messaged you," Harriet said around another yawn. "I'm so sorry. I can't seem to stop yawning."

"I understand, but you're going to make me start yawning in a minute," Brad warned her.

"I'm glad Caroline's going to be okay," Harriet surprised him by saying.

"How did you know that?" Brad asked.

"Oh. Jules messaged Jennifer, Liam, and Finn on their group chat, and Liam told me," Harriet explained. "I don't think Jennifer and Finn like me much."

"Why do you say that?" Brad sighed. Harriet acted tough and as if nothing got to her, but she was actually quite sensitive and very perceptive to people's feelings. "I'm sure they're just wary of strangers. You know how celebrities can be."

"Finn's the celebrity, and I guess I understand that," Harriet said. "But while Jennifer and I teamed up to watch Clover, she was still cold."

"She also gave me the icy treatment, so I wouldn't worry about it," Brad reassured her. "Editors and celebrity managers, which I believe she's now going to be, can be just as stand-offish as their clients."

"That's probably it," Harriet agreed.

"How the heck did you all get locked in the lighthouse?" Brad decided to move the conversation onto another topic.

"Clover locked us in!" Harriet's voice held hints of anger and annoyance. "She's so fired when I find her. I don't care who her brother is and how unhappy your father is with me for doing it either."

"I don't blame you," Brad wouldn't stop Harriet. "And this is *my* project. We run it how we see fit."

"Thank you," Harriet said sincerely. "I think Clover saw what Liam was messaging to Officer Crowley, who got stuck with a flat on his way to the lighthouse to take Clover in for questioning." She paused. "Her brother was wrong about her. Clover is an excellent actress. She started freaking out, pointing to the window and saying she saw a shadow out there like the one that dashed in front of her car earlier."

"Let me guess, so you all traipsed outside, and Clover thought they went into the lighthouse?" Brad guessed.

"The lighthouse door was open," Harriet explained. "Liam grabbed the keys, intending to lock it after we'd checked it out. Clover was acting very scared, so we went in first with Liam, telling her to get behind him. She knocked the keys from his hand, pushed Liam into us, and by the time we'd untangled ourselves from the heap on the floor, Clover had locked us in."

"Did you at least have flashlights?" Brad asked, knowing how much Harriet hated the dark.

"No, Liam had his phone." Harriet gave a laugh. "Jennifer and I left our phones charging inside the house."

"Oh!" Brad nodded in understanding. "Liam messaged an SOS to Finn when we were about to follow the ambulance taking Caroline to Newbury Port Hospital."

"Liam told us," Harriet said. "It was rather odd to be trapped in the dark and stop our panic for a few seconds to hear the news about Caroline."

"I can picture it." Brad smiled. "You all freaking out then getting the news, sighing in relief and nodding about how relieved you all are, then freaking out again."

"That's quite accurate," Harriet told him.

"I always knew Clover was a little weird, always staring at me," Brad admitted, his tone reflecting a mix of confusion and realization. "But breaking into someone's house? I didn't see that coming." He shook his head. "It doesn't add up."

"I guess there's more to her than meets the eye." Harriet yawned again. "Brad, I'm going to hang up now and get some sleep. What are you going to do?"

"I'm heading back to the Summer Inn, grabbing a shower, checking in on my son, then heading back to Newbury Port Hospital," Brad told her. "I did need you to clear my schedule for the day."

"I did that already," Harriet informed him. "Although I didn't think you would spend the entire day with Caroline." Her voice held a disapproving edge to it. "Brad, remember what I told you last night about starting anything romantic with Caroline. It won't end well."

"And I told you we have a purely professional relationship," Brad insisted. "So stop worrying."

"Uh-huh!" Harriet wasn't convinced. "Oh, and you won't find Connor at the hotel. He slept for a few hours and then took off to the beach to meet and hang out with his new Plum Island friends."

Harriet's update on Connor made him smile. Brad was glad to hear that his son was having fun and had made new friends quickly. It seemed that Connor was quickly steeling into small-town life with ease. Brad had to admit that last night, he, too, had felt the allure of the town embracing him like an old friend.

Brad must've dozed off as twenty minutes later Sam was giving him a gentle shake.

"Brad, wake up," Sam's voice broke through his dreamless sleep. "We're here."

Brad opened his eyes to find they were parked at the Summer Inn.

"Thanks, Sam." Brad rubbed his eyes and climbed out of the limo. "I should only be about twenty minutes, and then we need to return to Newbury Port."

"You're exhausted," Sam noted. "You should get a couple of hours of sleep. Caroline will understand."

"I promised I'd get back within two hours, and that's what I intend to do," Brad said determinedly. "I'll feel better after a shower and cup of coffee."

An hour later, they were driving back into Newbury Port and heading for the PC shop where Brad had ordered a new laptop for Caroline. He was walking into the shop when a woman with an oversized hat, sunglasses, and purse on her way out bumped into him.

Brad turned to apologize when a little dog's head popped out of the purse to growl at him.

"Dingle, no!" The woman's voice caught his attention.

Brad's frown deepened as he recognized her as Vanessa Turner, the actress playing the lead in Cobble Cover Mysteries.

"Vanessa?" Brad stared at her.

"Brad!" Vanessa purred, pulling off her glasses. "What are you doing in Newbury Port? Shouldn't you be working in Plum Island to get ready to start filming my new hit television series?"

"I *am* working, Vanessa." Brad's tone was clipped. "What are you doing here?" His eyes narrowed. "You're not supposed to arrive for another two weeks."

"I arrived yesterday. I *always* go to a new filming location at least two weeks ahead of my scheduled time to be there," Vanessa told him. "I like to fully integrate myself into the surroundings to become one with my part."

"I get it," Brad lied, thinking she was one of *those* actresses who liked to milk the production company for everything she could, including free vacation and a large hotel bill. "I hope you checked with the Summer Inn about having animals?"

"I did, and they made an exception for the show's star." Vanessa smiled prettily and batted her eyelashes. "As we're going to be on Plum Island together for a while, I hope we can have dinner and continue where we left off?"

"I don't think so, Vanessa," Brad's voice was flat and brooked no argument. "We have a rule at Danes Productions about romantic involvement with anyone involved in a production."

"You're the boss. I'm sure that silly rule doesn't apply to you." Vanessa ran a finger over his chest, and he instinctively stepped away from her.

Brad was focused on keeping his distance from her. He didn't see the flash of emotion that flitted through her eyes.

"As the *boss*, I'm the one that sets the examples," Brad told her firmly. "Unlike Ethan Blackwell, I believe I should practice what I preach."

"What are you implying?" Vanessa asked him icily. "I thought Ethan was your friend!"

"I'm not *implying* anything!" Brad's eyebrows rose. "And Ethan is a very good friend of mine. Let's just say he's no fool and gives as good as he gets."

"What does that even mean?" Vanessa's eyes flashed angrily.

"You're a—" Brad looked her over, "*clever* woman. I'm sure you'll figure it out." He looked at his wristwatch. "I have to run."

Brad stepped back to let Vanessa pass, giving her a tight smile when she glared at him, raised her chin, and stormed off. Brad blew out a breath and shook his head, suppressing a shudder. Vanessa Turner didn't care who she hurt to get what she wanted. She wanted to be a famous actress and marry someone influential in show business.

Unfortunately, she was also the daughter of a congressman on the *society's elite social invitation list,* as Harriet called it. This meant his mother, who chaired and organized most of the elite gatherings in New York, knew Vanessa's parents. The woman was a Jekyll and Hyde character who hid her ugly alter ego very well.

"Can I help you?" The shop assistant greeted Brad.

"Yes, Brad Danes. I ordered a laptop and was told I could collect it after nine this morning," Brad answered the man.

"Let me check." The man walked to the back of the store and disappeared through a door.

Brad wandered around the shop, checking out some of the gadgets. He spotted the Smartwatch Connor wanted for his birthday. Brad was about to pick it up and look at it when another man approached him, looking embarrassed.

"Mr. Danes, I'm Collin Jacobs, the store manager," the man introduced himself. "I am so sorry, but there's been a mix-up, and your order was given to someone else. We're contacting the person now and will have this cleared up quickly."

"How long is no time?" Brad's brows creased as he stamped down his irritation. "I have an appointment, and this delay makes me late."

"I don't know what to say other than I'm terribly sorry, Mr. Danes," Collin looked truly sorry.

"Was it you that made the mistake?" Brad asked.

"No, sir, that would be our temp, who has unfortunately left for the day, and we can't get hold of them," Collin explained. "I've already sent one of our staff to the warehouse to get another laptop for you in case we can't get the one we had ready for you back."

"And how long is it going to take to get ready as I asked for it to have specific programs installed on it," Brad's impatience was rising. He knew it wasn't Collin's fault, but someone at the store had to take responsibility for this mess.

"I can assure you, as soon as it arrives, I'll have my top people on it to get it ready," Collin promised. "Can we get it delivered for you? That way, you can get to your meeting."

"I needed the laptop *for* the meeting," Brad told him.

"Again, I'm truly sorry," Collin expressed.

The door to the shop flew open, and Vanessa flounced in, ripping her sunglasses from her face to reveal how angry she was. She had a box in her hands as she stormed toward Collin and Brad. Her sights set on the store manager.

"What is this?" Vanessa hissed, shoving the box at Collin. "I asked for a tablet, and your incompetent staff gave me a laptop." She ran her hand over the box the astounded man was holding. "How would I fit *that* clumsy thing into my purse?"

As she spoke, her dog popped its head out of Vanessa's purse to growl at the man.

"Oh, don't worry, Dingle Wingle, Mommy's handling this," Vanessa cooed at the animal and stroked its head. "You go back to sleep now as it's nap time, and you know how crazy you get when you miss nap time." Her angry eyes pinned a gaping Collin. "Thanks to your store's mistake, you've completely upset my dog's routine."

It was Brad's turn to gape at the drama queen standing before him.

If only she was that good at acting on screen! Brad thought before stepping in to defend the poor man who was still staring at Vanessa's doghouse purse. "Vanessa, it's not Collin's fault, and you should always check your purchases before leaving a store." His frown deepened. "You should've realized that box was too big to be a tablet."

"Who's Collin?" Vanessa looked at Brad, confused, before waving the subject off and saying, "I didn't take the box." Vanessa looked at him as if he'd grown two heads. "My driver took it to the car for me."

"Are you Miss Turner?" Collin finally got out of his astonishment and found his voice.

"Oh, as if you don't know who I am!" Vanessa looked at him with that look actors give people as if everyone in the world knows who they are.

Collin glanced at Brad as he hesitated and said, "So you *are* Miss Turner?"

Brad nodded, "Yes, she's Miss Turner."

"As if you didn't know who I was!" Vanessa sneered. "Your staff probably messed up my order deliberately to get me back in here to take more secret pictures of me."

"Uh..." Collin looked at Brad for help. "Are you a celebrity?"

"Sure!" Vanessa pulled a not-convinced face. "I'll dish out whatever autographs you want. Just hurry up and fix this!"

Brad glanced around the store and saw the other people who worked there staring at Vanessa's commotion as his eyes caught the posters that lined the walls. They were pictures of video games and sci-fi characters. Collin nodded and rushed off to sort out the mistake. He was back within a few minutes with Vanessa's tablet. "Here you go, Miss Turner, and again, I'm sorry for the mix-up."

"Fine," Vanessa waved her hand dismissively, glancing around the room expectantly, but no one approached her.

"I think you're in the wrong store looking for adoring fans, Vanessa," Brad told her, pointing to the walls. "If you're not a video game or Sci-fi hero, I doubt whether they'll recognize you."

"Noted," Vanessa said, raising her chin and shoving her sunglasses back on her face. "I best be going. I have a busy day."

As she flounced out of the shop, Collin turned to Brad, "I'm sorry, but should we have known who she was?" His eyes were filled with concern. "We didn't mean to offend her."

Brad sighed and shook his head, "Some actresses take it for granted that the whole world watches their movies."

Collin nodded in agreement. "The box Miss Turner brought back is your laptop. As she'd opened it, I'm getting one of my team members to quickly check it to ensure it's okay."

"That's fine," Brad told him. "While I wait, I wonder if you can help with a Smartwatch for my son."

"Certainly," Collin said, walking Brad to the watch counter.

Veiled eyes watched Brad from afar as the town car Vanessa had climbed into slowly drove away. The plan was coming together nicely. One obstacle had been removed, and there were only two more to go, and they were going to enjoy getting rid of those two.

AMY RAFFERTY

CHAPTER 15

"Mo...mmy!" Jules's voice sang through Caroline's dreams, drawing her back to wakefulness. "Wake up, sleepyhead."

Caroline was so relaxed and comfortable she didn't want to wake up. She wanted to stay wrapped in the peaceful arms of sleep. Caroline snuggled back into her dreams only to feel the dreamworld she was floating into start to shake, and the peacefulness shattered as she got sucked back to reality. Caroline's eyes opened, and the world around her was fuzzy and moving. She blinked to clear her sleepy eyes and realized she was being shaken. Caroline turned her head to see her daughter shaking her.

"I'm awake," Caroline grumbled. "Please stop shaking me. You're making me feel nauseous like I'm on a boat."

"Oh, sorry, Mom," Jules said sheepishly. "You have visitors who're not as patient as Brad was."

"Brad?" Her sleep-fogged mind cleared instantly as her heart shook away the cobwebs with a hard jolt. "Oh, no, what's the time?" Caroline tried to push herself upright only to grab her head as pain shot through her brain. "Ow!" She rubbed her temples.

"Take it easy, Caro," Finn's voice made her turn her head to find him and Jennifer sitting beside her bed. He leaned over and kissed her cheek. "I'm so glad you're okay."

"Hey, Sleeping Beauty." Jennifer stood and kissed her brow. "We were wondering if the doctors gave you a bit too much pain medication for a while there."

"How long have I been asleep?" Caroline's eyes took a turn around the room. Her heart dipped when there was no sign of Brad.

"The whole day!" Jules informed her. "I wanted to wake you hours ago, but Brad said to let you sleep, and I helped him finish setting up your new laptop." She held it up for her to see. "It's awesome, Mom." She gave Jules a smile. "Can I have your old one when the police give it back to you?"

"I'm not keeping that new one." Caroline slowly pushed herself into a sitting position. "When did Brad leave?" She glanced at the clock above the door and couldn't believe it was nearly four in the afternoon.

"He checked out about two hours ago," Jules told her.

"Oh, I'm sorry I missed him. We were going to go through the locations I had taken pictures of on my laptop." Caroline tried to hide her disappointment, squeezing her heart from her voice.

"I went through them with him," Jules told him.

"I helped," Jennifer said, holding up her hand.

"Sure, for the last five minutes." Jules raised her eyebrows at Jennifer.

"It's not my fault Brad clocked out soon after I arrived," Jennifer said haughtily and looked at Caroline. "Those locations you've pinpointed on the island are perfect for the scenes you've highlighted."

"Thank you," Caroline said, her mouth and throat dry and making her voice croaky. "Is there any water around?"

"Yes, there are water bottles beside your bed," Finn told her. "Apparently, your self-appointed guardian angel insisted they were put there as he thought you might need water when you woke up."

"The man clearly has feelings for you," Jennifer said, and Caroline could hear the reluctance in her friend's voice to admit that.

"He's not a bad guy," Finn stuck up for Brad and looked at his sister. "I'm sorry, sis. I know you and Brad have issues, but I like the guy, and his son and Tucker have become fast friends."

"I feel so bad that I slept through our meeting," Caroline said, taking a bottle of water Jennifer opened and handed to her. "I'll message him later and apologize."

"Or you could tell him when—" Jules stepped out of the way and pointed to the chair she'd been sleeping on earlier. "Brad wakes up."

Caroline's heart took off, rapidly dancing in joy at the site of Brad's long frame sprawled out in the recliner.

"The man was just as tired as you were," Daniella's voice came from the doorway. "Jules and Jennifer asked two male nurses to help them get Brad into the chair after he fell asleep beside your bed." She walked into the room with her tablet in her hand.

"Can you believe he fell asleep while discussing the script?" Jennifer shook her head.

"You were a little boring, Aunt Jen," Jules teased and giggled at the look Jennifer shot her. "I nearly dozed off myself."

"Why, you little traitor." Jennifer put her hand dramatically over her heart.

"I just need to give you a quick check, and if I'm satisfied and your headache is gone—" Daniella didn't finish her sentence.

"It's gone," Caroline told her. *It's almost gone.*

"Then you've only got a few more hours of observation left before you go home," Daniella told her and looked at the occupants. "Do you mind giving us a minute?"

"Sure," Jennifer rose with Finn.

"We'll get some coffee." Finn looked at Daniella. "Is that okay?"

"Yes, Caroline can eat and drink normally," Daniella told them.

Finn, Jules, and Jennifer left the room. Jennifer stuck her head back in. "What about the sleeping giant?"

"He can stay," Daniella told them. "Unless one of you want to wake him or move him to the cafeteria?"

"Nope!" Jennifer shook her head. "It was hard enough getting him into the chair. He's worse than Caroline when you disturb his sleep."

"Then he's fine where he is." Daniella checked her wristwatch. "And he should be out for another fifteen minutes."

"What's that supposed to mean?" Jennifer asked before Caroline did.

"When Brad returned to the hospital, he had a headache and asked if I could give him something for it," Daniella explained. "I gave him a quick exam and found he was exhausted, so I gave him an excellent headache pill that also helps a person get some sleep."

"You're sneaky." Jennifer's eyes narrowed suspiciously at Daniella before she disappeared.

"He's going to be angry," Caroline pointed out as Daniella started her examination.

"I did warn him the medication would cause drowsiness, and he was fine with it," Daniella said. She asked Caroline to look in a few directions as she did her tests. "He even signed the chart I opened for him."

"You are sneaky," Caroline agreed with Jennifer.

"No, I'm thorough and cover all my bases." Daniella jotted on her tablet before folding it in her hands and smiling at Caroline. "You're good to go."

"Thank you, Daniella," Caroline said. "I didn't know you worked at this hospital as well."

"I help out when needed or when I have a patient here," Daniella explained. "I'm not full-time or even part-time."

"You're such a good doctor. Why are you wasting away on Plum Island?" Caroline asked her. "And why on earth would you want to take over as head librarian?"

"When I was a kid, the library was my portal to so many different worlds," Daniella smiled. "No matter how lonely or upset I was when

I'd walk into the library, it was like stepping through reality into the realm of imagination and possibilities."

"I know exactly what you mean." Caroline nodded, relating to what Daniella was saying.

"Much to my stiff parent's horror, when I was in high school, I helped out in the library, and I did so again during college," Daniella told her. "When I was doing my internship, I took a part-time job working at a library so I could start to pay my own way in the world." Her eyes took on a faraway look. "My husband was my fiancé back then, and he was none too pleased either and sided with my parents."

Caroline noticed that mentioning her husband instantly dissolved the nostalgic look in her eyes. Caroline frowned as she was sure she'd seen a hint of fear flash in Daniella's eyes. But it was gone so quickly and replaced by a haunting sadness.

"Then, when Em was born, the library was the one place she'd actually settle down and sleep so well." Daniella's lips turned up into a warm smile. "When she lost her hearing," the fear flashed in her eyes, followed by anger and sorrow, "the library became more than just a quiet place. It was a place where Em felt normal, and it didn't matter if she couldn't hear because she didn't need to hear to escape between the pages of a book."

"Oh, Daniella." Caroline felt the tears sting the back of her eyes.

Daniella Thornton had moved to Plum Island five years ago with her daughter, Emily. While the community had quickly embraced her and her daughter, she didn't speak much about her life before Plum Island. All anyone really knew about her was that she was kind, a great doctor, an excellent mother, and Sam Donovan's goddaughter. Daniella had lost her husband five months before arriving on Plum Island, and she never spoke about the man either. As the locals assumed she was grieving, they respected her and her daughter's privacy.

"Are you going to be able to run the clinic, the emergency center, and run the library?" Caroline asked her worriedly. "While I know you can do it," she assured Daniella, "I worry that you're overdoing things, and what about Emily?"

"That's sweet of you to worry about." Daniella smiled warmly. "But I assure you I balance my time to ensure my daughter never lacks for any of mine and still make sure I have enough reserve time for emergencies."

"Pity you already have a job," Brad's voice startled them as their eyes shot to where she was stretching awake on the chair. "This chair is deceivingly comfortable. I slept the best I have in years."

"That's good," Daniella said, winking at Caroline. "Do you mind if I give you a quick check?" She walked toward him. "I gave you quite a strong pain pill for your tension headache."

"Sure," Brad said with a nod. "But my headache and sore neck are gone."

"It wouldn't have been if you hadn't moved to the recliner," Daniella pointed out as she began her quick exam of Brad's vitals. "I'm glad your headache is gone."

"I feel great," Brad admitted, and he tilted his head around Daniella and smiled at Caroline, making her lose her breath. "Hi, I'm glad to see you're back with us."

"I'm sorry I was out for the count when you came to discuss the locations," Caroline apologized.

"You needed your rest," Brad told her. "Besides, Jules and Jennifer filled in for you."

"I believe so," Caroline told him, feeling disappointed that she didn't get to spend the time with him.

"You're fine," Daniella told him and typed on the tablet. "But I'm recommending that you get more rest."

"Trust me, I try," Brad said. "But there is never enough time during the day to finish everything. So I push sleep back as much as I can to squeeze everything in."

"That's not good for your health," Daniella pointed out. "And, not to be rude, but you're no longer a spring chicken. Your body needs more rest and attention now more than it ever did before."

"I know." Brad sighed. "I promise to take my health more seriously."

"Good." Daniella nodded. Then turned to Caroline. "I've signed your release forms, and you're free to go as soon as you're ready. But I want you to take two days off work." She held up her hand, cutting Caroline's protest off. "Don't worry. I've already spoken to Tanith and I'll start at the library tomorrow."

"Thank you." Caroline breathed a sigh of relief. "But I should be there to help you through your first day."

"No, between Tanith and myself, we'll manage," Daniella assured her. "Besides, if we need you, you're only a phone call away." She checked her wristwatch. "I must return to Plum Island to collect Em from Carly."

"Thank you, Daniella," Caroline and Brad said in unison as Daniella left the room.

As the door clicked shut, an awkward silence descended on the room, and Caroline's eyes met Brad's. She watched him push himself from the chair and walk toward the bed. Taking her hand in his, he brought it to his lips and gently kissed it.

"I'm so glad you're okay." Brad's voice was soft and deep. "You really scared me when you collapsed last night."

"I'm sorry I put you out like this." Caroline didn't recognize her squeaky voice and cleared her throat. "You've wasted a whole day being here by my bedside."

"It wasn't a waste," Brad said, shaking his head. "Would you like to have lunch with me tomorrow?" His eyes held hers captive. "I'd still like to hear your perspective on those locations."

"I—" Caroline swallowed. Her throat felt like it had sand in it. "Of course." She nodded. "But only if you allow me to cook for you as a thank you for all you've done."

"I'd like that," Brad accepted her offer.

"Great." Caroline nodded. "Come to the lighthouse at twelve tomorrow?"

"I'll be there," Brad acknowledged as his head dipped lower and his lips were drawn to hers.

Caroline started to feel lightheaded and realized she was holding her breath, waiting for his lips to touch hers. But as they neared, the sound of Jules's laughter echoed through the hallway, and Brad straightened, letting go of her hand. Leaving her feeling like she was hanging suspended on a highwire with no net beneath her as the door burst open. Jules, Jennifer, and Finn ambled into the room with the smell of coffee and toasted bagels filling the air and making Caroline's stomach gurgle, reminding her she hadn't eaten the whole day.

"Hi, Brad," Jules greeted Brad with a big smile. "We thought you might be awake and got you a coffee and bagel."

Finn handed him a brown paper bag and a cup of coffee from the cut of a cardboard box he had the food and beverages balanced on.

"Thank you," Brad smiled gratefully. "I am hungry and dying for a cup of coffee."

He looked at Caroline and smiled. Brad's eyes held a promise that the moment they'd almost shared was to be continued. Despite herself, she smiled before forcing herself to look away from his hypnotic eyes and take her food from her brother.

Two hours later, Caroline was back home, showered, and grateful that Jennifer had cleaned the place after the late-night intruder had turned her living room upside down. Jules and Jennifer were rushing around Caroline, ensuring she took it easy.

It was both sweet and irritating as Caroline had work to do. She also needed to find a way to get Jules and Jennifer out of the house for her lunch with Brad the next day. Caroline's brows shot up.

"Shoot, I have to go grocery shopping," Caroline said out loud.

"We'll go for you," Jules offered, looking to Jennifer for confirmation.

"Of course we will," Jennifer agreed with her. "Write us a list, and we'll go to the store."

"I'd rather go myself," Caroline told them. "But thank you for offering."

"Mom, you can't go walking around a store on your own," Jules's voice was laced with concern.

"No, you can't," Jennifer stood behind Jules's resolve. "But, we can go with you."

"Oh, no!" Jules's eyes widened. "I'm supposed to meet Lila, Tucker, Connor, and Reef at Cobble Cove Beach."

"Oh?" Caroline looked at her daughter curiously. "You've been spending a lot of time with Reef Donovan."

Caroline ignored Jennifer's warning look.

"He's a friend of Tucker's." Jules shrugged and frowned at her mother. "I've been hanging out with him since he moved here with Carly three years ago, Mom."

"Yes, *Mom*," Jennifer's eyes narrowed on Caroline. "Jules and Reef have been *friends* for three years."

Caroline glanced at Jennifer, giving her a black look and reinforcing Jennifer's fierce one.

"Okay. Sorry, honey. This bump on my head is making me a little weird." Caroline hoped the smile she forced her lips to form looked warm, encouraging, and genuine. She looked at Jennifer. "Would you mind taking her to the beach?" She reached for her phone on the table beside the chair. "I'll ask Finn to bring Jules home later."

"Can I stay with Lila tonight?" Jules asked, and her eyes widened. "Sorry, Mom. Don't worry about that. I'll stay here with you."

"Don't be silly, sweety," Jennifer answered for Caroline. "I'm here to keep a watchful eye on your mother. It's summer vacation." She turned to Caroline. "My brother will ensure the girls are okay and *behave*."

Caroline's smile loosened into a genuine one, realizing what Jennifer meant. Liam was more strict with his daughter than she was with Jules. She made a mental note to message Liam and ask him to keep an eye on Jules and Reef.

"Is that okay with you, Mom?" Jules looked at her with pleading eyes.

Caroline's heart melted. Since their New York trip, her and Jules's relationship had started to mend, and they were becoming as close as they had been before the divorce. And before her daughter left childhood behind to become a teen.

"Sure, honey," Caroline said and received a big hug and kiss from her daughter as her reward.

"You're the best mom in the world," Jules told her, kissing Caroline's cheek again. "If you need me, message me." She looked at her mother. "Okay?"

"I will, I promise." Caroline's heart was filled to the brim with love and joy at the moment she would've pulled the moon from the sky if Jules had asked for it.

"I'm going to pack and let Lila know I can stay over," Jules said as she walked toward the stairs. "Thanks, Mom and Aunt Jen. You're the coolest adults."

"We're the coolest!" Jennifer and Caroline chorused, laughing.

"It's good to see you and Jules connecting again," Jennifer noted, plopping onto the sofa while she waited for Jules. "Do you want me to call Liam and ask him to keep an eye on Jules's budding relationship with Reef, or are you going to do it?"

"What makes you think I was going to do that?" Caroline sometimes hated how well Jennifer knew her as she started messaging Liam. "I'm merely making sure it's okay for Jules to stay the night."

"Uh-huh!" Jennifer nodded, not at all convinced. "Of course, that's all you're asking."

"Thank you for taking her to your brother's for me," Caroline said as she hit send on the message to Liam.

She put her phone on the table beside her as Jules rushed back into the living room.

"Ready!" Jules had her backpack slung over her shoulder, her tablet, her phone, and headphones in her hand.

"That's my cue," Jennifer said, standing and looking pointedly at Caroline. "I'm leaving those three in charge here."

Jennifer pointed to Melton, who was lazing in the sun by the window, Sandy, who was lying next to Caroline's chair, and Blue Beard, who was enjoying the sun with Melton.

"I'll be fine," Caroline assured them as Jules kissed her goodbye. "Be safe, honey, and listen to Uncle Liam."

"Always, Mom," Jules promised, leaving the room.

"I won't be long," Jennifer told her. "Do you want to come with me, and we can go to the store?"

"I need to figure out what I need first." Caroline wanted a few minutes of peace and quiet without watchful eyes tracking her every movement.

"Okay, then," Jennifer nodded. "I'll be back in half an hour."

"Take your time," Caroline called after Jennifer.

Caroline breathed a sigh of relief when she heard the kitchen door close, and the house fell silent. She loved her daughter and best friend, but they had been shadowing Caroline since she got home from the hospital, and she needed some space before she exploded.

She was about to lock the back door when her phone beeped. Caroline picked it up and froze at the message on the screen.

Keep your distance, or you won't like the consequences as I destroy you and ensure your series never gets made!

CHAPTER 16

Brad stepped into the Summer Inn, his thoughts still swirling with the near kiss he'd shared with Caroline. Anticipation bubbled within him, contemplating their lunch together the next day. He needed an excuse, a reason to see her again today, to bridge the gap between the lingering almost moment and the promise of tomorrow.

As he navigated through the foyer, the sight of Alex Blackwell at the front desk brought a heavy sigh to Brad's lips, and his heart sank. The Blackwell brothers had descended upon the tranquil Plum Island, disrupting the usual rhythm of life.

In Brad's mind, the question lingered like an uninvited guest: *Did no one in show business know the meaning of a schedule? They weren't supposed to arrive for another two days!*

Unfortunately, it was definitely Alex, the more extroverted half of the Blackwell Director and Production duo, who was the playboy, carefree and always ready for a good time, who was at the concierge desk.

Brad would've much rather have run into Alex's brother, Ethan, the reserved director, who shunned the limelight and evaded social gatherings whenever possible. Brad rolled his eyes as Alex explained his needs to the concierge.

"I need someone who can cook and cater for about fifteen to twenty people on short notice," Alex's voice carried across the foyer. "I'm hosting a dinner party tonight. My assistant will give you the menu."

Attempting to sidestep the impending invitation Brad knew was coming, he tried to sneak past, only to be caught in Alex's sights.

"Brad!" Alex's booming voice echoed through the foyer, and Brad knew there was no escaping the attention of his lifelong best friend. "There you are, old man!"

Alex walked over to Brad, greeting him with the hand shake-hug.

"Hey, Alex." Brad tried to keep the impatience from his voice. "I see you arrived early!"

"The warm shores of Plum Island beckoned, and we couldn't resist the call." Alex laughed. "I'm having an arrival in Plum Island dinner party on the yacht tonight. And I know you'll be there."

"Do I have a choice?" Brad asked hopefully.

"Everyone has a choice," Alex answered. "Yours are, yes, and definitely."

Brad sighed, realizing the inevitability of the situation. "Fine, I'll be there," he conceded, mentally preparing for an evening of Alex's extravagant festivities before a thought hit him. "But I'm bringing a date."

"Of course." Alex patted him on the back. "I never thought otherwise."

"I take it you have two or three dates?" Brad shook his head.

"Nah!" Alex surprised him by saying. "I'm taking a break from relationships for a while."

"Ah!" Brad nodded in understanding. "Your father finally made good on his threat?"

"Yup!" Alex confirmed. "I'm here totally solo, and I have to stay that way for the entire first season of shooting Cobble Cove Mysteries or else."

"Your father grounds you?" Harriet sneered from behind them.

Brad turned as he saw Harriet walking toward them from the direction of the dining room with a cup of ice in her hands.

"Hey, Harry." Alex's mouth lifted in a sexy smile as he eyed her like she was a prime steak. "Looking good as always, Princess."

"Don't call me Harry or Princess," Harriet said through gritted teeth, her cheeks starting to heat as anger sparked in her eyes. "You should be over there apologizing to Dawn."

She pointed toward the lounge, and Brad turned to see Dawn sitting there and not looking too good. Concern etched lines on his forehead as he looked at Harriet questioningly.

What has Alex done now? Brad asked Harriet. "What's wrong with Dawn?"

"Alexander here," Harriett gave Alex a smug smile, seeing him blanch at the mention of his full name, "insisted on Dawn accompanying them on the yacht to Cobble Cove, and she's been ill since leaving New York."

Brad's heart sank further–he knew Dawn's aversion to sailing and the inevitable seasickness that accompanied it.

"Alex, really?" Brad looked at him in disbelief. "You know Dawn hates sailing."

"I thought she'd grown out of that," Alex said nonchalantly. "Oh, come on. You're mad at me for her condition?" He looked surprised. "I gave her seasick pills."

"You know she can't take them!" Harriet's voice rose slightly with frustration as she glared at Alex. "You are such a jerk."

She spun on her heel and stalked back to Dawn.

"Wow!" Alex watched Harriet, a dark emotion flashed in his eyes for a few seconds before his attention returned to Brad. "Harry is still such a firecracker igniting at the slightest spark."

"You're no slight spark, Alex." Brad blew out a breath.

He knew he'd be breaking up a few of these spats between Harriet and Alex over the next few months of filming. The two did *not* see eye to eye, and when they were in the same space, sparks flew, and tempers flared.

"I'd better go see how Dawn is and take her to a doctor," Brad told Alex. "Please, Alex, can you try not to lose us our head screenwriter or my executive assistant this time?"

"Geez, cut off all my fun, why don't you!" Alex threw his hands in the air. "Between you, my father, and my stick-in-the-mud broody brother, these next few months will be like my own personal jail."

"All we're asking is that you tone down your larger-than-life personality and try to blend into the Plum Island way of life," Brad advised. "This is a small, tightly-knit community, and they aren't used to your extravagant lifestyle." He glanced worriedly toward Dawn. "Try to be more Ethan than Alex while you're here."

"Isn't that just the story of my life?" Alex's eyes flashed. "Always being unfavorably compared to the good Blackwell brother." He held up his hands. "Well, he's not as innocent and angelic as the world thinks." Bitterness laced his voice.

Brad's attention returned to his friend. "Alex, that's not fair." He raised his eyebrows. "Ethan's been through a lot, and no one expects you to be like him. That's not what I meant. I simply need you to keep a low profile like Ethan does. Just while you're here."

"I said I would!" Alex snapped, startling Brad momentarily, as Alex had never done that and had hardly ever lost his temper. "I have to go finish organizing dinner."

Alex turned and walked back to the concierge desk while Brad's brow furrowed curiously.

Alex's father must have really come down on him. Brad thought as he went to join Harriet and Dawn.

"Hello, Dawn," Brad greeted her as she lifted her head and gave him a weak smile.

"Hello, Brad." Dawn rubbed her temples.

"Why did you agree to sail here with the Blackwells?" Brad asked.

"My father, their father, and your father thought it would be good publicity for the new television show." Dawn popped some of the ice chips into her mouth. Her eyes glanced behind Brad.

Brad followed her gaze to see the Dark Ocean, Alex Blackwell's extravagant superyacht now gracing Plum Island's shores and docking on the jetty built explicitly for it.

Brad pinched the bridge of his nose. *The residents of Plum Island are never going to be the same!* "Dawn, I can take you to see a doctor on the island. You don't want to feel like this for the next few days."

"Usually, I'd put up a fight about going to the doctor," Dawn stated. "But I want to see the island as soon as possible, so I won't say no."

"Great." Brad looked at Harriet, who nodded and helped Dawn up. "Can you organize a bag in case Dawn feels sick on the drive?"

"Sure," Harriet said and rushed to the front desk, carefully avoiding another encounter with Alex.

"This project is going to be full of fun and games!" Brad said sarcastically.

"It's quite the team your father has assembled," Dawn agreed. "My father says that Travis Danes always has ulterior motives for everything he does."

"I agree with your father on that point," Brad told her as Harriet rejoined them with a bag. "My father always has some sort of plan going on in the background."

"Here you go." She gave it to Brad. "I'd go with you, but I must get to the police station. Clover's brother's in town, and he isn't happy that Clover is being held for questioning."

"Awesome." *Can this day get any worse?*

"Clover insists that she's innocent and hadn't been to the lighthouse before she'd followed us, and she was bitten by a dog here in the hotel," Harriet informed him.

"It's easy enough to prove," Alex joined the conversation. "Ask Clover if she can remember what type of dog it was and then compare the bite marks."

"That's amazing!" Harriet said.

"It's a logical thing to do," Dawn told her.

"Oh no, I meant it's amazing that Alex has actually been useful for once!" Harriet gave Alex a tight smile. "But I didn't think dogs were allowed in the hotel?"

Brad's chance meeting with Vanessa flashed through his mind.

"There is a dog in the hotel," Brad said. "Vanessa Turner—"

"Hey, she's not a dog!" Alex defended the star of their show.

"He didn't mean she was a dog!" Harriet growled. "Vanessa has that purse dog of hers she carries around."

"Yes, that dog is horrid." Dawn shuddered. "I love animals, but that's a little terror with sharp teeth and a bad attitude."

"I'll go find out what dog bit Clover," Harriet told Brad. "And sort out the Ashtons." She smiled warmly at Dawn. "Brad, you take care of our head screenwriter."

"Good luck getting Vanessa to take her purse dog for a bite test," Brad said as he and Dawn walked to the exit where Sam was waiting by the limo.

As they stepped outside, they were bombarded by the relentless flash of cameras as a group of paparazzi stormed them like a pack of hungry wolves. Brad instinctively wrapped his arms around Dawn, shielding her from the invasive lenses. With practiced ease, he guided her toward the waiting limousine, leaving the chaos of the Summer Inn behind.

Sam, Brad's trusty driver, awaited their departure inside the limo. "Where to?" Sam inquired.

"The Plum Island Library," Brad replied, looking at Sam in the mirror. "Sam, this is Dawn, the head screenwriter for the Cobble Cove Mysteries. She's not feeling too well, and I'd like her to see Daniella."

"Hello, I'm Sam." He smiled at her in the mirror. "Daniella is an excellent doctor and will have you feeling better soon."

"Hello, Sam," Dawn greeted him. "Thank you for taking me."

"I'm here if you need me," Sam assured her. "We'll be at the clinic in a few minutes. There's some ginger ale in the fridge. If you sip on it, it will take any nausea away."

"How do you know I feel nauseous?" Dawn looked at Sam in surprise.

"You're green around the gills," Sam told her honestly.

"Thanks, Sam," Brad said, opening the small refrigerator before him to get a bottle of ginger ale that he opened and offered to Dawn.

"I'll try it," Dawn said. "Do you have the barf bag handy?"

"There are a few of those in the back pocket of my seat," Sam told her.

As the limo glided through the quaint streets of Plum Island, Brad pointed out a few landmarks to Dawn, attempting to distract her from her motion sickness and the paparazzi-induced stress. The picturesque surroundings of the island, with its charming houses and vibrant greenery, served as a soothing backdrop to their journey.

Upon arriving at the library, Brad escorted Dawn inside, the quiet ambiance starkly contrasting with the chaos they had left behind. The scent of old books and the soft murmur of hushed conversations surrounded them as they made their way to the front desk, where Tanith was busy with a few books.

She looked up as they approached. "Hello, Brad." Tanith looked curiously at the woman with him.

"Tanith, this is Dawn, she's the screenwriter," Brad introduced them. "Dawn needs to see Daniella as she isn't feeling well."

"Hi," Tanith greeted Dawn. "Welcome to our little town." She glanced toward an office. "Why don't you have a seat over there." She pointed to a row of seats that looked onto the front desk. "I'll go see if Daniella is available."

"Thank you," Brad and Dawn said in unison.

They sat on the chairs, and Dawn rested her head on Brad's shoulder.

"When last have you been in a library?" Dawn asked Brad.

"A few days ago," Brad surprised her by saying. "I came here to meet Carrie Lines."

"Harriet told me you'd met her," Dawn said. "She also told me she thinks you like Carrie more than you should." She tilted her head back on his shoulder to look at him. "Brad, you can't mess around. Especially if this series goes as planned because your father will want at least another season."

"Harriet exaggerates," Brad assured Dawn and was saved by Daniella and Tanith walking toward them.

"Brad, what is it with you?" Daniella teased.

"He obviously makes women sick!" Tanith gave him a cheeky smile.

"He's not that bad," Dawn surprised Brad by sticking up for him. "He has a good heart."

"Thank you." Brad smiled down at her as a flash blinded him.

"Hey!" Tanith yelled. "You can't take pictures in here."

As Brad's eyesight righted itself, he heard running footsteps.

"Come on." Daniella helped Dawn up. "Let's get you out of the way of the press."

"Thank you," Dawn said weakly as they followed Daniella down the long corridor to the door at the end, which was labeled *staff only*.

Brad reached over and opened it, letting Daniella and Dawn enter first.

"Please hit the latch," Daniella told Brad before leading Dawn to one of the few overnight rooms.

Brad latched the door, checked the others that led into the clinic, and pulled the blinds. He sat in the waiting room and pulled out his phone to call Harriet to find out how it was going at the police station.

"Hello." Harriet's tone was clipped.

"I take it things aren't going too well there?" Brad sat back and rested his ankle on his knee.

"Something like that." Harriet's voice was laced with anger. "Whoever thought that Vanessa Turner and Rowen Ashton could work together on a movie was very, very wrong."

"What's going on?" Brad asked.

"The police detective interviewing Clover doesn't believe that the dog bite on her arm is from a large dog like Caroline's," Harriet informed him. "Alex found Vanessa and dragged her and her purse dog to the police station, and now she's threatening to sue everyone and throwing her father's name around."

"That sounds like something she'd do." Brad drew in a calming breath and closed his eyes.

"Rowen is accusing Vanessa of trying to get his sister fired to make him look bad so we'd kick him off the show," Harriet continued the story. "Rowen threatened Vanessa if she didn't hand over her dog to the local vet to check its bite."

"What did he threaten her with?" Brad felt his headache coming back.

"I have no idea." Harriet paused, and Brad could picture her physically gathering her control. "Something about exposing who she really was to the world. Vanessa told him to go ahead, and she'd make sure her father destroyed his career."

"So, a typical society catfight?" Brad rubbed his temples as he felt his shoulders tensing. "What do you think about Clover's story?"

"I know you don't like her," Harriet said, "but I think Clover's telling the truth. Oh, and the police technical support went through Caroline's laptop and found some sort of program that allowed for remote access to her laptop."

"Many people have remote access software on their computers," Brad pointed out.

"Not this sort of remote access software," Harriet's words alarmed him. "The tech guy said that it was the sort of tool used to hack into a person's computer, and it could enable the camera."

"I doubt Caroline would've had something like that on her laptop," Brad said.

"It was installed the night of the break-in," Harriet's words made his spidey senses tingle.

"Maybe Caroline and Jennifer didn't interrupt the burglar taking the laptop but returning it," Brad suggested. "After installing the spyware on it."

"That's what the detective thinks," Harriet told him. "They're keeping the laptop until the case is resolved and using the software to trace its source."

"It's just as well I bought Caroline a new laptop," Brad said, relieved at his decision.

"Yes, thank goodness," Harriet agreed. "I'd better get back to the circus to try and moderate the negotiation to get Vanessa's dog's teeth tested."

"Keep me informed," Brad told her. "Oh, and if you have to fire anyone, and you believe Clover is telling the truth, fire Vanessa."

"I was thinking the same thing," Harriet said, her voice filled with disdain for the woman. "And I am beginning to believe that Clover has been set up."

"It seems that way to me as well," Brad admitted. "Set a meeting for me with Rowen for later this afternoon." He looked at his wristwatch. "Dawn and I should be finished at the clinic in an hour or so."

"Sure, I'll see what I can do," Harriet promised. "How's Dawn?"

"I'm waiting for Daniella," Brad told her. "I'll let you know."

"Likewise," Harriet said before hanging up.

Brad stretched out his legs and leaned back in the chair, rubbing his face warily. This was what happened when people didn't stick to his carefully mapped out schedule. Pieces got bumped out of order and flew everywhere, and that's what he felt was happening to his carefully laid-out project. It was unraveling, with pieces flying in all directions every time another tightly pulled project string snapped.

"Brad?" Daniella's voice caught his attention. "I'm going to be keeping Dawn here for a while. She told me to tell you to go."

"How is she?" Brad asked.

"Dehydrated," Daniella told him. "I have her on a drip at the moment, which will replenish her, and it has medication to relieve her nausea and headache."

"Thank you." Brad sighed with relief. "May I see her?"

"She was drifting off to sleep when I left her," Daniella said. "Besides being severely ill and dehydrated, Dawn was also exhausted." She shook her head. "Don't any of you showbiz types sleep?"

"Not when we're stressed!" Brad smiled, running his hand through his hair. "Let me know when Dawn's ready to be released, and I'll send Sam to get her."

"I will," Daniella promised, showing Brad through the door they'd entered the clinic.

As Sam drove Brad back to the Summer Inn, he decided to visit Caroline and find out if she was feeling well enough to attend a dinner party. He was about to lean over and ask Sam to take him to the lighthouse when the memory of the last time Brad had invited her to a party on the yacht flashed through his mind.

Brad closed his eyes and hesitated momentarily, remembering how they'd almost kissed earlier that day. He was sure he hadn't imagined the look in her eyes, which mirrored his as they'd drawn closer. Brad glanced out the window and noticed they were nearing the Summer Inn.

"Sam, can you please take me to the Cobble Cove Lighthouse?" Brad decided to take a chance.

Sam nodded, overshooting the hotel as he headed for Caroline's house. Brad would feel out the situation before asking her to go to Alex's dinner party with him. He did have some news to tell her about the intruder and what the police had found on her laptop. That was the excuse Brad had been looking for to see Caroline.

If you'd be honest with yourself and Caroline, a nagging voice in his head said, *you wouldn't need excuses to see her.*

Brad shook the thought away and let himself get caught in the breathtaking scenery to relax the nerves that were suddenly worrying him as they drove to the lighthouse. His heart lurched when they turned into Caroline's driveway a few minutes later, and Sam pulled to a stop near the barn-style door Brad knew led into the kitchen.

"Thank you, Sam," Brad said as he slid out of the car.

"I'm going to take a walk down by the cove," Sam told him. "Let me know when you need to get back."

"Will do," Brad said as he knocked on the back door.

He heard Sandy start to bark and absently ran his hand over the scratches on his face. They still stung and made him look like he'd had a fight with a cat, but Daniella had assured him they were healing nicely when she examined him earlier for his headache.

"Sandy, Blue Beard, shh!" Brad smiled, hearing Caroline's voice call to the animals a few seconds before a key turning in the lock and bolt sliding echoed to him.

The door opened slightly, and Caroline peeked through the crack. Her face showed relief when she saw it was Brad, and she opened the door wider. Before Brad could step into the house, Blue Beard flew at him, but he managed to duck, only to be bowled over by Sandy, who leaped at him.

"Sandy!" Caroline yelled. "Blue Beard! No!"

She reached out to grab Brad as he toppled. He held onto her hand, and they landed in a heap on the ground. Caroline pushed herself up onto her arms, looking down at him. Their eyes met, and before Brad realized what he was doing, their lips met and melded together. Time and their surroundings started to fade around them until the crunch of wheels in the distance yanked them back to reality, and they sprung apart.

Caroline shot to her feet, as did Brad, as a town car pulled up alongside Sam's limo. Brad and Caroline stood side by side as Sandy's hair stood on end, and a low warning growl rolled in her throat.

"Sandy," Caroline warned the snarling dog, looping her hand through Sandy's collar.

"Onward!" Blue Beard squawked as the car driver got out to open the back door. "Onward!"

As Vanessa Turner stepped out of the car, anger sparked in Brad's chest.

What is she doing here? Brad's eyes narrowed suspiciously as she started walking toward them.

Sandy's growl turned into a vicious bark. The dog yanked herself free of Caroline and rushed at Vanessa while Blue Beard swooped down at her. The parrot stole her hat as Sandy pounced, knocking Vanessa to the ground.

"What the..." Vanessa screamed, landing with a thump. Her purse went flying, and the Yorkie was dumped out of it with an indignant yelp before Blue Beard dropped the hat and attacked the little dog. The Yorkie took off yelping, running away from a squawking Blue Beard.

"Sandy!" Caroline's eyes were huge with shock as she ran after her dog.

Brad stood watching the scene unfold like a slapstick comedy of errors and had to try not to laugh at the absurdity of it.

"Get this vicious mutt off me!" Vanessa yelled angrily.

Her driver and Caroline looked at each other in disbelief before springing into action. Caroline battled to pull Sandy away from Vanessa. The dog didn't like the woman, which made Brad frown as a troubling thought rushed through his mind, but he pushed it aside.

No, why would Vanessa have stolen Caroline's laptop? Brad gave himself a mental shake and went to help Caroline pull Sandy off Vanessa so her driver could help her up. She was spitting mad as she dusted off her soft yellow flowing cotton pants and cream top, now smeared with dirt. Her driver picked up her one yellow sandal she'd lost when she'd fallen, which Vanessa snatched from his hand.

"Is this how you greet all your visitors?" Vanessa looked down her nose at Caroline.

"I'm sorry, they don't usually do this," Caroline apologized, turning to see Brad holding a snarling Sandy. "I'll put her away."

"I'll put her in the house," Brad offered. He reached down, ran his hand over Sandy's soft fur, and felt the echo of her growls rumble through her body. "It's okay. I know how you feel, though. Vanessa does have that effect on a *lot* of people." He cooed as he managed to get Sandy into the house and close the back door.

"Where's Dingle?" Vanessa's voice was filled with urgency when Brad turned to see her snatching her purse from the driver's hand and frantically looking for her dog. "Dingle!"

A squawk caught their attention, and they turned to find the little dog cowering beneath a bush on the side of the driveway with Blue Beard perched on a branch, keeping a watchful eye on the dog.

"What is this place?" Vanessa stormed over to the bush, grabbing her shredded hat along the way.

"Don't!" Caroline and Brad shouted in unison as Vanessa reached down to get her dog.

Blue Beard swooped at Vanessa, who ducked and landed face-first in the Rugosa Rose hedge that lined one side of Caroline's driveway.

"That's going to hurt!" The driver pulled a face and put a hand to his mouth.

CHAPTER 17

Caroline stood staring at the woman stuck in her rose bush in horror!

What on earth had just happened? Caroline watched as the town car driver and Brad rushed to help the furious woman from the rose bush. Luckily, the woman had shielded her face with her hands, which had taken the brunt of the scratches from the thorns.

"This place is a dangerous hazard of crazed wild animals and prickly bushes!" she raged, pushing the driver aside and throwing herself into Brad's arms, wailing. "What are you doing here?"

Brad pushed the woman away from him as another car arrived. Caroline was relieved to see it was Jennifer. She pulled into a space and jumped out of the vehicle, hurrying to Caroline's side.

"What the heck is going on?" Jennifer demanded, her eyes narrowing on the woman in Brad's arms.

"That woman's animals and hedge viciously attacked me!" The woman's eyes pinned Caroline and were brimmed with malice. "I'm going to report you to the police for this abuse."

"Vanessa!" Brad barked. "You're on Caroline's property." He looked at Caroline questioningly. "And uninvited?"

"Of course, uninvited!" Jennifer chimed. "Who are you?" She frowned at the woman Brad had called Vanessa before looking at Caroline. "Do you know her?"

"No," Caroline shook her head. "She arrived here just after Brad did." She swallowed as the memory of their kiss made her breath catch. Caroline forced her mind back to the situation at hand. "Then her car pulled up, and Sandy and Blue Beard pounced on her as she got out."

"Pounced?" Vanessa spluttered. "They attacked me." Her voice rose dramatically. "I swear I heard you tell them to." Her eyes narrowed as she glared at Caroline.

"No, she didn't!" Brad dropped his hands around Vanessa's arms and stepped away from the woman. "What are you doing here, Vanessa?"

"I was told you were here checking out the old lighthouse from the script, and I wanted to join you." Vanessa turned her attention to him and smiled suggestively while purring, "I was hoping you'd ask me as your plus one to Alex's dinner party tonight." Her eyes dropped to her hands, and her head shot to Caroline. "Look at my hands."

"Were you picking roses?" Jennifer asked her innocently.

"No!" Vanessa sneered and pointed a scratched hand at Caroline. "She sicced that ... that..." She turned, and her eyes widened as she saw Blue Beard perched near her. "Get it away from me."

Vanessa launched herself back into Brad's arms.

"Intruder alert!" Blue Beard squawked. "Intruder alert!"

Brad looked at Caroline as Vanessa clung to him like a vine to a wall. "Please, can you put Blue Beard away?"

"Here's a thought!" Jennifer answered. "Why don't you put *her* away into that gas-guzzling car of hers and send her back to where she came from?"

"How dare you!" Vanessa stated dramatically. "I came here to see my..." She turned and gave Brad a shy smile. "Brad, only to be attacked and humiliated." She indicated to her clothes with a sweep of her hand. "Look at my new outfit. It's ruined. Now I have to go back to the hotel and change."

"I can see how that's a dilemma for you." Jennifer pursed her lips and nodded, feigning compassion. "But here's the thing, lady, you've come into my friend's home, upset her animals, and accused her of attacking you."

"I get tired of jealous females being spiteful to me all the time," Vanessa said, sidling closer to Brad and giving him a look that spoke volumes to Caroline and Jennifer. "I've just never suffered this kind of abuse before."

"I think you should go, Vanessa," Brad suggested, pushing her away and stepping out of her reach. Something bumped his leg, and he saw Dingle cowering near him. He bent down and scooped the dog up. "Here's your dog."

"Dingle, my poor baby," Vanessa cooed, indicating for her driver to bring her purse, which he did, and held it open. "Please put him in there for me." She batted her eyelashes at Brad, pouting as she held up her hands. "My hands are sore and bloody."

"Here you go, Mr. Danes." The driver held the purse for Brad to put the dog inside.

"Intruder, intruder, intruder, intruder, intruder, intruder," Blue Beard squawked.

"Get that horrible creature away from me!" Vanessa demanded. "Or I'll call animal control to do it."

"I doubt they'd do that, Miss," Sam told her as he strolled up to them from the Cobble Cove entrance to the back garden. "Blue Beard's a hero around these parts."

"He nearly killed me and tried to eat my dog!" Vanessa snarled.

"He's a Macaw. They don't eat meat," Sam corrected her. He walked nearer to them and tilted his head to the side as Vanessa raised a hand to push aside a stray lock of hair that had come loose. "That's a nasty bite you have on your wrist."

He pointed out, making Caroline's eyes widen as they fell on Vanessa's wrist, now visible as the decorative band she'd worn around it had slipped from her fall.

"My dog bit me," Vanessa admitted grudgingly. "Dingle can be a little temperamental at times."

"Maybe he doesn't like being shoved in a purse," Jennifer suggested and said beneath her breath, "Even if it is Gucci."

"You should get it looked at," Sam told her again. "If you go to the library in town, they have a clinic on the side. My goddaughter, Dr. Thornton, will look at it for you."

"It's fine," Vanessa waved it off.

"She can look at those cuts for you as well." Sam pointed to her hands. "You're lucky you covered your face when you tripped into the rose bush. Those thorns can cause an infection."

"I'll ask the on-call doctor at the hotel to take a look," Vanessa glanced at her hands again before turning to Brad. "I have to go change for the party. What time should we meet?"

"I'm not going to the party!" Brad's jaw clamped, and his eyes narrowed angrily. "But I agree that you should leave."

"Alex is going to be disappointed if you don't show up," Vanessa said.

"He'll get over it," Brad said through clenched teeth.

She turned, raised her chin, and flounced to the car. Her driver pulled the back door open as she got to it. She stopped before climbing in to glare at Caroline and Jennifer.

"You'll be hearing from my lawyer and *animal control!*" Vanessa said spitefully. "Those vicious creatures shouldn't be allowed to roam freely."

She slid into the car, and the driver closed the door. He looked at Caroline and Jennifer, his eyes shining with apology, before tipping his hat and getting into the driver's seat. As they watched the car pull out of the driveway, Caroline felt like she was having a bad dream.

Maybe I'm still in the hospital? Caroline reasoned. *It must be because stuff like this doesn't happen in real life.*

"Don't worry about her, Caroline," Sam's kind voice broke through her thoughts. "I know her kind. She's all about the publicity."

"That's what worried me," Jennifer told Sam and looked at Caroline. "We don't need bad press while launching this new series."

"I don't understand why my animals would go for her like they did!" Caroline was still astounded by how they'd reacted.

A shadow covered hers as Brad stepped up behind her. "I'll deal with Vanessa," he told them.

"Who is she?" Jennifer asked him. "Your current girlfriend? Don't you have two of those here already?"

Caroline's head started to swim as Jennifer and Brad took a stand against each other.

"Excuse me?" Brad's face crumpled in confusion at the hostility and accusation in Jennifer's voice.

"You heard me!" Jennifer glared at him accusingly.

"That's Vanessa Turner." Brad pointed down the driveway.

The name rang in Caroline's ears, and her brow furrowed as she tried to remember where she'd heard Vanessa's name. But her mind was still a little foggy from the bump on her head, and she didn't want to admit to anyone that she felt like she had holes in her memory after the knock on her head. She remembered pieces of the day leading up to the incident and flashes of the incident. Luckily, her friends and family were so astounded by what had happened and caught up in the thrill of the movie crew in town that they hardly noticed that Caroline had taken a back seat and let them fill in the gaps for her.

"Are we supposed to know who she is?" Jennifer's slightly raised voice drew Caroline back to the present.

She was in the middle of a heated conversation between Brad and Jennifer.

"She's the ..." Brad's voice faded away as an article Caroline had read a few days before Brad had come to town came to mind.

Jules had bought Television Magazine for Caroline as it had an article featuring the up-and-coming Cobble Cove Mystery series. Caroline had kept the magazine and underlined some of the troubling bits she wanted to discuss with Jennifer.

There were no pictures of anything but the Cobble Cove lighthouse attached to the article, only names.

In a surprising turn of events, Danes Productions, renowned for its stellar track record in the entertainment industry, has announced an upcoming television series that has set tongues wagging. The production, an adaptation of the best-selling book series by emerging author Carrie Lines, will be spearheaded by none other than Brandon Danes. This move has left industry insiders speculating about the dynamics at play within the Danes family.

THE LIGHTHOUSE ON PLUM ISLAND

Television Magazine recently delved into the casting decisions that promise to make this production stand out. Of particular note is the appointment of Vanessa Turner, a figure known for her diva tantrums and second-rate acting, to a significant role. The magazine has already given Brandon one strike for the controversial hiring, leaving readers to wonder if he's playing with fire or orchestrating a strategic masterstroke.

In an interview with Travis Danes, Television Magazine was told that he supported his son's decisions and that we should give Vanessa a chance. We at the magazine would like to know a chance for what? Is the legendary King of Danes Productions putting Brandon in the position to choose between Dawn, a scion of one of the industry's oldest families, and Vanessa, the daughter of a congressman, as the future Mrs. Brandon Danes?

Another question burning through the show business industry's minds is: Can Brandon Danes prove himself capable of taking the reins of Danes Productions? With his career trajectory back on track now that he's back in the fold of the Danes family. Rumors are flying around that this production is Travis Danes's test to ensure his son is finally ready to lead the family business. The stakes are high for Brandon, who needs to make this production a resounding success by any means if he wants to prove he's fit to take the crown from his father, the industry icon Travis Danes.

The stage is set, and all eyes are on Brandon Danes as he steps into the limelight, navigating the complexities of family, relationships, and the entertainment business. Let's hope you make the right choices this time, Brandon!

Caroline still couldn't believe the Brad she'd met in New York six weeks ago and let her heart get caught by was Brandon Danes. Her head started to ache, and bile rose in her throat, and where his lips had met hers, she felt their sting of betrayal. Caroline's mind reeled, and her stomach lurched. She clasped her hand over her mouth, spun on her heel, and rushed inside, heading for the bathroom. Caroline decided against the downstairs guest toilet and ran to her bedroom, where she locked the door behind her and just made it to the bathroom before she got sick.

"Caroline!" Jennifer cried through the door, concern ringing in her voice.

Caroline collapsed on the bathroom floor for a few seconds, letting her stomach settle and the fog lift in her brain while trying to ignore the pain stabbing her heart.

I can't believe I let myself get pulled in by Brad's charm and feigned compassion! Caroline seethed. *I'm beginning to think he knew who I was when we were in New York.*

Hurt and anger mixed together, fueled by betrayal, as tears started to sting her eyes while trying to squeeze through her closed eyelids. She nearly jumped out of her skin when there was a pounding on her bedroom door.

"Caroline!" Brad's voice echoed through to her.

His voice was like another arrow through her heart because she knew the panic in his voice was just a lie. How could she have been so naive?

"Caroline, if you don't answer me, I will let Brad break this door down!" Jennifer warned.

Caroline sat up, ignoring the pain starting to pound in her brain.

"I'm fine," Caroline called. "Just give me a minute."

"Please, Caroline, open the door so we can see that you're okay," Brad pleaded.

"I said I needed a minute!" Caroline couldn't stop the anger that spurted into her voice.

"Let's give her a minute," Caroline heard Jennifer say.

She leaned over the basin, taking a few steadying breaths, wishing no one was in her house as Caroline needed to be alone with her thoughts and pain. Her life had blown up in the past year, starting with the publishing company wanting to publish her series. Then, eight weeks ago, she got an invitation to meet Travis Danes, who was interested in making her book series into a television series.

Caroline splashed water on her face and rested her head against the bathroom mirror.

How has my life become this? She swallowed down the tears threatening to spill over from her bruised heart. *Why do I keep falling for men like Robert and Brad?* She leaned over and grabbed some toilet paper to blow her nose.

Caroline looked at her reflection in the mirror. Her shoulder-length sandy blonde hair was pulled back and confined with a band showing the raised bruise on her temple—the current source of pain in her head which only amplified the pain in her heart. She sighed and splashed more cold water on her face, trying to get rid of her red eyes.

She patted her face dry with a towel and shook her head at her reflection. Caroline hardly recognized herself or the life she felt like she was being sucked into. She felt like she was swirling around in the vortex of a whirlpool, shaking everything she was away. She ran her hand over her cheeks, trying to rub some color into them as she worried what would be left of her when she came out the other side.

Caroline realized she may not be able to control everything the future held, but she knew one thing—she was going to harden her heart against the likes of Brad Danes. Caroline *would not* be another

Brad Danes conquest to get splashed in the media as another of his cast-aside failed relationships.

As Caroline pulled her hair from its confines and ran a brush through it, she wondered about Connor's mother—Brad's first wife. Caroline could remember Brad telling her when they'd met six weeks ago that he'd come home to find she'd left.

"He was probably cheating on her!" Caroline said to her reflection, giving her cheeks a final pat before heading out of her room and downstairs.

"Caroline!" Brad stood up from the chair he'd been sitting in, followed by an anxious Jennifer.

They rushed at her, but she held up her hand to stop them as a warning growl came from her knee. Caroline looked down to find Sandy standing protectively beside her with Blue Beard perched on her back. She looked around to find Melton sitting on the back of the chair Brad had vacated, swishing his tail as he eyed out the scene. Her heart swelled at the love her pets protectively exhibited toward her. They weren't vicious. They were merely picking up on Caroline's need for space.

"Please, I'm okay," Caroline forced a smile on her face. "I felt a bit giddy and ill for a moment. I think I may have overdone the excitement."

"Then sit," Jennifer pulled a reluctant Brad aside. "Brad and I ordered some takeout for dinner."

"Seriously, I'm fine and not very hungry," Caroline admitted. "I think I'm going to have a shower and climb into bed."

"Then that's what you must do," Brad said. "But after you've eaten."

"I find myself agreeing with Brad," Jennifer told her. "The food should be here soon. So come sit, and I'll make us some tea."

"That sounds good." Caroline could use some tea.

She sidestepped Brad and Jennifer as she headed for her chair, which happened to be the one Brad had recently vacated. She could still feel his warmth and smell his lingering cologne as she settled into it. Caroline pushed the thoughts of him aside, which was hard as he was standing a few feet away from her.

"Would you sit?" Caroline said to Brad. She hadn't meant to sound snappy.

"Sorry, I don't mean to hover." Brad's voice was soft, and his eyes were shadowed with concern. He glanced toward the kitchen. "We need to talk."

"About?" Caroline tilted her head slightly and frowned, hoping he couldn't hear her pounding heart.

"Everything that happened outside," Brad said. "Including Vanessa!"

"Really, Brad, you don't have to explain anything to me," Caroline assured her, trying her best to feign nonchalance, something she wasn't good at. She glanced at the clock on the mantle. It was almost six. "I know you have a dinner party to get to. You don't have to stay here. Jennifer is here and I have my trusty protectors."

As if on cue, Melton plopped into her lap. Blue Beard perched on the arm of her chair, and Sandy curled up by her feet.

"I'm not going to Alex's dinner party," Brad told her. "I was going to ask if you felt well enough to attend..."

"You know who'd love to go to Alex's party," Caroline said, cutting him off as an idea formulated in her head. "Jennifer. It would be good for her to meet your production team as she is my manager."

"I can't leave you," Jennifer said, walking into the living room. There was a tray of steaming tea mugs. She handed the mugs out, took one, and sat on the sofa beside Brad. "Especially not after the break-in."

"I promise I'll be fine!" Caroline stated again.

"I'll stay here," Carly Donovan walked into the living room carrying take-out bags. "Sorry, I knocked, but there was no answer. I saw the lights on, and the back door was open."

"Open?" Caroline felt alarm jolt through her.

"I left it open for when Carly delivered the food," Jennifer explained.

"It's okay, Carly," Caroline smiled at the petite woman with the wild, unruly copper hair and thick black-framed glasses as she handed Jennifer the take-out bags.

"It's no bother," Carly assured her. "We haven't spent much time together this past year. It would be good to catch up." She smiled shyly, her eyes darting toward Brad, her head bowed slightly like she was trying to shrink into a shell and hide.

"You look so familiar." Brad's voice drew Caroline's attention, and she could see him staring at Carly, a deep, thoughtful frown creasing his brow.

"This is my niece, Carly Donovan," Sam walked in, carrying another food bag. "Sorry, honey, I got a phone call."

Jennifer took the last of the bags of food and walked into the kitchen with them.

"Oh!" Brad stood and was about to shake Carly's hand but noticed how she stepped behind her uncle. So he smiled and gave a slight bow as he introduced himself. "Brad. It's nice to finally meet you. Your uncle talks about you all the time."

"Uncle Sam," Carly berated him. "You know I don't like it when you talk about me."

"I can't help it. I'm so darn proud of you and my great nephew," Sam grinned.

"Rather talk about Harley." Carly shook her head. "You are proud of him too."

"Harley's my nephew," Sam explained. "Carly's older brother. He moved here about six months ago."

"Eight months ago, Uncle Sam," Carly corrected. Her eyes moved to Caroline as her words became more forceful this time. "I'll stay and keep you company while Jennifer attends the dinner party." She smiled. "Uncle Sam and Danny told me what happened. I'm glad you're alright."

Caroline nodded. "Thank you, Carly." She looked at Brad and Jennifer before accepting Carly's offer. "I do have a lot of food, so I hope you're hungry?"

"I could eat," Carly admitted. "Reef is with Tucker and ..." Her eyes widened, and she looked at Brad. "Is Connor your son?"

"Yes," Brad confirmed. "I hope he's behaving himself."

"Oh, yes, they're all at Liam's house, watching surfing videos of Liam and Finn," Carly told them.

"I bet Connor's loving that." Brad laughed, and Caroline couldn't believe how duplicitous the man was.

"Jen, I know you'd love to go to the dinner party on the yacht," Caroline enticed her friend. "Carly's going to be here, so go."

"If Brad doesn't mind, I'll bring you home afterward," Sam offered.

"Not at all," Brad said, and Caroline noticed his tight smile.

"If you don't mind waiting for me to get ready?" Jennifer looked at Brad.

"I can take Brad to the hotel as I'm sure he wants to get ready too," Sam suggested. "I'll come back to pick you up, Jennifer."

"I'll meet you in the hotel's foyer," Brad told her.

Jennifer's eyes flashed excitedly, overshadowed by concern when they met Carolines. "Are you sure you're okay with me going?"

"One of us should be there, I guess?" Caroline looked at Brad. "Are there going to be a lot of production team members there?"

"I'd imagine," Brad told her. His eyes flashed with a touch of confusion and concern.

"Then that's settled," Caroline said, forcing another smile and feeling her face starting to ache from all the false bravado she was trying to purvey. "You two go and have a wonderful evening. I'll feel much better knowing I'm not holding you back by having to babysit me."

"You're not holding us back," Brad assured her. "I want to stay here with you."

"That's how I feel as well," Jennifer told her.

"Maybe Caroline is trying to tell you that she needs some space," Carly said softly.

"Is that true?" Brad and Jennifer said in unison.

"I'm grateful to you both for how much you've cared for me," Caroline told them honestly. "I love how you're both so concerned and appreciate everything you've done for me." She put her hand on her heart. "It means the world to me. But it also makes me feel awful that I'm wasting your time. So do this for me and go have some fun."

"Okay, we get the hint." Jennifer laughed, lightening the mood. "Brad and I can be a bit overbearing when someone we care about gets hurt."

"What she said." Brad didn't take his eyes off Caroline as he tilted his head toward Jennifer. "Are we still on for lunch tomorrow?"

"I—" *Oh no, I forgot I invited Brad to lunch.*

"Oh, that's why you wanted to go grocery shopping?" Jennifer raised a knowing eyebrow as she looked at Caroline.

"Sure," Caroline said quickly, needing to get them out of her house as soon as possible.

Brad looked at Carly. "Will you take my number and call me if you need to anytime during the night?"

"I'm quite capable of calling for help," Caroline said, not liking how they made her feel like an invalid. "I have your number and Jen's on my phone."

"Along with everyone else's on Plum Island." Sam snorted.

"I'll see you tomorrow," Brad said, turning to Jennifer. "I'll meet you in the foyer of the Summer Inn in an hour?"

Jennifer nodded, and they watched Brad leave with Sam trailing behind him after saying goodbye.

"Are you really fine with me going?" Jennifer asked Caroline.

"One hundred percent," Caroline answered.

Jennifer kissed her cheek. "I'll fill you in on how it goes tomorrow."

"I can't wait," Caroline lied.

As soon as Jennifer left the room, Carly sat on the sofa beside Caroline. "Caroline, my uncle told me what happened here earlier with Vanessa Turner." She squeezed Caroline's arm affectionately. "Trust me when I tell you this: Brad is not what the press and everyone makes him out to be." She looked pointedly at the Television Magazine on the table beside the chair. "He's a good guy."

"How would you know that?" Caroline asked her.

Carly sighed, "Can you keep a secret?"

Caroline nodded.

"I've met Brad before. I even know his ex-wife," Carly shocked her by saying.

"How?" Caroline knew it was rude to pry into other people's lives, but she couldn't stop herself. She'd known Carly for three years but didn't know much about her.

"I'll tell you someday," Carly promised with a wink. "I'm starving." She stood and looked questioningly at Caroline. "Can I dish up for you?"

Caroline nodded and frowned, staring at Carly, wondering how she knew so much about Brad and why he'd think she looked familiar. All thoughts of that disappeared when Carly brought her a plate of mouthwatering food. They spent the rest of the evening chatting about the restaurant and lighthouse while Caroline tried to stop herself from thinking about the yacht party.

CHAPTER 18

Brad Danes stood outside Harriet's door dressed in casual evening wear attire. His clothes exuded a mix of sophistication and ease: a tailored black blazer worn over a crisp white shirt and black trousers. A subtle, expensive cologne enveloped him as he knocked, expecting an answer from Harriet's suite.

To his surprise, there was no response. Frowning, Brad wondered if she'd already gone to the yacht. He looked at his wristwatch and realized it was time to meet Jennifer, so he went to the foyer. He arrived at the same time Jennifer walked in, looking stunning in an elegant, floor-length navy blue gown that hugged her lithe figure gracefully. The dress boasted intricate beadwork that sparkled in the dim lighting, and her auburn hair was styled into loose waves, cascading over one shoulder. A pair of diamond earrings adorned her ears, adding a touch of glamor.

"Brad," she greeted him with a tight smile.

"Jennifer," Brad replied. "You look breathtaking."

"Thank you," Jennifer looked him over. "You don't look too shabby yourself."

"I'll take that as a compliment." Brad frowned, offering her his arm.

As they started walking, Jennifer steered them toward the lounge bar. "Would you mind if we had a drink at the bar first?" He looked at her curiously. "I think you and I need to have a chat."

"Sure," Brad nodded. He had a hunch what the conversation was about—Caroline!

Brad noticed the staff greeting Jennifer warmly as they made their way to the bar, and she returned the greetings. And to his surprise, she knew each one of them by name.

"That's impressive," Brad said, pulling out a high-back bar chair for her before taking the one beside hers.

"What is?" Jennifer looked at him curiously.

"The way you know each person who works here," Brad told her, getting the bartender's attention. "And not just their names but their families."

Jennifer shrugged, placing her clutch purse on the bar before her. "My brother owns the place, and I helped him hire most of them. The others have been here since—" She stopped and cleared her throat. "Since Caroline's father owned the place."

"Sam told me that Caroline's family owned most of Cobble Cove before times got tough," Brad said.

"Caroline's father had a rough time of it," Jennifer explained. "First, it was his father, then his mother, and then his first wife." Her eyes misted over, and she looked away.

"Good evening," the bartender greeted them. His smile broadened when he saw Jennifer. "It's good to see you again, Miss Gains."

"How many times must I tell you to call me Jennifer, Basil," Jennifer told the young man.

The young man blushed and nodded. "What can I get you to drink?"

"I'll have a white wine," Jennifer told him.

"The usual one?" Basil asked, and Jennifer nodded. He looked at Brad. "What can I get you, sir?"

"I'll have the same," Brad told him. "What would you like to talk about?"

"I'm going to cut straight to it," Jennifer warned him. Her eyes darkened as they narrowed slightly. "I know about your romantic fling with Caroline in New York. I was there through it all. She's unlike the women you know, who move in your social circle." She paused as Basil brought their wine.

"I know that!" Brad's jaw had clamped when Jennifer referred to his time with Caroline in New York as a fling. "And I can assure you, it was not a *fling*!"

"Really?" Jennifer's brow rose in disbelief as she sipped the wine. "Then what would you call it?" She put the glass on the bar and looked at him expectantly. "Because that move you pulled—waiting for her to arrive at the party and then flaunting your relationship with another woman in her face to break it off—says *fling* to me."

"What?" Brad nearly spewed the wine he'd sipped all over the place at Jennifers' words. "I have no idea what you're talking about." He took a napkin from the bar and dabbed his chin. "If you're talking about Alex's birthday party, I invited you both to? I remember neither of you showing up to it."

"Sure!" Jennifer said sarcastically, having more wine. "Oh, we were there," she assured him, and Brad's eyes widened in surprise.

"I waited for Caroline," Brad said, his brow furrowing as he shook his head. "I even walked to the host several times asking if she'd shown, and he said you hadn't."

"That's weird because we spoke to the host. He found our names on the list and let us board Alex Blackwell's mini cruise liner." Jennifer turned her wine glass as she spoke.

"Did Caroline look for me?" Brad asked, wondering why the host hadn't told him that Caroline and Jennifer had arrived at Alex's party six weeks ago.

"Caroline did." Jennifer nodded, pausing to enjoy more wine and making him want to shake the information from her.

"Why didn't she say hello?" Brad had to stop from gritting his teeth and took a breath.

"She was going to," Jennifer's eyes narrowed. "Right up until one of your friends likened her to a nag, and your other date branded you with a kiss."

Brad's eyes widened, and this time, he choked as waves of shock vibrated through him. He remembered that conversation, but he didn't remember anyone branding him with a—

"It was Harriet," Brad exclaimed. "Harriet kissed me goodbye as she'd come to the party to help me talk the Blackwells into directing Cobble Cove Mysteries."

"I thought they were your big buddies?" Jennifer's chin dipped.

"They are," Brad said. "But Harriet is more adept at getting people on board with projects than I am."

"So you weren't there with Harriet?" Jennifer asked, looking at him for confirmation.

"No!" Brad shook his head. "Harriet is one of my oldest and dearest friends. She grew up with myself and the Blackwells."

"Does she usually kiss you?" Jennifer still wasn't convinced.

"Not a romantic kiss," Brad answered. "It's a kiss you give a relation not a partner."

Jennifer nodded. "What about the viper from this afternoon?"

"You don't want to get me started about her," Brad warned. "I don't like her and never have. Vanessa's father is a congressman and a friend of my parents. Besides being forced to reintroduce her to New York society when she moved back two years ago, I barely know her."

"The tabloids have practically married the two of you off," Jennifer informed him.

"They try to get me married off at least three or four times a month." Brad sighed and drank some wine. "I admit I've sowed my wild oats, but not since I married. Even after my divorce, the only person I was serious with was..."

"Me!" Dawn Vanderbilt popped up behind them. "Hi!"

"Dawn?" Brad looked at her worriedly. "What are you doing here? Shouldn't you be resting?"

"I'm fine," Dawn assured him. "I just needed to be rehydrated and vowed never to sail again."

"Dawn, this is—" Brad started to introduce Jennifer.

"Jennifer Gains." Dawn smiled warmly. "How are you?"

"I'm fine, thank you, Dawn." Jennifer gestured to Dawn's dress. "I love your dress."

"Thank you," Dawn said. "And I love yours."

"You two know each other?" Brad asked.

"We've met many times," Jennifer confirmed.

"I hear you've left the publishing business to start your own management firm?" Dawn looked at her questioningly.

"I have," Jennifer nodded.

"Then we need to talk," Dawn told her. "We'll have lunch soon, as I'd love to hire you."

"Of course," Jennifer said.

"Great, I'll give you a call next week." Dawn glanced at where the yacht was. "I can't believe I allowed Ethan to talk me into going to that dinner party."

"Ethan's at the party?" Brad looked at the boat in astonishment.

"Yup!" Dawn nodded. "He messaged me a few minutes ago demanding to know where I am because some woman is suffocating him and following him around."

"You know you shouldn't let Ethan rely on you as his social buffer," Brad told her.

"He's had a rough time," Dawn reminded Brad.

"I know, but it's time he moved on," Brad pointed out.

"I don't think you ever move on after losing someone the way he lost his ex-wife," Dawn's voice dropped, and her phone buzzed. "That's him, again." She sighed. "I'd better go." She smiled at Jennifer. "I'll see you on the yacht."

Dawn walked off toward the jetty.

"I didn't know you knew Dawn," Brad said, looking inquiringly at Jennifer.

"I met her years ago," Jennifer explained. "She's lovely."

Brad nodded and moved the subject away from Dawn as he didn't like trying to explain what had happened between them, which was inevitably the way a conversation went when someone puts him and Dawn together.

"I thought the two of you hated each other?" Jennifer looked to the door Dawn had disappeared through.

"Dawn hated me, and I stayed away from her because I felt so guilty about how things ended between us," Brad admitted.

"You don't seem at odds now?" Jennifer noted.

"That's because I apologized and have since realized that it's better to get things out in the open, no matter how someone feels about you, rather than bottling it up." Brad took a big sip of wine. "I'm glad Dawn and I were able to mend our friendship. She also grew up with us."

Jennifer stared at him for a few seconds. Her eyes bore into him as if she was trying to see into his mind.

"What?" Brad asked after a while, starting to feel uncomfortable beneath the weight of her gaze. "Do I have something in my teeth or hair?"

"No." Jennifer shook her head. "You just surprise me, that's all."

"How so?" Brad raised an eyebrow.

"I came here intending to give you a piece of my mind about what you did to Caroline in New York and to warn you to stay away from her," Jennifer confessed. "I had you pegged as an Alex Blackwell."

"I gathered that." Brad tipped his glass toward her. "You made it quite clear with your frosty looks and warning glares."

"Caroline is my oldest and dearest friend," Jennifer explained. "She's family, and I'd do anything for her, including keeping men like her ex-husband away from her."

"I'm nothing like Caroline's ex-husband," Brad assured her. "Contrary to what the press likes to print, I've never cheated on anyone I was in a relationship with."

"I want to believe you," Jennifer put the wine glass on the bar. "But I keep picturing you with that drama queen in your arms."

"I take it you mean Vanessa?" Brad asked, and Jennifer nodded. "Trust me, if it were up to me, I wouldn't have hired her for the part. But my first and second options weren't available."

"I Googled Vanessa Turner before I came here tonight," Jennifer told him. "I must admit being surprised that she was even in your top ten." She gave her head a shake. "She doesn't even resemble the female lead in Caroline's books."

"I know," Brad agreed. "Trust me. I have also been putting off signing contracts with Vanessa, but I will have to in the next two weeks if at least one of the other two actresses doesn't arrive."

"You mean Vanessa hasn't officially been offered the part?" Jennifer frowned.

"We told her it's between her and two others," Brad told her. "Vanessa told the paparazzi that she'd landed the part." He ran a hand through his hair. "It's not official yet. Before deciding, Ethan wants to screen-test the three actresses Alex short-listed here on Plum Island."

He leaned his elbows on the bar. "There is an actress I want for the part who'd be perfect for it, but no one seems to know where she is."

"Which actress?" Jennifer looked at him questioningly. "Maybe I can help find her."

"She hasn't made a movie or television show in about three years," Brad twirled the glass on the bar. "Stella Hart."

Brad frowned when he saw the shock on Jennifer's face before she quickly looked away. "Do you know where she is?" he asked, looking at her suspiciously.

"I know of her," Jennifer glanced at him and then back at her wine glass.

She seemed nervous, making Brad even more convinced that Jennifer was hiding something.

"Do you know where Stella is?" Brad pushed her for information.

"Nope!" Jennifer lifted her glass and stared at the remaining wine before turning and looking him in the eyes. "I can honestly say I don't know where Stella Hart is. The last I heard, she was giving up acting and moving to a remote island to write a book."

Brad watched Jennifer finish her wine and knew without a shadow of a doubt she knew something about Stella Hart that the rest of the world didn't know. He also realized that he wouldn't get any more information about the actress from Jennifer, but he would keep trying to.

"About Caroline," Brad moved the topic back to why they were at the bar. "She was more than a fling to me, Jennifer. When she disappeared in New York, I tried to find her."

"Before we talk about Caroline, I need you to answer a question for me honestly," Jennifer's eyes searched his as if trying to pull the truth from them. "Did you know Caroline was Carrie Lines when you met her in New York?"

"No!" Brad answered her honestly. "I had no idea. I didn't even know Caroline's last name. Your doorman eventually told me after about the one-hundredth time I called around to get you to talk to me and tell me where I could find her."

"I need to get this straight!" Jennifer held up her hands. "You thought Caroline ghosted you?"

"I guess you can call it that!" Brad wondered where she was going with her line of questioning.

"But you still tried to track her down, even when I refused to speak with you?" Jennifer looked at him in disbelief.

"Yes." Brad nodded. "Harry, your doorman can back me up on that."

"I'm sure he can." Jennifer gave a soft laugh. "I'm sorry. I'm not laughing at you." She touched his arm. "I'm laughing at how absurd we humans are." She shook her head. "Our lives are like a comedy of errors."

"I have to agree with you on that point." Brad snorted. "When I walked into Caroline's office at the library, I was expecting to find Carrie Lines, not Caroline." He blew out a breath. "I thought I was dreaming."

"Fate sometimes has a sick sense of humor," Jennifer said. "One of its favorite tricks is yanking the rug out from under your feet only to slap you with it as you get back up."

"Isn't that the truth?" Brad drank the last of his wine. "Every time I think I'm reaching Caroline, she pulls away, and I feel like fate is punching me in the face."

"Caroline had a hard time with her ex-husband and then her daughter after the divorce," Jennifer explained. "She needs time to build her trust in you again."

"I seem to keep knocking that block of trust down as soon as it just starts to get to the top," Brad sighed.

"I noticed." Jennifer widened her eyes and nodded. "But give it time and be honest with her—always."

"Noted," Brad said. "And thank you."

"I haven't done anything." Jennifer raised her hands before warning him. "And I'm not going to do anything but keep a watchful eye on you."

"Fair enough," Brad agreed. "What do you suggest I do?"

"Not hurt her!" Jennifer stated. "That's a good start." She turned, readying herself to get off the chair. "And talk to her. Keep an open line of communication."

"Okay." Brad nodded. "Be honest and talkative." He grinned at the look Jennifer gave him. "I take it by your pose you're ready to join the party?

"I'm starving and dying to get back on that yacht," Jennifer confessed. "I didn't see all of it the last time I was on it."

"Then I shall give you the grand tour." Brad got off the chair and called the bartender, showing him his room card. "Put it on my tab."

Brad helped Jennifer off the chair and gave him her arm as they walked to the yacht.

"Who do you think broke into Caroline's house?" Brad asked Jennifer as they made their way down the path to the jetty.

"I'm not sure," Jennifer said. "But it is worrying that it happened the day the film crew arrived in town."

"I know." Brad glanced at the yacht gently bobbing next to the dock. The sounds of laughter, music, and conversation got louder the closer they got to it. "That's been worrying me too."

"I thought the police had someone they were questioning?" Jennifer's eyes narrowed thoughtfully. "Clover, was it?"

"We're not convinced it was her," Brad informed Jennifer. "The police think she was set up."

"To be honest, she didn't look like the type to break into someone's house," Jennifer looked at the yacht as they neared it. Her brow creased as she turned to him. "And I think she was too short to be the intruder."

The conversation stopped as they walked up to the yacht. The night air was alive with the sounds of the ocean. As they climbed aboard the boat, the gentle lapping of waves against the yacht's hull harmonized in a soothing melody to the tunes above. The lights aboard the vessel danced across the water, casting an ethereal glow that painted the night in shades of luxury.

Dark Ocean was an opulent engineering masterpiece that stood tall and proud against the backdrop of the night sky. Its sleek design boasted a seamless blend of cutting-edge technology and timeless elegance. The yacht's lights were strategically positioned to accentuate its curves, creating an aura of mystique.

THE LIGHTHOUSE ON PLUM ISLAND

The soft murmur of conversations and laughter echoed from the various decks above as Brad and Jennifer walked up the gangway. The vessel seemed to pulse with life, each deck offering a unique ambiance. The lower decks resonated with the upbeat tempo of a live band, the music drifting down like a siren's call. The rhythmic thud of the bass reverberated through the yacht, enticing guests to sway to its infectious beat.

Ascending the grand staircase, Brad and Jennifer emerged onto the main deck, where a sea of fairy lights adorned the railings. The air was infused with saltwater and the delicate fragrance of exotic flowers strategically placed around the deck. As Brad led Jennifer towards the upper deck, the atmosphere shifted. The soft glow from strategically placed lamps illuminated plush seating areas, inviting guests to relax and enjoy the view.

Reaching the sundeck, Brad and Jennifer found themselves surrounded by the mesmerizing skyline. The deck was transformed into an open-air lounge with a stylish bar. Brad guided Jennifer towards the bar. The bartender, a maestro of mixology, skillfully crafted champagne cocktails. The clinking of glasses and the effervescent pop of the champagne bottle harmonized with the music.

With glasses in hand, Brad and Jennifer resumed their tour of Dark Ocean's luxurious interiors. The lower decks housed private lounges and a state-of-the-art cinema. The mid-decks featured elegantly designed dining spaces, where a team of culinary artisans prepared a feast for the senses.

Eventually, they went to the upper deck lounge, where they found Dawn and Harriet.

"Hello, Jennifer and Brad," Harriet greeted them. "Dawn said you were on your way." She looked at Jennifer. "Have you had something to eat?"

"No." Jennifer shook her head.

"Neither have I," Harriet told her. "I'm trying to avoid Alex and his annoying new friend."

"Harriet has already threatened to shove them both overboard," Dawn told him, grinning.

"Please don't!" Brad rolled his eyes. "Do you remember the last time you pushed Alex overboard?"

"Which last time?" Harriet asked him. "The latest last time or the last, last time?"

"The week before his birthday!" Brad said.

"Oh!" Harriet's eyes widened, and humor flashed in them. "That was when he nearly got run over by that jet ski."

"What?" Jennifer looked at her wide-eyed.

"Alex and Harriet have a dislike, an intensely dislike relationship," Dawn explained to Jennifer. "Whenever the two of them are together for too long, one of them ends up being pushed from a boat."

"Having a drink thrown over their head," Brad added.

"Being slapped!" Dawn looked at Jennifer. "Harriet nearly pushed him out of a party bus once."

"Is he that obnoxious?" Jennifer looked at the three of them.

"He has his moments," Harriet told her, linking her arms through Jennifer's. "Let's get something to eat, and you can keep me from drowning him."

Dawn and Brad watched Harriet whisk Jennifer away, leaving them beneath the million stars that studded the night sky.

"I don't think I've seen this many stars," Dawn noted, staring at the sky. "And the moon is so big it looks like you can reach out and touch it."

"I can't get over how quiet it is," Brad looked back over Cobble Cove Bay, formally known as Cobble Cove Beach. "It's a different world."

"It is." Dawn followed his gaze, and they fell into a companionable silence that Dawn broke. "I thought it was Caroline you were interested in?"

"I didn't tell you that," Brad pointed out, realizing he was being tricked into admitting his feelings for Caroline. "And before you say anything, let me assure you that Jennifer and I are not romantically involved."

"Good," Dawn said. "Because I'd hate to have to push you off the boat if you were."

"Please don't pick up Harriet's bad habits." Brad rolled his eyes.

"Brad, I have one of my bad feelings," Dawn admitted.

"No, no!" Brad looked at her and shook his head emphatically. "You're not allowed to say that. Take it back."

"I'm afraid I can't," Dawn bit her lip. "I think someone's trying to sabotage the production."

"Is that just a feeling, or has something happened?" Brad needed to clarify.

"Both!" Dawn rubbed her chin.

"What's happened?" Warning bells started ringing in his head.

"This, for starters." Dawn pulled out her phone and showed him the message she'd gotten earlier.

Keep your distance, or you'll have to deal with the consequences, and this time, I will destroy you.

"Dawn!" Brad looked at her in alarm. "When did you get this?"

"Just after I left the clinic," Dawn told him. "When I got to my room, my first draft of the script I'd printed had been shredded." She looked at him. "Some of the equipment has been taken from the one truck, and the equipment in the second truck has been vandalized."

"Why am I only hearing about this now?" Brad stared at her in disbelief.

"Because I only got the message about it now!" Dawn told him. "Your father messaged me right before you and Jennifer arrived. I was just about to show Harriet the message."

"Why is my father messaging you?" Brad asked, confused.

"He's been trying to call you and Harriet all afternoon," Dawn told him.

"That's strange," Brad pulled out his phone. "There are no missed messages or calls from my father." His frown deepened as he realized there were no missed calls or messages at all. "That's strange."

"What is?" Dawn looked at him.

"I've had no calls or messages for most of the day." Brad scratched the back of his neck as he looked at his phone.

"Do you have a signal?" Dawn looked over his shoulder at his phone.

"Yes." Brad nodded. "It has full bars."

"You didn't drop it into the toilet again?" Dawn raised her eyebrows.

"No!" Brad said, rolling his eyes. "I don't keep it in my top pocket anymore."

"Let me test it." Dawn dialed his number.

Brad's phone never rang and instead went straight to voicemail. Dawn messaged him:

Hi, Brad. It's Dawn.

No message came through on Brad's phone.

"There must be something wrong with it," Brad looked at the device in frustration. "I'll have to take it to a phone shop in the morning."

"Uh, Brad," Dawn held out her hand to him while she stared at her phone. "If your phone is broken, why are the typing dots bouncing around on my screen?"

She held her phone up for Brad to see, and to their surprise, a message from Brad appeared on her screen.

What do you want, Dawn?

CHAPTER 19

Caroline awoke to the gentle touch of the sun's rays weaving through the gaps in her curtains like silver threads reaching across the room. She stretched and winced as the bump on her temple brushed against a pillow.

The room greeted her with a muted stillness as she sat up. Her fingers instinctively sought the bump on her temple. The dull ache in her head that had lingered the previous day was gone, leaving only the tender bump that had caused the pain.

Caroline's brow furrowed with a mixture of confusion and curiosity as her eyes scanned the room, searching for the familiar forms of her pets, but they were conspicuously absent. Her head moved toward the door to her bedroom, which stood slightly ajar, fuelling a sense of unease after the last two days' events.

Caroline shook the feeling away.

"This is Cobble Cove, Caroline. Not New York!" She reminded herself.

Caroline rose from the bed and walked over to the door poking her head through it to listen for sounds, but there were none. The upstairs was quiet. Her eyes narrowed as a frown creased her brow.

"Jennifer must've let the animals out," Caroline reasoned, closing and locking her bedroom door. "Just in case!" She looked at the lock and shook her head. "What have I done to our little community?"

Guilt washed over her as she went to the bathroom to shower. Caroline had thought she was doing the town a favor and bringing in much-needed revenue and tourists. Instead, she felt like she'd not only brought the glitz and glamor of a society that didn't belong there but the other elements of it that tended to follow the high life around.

After a shower, she felt refreshed. She looked around the room for her phone but couldn't find it.

"I must've left it downstairs." Caroline bit her lip, confused. "Although I'm sure I put it beside my bed before I fell asleep."

She sighed. *That knock on the head has knocked out my senses.* Caroline laughed at her musings as she left her room and followed the soft creaking of the staircase to the ground floor. The sound of muted voices and the subtle clinking of dishes made her pause on the last step as she stood listening and wondering if Jules had come home and brought friends. Although she didn't think any of Jules's friends could cook. The aroma of a mouth-watering breakfast teased her senses and made her empty stomach rumble.

Caroline walked into the living room and her eyes widened in surprise to see Jennifer conversing with Harriet. A noise from the kitchen caught her attention. As she turned to look that way, Caroline found her pets scattered around the room, seemingly at ease in the company of the visitors.

"Good morning," Carly appeared round the corner with a warm smile, looking like the ordinarily shy, reserved Carly once again. "I made breakfast."

She pointed to the dining room table beside the kitchen at the far end of the living room. Caroline glanced at the breakfast spread.

"Good morning," Jennifer and Harriet chorused.

"Morning," Caroline greeted. Her eyes fell on the computer Jennifer and Harriet were leaning over. "Is that my new computer?"

Caroline pointed to the device on the coffee table. Everyone in the room was gathered around.

"Yes," Jennifer answered. "We hope you don't mind, but Jules helped us log in to review your suggested location photos."

"That's fine." *No, it was not okay!* Caroline gave herself a mental shake and stern talking to. *Don't be petty, Caroline.* "Is Jules home?" She glanced toward the hallway.

"No," Jennifer shook her head. "But she asked if you'd call her as soon as you were awake."

"Have you seen my phone?" Caroline's head swiveled around the room.

"I have it!" A young man with a plate piled with breakfast food in one hand and holding up her phone in the other walked through from the kitchen.

"Why do you have my phone?" Caroline looked at the young man in amazement.

"That's Simon, the tech guy on the film crew," Harriet introduced the young man.

"Hello, Simon," Caroline acknowledged him before asking again, "Why do you have my phone?"

"Simon was checking it to ensure it hadn't been cloned," Jennifer explained.

"Cloned?" Caroline took her phone from Simon, squeezed her eyes shut, counted to ten, and opened them, but everyone was still in her living room.

"You're not dreaming, Caro," Jennifer assured her. "Sit down." She gestured to Caroline's favorite armchair.

"I'll bring you a plate of food and coffee," Carly offered.

"It's okay, Carly, you don't have to wait on me. I'll get it," Caroline ignored Jennifer and walked to the dining room table.

Her mind was reeling as she glanced at her phone. What did cloning her phone even mean?

"Miss Lines?" Simon appeared beside her, startling her from her thoughts, and she nearly dropped her phone. "Sorry, I didn't mean to startle you." He smiled. "Mr. Danes asked me to check all your devices. The police techs found a sort of spyware on your laptop that was stolen the other night."

"Isn't that like a virus?" Caroline didn't understand cybersecurity and threats.

"Kinda," Simon told her. "But what the police found on your laptop was high-level coding. The type you'd expect the NSA to have."

Caroline's jaw dropped slightly as she stared in bewilderment at Simon. "Why would the NSA put spyware on my laptop?" She blinked, and her eyes widened in fright. "Oh, no. You don't think it's because of the research for chemical weapons I did for a new series I'm writing?"

Simon grinned and shook his head. "No, I doubt that," he said encouragingly. "While the software I found on your laptop was NSA level, it was more a watered-down version of the type of top secret spyware."

"You should've said that!" Caroline slid the phone into the back pocket of her cutoff jeans and started dishing up a plate of food. "You had me in a panic for a moment about my search history for my next book."

"I'm sorry," Simon apologized. "I'd love to read it."

"You're not reading it before I do," Jennifer joined them at the table. "Carly's breakfast is just so good I have to have another bagel with her homemade cream cheese."

"Simon was explaining the spyware-type program the police found on my stolen laptop," Caroline told Jennifer. "How long have you known about that?"

"I found out last night after Dawn got a threatening message on her phone," Jennifer answered.

"Then Brad found out he hadn't got calls or messages that day, even though he'd made a few and sent some messages." Harriet walked to the table and poured coffee into a mug.

"Miss Vanderbilt tried to message Mr. Danes, but it didn't go through," Simon added.

"Maybe his phone doesn't work in New England." Caroline shrugged.

"Brad messaged Dawn back," Harriet explained.

"I don't understand." Caroline's brow furrowed in confusion. "You said Brad didn't get the message."

"He didn't!" Jennifer told her. "Nor was Brad the one who rudely answered Dawn's message."

"Oh!" Caroline suddenly realized what they meant about cloning, and shock waves made her nerve ends tingle. "Someone cloned Brad's phone."

"Yeah." Simon nodded. "Again, it was professionally done."

"Why would anyone want to clone my phone?" Caroline was trying to absorb what they were saying.

"For the same reason, someone installed that program on your laptop," Simon told her. "They were trying to monitor you both for some reason." He took more bacon. "Miss Vanderbilt's threatening message was similar to the one on your phone."

"You went through my phone?" Caroline was flabbergasted. That was her personal information, and he may as well have told her he'd rifled through her purse.

"I'm sorry, Miss Lines, but I had to." Simon's eyes flashed with regret. "I don't like doing it, but I did find out that your message was sent before Miss Vanderbilts, and I was able to trace the vicinity where the message was sent from."

"And that helps you how?" Caroline was trying to bite back her annoyance at having her phone tampered with.

"It was sent from the internet cafe near the library," Harriet told her.

"Those computers have cameras that take photos of whoever used the laptops," Simon explained. "Because of the time stamp on your message, I can trace the PC and get a photo of whoever used it."

"We think that whoever's been threatening you and broke into your house is trying to sabotage the series," Harriet told her.

"Why?" Caroline's voice was filled with outrage. "I don't have enemies."

"No, but the rest of us do," Brad's voice had her spinning around to find him standing in the kitchen doorway. "Hi!" His eyes softened as he greeted Caroline.

"So what you're saying is that I'm caught in the middle of a vendetta that has nothing to do with me but is about to tank my television series before it's even begun?" Caroline stared at him in disbelief.

"We're sorry, Caroline," Jennifer's hand touched her arm, and suddenly it was all too much.

She needed time to clear her head and put some space between her and Brad. Her world tilted whenever he was near her, and she couldn't think straight. That cologne of his filled her senses, made her heart beat more rapidly and excited the butterflies in her stomach.

"Wait! Stop!" Caroline held up her hands and pulled her arm away from Jennifer. "This is all just too much. It wasn't supposed to be like this." She stormed into the kitchen, giving Brad a wide berth and opening a drawer to pull out a ziplock bag and a mug flask. "I was just supposed to be this author sitting in my lighthouse tower writing gripping mysteries that Fern McBride solved." She walked back to the dining room table. "You know, like a younger Jessica Fletcher."

Caroline stuffed two bagels with cream cheese and a fist full of bacon into the bag while four pairs of eyes watched her without saying a word. She filled the mug flask with coffee.

"I was happy with just having the books published and the publishing house interested in the next installment of the series." Caroline forced the lid onto the mug. "I wasn't supposed to capture the attention of a production company or go to New York and get swept up in the romance of it all."

Caroline took her beach bag hanging on a hook near the kitchen door and shoved the items into it before hooking it over her shoulder. She stood staring out the living room window at the sparkling sea ahead.

"My life was supposed to be quiet as I dealt with my moody teenage daughter while getting lost in my writing." Caroline shook her head and moved through the living room. "Instead, I feel guilty about bringing chaos to my little hometown. I don't recognize myself in the mirror, let alone the life I'm being propelled into." She clicked her fingers, and her three pets stood to attention. "And I wanted to *write* mysteries, not *live* them."

With that, Caroline left four people staring after her as she and her pets left through the front door and headed for the one place where she always found peace—Cobble Cove. As she descended the stairs toward the beach below, the sound of construction caught her attention. She turned to see there was a team working on the boardwalk.

"Really!" Caroline moaned, throwing her hands in the air as Blue Beard squawked his agreement of her sentiment. "Come on, guys, let's go to the throne. No one will find us there."

Caroline kicked off her shoes and let the cobbles tickle her feet as she carefully trod along the water's edge, allowing the cool sand and sea to wet her feet. Sandy and Blue Beard chased the waves and gulls as they touched the shore while Melton kept a safe distance from the water. He didn't mind swimming, but only on his terms.

As she walked toward the far end of the cove, Beach Plum Cottage came into view. It stood silent and alone as it looked out over the cove. Caroline wondered where Aunt Betty was and made a mental note to ask Jennifer if she'd heard from her aunt. Caroline squinted as something glinted from one of the windows and then disappeared.

"Maybe Aunt Betty is back?" Caroline mumbled, covering her eyes to get a better look. She could've sworn she saw the curtains rustle. "I'll ask Jennifer when I go back home."

Caroline pushed the incident to the back of her mind when she came across the part of the cove that changed into a shelf of smooth dark rocks that extended to the caves that disappeared beneath the cottage.

She carefully maneuvered around the one large rock until it opened into a flat shelf that was closed on the right side and far enough from the sea that she didn't get splashed by the sea. At the back of the opening were three grooves with flat rocks that resembled a small bench. In the middle of them was one that looked like a giant's armchair that they had called the throne.

Caroline made her way to it. She plonked her bag next to the throne, pulled out the beach towel she kept in the bag, and placed it on the seat before she sat on it. Her pets joined her, gathering around her, and settled down to enjoy the peace with her. Caroline closed her eyes and lifted her face to the warm morning sun.

This was what she needed. Peace and quiet to sort her head out. As if on cue, her phone rang. Caroline pulled it out of her pocket and saw it was Jules.

"Hi, honey," Caroline felt herself relax hearing Jules's voice.

"Hi, Mom." Jules's cheery voice was like a soothing balm on her frayed nerves. "How are you feeling?"

"A lot better." Caroline wasn't lying this time. "How was your night at Lila's?"

"Fun, we watched Uncle Finn and Liam's old surfing videos," Jules told her. "They were both quite handsome back in the day," she teased.

"Hey!" Caroline grinned. "I guess they were." She lay her head against the rock and closed her eyes, letting the sound of the sea create a meditative vibe. "When are you coming home?"

"That's what I wanted to talk to you about," Jules told her. "Uncle Finn wants to talk to you."

"I'd rather you spoke to me," Caroline told her.

"Yes, but then you'd try and find an excuse not to let Jules come have some fun with us," Finn's voice replaced Jules.

"What are you up to, big brother?" Caroline sighed.

This was the type of drama that she could handle. The everyday drama of living and making sure your kid is doing alright. Because that's all you had to worry about—getting you all through the day.

"The Fish and Wildlife services have closed the beach due to a suspected bacterial outbreak after some kids found a bunch of dead fish on the shore."

Finn's words made Caroline sit up straight as she stared out at the sea. "I'm at the cove."

"Maybe don't go in the water and keep the animals out of it," Finn advised.

"They haven't gone swimming yet," Caroline said as she looked at her pets lying by her. "I'll keep them away."

"It's probably nothing, but they must be vigilant, especially when movie stars are throwing a hissy fit about diseased small towns." Finn's voice was filled with disgust.

"Tall blonde woman with a purse as big as her ridiculous hat?" Caroline guessed.

"Yes, although she didn't have a hat," Finn's words elicited a giggle from Caroline as she pictured the large hat with talon shreds through it. "Are you okay?"

"Yes, just picture the woman's hat with Blue Beard shreds through it." Caroline snorted.

"Oh!" Finn dragged out the word. "That's the rose bush lady."

"The who?" Caroline giggled again as an image of Vanessa stuck in the rose hedge came to mind.

"Jennifer was regaling us with the story of the woman's visit to the lighthouse yesterday," Finn told her.

"When did you see Jennifer?" Caroline wondered when her friend had had the time.

"Liam and I stopped by that monstrous super yacht party last night," Finn told her, alarming her.

"Who was looking after the girls staying at Liam's house?" Caroline asked.

"Relax, helicopter mom!" Finn teased. "T and T were at Liam's house."

"T and T?" Caroline's mind immediately conjured images of Wile E. Coyote laying TNT dynamite. "You had Wile E. Coyote look after them."

"Not TNT!" Finn laughed. "T and T is what we call the latest romantic pair in town. You know Tanith and Tanner?"

"They're dating?" Caroline wondered how long she'd been concussed for. "Did I fall asleep for a couple of months while the world moved around me, and no one told me?"

"No, you've just had a lot happening lately and been caught up in the big-time allure, losing touch with us mere islanders." Finn's voice was light and teasing.

"Can we move to why you're talking to me and not my daughter?" Caroline was feeling guilty enough about her life and dragging the town into what she thought of as the darkness.

"Liam and I want to take the teens to Nantasket Beach," Finn told her. "They've never been there, and we thought we'd spend a night or two in my friend's beach house in Hull."

"Corey Highland's beach house?" Caroline's eyes widened. "You mean his beachside holiday mansion!"

"Okay, if you want to call it that!" Caroline could picture her brother rolling his eyes. "It's not a mansion, just a large old house."

"That you could fit my house into a few times," Caroline pointed out. She was missing spending time with Jules, but having her daughter as far away as possible was also a good idea until whatever feud Caroline had been dragged into was sorted out. "Who all is going?"

"Myself, Liam, Connor, Tucker, Maggie, Lila, Reef and hopefully Jules," Finn told her.

"Are you going in the Summer Inn bus?" Caroline picked up a bit of driftwood and made squiggles in the patches of sand on the rock.

"Yup," Finn confirmed. "Is the interrogation nearly over because we want to leave soon?"

"Funny." Caroline pulled a face. "Put Jules on."

"Hey, Mom," Jules sang into the receiver. "Please, please, please, can I go. I'll do the dishes for three months and make sure my room is clean every day for the rest of my life."

"Wow, you really want to go!" Caroline laughed. "You can go. But please be careful and listen to Finn and Liam."

"I will." Jules's voice radiated with excitement. "Thank you. I love you!"

"I love you too and miss you, sweetheart," Caroline said. "Put your uncle back on the line."

"Hey," Finn said. "Thank you for letting her come with us. I promise to look after her as I always do."

"I know," Caroline said. "Just keep an eye on her and Reef."

"Reef?" Finn sounded surprised. "You don't think they're sweet on each other, do you?"

"Sweet on each other?" Caroline rolled her eyes. "I think they have a crush on each other."

"Don't worry. Liam and I have got this," Finn assured her.

"Don't be too harsh," Caroline warned. "Be careful. You have all my loved ones on that bus."

They said their goodbyes and hung up. Caroline sat back against the warm rock and stared at the ocean, her mind going to the bacteria scare. She reached over and scratched Sandy's ears, receiving a jealous meowl from Melton, who dropped onto her lap.

"You are such a baby." Caroline laughed, scratching his belly and being rewarded by a purr. She looked at the sea again. "I wonder if it is a scare or just another ploy to somehow sabotage the filming of my series."

"That's what we were wondering!" Brad's voice startled her, and she yelped.

Caroline's fright caused a chain reaction as her pets felt the change in her demeanor.

"Intruder, intruder, intruder." Blue Beard started flapping his long wings warningly.

Sandy's hair stood up on her back, her body rumbled in a low growl as she bared her teeth at Brad while Melton stayed on his back like a dead possum enjoying his belly scratches.

"So much for no one finding me here!" Caroline hissed, her heart hammering in her chest with fright.

"If Jennifer hadn't drawn me a map of how to get to the throne, I wouldn't have found you," Brad told her. "May I come in?"

Caroline's eyes narrowed on him. Her flighty heart skipped a few beats and started hammering so loud in her chest that it woke the pesky butterflies in her stomach. But she felt much more relaxed, knowing her family would be out of town and safe soon. Being in her and Jennifer's hiding place always relaxed her, so she smiled at him.

"Before I let you in, you have to promise never to tell anyone else about the throne," Caroline said playfully.

"I already had to do this before Jennifer would draw me this map." Brad held up the crude drawing.

Jennifer was never good with drawing maps or directions. Caroline was amazed Brad had managed to find the place. Caroline had often worried that Jennifer had managed to relocate people after they'd given up trying to find their original destination while following her friend's directions.

"Wait a minute!" Caroline leaned forward, squinting at the map. "That doesn't look like one of Jennifer's maps."

"No." Brad shook his head and looked at it. "Sam stopped me as I headed out and fixed it for me."

"Sam knows our super secret hiding place?" Caroline feigned outrage.

"Sam knows *everything*!" Brad grinned, playing along. "He's like the Wiseman of Plum Island."

"That he is," Caroline agreed and sighed. "Fine, you may enter." As she relaxed, Sandy and Blue Beard settled down but still kept a watchful eye on the newcomer.

Brad folded his long frame onto the smaller rock bench beside her. Caroline swallowed as she could feel his warmth while his subtle scent tantalized her senses. She hardened her resolve and forced herself to concentrate.

"Jennifer sent you, huh?" She looked at him with a lopsided knowing grin.

"I lost the coin toss," Brad told her honestly. "But I must tell you that your friend Jennifer is a cheat."

"Yup!" Caroline nodded, enjoying the light banter between them. "I know. She also hasn't got a good sense of direction, so you're lucky Sam redrew that map for you, or you'd be trudging around the sanctuary."

"I thought she was deliberately trying to confuse me." Brad laughed, ran a hand through his hair as he turned, and their eyes locked. "But I'm glad I lost." His voice grew hoarse. "I wanted to apologize for Vanessa and—" He broke eye contact and looked out at the sea. "Everything."

"Everything?" Caroline's eyes widened. "That's a lot to apologize for."

"I have a lot to apologize for," Brad told her. "I'm sorry that you've gotten pulled into whatever trouble is following me around."

"That's not your fault." Caroline shook her head. "Unless you did something bad to someone, and now they're retaliating."

Brad let out a breath. "I'm not sure!" He looked at her. "I hate that you got hurt because of me." His eyes searched hers. "Caroline, you're the last person I ever wanted to hurt."

"It's okay," Caroline's voice was barely a whisper as she started getting lost in his eyes. "I'm sorry I've been Miss Overreacting."

"There's nothing between Harriet and I," Brad blurted out. "There never has been and never will be. She's like a sister to me. Dawn and my engagement ended rather publicly two years ago, but we've patched things up and are getting back to being friends."

"Brad, you don't have to explain anything to me." Caroline's heart started hammering in her chest as excitement tickled her stomach.

"Yes, I do!" Brad told her, not breaking eye contact. "I hardly know Vanessa other than having had to take her out on my mother's insistence once to reintroduce her to New York society." He shuddered. "Contrary to what the tabloids love to write about me, I don't cheat on someone—" His eyes pierced hers, and his eyes darkened with emotion. "Someone that I love."

THE LIGHTHOUSE ON PLUM ISLAND

Caroline's breath caught in her throat. She didn't know who made the first move, and as their lips met and melded together, it didn't matter as time and space spun away. The world came crashing back a few minutes later when Sandy's angry bark made them jump apart.

Dazed, they turned and watched the German shepherd growl and bark at the cliff above before taking off toward it as they saw a figure turn and flee.

CHAPTER 20

The rocky steps leading to Beach Plum Cottage felt treacherous under Brad's hurried steps. Caroline kept pace beside him as they followed Sandy, who had bolted up the path with an urgency only animals seemed to possess. Blue Beard's frantic squawking added to the chaotic atmosphere.

Reaching the cottage, they found Sandy attempting to get inside, her paws scraping against the door. Blue Beard circled overhead, wings flapping, and announced, "Intruder on the other side!" His squawks echoed the tension building in the air.

Rushing to the front door, Brad and Caroline heard desperate banging and muffled cries from the other side. It was evident someone was trapped within. Blue Beard's warning cries intensified.

"Intruder!" the Macaw continued, flapping off toward the rear of the cottage with Sandy hot on his tail.

The situation escalated as the person behind the door grew increasingly desperate. Brad and Caroline exchanged a worried glance, unsure of their next move. Caroline made a swift decision.

"Go around the back in case there are two, as Blue Beard and Sandy seemed pretty excited," Caroline instructed.

Responding to her directive, Brad hesitated momentarily, not wanting to leave Caroline. "I don't want to leave you here alone."

"Trust me, I yell really loud," Caroline promised.

Brad nodded and hurried around the cottage, his heart pounding with a mix of adrenaline and uncertainty. As he rounded the corner, he saw a dark figure flash toward the stairs. Brad was about to follow the figure when he heard a whine. He frowned as he realized Blue Beard had gone quiet.

Brad turned and saw Sandy desperately trying to free her feathered friend from a nylon fishing net in which the beautiful bird was entangled. His heart dropped when she saw the blood-staining Blue Beards on the blue wing that was squashed awkwardly through the lethal net.

"Calm down, Sandy," Brad drew in a steady breath as he neared the animals and went onto his knees beside Sandy. "There you go, girl." He raised a hand and stroked her fur, gently pushing her aside.

Sandy barked but stayed lying as if giving him permission to help her friend. Brad hoped the moody macaw wouldn't try to bite or claw him as he gently went to lift him, but he didn't know how, as Blue Beard was panic-stricken.

Brad took off his cotton shirt that he had over a white t-shirt. He looked at Sandy.

"I'm going to put this over Blue Beard to stop him from struggling while I try to cut the net off him," Brad explained to the German Shepherd, who watched him tilting her head from side to side and softly whining.

Brad held his breath, bracing himself for an attack from either the dog or the bird. Although his money was on the bird attacking him first. Brad gently covered Blue Beard with his shirt and wrapped it around the bird, carefully folding the wings against the body.

"Blue Beard, stay still, boy." Brad's deep voice took on a soothing tone. "There you go, boy," he cooed.

While gently holding Blue Beard beneath his arm, Brad reached into his back pocket with his free hand and pulled out the Swiss Army knife his grandfather had given him when he was sixteen. Brad had brought it along on the trip to give it to Connor, who had been eyeing it out since he'd seen it in the display cabinet at the age of eight.

"Let's hope one of these blades is still sharp enough to cut through nylon," Brad said, and Sandy whined as if understanding him.

Brad lifted the side of his shirt where the damaged wing was, and keeping his hand as steady as possible, he cut around the feathers that were painfully jammed through the net. To his amazement, Blue Beard kept perfectly still while Sandy watched him with big, soulful eyes.

Cutting the bird free once he'd loosened the damaged wing didn't take too long. He gently put Blue Beard on the ground and lifted his shirt off him. To Brad's surprise, the bird jumped onto his lap and rubbed his head on Brad's arm while Sandy sprung to her feet and covered his face in doggy kisses.

Brad examined Blue Beard's wing when the bird tried to fly but couldn't. "I'm no vet, but it might be broken, buddy." Brad stood with his shirt wrapped around his arm and Blue Beard perched on top of it. "As soon as I've helped Caroline, we'll take you to the vet."

Blue Bird squawked and nuzzled Brad's arm again while Sandy walked by his side. He returned to the front of the cottage as he saw Caroline talking on her phone. Her brow was creased worriedly.

Caroline had tried the door, but it was locked, and she was sure Brad had tried the back door. She also knew that Aunt Betty would've locked the window latches on all the windows before leaving town.

"And everyone calls me paranoid about security," Caroline mumbled.

She held her breath as she stuck her hand in the knot of the creepy old plum tree that had given her and Jennifer nightmares as kids. It actually still gave Caroline nightmares. Her fingers finally touched the cool metal of what she hoped was the key, not some weird metal-feeling bug.

As Caroline pulled the key from the tree, her phone rang. It was Jennifer.

"Hello!" Caroline answered, dusting off the key.

"Where are you?" Jennifer's voice sounded frantic.

"Beach Plum Cottage," Caroline said, causing a drawn-out pause from the other end of the line.

"Why are you at my Aunt's cottage?" Jennifer asked, but before Caroline could answer, Jennifer spoke again. "You can tell me later. This is more urgent."

"What's happened?" Caroline froze on her way to the front door and held her breath as thoughts of what could've gone wrong flashed through her mind.

"You and Brad." Jennifer paused again. "He did find you, didn't he?"

"Yes, he did," Caroline told her, hearing the sigh of relief Jennifer breathed.

"Great, the two of you need to return here *now!*" Jennifer's voice took on an urgency. "We've just found out why the intruder took your laptop and shredded the screenplay of it in Dawn's hotel suite."

"I can't come back right now," Caroline told her, her head turning toward where the banging on the front door was getting louder.

"Look, I know you and Brad have a lot to sort out," Jennifer said. "But Caro, Travis Danes, and the publishing house are freaking out."

"About what?" Caroline was confused.

"Whoever took your laptop has called the publishing house and Travis Danes. They are claiming that you stole their manuscript," Jennifer's words bounced off her system initially as Caroline didn't quite believe what she was hearing. "Caro, someone called Tan King is accusing you of plagiarism and demanding that the book and series get pulled."

"We have to go on a conference call and tell Travis and Jen's previous employer what's been going on," Harriet's voice came through the receiver.

"What?" Caroline felt the world shrink around her as shock engulfed her. "Why would they do that?" She frowned. "I don't know any Tan King."

"I got your old laptop from Jules's room," Jennifer told her. "Caro, that spy program thingy was on it, and whoever's doing this has been stealing your manuscripts since the publishing house requested the rewrites."

"But that was nearly a year ago," Caroline's confusion grew, and something registered. "Wait, is that why they stole my laptop? To put the spyware on it?"

"We think so," Jennifer confirmed, and her voice dropped. "And Caro, I got word from another publisher friend of mine that someone tried to sell them Newbury Dawn."

"But I haven't even finished that series yet." Caroline struggled to comprehend the unfolding crisis. "That's the real reason they wanted my new laptop because Newbury Dawn isn't on the old one, nor is it in my cloud."

"Did you give a draft of Newbury Dawn to Dawn?" Jennifer asked her.

"Yes, when we were in New York," Caroline told her. "It was only the first five chapters of the first book. Why?"

"Dawn had written a sample screenplay of it for you, but it was stolen from her suite the night whoever did this shredded the screenplay for Cobble Cove Mysteries," Harriet told her.

The banging on the door resumed a little more frantically, pulling Caroline from her state of shock.

"You and Brad need to get back here," Jennifer told her.

"I can't," Caroline's head swiveled to the door. "We may have whoever's behind this trapped in your aunt's cottage."

"You... you... What?" Jennifer spluttered.

Caroline gave her a quick rundown of the events. "And now someone's locked inside the cottage."

"How do you get locked inside a cottage?" Harriet's voice echoed her confusion.

"I love my aunt dearly," Jennifer explained to Harriet. "But she is crazy paranoid and has these weird fail safes everywhere in her house. She reasoned that if someone was trying to get her and she ran out of the cottage, she could trap them inside until the police came." Caroline could picture Jennifer holding up her hand to ward off questions. "Don't ask," she said to Harriet.

"Can we get to the cottage or call the police?" Harriet asked.

"If you could call the police, that would be great," Caroline told them. "We think there may be two people and that one has escaped toward Cobble Cove. Brad, Sandy, and Blue Beard have gone after them while I'm about to see who's behind door number one."

"Caroline, you can't do that! The last time you were knocked flying," Jennifer reminded her.

A meow made her look down to see Melton had finally joined the party. "Don't worry, I have Melton with me."

"You're going to throw a cat at them?" Harriet asked in disbelief.

"Oh, no," Jennifer told Harriet. "Melton throws himself at strangers."

"I'm going to go. Call the police and get them out here as soon as possible," Caroline hung up and edged her way to the door. "Hello?"

Before the person could answer, Caroline's phone rang again. It was her ex-husband, Robert. Juggling the chaos around her, she answered.

"Robert, now isn't a good time. I'm going to have to call you back," Caroline told him impatiently.

"Wait! I was wondering where Jules was," Robert asked.

"She's out with her uncle and friends," Caroline told him.

"Oh, that's a shame," Robert sounded genuinely disappointed. "We're here on Plum Island, and I wanted to introduce Jules to her four-week-old baby sister."

"Robert, I'm sorry you came all this way, but you know the rules. You have to call first if you plan to visit Jules." Caroline jumped as the thumping started again. "I have to go. Call Jules. I'm sure she'd love to hear from you."

"No, Caroline please wait!" The desperation in Robert's voice made her hesitate. "Tanya hasn't, perchance, dropped by for a visit, has she?"

"No," Caroline said. "Have you lost your new wife?" Her eyes narrowed suspiciously.

"What? No!" Robert stressed.

"Robert, what is going on?" Caroline asked, sensing he wanted to tell her something.

"Nothing," Robert said, but she could hear in his voice it was something. "Look, if Tanya shows up, please call me immediately." The baby started crying in the background. "Thank you, Caroline."

"I will," Caroline promised, and they hung up. She didn't have time to ponder over the phone call when the thumping began again.

"Please let me out!" Caroline's eyes widened as she recognized the woman's voice.

Before she could react, Brad called her.

"Caroline, Blue Beard's been hurt," Brad called as he popped out from the side of the house with Sandy at his side and Blue Beard perched on his arm, his one wing splayed out awkwardly.

"Can you get me out of here!" The voice on the other side of the door yelled.

Caroline was about to run to Brad and hesitated. Brad made the choice simple as he came to her.

"Oh, no!" Caroline's heart lurched in alarm when she spotted the bloodied wing. "What happened?"

"He got caught in a net," Brad explained. "Sorry, but the figure got away. I had to free Blue Bird from a nylon fishing net."

"You let that crazy person get away to save a stupid bird," the angry voice hissed from the other side of the door.

"Is that?" Brad pointed to the door and blinked at Caroline, who nodded.

"I believe so," Caroline said, nodding. "I've asked Jennifer to call the police."

"Good," the person on the side hissed. "I want that crazy person arrested along with the both of you and your dumb animals."

"Ah, look, there's the police," Caroline said as the flashing lights came down the driveway. "Should we let her out?" She held up the key.

"Yes, why not," Brad said. "I can't wait to see her face when she gets taken away for everything she's done."

Caroline unlocked the door, and Vanessa came barging out dressed from head to toe in a black cat burglar outfit.

"Nice outfit," Brad told her.

"Don't you talk to me," Vanessa sneered. "I'm getting hold of my father and lawyer, and when we're done with you," she pointed at Brad and then swung toward Caroline, "and you, you'll have nothing left."

"Your threats didn't scare us off before," Caroline pointed out. "They're not going to now." Her eyes narrowed angrily at Vanessa. "And your latest stunt accusing me of plagiarizing your work will not work either."

"What are you blabbering on about?" Vanessa looked at Caroline as if she'd grown two heads. "Why on earth would I want to take the credit for the drivel you write?" She looked at Caroline in disgust. "The only reason I took the job was to be close to Brad."

"I told you, Vanessa," Brad shook his head impatiently. "I don't date co-workers."

"I guess you would say that around *her*!" Vanessa looked down her nose at Caroline. "Maybe I should show her all your late-night messages?"

"What?" Caroline felt the shock zing through her as she looked at Brad in disbelief.

"I haven't sent her any messages." Brad held up his hands. "I swear."

"Really!" Vanessa sneered at him, pulling her phone from her pocket, scrolling to Brad's messages, and handing her phone to Caroline with spite shining in her eyes.

Caroline took the phone and felt the world around her start to spin as she scrolled through all the messages Brad had sent her in the past few days since he'd arrived on Plum Island.

"I didn't send those," Brad's voice pulled her back from her thoughts. "I can prove it." He pulled his phone out of his pocket. "Send me a message," he told Caroline.

She typed a quick message and sent it from Vanessa's phone.

"See, there's no message on my phone," Brad showed them. "Wait for a few minutes."

The three stood staring at the phone, and soon, the wiggling dots danced on the screen, indicating a reply was being typed.

"That's not me!" He held out his phone for them to see.

Hey, baby. I can't message you right now. I'm in a meeting. Did you go to the cottage and meet the author?

"What are they talking about?" Caroline looked at Vanessa.

"I got a message from Brad this morning to dress like a cat burglar and meet Carrie Lines at this cottage as she was going to do one of my screen tests," Vanessa told them. Her eyes narrowed angrily. "Only, when I got here, there was another person dressed just like me that pushed me into that creepy old cottage and locked me in."

"Who told you I was at the lighthouse yesterday?" Brad asked her.

"You did!" Vanessa pointed to her phone. "Go ahead. It's all on there."

Caroline and Brad scrolled through the messages that Brad allegedly sent.

"You told her to arrive on the island the same day you did." Caroline pointed to the message. "To meet her at the lighthouse yesterday." Her eye caught another message. "You bought her a tablet for easier communication throughout the production?"

"Not me." Brad shook his head. "I didn't buy her a ..." His eyes widened, and he looked at Vanessa. "You were being set up."

"For what?" Vanessa asked impatiently.

"Vanessa was given the wrong box when she went to pick up the tablet." Brad looked at Caroline as the pieces fell into place. "When I went to get Caroline's new laptop, a temp had given it to you and then left the shop, and they couldn't get hold of them."

"I'm not following," Vanessa told them.

"There was spyware on my laptop that got stolen the other night," Caroline explained. "The thief was setting you to take the fall for it by giving you access to the new laptop replacement Brad bought for me."

"Oh!" Vanessa's eyes widened. "Why would someone want to do that to me?" she asked in shock. "Everyone adores me."

"Hi, Caroline," the officer exited the car and approached them. "I believe there's been an intruder at Betty's cottage?"

"Yes," Vanessa answered before they could and started blabbing on about what they'd been discussing with the poor, confused officer. "I think it's Clover."

"Why would you say that?" Caroline asked Vanessa in exasperation.

"Because the first night I was here, she made me smell like old rotten fish, and Dingle bit me because he can't stand the smell of it," Vanessa told them.

"How did Clover make you smell of fish?" Brad sighed.

"When I arrived here a few days ago, I ran into that wannabe author and screenwriter that's been trying to lobby their work around the New York movie scene these past few months." Vanessa shuddered. "They were carrying a box of stinky fish out of the hotel."

"What author?" Caroline's eyes narrowed suspiciously.

"I don't know their names?" Vanessa flapped her hand in the air. She looked at Brad. "Ask your friend Alex. He was trying to woo her."

She clicked her fingers. "She's Clover's cousin as far as I know. She was introducing the author to everyone."

"Her?" Caroline and Brad said in unison.

"Yes!" Vanessa nodded, then continued with her dog story. "While I waited for the slowest elevator in the world, I noticed Clover coming into the hotel. She stopped and hugged the author, then got into the elevator with me, reeking like a dead fish." She pulled a face. "That's why Mr. Dingle bit her and then me because I tried to stop Clover from patting him and got the fish juice on my hands."

"Dead fish?" Caroline and Brad looked at each other before turning to Officer Crowley. "Is there news about the bacteria scare at the bay?"

"It hasn't been made public yet, and the beaches are only being reopened tomorrow. But it was a false alarm, just some dead fish that were..." Officer Crowley's eyes widened as he realized what was going on. "Dumped there." He looked at Vanessa. "You say you don't know the author's name?"

"No, only her face," Vanessa told him.

"The stolen laptop was only two weeks old," Caroline said out loud. "That's why it was stolen because the thief needed to put the spyware on it." She looked at Vanessa. "Did you notice anything about the person who locked you in the house?"

"Yes, at first I thought it might have been Harriet as she was about the same height as Harriet but was tubbier," Vanessa said and ran a hand over her chin. "Oh, and she smelled like..." She clicked her fingers.

As Vanessa said that, a memory of the night Caroline was attacked flitted through her mind. "Clean sheets having been dried in the warm sun!"

"I guess so." Vanessa agreed.

"So we're looking for a woman that's about five-seven, that's slightly tubby, and smells like clean sheets," Officer Crowley looked from one to the other.

The three people staring back at him nodded.

"I'm going to need Miss Turner to come to the station with me and sit with our sketch artist," Officer Crowley sighed.

"Gladly," Vanessa told him.

"Where's your town car?" Officer Crowley asked her, glancing around.

"I told my driver to go because I thought I was meeting Brad," Vanessa answered.

"Do you need a ride back to the lighthouse?" Officer Crowley asked Brad and Caroline.

"We could use a ride to the vet," Brad told him, pointing to a suspiciously quiet Blue Beard.

"I'm not riding in the car with that crazy bird." Vanessa pointed at the macaw and took a few steps back.

"He's hurt," Brad pointed out.

"We can take you," Jennifer and Harriet rushed toward them.

They'd been so engrossed in conversation they hadn't heard them pull up.

"Thank you," Brad said.

Officer Crowley took Vanessa to the station while Brad, Caroline, Blue Beard, Sandy, and Melton piled into Caroline's SUV that Jennifer had used. They discussed the day's events as they drove toward Newbury Port, where the nearest vet was.

Forty minutes later, Caroline, Brad, Jennifer, Harriet, Melton, and Sandy sat in the veterinary clinic waiting for Blue Beard.

"I'll call my father," Brad offered.

"I already did," Harriet told him. "He's waiting to hear back from us before deciding whether or not to pull the production."

"I didn't plagiarize Cobble Cove Mysteries!" Caroline said in frustration.

"We know that," Jennifer assured her. "We just have to find this author claiming you stole their work."

"Did you get their name?" Sitting next to Caroline, Brad leaned forward to ask Harriet, seated on the other side of Jennifer.

"Tan King," Harriet told him.

"Never heard of them," Brad shook his head.

"Yes, you have. I introduced you to Tan last night as my date." Alex Blackwell's voice had them turning toward the clinic door.

CHAPTER 21

"What did you say?" Brad stared at Alex with narrowed eyes.

"It was one date," Alex told him. Stopped, thought about it, and admitted, "Okay, so we've been out on a few dates."

"You're supposed to be taking a relationship break!" Brad raised his eyebrows.

"I started dating Tan a few weeks before I was told I had to stay away from romance," Alex told him, turning toward Harriet and Jennifer to glare at them. "Oh, it's you two."

"How did you find us?" Harriet asked Alex.

Alex held up his wrist. "Our watches."

"So it is waterproof!" Harriet and Jennifer laughed.

"What is going on with you two?" Caroline eyed them suspiciously.

"They bonded over ganging up on me last night," Alex told her. "They pushed me off my yacht. Unfortunately, I wasn't the only one they pushed as my date tried to catch me and was pulled overboard with me."

"Seriously?" Brad glared at Harriet. "I told you not to pick on Alex last night."

"Hi, I'm Alex. We haven't met," Alex introduced himself to Caroline, holding out his hand, which she left hanging there, and he retracted with a shrug.

"Not officially," Caroline told him icily. "But I believe you once compared me to a nag."

"What?" Alex looked at her, confused, and she heard Brad breathe beside her. "I'd never compare you to a nag. You're more like a graceful thoroughbred."

"Alex, this is Carrie Lines," Brad said pointedly.

"Oh!" Alex nodded. "It's great to meet you, and I want you to know that I'm on the fence about who wrote Cobble Cove Mysteries."

"I wrote Cobble Cove Mysteries," Caroline's voice rose, and anger flashed in her eyes. "Where is your girlfriend? Tell her to come here, and we can have this out face to face instead of hiding behind the cowardly stunts she's been pulling."

"Okay…" Alex's head pulled back slightly as he looked at Caroline like she'd gone insane. "Whatever you say."

"I wish I'd have been on your yacht last night so I could have thrown you an anchor instead of a lifejacket." Caroline stood up. "I'm going to check on my macaw."

""Wow!" Alex watched Caroline storm off. "She's *hot*!"

"What are you doing here, Alex?" Brad said through gritted teeth, balling his hands into fists so he didn't punch his friend in the face.

"I was wondering the same thing about you?" Alex glanced around the vet's clinic before innocently looking at Harriet. "Or is it time for Harry's check-up again?"

"Why you…" Harriet hissed.

"Don't let him bait you!" Brad growled. "Alex, you promised."

"I think you need to give the same speech you gave me to Princess Harriet." Alex pointed his head toward her. His eyes narrowed as he looked at Harriet then shook his head. "You know what? Forget it! I'll find out if the front desk will lend me their phone to get a cab back to the hotel. My stupid phone hasn't worked in days." He shook his head. "This has been the worst week *ever*. My father denies asking me to take Dawn with us on the yacht. My broody, moody brother blames me for trying to sabotage Dawn. You hire the worst actress in the world for the lead part in this amazing series…"

"Whoa!" Brad stood up and stopped him. "You were the one that put Vanessa on the top three list."

"No!" Alex shook his head and pointed at Brad. "You did that. Your father and I just endorsed your decision as you're running this show."

"Can I see your phone?" Harriet asked him, holding her hand out, but he pulled it away.

"No way!" Alex shook his head, eyeing her mistrustfully.

"Oh, for heck's sake," Harriet breathed, pulling out her phone and messaging Alex.

Nothing happened, and a few minutes later, she got a reply.

Looking to dump me in the water again? Luckily, the contamination scare was just that, or you'd be hearing from my legal team.

"I did not write that!" Alex looked at Brad and held up his hands.

"We know you dope!" Harriet shook her head in dismay. "I can't believe you're a genius at times."

"I can't believe you're a p..." Harriet shot off her seat and shoved a hand over his mouth. "Seriously, if you say that word..."

"Sorry, I forgot!" Alex held up his hands. "I'm going to get a cab."

"Here, you can use Harriet's phone," Brad took it out of her hands and handed it to Alex.

"Hey!" Harriet glared at Brad.

Alex walked back toward them, handing Harriet her phone as something dawned on him. "Oh!" Alex nodded, looking at Brad. "Carrie Lines is the mousy librarian Brad's in love with."

A gasp had them turning to where Caroline stood, gaping at Alex from the hallway.

"This is why people push you off boats," Harriet told him through gritted teeth as she started to drag him out of the clinic.

"What? She's hot now!" Alex looked at Harriet innocently.

"Shut up, Alex," Harriet hissed and yanked him out of the clinic.

And awkward silence descended over Caroline, Brad, and Jennifer.

"You know, I'm going to make sure that Harriet doesn't end up in jail for pushing Alex into the traffic." She stood. "Or anywhere that isn't here."

"How is Blue Beard?" Brad asked, his mind grappling for something to say that would smooth over the tension between them.

"The vet is still busy with his wing," Caroline said, sitting beside Brad and letting Melton climb onto her lap.

"Caroline, about what Alex said," Brad decided to get it out in the open, so he dove right in. "He's not always an idiot; deep down, he's actually a nice guy."

"I can only go on what I've seen," Caroline told him.

"Well, hopefully, you'll get to know him during filming and socializing over the next few months," Brad suggested.

"That's if there is going to be a series now that I've been accused of plagiarism." Caroline pinched the bridge of her nose. Brad could see this rollercoaster ride was taking its toll on her. She leaned back and folded her arms. "I've worked so hard for everything I have." She looked at him, her eyes flashing with anger. "How dare someone try and steal that from me!" She shook her head, and tears misted her eyes. "Why would someone try and steal that from me?" She sniffed, and a tear rolled over her eyelid.

Brad leaned over and wiped it away with his thumb. "We're going to sort this out," he promised, hoping he'd be able to keep it. He didn't know how they got to this but hoped Vanessa came through for them.

"What am I doing, Brad?" Caroline drew in a shaky breath. "Look what happened today. Blue Beard got hurt and could've died."

"That's not your fault," Brad pointed out. He put his arm around her and drew her to him. Caroline snuggled into him, and he kissed her head.

"What if that had been Jules, Connor, you, or someone else I loved?" She sucked in another shaky breath, not feeling the slight stiffening of Brad's shoulders upon hearing her words.

"I promise we're going to get this sorted out," Brad concreted his promise and swore he'd find a way to keep it.

She went quiet briefly before saying softly, "I'm sorry, Brad." Caroline lifted her head to look at him. "It seems I owe you an apology for everything, as I've somehow pulled you into whatever vendetta someone has against me."

"I don't think either of us owe anyone an apology." Brad hugged her. "Only a coward hides behind these kinds of malicious games." Anger reverberated through his system.

They fell into a comfortable silence, each lost in thought before Caroline looked at him. "I did go to Alex's yacht party in New York." His eyes met hers. "I saw you kissing Harriet. I didn't know who she was, and I heard Alex talking about me and comparing me to a nag while you didn't say a thing. You only told him I was just a friend."

"The only reason I did that was because I was trying not to punch him in the face for daring to say that about you, and if I had said anything, Alex wouldn't have let up about it," Brad admitted. "And before you ask, I didn't know you were Carrie Lines."

"I didn't know you were Brandon Danes," Caroline told him.

"I hadn't dated seriously since my divorce until Dawn," Brad told her. "I was with Dawn for three years before our breakup." He drew her a little closer. "The first time you smiled at me in A Cup of Soho, it was like your smile had lassoed my heart." He gave a soft laugh. "I floated home that day feeling like a schoolboy with his first big love. The more time we spent together, the tighter your lasso became around my heart. When you didn't show up at Alex's party, I spent the next few weeks trying to track you down." He grinned at her when their eyes connected. "I even became good friends with Harry."

"Jennifer's doorman at her apartment?" Caroline's eyes widened.

"Yup." Brad nodded.

"I wonder if his granddaughter has had her baby yet?" Caroline said.

"Yes, he messaged a few days before I arrived on Plum Island to tell me Thelma had a healthy baby boy." Brad's heart grew a little bigger at the beautiful smile she gave him.

"You and Harry message?" Caroline sat up and looked at him.

"Yes," Brad nodded.

"You are a good man, just like Carly said you were," Caroline told him, kissing him softly. "I'm sorry I skipped town with my broken heart and didn't contact you again."

"To be honest, if our roles had been reversed, I'd probably have done the same thing," Brad admitted. "I know my friends can be a bit much, and some of them, like Alex, can come across as jerks. But he has a good heart, just like all my special friends do, and I'm hoping you'll let me introduce you to them."

"I'd like that," Caroline said, their eyes locking as their lips drew them together.

Caroline's arms wrapped around Brad's neck as he locked his arms around her waist, drawing her close as their kiss deepened. For the first time in days, the world seemed to right itself for those moments they were locked together.

But like it always did, reality came crashing back when Caroline's phone rang. She sighed and pulled it out of her pocket.

"Oh, no!" Caroline's eyes widened. "I forgot to call Robert back." She hit answer. "Robert, I'm sorry I didn't call you back, but Blue Beard got hurt, and I'm at the vet with him."

Brad knew it was wrong, but he tilted his head slightly to hear what the man had to say.

"She's gone, Caroline," Robert sounded like he was having a meltdown. "This is my fault. Why do I do this?"

"Robert, calm down, where's your baby?" Caroline turned and mouthed sorry to Brad, and he kissed her forehead.

"She's with the nanny," Robert told her. "But Tanya has disappeared again!"

"What do you mean again?" Caroline's brow furrowed.

"The week before our daughter was born, we attended this red carpet-party," Robert explained. "I may have flirted with a few actresses or models."

"Robert!" Caroline hissed in disgust. "Your wife was nine months pregnant, and you did that to her?"

"I didn't mean it as an insult," Robert defended his actions. "You know me, I'm just overly friendly."

"Call it what you want," Caroline said hotly. "You were cheating on Tanya with your mind."

"That's not a thing," Robert said in frustration. "Anyway, since that night, she got fixated on me having an affair with a few of the women I met that night."

"And were you?" Caroline asked him ruthlessly.

"No!" Robert denied. "She's been acting crazy ever since you showed up at the house six weeks ago looking like a supermodel."

"Robert, you didn't tell her that, did you?" Caroline sighed.

"I may have mentioned how drop-dead gorgeous you were looking and how proud I am of you for having exceeded your dream of writing and publishing a book series," Robert confessed. He gave a snort. "Tanya once fancied herself an actress that produced a few television series." He paused for a few minutes. "For the past five weeks, we've done nothing but fight, and she kept throwing how I stole her dream from her in my face. I went to lunch with some actresses I met on the red carpet. It was a business lunch."

"What business do you have with celebrities, Robert?" Caroline shook her head. "Aren't you in real estate now?"

"Yes, celebrity real estate," Robert explained. "I had to spend time with the actresses and take them to the properties they wanted to see, and I'm telling you the truth when I say that's all it was." He blew out a breath. "But Tanya has refused to believe me, and the other day, I found a magazine picture of Brandon Danes in her purse."

Brad and Caroline looked at each other wide-eyed. "She's probably just trying to get back at you for the actresses."

"Perhaps," Robert sighed. "Please, can you help me find her? Tanya insisted we go to New England to introduce Jules to her baby sister this week, and I've hardly seen her."

"Tanya used to love to walk before and she couldn't because of the pregnancy," Caroline consoled him. "I'm sure she's trying to walk off the baby weight."

"I hope so," Robert said. "Please don't let her know I told you this, but she's suffering from postpartum depression. I'm worried about her, Caro. She's become like two completely different people, and I never know who I will wake up to each day. I'm even more worried about her being around her newborn daughter."

"Have you found help for her?" Caroline asked him.

"Yes, but she says she's going to the appointment and doesn't show," Robert told her.

Brad heard Caroline's phone beep.

"Can you hold on a minute, Robert? I've got to check my messages in case it's from Jules," Caroline told him.

Caroline opened the message and looked at Brad in wide-eyed shock.

"What is it?" Brad asked her.

"Officer Crowley sent over the sketch from Vanessa's description," Caroline told him.

"Let me see," Brad looked at the sketch and frowned. "She looks familiar."

"That's because I introduced you to her last night," Alex appeared in front of them. "That's Tan King."

Brad watched Caroline's eyes widen even more as she gaped at Alex in disbelief.

"It was baby powder," Caroline said.

"What was baby powder?" Brad asked her worriedly.

"The smell of the intruder that I thought smelt like clean linen, and Vanessa agreed," Caroline told him. "It was baby powder."

"Okay..." Alex looked at Caroline like she had two heads. "Why do you have a sketch of my date on your phone?"

"Robert, when did you get to Newbury Port?" Caroline asked him.

"About two days ago," Robert said, and Caroline's eyes flew to Brad's.

"I'll call you back, Robert."

Before the man could reply, Caroline hung up.

"What's going on?" Jennifer asked as she and Harriet walked back into the clinic with coffees for everyone.

"Vanessa sat with a sketch artist to draw a picture of who we thought was Tan King," Caroline told them. "Alex has just confirmed it is her."

"Great, let's see her picture," Jennifer said.

Caroline held it up.

"No!" Jennifer's reaction was on par with Caroline's.

"What's going on?" Brad demanded.

"Yeah, I'd like to know why a picture of my date has you two so spooked," Alex said.

"Because she's not your *date*." Caroline's eyes flashed at him. "Tan is my ex-husband's new wife! My daughter's stepmother."

The information silenced the room until the vet came to let them know that Blue Beard would be okay, but the vet would keep him for a few days.

Caroline was still reeling from finding out Tanya was behind trying to sabotage Caroline's success and stop her television show from going forward. Caroline tried to figure out if she'd ever done anything to warrant what Tanya was doing to her.

It was Tanya who'd had an affair with Robert and stolen Caroline's husband. She had suspected that Tanya had made Jules believe the divorce had been Caroline's fault. Tanya and Robert were the innocent parties. Tanya insisted she and Robert lived in the brownstone and didn't care that Caroline and her daughter would be homeless.

But through all Tanya's malice and spite, Caroline had never said a bad word about her to Jules. She had helped the woman whenever Tanya would call at all hours of the day in tears because she believed Robert was cheating on her. It was Caroline who talked Tanya through her first pregnancy.

"What did I do to deserve this?" Caroline asked aloud as she stared out her living room window at the ocean while hugging a mug of tea

"You took everything I wanted!" Tanya's voice came from behind Caroline, making her spin around.

"Tanya!" Caroline breathed. "Where have you been?"

"Why?" Tanya sneered. "So you can take that away from me too?"

"What have I taken from you, Tanya?" Caroline frowned. "You're the one that stole my husband and tried to turn my daughter against me."

"Yet you still landed up with everything!" Tanya's eyes looked glazed as she looked around the living room. "I don't understand how such a ..." She eyed Caroline disdainfully. "Someone like you would get everything someone like me should have." She gave an evil laugh. "I couldn't even get that brat of a daughter of yours to turn against you and tell child services you were abusive so they'd give Robert custody, and he wouldn't pressure me into having a child."

"You did what?" Caroline couldn't believe her ears.

"I tried to get Jules to turn you in so you'd lose custody of her." Tanya laughed. "But no. Even when the two of you were at odds you were still the best mother in the world to Jules." She shook her head. "I'm so sick of hearing how great Caroline is. Do you know Robert even compared our beautiful baby girl to Jules and her birth?"

"I was finally rid of you when I came back here to the back end of nowhere, and you faded into the background," Tanya breathed.

"Then all of a sudden, boom, you explode into the light like a supernova once again, getting everything I should have."

"You have so much, Tanya," Caroline said, biting back her anger as she realized Tanya was unstable. "A beautiful home, a new daughter, and a husband that loves you."

"He *loves you!*" Tanya yelled. "You don't even remember me, do you?"

"You worked at the same firm as Robert," Caroline humored her. "I do remember you if you're talking about before you had an affair with him."

"*You were the one having an affair with the man I was supposed to marry!*" Tanya's voice rose to a hysterical level. "I was Roberts's fiancée before he met you."

"Robert wasn't engaged when I met him." Caroline's brow furrowed.

"Yes, he was," Tanya said.

"No, Robert had come out of a long-term relationship when we met," Caroline told her. "Childhood sweethearts that had outgrown each other."

"No, we hadn't outgrown each other." Tanya's anger boiled through her vocal cords, and her hate shone in her eyes. "You stole my life, and all I did was take it back again until you exploded like that supanova and stepped out looking like this." Her eyes narrowed. "Did it feel good to get your celebrity friends to tempt my husband away from me and make me feel horrible about myself?"

"What are you talking about?" Caroline frowned.

"Don't play dumb!" Tanya snarled. "You knew what you were doing when you set Dawn Vanderbilt and that Vanessa Vamp Tramp on my husband."

"Dawn and Vanessa were Robert's celebrity clients?" That made sense, but what about Alex and Brad. "I didn't even know Robert was selling celebrity real estate," Caroline told her honestly. "Is that why you went after Vanessa and Dawn? You think they're having an affair with Robert?"

"I know they are!" Tanya nodded. "That's why I went after Alex and Brad. Until you caught Brad's eye. But then I realized it made my revenge on you even sweeter when I took away your newfound fame and the man you were in love with."

"Tanya, that's enough," Robert's voice startled them.

Before Caroline knew what was happening, Tanya grabbed Caroline like a lightning bolt. Tanya held a knife to Caroline's throat.

"Stay away, or I will kill her," Tanya warned.

"Tanya, you don't have to do this." Brad walked in after Robert, his eyes filled with fear as they caught Caroline's for a few seconds. "Let her go, and we can talk this through."

"No, she won't win this time," Tanya told them. "I'm taking my life back from her."

"Tanya, please, sweetheart," Robert pleaded with her. "Think about our daughter."

"I don't have a daughter." Tanya looked at Robert as if he was mad. "I'd never ruin my body by having a child." She shuddered, and Caroline's fear grew as she felt the blade of the knife dig deeper into the delicate skin on her neck.

"Listen to them, Tanya. It's not too late for you," Caroline said, pushing her fear aside. "You can have everything you want."

Tanya started inching Caroline toward the front door. "I'll have everything I want when you're no longer in my way."

"Tanya, don't do this." Brad and Robert tried to get closer, but Tanya pushed the blade a little closer to Caroline's throat.

As Tanya got to the front door, she had to loosen her grip on Caroline's neck for a few seconds to open it, then screamed. Melton pounced at her, knocking her backward. At the same time, Sandy sprung at Tanya, toppling her to the floor, and then stood over Tanya with bared teeth.

THE LIGHTHOUSE ON PLUM ISLAND

Brad rushed toward Caroline, who ran into his arms. Her heart was pounding with fear until she was in the shelter of his embrace. Robert went to Tanya as Jennifer and Officer Crowley stormed into the house.

The next couple of hours went by in a blur as Caroline gave her statement, and Tanya was taken to a secure mental health facility. Once the house had quieted down, Brad and Caroline sat on the sofa in her living room, resting in the comfort of each other's arms.

"I was so scared when I saw her grab you," Brad admitted and kissed her. "I don't know what I'd do if I ever lost you."

Caroline turned to look at him, her eyes locking with his. "I feel the same way about you."

"I don't know if I've made this clear," Brad told her. "But I'm head over heels in love with you, Caroline Shaw."

"And I'm crazy in love with you, Brad Danes," Caroline confessed and was rewarded with a heart stopping kiss.

EPILOGUE

Six Months Later

Caroline sat in the chair, watching the last scene for the final episode of the first series of Cobble Cove Mysteries. It had been a long, harrowing six months, and Caroline had learned a lot. She'd worked on most sections of the production process and loved every minute.

Brad and Connor had been on Plum Island for the first three months after filming started. Brad and Caroline had been nervous about how their teens would react to the news of their relationship. They had been pleasantly surprised when Connor and Jules had been happy for them and promptly told them they'd won a bet with Liam and Finn about it.

They had spent three months getting to know each other as a family unit. Caroline and Brad had even taken up surfing as an activity to do with their kids. Connor and Jules quickly became a brother-sister team as Connor became Jules's protective brother. Caroline and Jules had been heartsore when Brad and Connor had to go back to New York, but today they were due back home.

Caroline sighed. She couldn't wait to feel Brad's arms around her again or hear Connor's joyous laughter. The four of them had chatted on the phone three to four times a day since they'd left, and Caroline had found solace in Brad's voice over the phone or seeing his face on the screen. Caroline longed to touch his warm cheek and not the cold glass of her tablet or feel his warm breath against her ear when he whispered I love you.

Caroline glanced at her wristwatch as the crew wrapped up. She had to get going if she was going to have a shower and be ready in time for when Brad and Connor arrived home. Home was such a meaningful word when it was filled with love.

As Caroline hurried to her car, her phone rang. She pulled it out of her purse to see Robert calling. Caroline put her phone on its cradle and turned on her car, letting it take the call.

"Hello, Robert," Caroline said as she pulled out of the parking lot. "How are you and baby?"

"Doing great, thank you, Caroline," Robert told her. "I'm looking forward to finally figuring out who dunnit in the two-part episode of Cobble Cove Mysteries."

"No spoiler alerts, Robert." Caroline laughed.

"I just wanted to say hi and find out how you felt now that production has finally wrapped up for the first season?" Robert told her.

"Exhausted and sad," Caroline told him honestly. "How's Tanya doing?"

"No change," Robert's voice dropped. "She's still in a coma after her last episode."

"I'm sorry, Robert," Caroline said with compassion.

"It's going to be okay," Robert said positively. "Let Jules and Connor know I'm here for the weekend, and I hope they pop around."

"Will do," Caroline promised and hung up.

Her mind shifted to Robert. He'd moved to Newbury Port from New York after Tanya had been committed. Two months later, Tanya had her first seizure, and they'd snowballed after that until her last seizure episode had put her in a coma. Robert had stuck by Tanya and visited her every day as she was in a mental health facility close to Newbury Port.

Jules had repaired her relationship with her father, and Robert had embraced Connor like a son. Jules and Connor had often visited

Robert when he'd first moved to Newbury Port. They'd even taught him to surf and babysat for him.

Caroline sighed happily as she pulled into her driveway and parked the car. She was greeted by her pets as she climbed out of the vehicle. Blue Beard's wing had mended nicely, and Brad was his new hero. Sandy also doted on Brad and Connor. Even Melton had warmed up to them.

Caroline couldn't help the smile that spread across her lips as she walked into her house. Her heart did a few flips at the thought there was only another hour to go until she saw Brad. Caroline had missed him so much, and today, she didn't think she could be happier.

"Jules, I'm home," Caroline called, hooking her keys on the key rack.

Caroline frowned and listened, but there was no sound.

"Jules," Caroline called again as she stopped in the living room.

Her frown deepened when she saw what appeared to be bunny footprints etched in flour leading from the living room through the open front door and into the lighthouse. Caroline's frown deepened as she noticed the prints went up the winding staircase. She felt like Alice following the bunny into the rabbit hole. She even had an urge to start chanting. She didn't have time for this; she was going to be late for a very important date. But she was intrigued to find out where floury bunny prints were leading up the winding staircase into the glass dome tower of the lighthouse.

As she got to the top and stepped inside, she nearly had a heart attack when Jules and Connor jumped out at her.

"Surprise!" Jules and Connor chorused.

"Good grief! Are you trying to kill me?" Caroline stared at the two of them before it dawned on her that she was looking at Connor in person. "Hello!" She grabbed the teens and pulled them in for a hug.

"Did you two do the bunny prints?" Caroline looked at them sideways with a raised eyebrow.

"Yes." They nodded with goofy grins, making Caroline suspicious. "What are you two up to?"

"It's a surprise," Connor told her, his grin widening.

"Wait, where is your father?" Caroline asked him.

Connor and Jules said nothing, just pointed behind her. Caroline turned, and her eyes widened as she found Brad on one knee with a blue velvet box in his hand.

"Caroline Shaw, I'm not the writer in what I hope will officially become mine and Connor's family," Brad told her. "I wish I had the words to describe how I feel about you and that I never want to spend another minute apart from you. I felt like I couldn't breathe until I saw you again." He opened the box. "Will you marry me and accept Connor and me as part of your and Jules's family?"

Caroline felt like her heart would explode as she stared into the loving eyes of the man that made her world feel so much brighter. "Yes!" Caroline said as tears of joy sparkled in her eyes.

Brad stood and slid the ring onto her finger, pulling her into his arms for a kiss she longed for for three months while Connor and Jules cheered behind them.

CONTINUE THE SERIES

COBBLE BEACH ROMANCE SERIES - BOOK 2

THE COTTAGE ON PLUM ISLAND

CHAPTER 1

Jennifer Gains's head throbbed from the five-hour Los Angeles to Boston flight. The idea of checking into a cozy hotel for the night crossed her mind, but her aunt's urgent need pulled her toward Plum Island. She adjusted the rental car's mirror and watched Boston recede into the distance.

Jennifer wasn't due back in Plum Island for another two weeks as she was supposed to fly from Los Angeles to New York to pack up the last remnants of her life in New York. She was moving home to

Plum Island. But her Aunt Betty had fallen off a ladder and broken her leg. Jennifer's older brother, Liam, would've usually been there to help their aunt, but he was off on a cruise.

Luckily, Sam Donovan, a key figure on Plum Island and one of Betty's oldest friends, had gone to her rescue. Sam's goddaughter, Doctor Daniella Thornton, ran a small clinic on Plum Island. Sam had taken Aunt Betty to Daniella, and she'd gotten Betty transferred to Newbury Port Hospital. That was two days ago, and Aunt Betty was ready to be released. Jennifer was going to fetch her on the way through.

Jennifer was still unclear as to why her aunt would be trying to climb onto the roof. She had forbidden Betty to try to clean out the gutters two years ago after Betty's last fall. She sighed and put her hand over her mouth as she yawned.

The past week in Los Angeles had been a whirlwind of meetings with various celebrities, courtesy of her new friend, Harriet Joyce. Jennifer had found herself at countless functions and parties with her new friend. For a woman who didn't like to socialize much, Harriet had dragged Jennifer to their fair share of social gatherings.

Although they were select functions and the parties were tasteful garden or yacht ones. They also never stayed at a party long. A smile touched Jennifer's lips as she thought about Harriet's mantra: *You just need to show your face, mingle for a while, and then discreetly leave, and don't forget to grab a bottle of champagne on the way out.*

Jennifer yawned once again and glanced at the dashboard clock. She'd been traveling for forty minutes. Jennifer didn't have much further to go. As she yawned again, Jennifer decided she needed water to refresh and rehydrate her. She'd read somewhere that sometimes fatigue meant you could be dehydrated. Jennifer reached into the cup holder in the door to get her bottle of water, and as Jennifer opened the lid, it took a nosedive to the floor.

"Shoot!" Jennifer cursed, glancing down to see where the runaway cap had gone.

She spotted the white lid next to her pedal foot. Jennifer managed to maneuver the lid back to where she could reach down to grab it. She placed the opened water bottle in the dashboard cupholder and bent down to grab the lid. A terrible crunching noise resonated through the vehicle as her fingers closed around the little troublemaker.

"Darn it!" Jennifer exclaimed as the clatter-clatter noise mimicked the sound of a flat tire. "That's all I need!"

Wondering what she could've hit that would given her a flat, she glanced in the mirror. As her eyes were drawn back to the road ahead, they widened as a man appeared in front of her, flapping his arms widely in the air. Instinct kicked in, sending pinprick shockwaves to zap through her nerve endings, and she swerved sharply to avoid him. As she turned the wheel to right the car, water and the other items on the passenger seat flew everywhere.

As she pulled to the side of the road, Jennifer barely heard the clatter-clatter noise coming from the front of the car as a whooshing noise echoed through her ears. Shaken, Jennifer sat for a few seconds staring ahead, unblinking, and her hands attached to the wheel in a death grip.

Her chest rose and fell as her heart hammered against her ribcage. She nearly jumped out of her skin when the crazy man who'd been flapping his arms in the middle of the road banged on her window.

Jennifer turned to see a handsome man with stormy aquamarine eyes glaring at her accusingly.

"You nearly killed me!" The man was so close to the window that his breath misted a spot on the window. "Are you crazy, lady?"

The shock cleared and was replaced by instant boiling anger being called crazy by a man flapping about in the middle of the road. *He just called me crazy?*

"I'm crazy?" Jennifer seethed, her eyes narrowed as she shoved her door open with a force that sent the man stumbling backward. She pushed herself out of the car.

"What the—" The man stared at her in disbelief, holding his chest where the door had hit it.

His eyes widened as Jennifer advanced on him, enraged. Index finger at the ready, she pointed at him accusingly and hissed, "Who jumps around in the middle of the road on a *bend?*"

"It's a slight curve, and you can see around it," the man's shock eased, and he retaliated, giving as good as he got. "For *your* information, I wasn't in the middle of the road. I was on the curb, which is where *you* were driving!"

"It's natural to go slightly into the curb when taking a *bend!*" Jennifer exclaimed, her voice raising slightly. "Why on earth would you be jumping around on the side of the road?"

"Oh, I don't know!" The man said sarcastically. "Why do people usually try to flag people down from the *side* of the road?" He turned to glance at his blue pickup parked on the grassy verge with its hood up. "I was trying to get help."

"What century are you from?" Jennifer sneered. "Because in this one, we have cell phones to use that don't require us to jump out in front of moving vehicles."

"I *didn't* jump out in front of you," the man said through gritted teeth. "And my phone has died. That's why I was trying to flag down the only car I've seen in an hour. I didn't expect to nearly get killed by a crazy person swerving all over the road."

"I swerved to miss the idiot standing in the middle of the road flapping his arms about like Peter Pan trying to fly!" Jennifer was seething. "And anyone with any *road sense* would've put an emergency triangle out to warn vehicles!"

"I did have one out!" The man snarled, storming to the front of Jennifer's car and going down on his haunches.

Alarmed, Jennifer moved to see what he was doing, and her eyes widened as she watched the man untangle something from between the tire and fender of her car. He stood with a mangled piece of orange plastic in his hand and held it up for her to see.

"Here's my triangle!" He exclaimed. "You killed it!"

Oh! That's what I drove over! Jennifer realized. *Oops!* She had to bite her lip not to laugh at the crunched-up triangle and cleared her throat.

"Again!" She pointed at the mangled mess in his hands and arced her index finger through the air. "It needs to be placed on the—" She leaned forward, saying forcefully. "*SIDE OF THE ROAD*!"

"Here's a little tip for you, *sweetheart*," the man's eyes narrowed. "That mirror attached to the windshield is for *glancing* behind you, *not* staring at yourself or putting on lipstick. And those signs with the numbers on the side of the road indicate the speed limit, which is the law and not a suggestion of what speed you should be doing."

Jennifer's chest rose as fury exploded in her chest. *Who does this arrogant jerk think he is?* She was about to give him a piece of her mind, but she'd already wasted enough time with him.

Jennifer raised both her hands. "You know what? I don't have time to stand here and argue with a crazy stranger. I have to get to Newport Hospital."

She pushed past him and was about to climb into her car when he called from behind her.

The man called from behind her. "You may want to change your skirt before going to the hospital!" He laughed. "I think you may have wet yourself when you nearly killed me."

Jennifer glanced down at her navy skirt, and her cheeks burned with humiliation as she saw a large wet patch strategically placed on it.

She raised her chin, her eyes narrowing dangerously as she turned to him. "Here's a bit of advice for you, *sweetheart!*" She mimicked his tone. "Always ensure you have a phone charger in your car and a fully charged phone while driving on—" She glanced around the quiet road. "Quiet country roads." She gave him a smug smile as she slid into the car and closed her door. She started her engine and rolled down her window. "Good luck with the *next* vehicle."

With that, she pulled off, leaving the man staring after her. Jennifer's humiliation and anger melted into a delightful feeling of satisfaction as she watched him fade into the distance.

"Take that you, rude, arrogant, insufferable," *gorgeously handsome* voice whispered in her head, but she pushed it aside, "jerk. I hope you're stranded there for hours and hours!"

Five minutes later, Jennifer's conscience got the better of her, and she called the roadside rescue service.

"I didn't do that for him," Jennifer spoke to no one in particular as she hung up. "I did it because it was the right thing to do. My Aunt didn't raise me to be petty. And besides, I wouldn't want to live with it on my conscience if I read about a man dying on the side of the road."

Two hours later, Jennifer was pulling away from Newbury Port Hospital with her aunt propped up on the back seat and heading to Cobble Cove on Plum Island.

"Are you okay in the back, Aunt Betty?" Jennifer glanced at her Aunt as they made their way to Plum Island.

"I'm fine, honey," Aunt Betty assured her. "I feel awful that I've put you out like this. You didn't have to interrupt your plans to babysit me."

"It's not babysitting, Aunt Betty." Jennifer slowed down as they neared Plum Island town center. "I can get to New York any time."

She glanced at the library as they drove past it. "It's hard to believe that just ten months ago, Caroline was still the head librarian there."

"Yes, we miss her at the library," Betty told her. "Although we do like Daniella as well."

"I'm surprised Daniella has the time to run the library and the clinic," Jennifer commented as they turned onto Cobble Cove Road.

"She's a remarkable woman," Betty remarked. "Sam said she'd had a hard time of it before moving to Plum Island with her daughter."

"Oh?" Jennifer looked at her aunt in the mirror. "Daniella doesn't speak much about her past."

"Not many of us do, dear," Aunt Betty pointed out. "When is Liam getting back from his cruise?"

As they drove past, Jennifer turned to see the Summer Inn, the hotel her brother owned.

"I'm not sure," Jennifer frowned. "I think he said he wasn't due home for another two weeks."

"He needs a break." Betty nodded. "Oh, Jen, honey, I nearly forgot to tell you. I've invited Sam to dinner tonight. He's going to quote on the work that needs to be done on the cottage."

"Aunt Betty, I told you I'd take care of the repairs when I was back in town," Jennifer reminded her. "Sam can't possibly handle the amount of work that needs to be done on his own."

"Don't worry about it, Jen. Sam has help," Betty told her as they turned onto Middle Point Road, which led to Beach Plum Cottage's driveway. "His nephew Harley, a wonderful man, helps him out now." She paused. "Harley will be at dinner too." She gave Jennifer a look.

"Seriously, Aunt Betty, I know that look, and I'm not going to tell you again," Jennifer warned her. "I don't like being set up."

"I'm not getting any younger, Jen," Betty started with the guilt trip. "I want great nieces or nephews."

"You have a great-niece," Jennifer reminded her. "With compliments of Liam."

"It was such a joy raising you and your brother." Betty sighed, her eyes misted with crocodile tears, making Jennifer roll her eyes as she glanced at her in the mirror.

"Oh, look at that, we're home!" Jennifer breathed a sigh of relief.

As they pulled up to the cottage, Jennifer frowned, noting a blue pickup parked beneath the old plum tree where she usually parked, sparking a spurt of irritation.

What is it with blue pickups today?

"Oh, Sam's here already," Betty said. "Be a dear and ask him to help you get me inside."

"I can get you inside, Aunt Betty," Jennifer assured her, unbuckling her seatbelt. "Let me ask Sam to move his pickup, and we'll have clear access to the front door."

She looked around as she pushed her door open, looking at her aunt, "Where is he?"

"He must be assessing what needs to be done to the house," Betty guessed.

"Wait here, I'll be right back." Jennifer climbed out of the car.

She walked around the side of the house, calling, "Sam?" She craned her head and saw two figures disappear around the other side of the house. "Great!" She sighed, looking at her two-inch pumps. "These shoes are not meant for working in the dirt."

Jennifer hurried after them.

"Sam!" Jennifer called.

As she rounded the corner, Jennifer skidded in the dirt and flew into a solid wall of muscle. Strong arms clamped around her as she plowed into him like a bowling ball. He flew backward, taking her with him as they landed in the dirt.

"Oh, my word!" Sam said, rushing to help untangle Jennifer from the man she'd plowed down. "Jen, are you okay?"

Sam helped her up as she dusted off her skirt.

"I'm so —" Jennifer turned to apologize to the man, and the apology froze on her lips.

"*YOU!*" The man and Jennifer hissed in unison.

He rose like a bear unfolding itself to tower over her. Aquamarine eyes bore into her.

"Do you two know each other?" Sam looked from one to the other.

"Yes, she tried to run me over earlier!" The man dusted off his clothes.

Jennifer gaped at the man, frozen in disbelief. *Was he this tall before?* She couldn't remember.

"Jen?" Sam's voice cut through her shock. "Are you okay?"

"I'm sure she is!" The man grunted. "She finally finished what she started on the road."

"Excuse me?" Sam's brow furrowed in confusion.

"She's the crazy lady—" The man started to talk at the same time Jennifer said. "He's the crazy man that—"

"Whoa!" Sam stepped between them and raised his hands. "I'm sure this is just a misunderstanding."

"Misunderstanding?" The man snorted. "Uncle Sam, she nearly rode me over on the side of the road a couple of hours ago and then left me stranded."

"I called a tow truck," Jennifer told Sam as the man's words sank into her head. "Did you say Uncle Sam?"

"Yes!" Sam nodded. "Jennifer, this is my nephew, Harley." He looked at Harley. "Harley, this is Betty's niece, Jennifer."

"No way!" Jennifer and Harley growled in unison.

AVAILABE SOON ON **AMAZON**

AUDIO BOOK OUT SOON

Watch out for The Lighthouse on Plum Island to be released soon as an Audio Book published by Podium Publishers.

COBBLE BEACH ROMANCE SERIES

Series Books:

The Lighthouse on Plum Island – Book 1

The Cottage on Plum Island – Book 2

The Restaurant on Plum Island – Book 3

The Library on Plum Island – Book 4

The Beach Hut on Plum Island – Book 5

The Summer Inn on Plum Island – Book 6

AVAILABLE SOON ON **AMAZON**

ALSO FROM AMY RAFFERTY

COLORADO CHRISTMAS TRILOGY

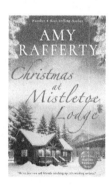

CHRISTMAS AT MISTLETOE LODGE – BOOK 1

"Walking away from you, leaving you standing there at the altar... it tore me apart. But I thought it was the right thing to do."

Avery Hawthorne left behind a lot when she moved to California.

Her family, the familiarity—and a small-town romance with an enigmatic ex she's tried to forget.

As the holidays roll around, she's determined to earn a promotion from her boss and make the sacrifices all worth it.

But this new task means going back to the place she fled twelve years ago.

Her boss is confident the deal for Mistletoe Lodge will be easy. The owners are drowning in debt and Avery has 'history' with the Carlisle family. What he doesn't know is that her history with them is anything but good.

Avery's ex, Ryder Carlisle, is determined to keep his family's inn afloat and has ideas to revamp it. The last thing he wants is to give in to some big corporate hotel chain. But he never imagined they'd send the one person he couldn't say "no" to!

Avery just wants to celebrate Christmas with a promotion.

Ryder wants to keep Mistletoe Lodge in the family.

In a battle of wills over Christmas festivities, Avery and Ryder reignite old flames as they wrestle with their wills—and their own feelings, which remain just as strong twelve years later.

It was official. Fate really had hijacked her festive season and was busy toying with her…

CHRISTMAS AT MISTLETOE LODGE is Book 1 of the Feel Good Holiday Romance series, a powerful women's fiction saga in which Avery and Ryder have a second chance at romance if they can push aside their stubbornness and the wrongs of the past...

AVAILABLE ON **AMAZON**

MORE BOOKS BY AMY RAFFERTY

SERIES

Christmas at Mistletoe Lodge ~ *A Feel Good Holiday Romance*

New Year at Mistletoe Lodge ~ *A Feel Good Holiday Romance*

Reunion at Mistletoe Lodge ~ *A Feel Good Holiday Romance*

The Bakery in Bar Harbor ~ *Secrets in Maine Series*

Cupids Bow Ranch ~ *Montana Country Inn Romance Series*

Starting Over in Nantucket ~ *Cody Bay Inn Series*

Leave a Rose in the Sand ~ *Starting Over in Key West Series*

A Mystery at Summer Lodge ~ *A Coastal Vineyard Series*

Charming Bookshop Mysteries ~ *Small Town Beach Romance*

Moonlight Dream ~ *Honey Bay Cafe Series*

Nantucket Christmas Escape ~ *Second Chance Holiday Romance*

Retreat ~ *Manatee Bay Series*

Secrets of White Sands Cove ~ *A San Diego Sunset Series*

The Seabreeze Cottage ~ *La Jolla Cove Series*

STANDALONE NOVELS

The McCaid Sisters ~ *A Second Chance Romance Mystery Novel*

BOX SETS

Montana Country Inn: The Complete Collection ~ *Montana Country Inn Romance Series*

Cody Bay Inn: The Complete Collection ~ *Nantucket Romance Series*

Starting Over in Key West: The Complete Collection ~ *A Florida Keys Romance Series*

A Mystery at Summer Lodge: The Complete Collection ~ *A Coastal Vineyard Series*

Charming Bookshop Mysteries: The Complete Collection ~ *Small Town Beach Romance*

Honey Bay Cafe Series: The Complete Collection ~ *Second Chance Beach Mystery Romance*

Nantucket Christmas Escape: The Complete Collection ~ *Second Chance Holiday Romance*

Manatee Bay: The Complete Collection ~ *Treasure Seekers Beach Romance Series*

Secrets of White Sands Cove: The Complete Collection ~ *A San Diego Sunset Series*

The Seabreeze Cottage: The Complete Collection ~ *La Jolla Cove Series*

THREE IN ONE

Coastal Collection: Sea Breeze Cottage, Mystery at Summer Lodge, Secrets of White Sands Cove ~ *Three Series in One Book*

SPANISH VERSION

El Café de Bahía Honey ~ *Honey Bay Cafe (Spanish)*

Escapada Navideña a Nantucket ~ *Nantucket Christmas Escape (Spanish)*

Bahía de Manatee ~ *Manatee Bay (Spanish)*

La Posada de la Bahía Cody – *Cody Bay Inn (Spanish)*

BOOKS BY AMY RAFFERTY & ROSE RYAN

Scott Sisters Series Books:

The Beach Hotel on Marco Island – Prequel

The Bookstore on Marco Island – Book 1

The Baby on Marco Island – Book 2

The Bachelor on Marco Island – Book 3

The Restuarant on Marco Island – Book 4

The Studio on Marco Island – Book 5

The Bride on Marco Island – Book 6

AVAILABLE ON **AMAZON**

VIP READERS

Don't want to miss out on my giveaways, competitions, and 'hot off the press' news?

Subscribe to my email list.

It is FREE!

Click Here!

FOLLOW ME ON MY SOCIALS HERE

Not only can you check out the latest news and deals there, you can also get an email alert each time I release my next book.

Follow me on BookBub

I always love to hear from you and get your feedback.

Email me at ~ books@amyraffertyauthor.com

Follow on Amazon ~ Amy Rafferty

Sign up for my newsletter and free gift, Here

Join my 'Amy's Friends' group on Facebook

ABOUT THE AUTHOR

Hi, wonderful people,

Having been described as "The Queen of Gorgeous Clean Mystery Romance," I am delighted that you are here.

I write sweet women's romance fiction for ages 20 and upwards. I bring you heartwarming, page-turning fiction featuring unforgettable families and friends and the ups and downs they face.

My mission is to bring you beach reads and feel-good fiction that fills your heart with emotion and love. You will find comfort in my strong female lead role models, along with the men who love them. Fill your hearts with family saga, the power of friendship, second chances, and later-in-life romance.

I write books you cannot put down, bringing sunshine to your days and nights.

Thank you for being here and reading my books x

Made in the USA
Monee, IL
20 September 2025